PETE DAVIES'S
THE LAST ELECTION

"Davies writes with great pace and style....The strength of the book is the depiction of an anti-utopia, every bit as unpleasant as *1984*."
—NEW SOCIETY

"A novel of considerable power, written with a kind of visceral fury in a prose that scorches and sings....Subtle as a flying mallet, *The Last Election* introduces a brilliant wordsmith fuelled on political anger and makes him a natural choice for Best First Novel."
—BOOKS & BOOKMEN

The Last Election glows with an unstoppable phosphorescence, gutsy, scatological, unswerving."
—NEW STATESMAN

"Highly talented....The close-knit writing, the spare though exuberant style, the exhausting action, the Jacobean horrors in the most modern of disguises, all combine to great ghoulish effect."
—THE FINANCIAL TIMES

"Very impressive…a highly original and chilling satire. It is comedy of the blackest kind, yet it always has an underlying edge of seriousness."
—THE LITERARY REVIEW

THE
LAST
ELECTION

P E T E   D A V I E S

VINTAGE CONTEMPORARIES

Vintage Books
A Division of Random House
New York

Library of Congress Cataloging in Publication Data
Davies, Pete, 1959–
    The last election.
    (Vintage contemporaries)
    I. Title.
PR6054.A89144L3   1987   823'.914   86-40155
ISBN 0-394-74702-X

THE LAST ELECTION

For Rebecca

In Nazi Germany,
old people were
referred to as
'cemetery weeds'

PROLOGUE

A week from today, the polls will be open and the voting will commence. It is the time of the Last Election.

Wally Wasted is one of many who won't be voting. Unlike the others, however, this won't be due to apathy. Wally won't vote, because Wally will be dead.

We are in the ruins of Wally's apartment. It is one room, a vast open space with a thick, deep blue carpet wall to wall. The carpet is littered with books, records, video cassettes, floppy discs, and shredded venetian blinds. These last have clearly been torn away from the floor to ceiling windows that run the length of the room on our left and right; and the windows have all been smashed. Broken glass lies along the edge of the floor; from the edge to the street far below is a long, long drop.

A tiny island of functional furniture and hi-tech equipment floats in the centre of the ocean-blue room. This too has been savaged. At the heart of the cluster, a big low bed smoulders where a small fire has died on it; there is a reek of lighter fuel. At the head of the bed, shelving has been thrown over; to one side, a neat little kitchen unit has been destroyed. At the foot of the bed, two arc lights have been knocked over and broken, and a video camera hurled off its stand and battered into pieces. On the other side, a dense bank of what must once have been sophisticated and expensive electronic hardware has been completely stoved in. The button-packed surface of a video editing console has been ripped open in many places by the repeated hammering of a crowbar through its thin metal cover; jagged little triangles of the metal stick up where the bar has sunk in and torn out, and these are stained with blood. Not yet dry, it runs down between the knobs, grooves, dials, and type-keys. Wires spill out; chip circuitry lies shattered and exposed. Monitor screens have been kicked in, sound mixing equipment beaten in, and tape spools strewn in festoons over everything. Somewhere under this heap of debris, a humble television set has escaped the onslaught;

1

calmly and firmly, the voice that still speaks from it is denouncing acts of terrorism.

On the far side of his smashed nest lies Wally on the floor. He is naked, bunched up in the foetal position except for his bad leg, which sticks out at its usual awkward angle; thin, white, hairless, and pocked all over with vivid stringy scars. His chest and belly are ripped and gashed, bubbling blood. His arsehole is horribly burnt, and bleeding profusely. He's still breathing; but only just.

Given that Wally is the people's favourite — with nice big numbers at the top of the ratings chart weekly to prove it — what on earth can he possibly have done, to get himself into a fix like this?

FRIDAY

ONE

In the run-up to the election, there was a fortnight to go. At six o'clock, the telly alarm bip-bipped, and up popped a smooth white face to tell this news to Inspector Bludge of Youth Surveillance. It was a matter of complete indifference to her, so she flicked over to the cooking channel, where bright young people were discussing instant curries. 'Now these Taj Mahals,' said a smiling presenter, 'took the market by storm two years ago; so what does our panel think of them now?'

'Watery, dodgy colour, short on meat,' said a chirpy little girl with bright green hair. Beside her, the man from Doo-wop Dupeaza PLC opined (promoting heavily) that Taj Mahals were a thing of the past.

'God help us,' said Bludge, sitting up in bed and flicking over to the private police teletext board. The screen clocked up the latest tally of London arrests — nothing special — and a fussy security bulletin about the arrangements for Nanny, who was going into hospital for a minor op over the weekend. A footnote from the Health Minister reassured all you loyal servants of the law that Nanny was fine, the op was routine, and she'd be back in press conference as usual on Monday.

'Big deal,' muttered Bludge, killing the screen with a touch on the remote. She rested against the headboard, unrumpling her nightie from the folds of her stomach, and considered the day. That morning, she remembered, she was due a visit from Grief, and that at least was something to look forward to. The snotty little bastard wasn't ever going to like her, she was altogether too gauche and prole; but she didn't mind knowing it, as his visits did add that touch of finery to the otherwise nasty, macho bustle of the City station. And then, screwing names from the poor guilty wimp was a minor thrill of cunning, when he thought her so stupid. She heaved herself out from under the sheets and examined her pink fleshy feet. One of the few good things about being so porky and moist, she decided, was you never had to spend money on all those lotions and creams for dry skin. Although the best thing about her bulk was, of course, that it hurt more when she hit people.

Bludge lived in North Kensington, in a dilapidated mews cottage completely surrounded by suspect garages, scrap-iron dealers, and crumbling bedsit warrens for the rootless, the dole kids, and the blacks. She could have had far better, naturally; police accommodation on their special estates was simply unbeatable. Perhaps it might have been safer, too; but she never got serious trouble. Considering her predilection for a juicy spot of violence, this mystified her at least as much as it did all the others down the shop. But it wasn't bad, to be close to her roots; and, in her idiosyncratic sort of way, she was amenable to those more dubious kinds of reason that come with the deals, the let-offs, the tips and the back-handers. Generally speaking, Bludge was thought of as a good copper — or as near to such a thing as it was possible to be.

Perhaps it was just that, locally, everyone knew she only stayed there for her mother's sake. The lefties wound her up, and the blacks of course were scum; but mostly the place would stay OK, until her mother'd got on with it and died. The only obvious sign of an understandable distaste for her presence in the area was the regular daubing of the jam sandwich parked outside; and secretly, she rather liked that. Sprayed all over the side of her car, sad comments, like whether anyone had ever found her vagina under all that belly, simply made her feel important. Bludge had a shitty job, and wasn't often noticed.

She forced her way into her uniform — the Clothing Dep still hadn't bothered to do her up with something that fitted — and trundled down to make herself breakfast. Then she banged about with the washing up, to wake her mother. Sure enough, right on cue, the same silly question whined its way across the tiny hall from the downstairs bedroom. 'Is that you, dear?'

She replied — as she did every morning, squeezing across the hall with the tray of warm milk, porridge, and tablets — 'No Mum, it's Nanny come to see us 'cos we're so vital to the nation.'

And when she was into the bedroom, her vacant and immobilised mother finished the ritual, dreamily saying, 'Oh I wish Nanny would. She's such a strong woman. I'd like to see her, to know how she does it.'

Bludge gave her the tray, hauling her up so she could dab at her food, then turned on the telly. 'Would you like snooker today?' she asked, pressing buttons until she'd found her way to 147. But the commentator on air was that socialist thug Thor Thunders, whom her mother disliked as much as she did; so she left it on the oldies' channel instead, where there was a nice show on about dogs.

Going back across the room, Bludge looked out the window. It was beginning to get light, and she could just see some rather less pleasant dogs, strays, crowded on the roof of an unfinished building. They scrabbled about amongst the concrete and metal, snarling and barking; she wondered if any of them were rabid. Perhaps she should get them down here, to bite her mother. Time was, until a few months ago, when the old cow could still at least potter a bit, and get her own food, and even stretch to attempts on the housework on her better days. Then she seized up, went to bed, and whined non-stop for a truly wearing three months. If it hadn't been for the police welfare, Bludge would never have managed it. Against all her deepest working-class principles, she'd have dumped the old bag in an oldies' hostel. But mercifully the police had proper social services, even if no one else did. There was a lot that Bludge could take, but cleaning up a shit-filled bed every day wasn't part of it; there was too much that was like that down the cells as it was. But it paid, to be in the law, it was as good as being rich. Why, they didn't just clean and feed her mother, they'd come up with those little grey tablets, too, that had shut her up good and proper, killed the pain and stopped her moaning something wonderful. Anyway, Bludge consoled herself, she was fading fast now, ageing all in a rush and would soon be gone. Bludge felt guilty, of course, but knew it'd be a blessing.

She made sure her mother had swallowed the pills, and was on her way out when the phone rang. A Latin voice, asking, 'You want a good catch?'

'Yeah, yeah,' said Bludge. 'What is it and where?' She got this sort of stuff all the time.

'It's the new drug,' hissed the voice, 'that's been selling down the Barn. You want the supplier's main agent?' Bludge perked up — this sounded like good news. An address followed, a disused warehouse on the other side of the City, and a time that she realised was only an hour away. She asked who she should thank for the tip. 'Ramon,' said the voice, 'and what will you give me? Like, how about a month off my back?'

Bludge answered, 'I'll give you what I feel like. You're only telling me this because when the kids buy new drugs, they don't buy your grass. But thanks, I'll remember it.'

She hung up, and bustled out to the car. Someone had written on it during the night, 'When Bludge goes down on you, you don't never get up.' She liked it, and smiled; she'd leave it on for a while. Then she banged on her cherry top, and all the blue roof lights, and cannoned off into the gnarled crush of traffic, calling up two subordinates as she went and telling them where to be. She hoped she'd be back soon enough not to miss Grief.

TWO

Another person not troubled in the least by the imminence of an election was Cairo Jones. What with everything that he had on his mind, and the contingent fact that his mind was very small, Cairo'd hardly noticed it. Cairo was only good at three things — sex, thoughtfulness, and riding a motorbike — and seeing how Marl was mostly too faded for the first these days, it was the second and third that were called into play this morning.

'Look,' Cairo, changing channels, happily remarked; 'Thor's on 147 today.' He knew this would please her — that show, Marl said, was 'the only outlet left in the corrupt capitalist media for an alternative point of view.' Unfortunately, as Cairo tuned in, Thor was playing a heavy metal video in between frames of the snooker. Marl turned her head away, moaning — the music, she said, was sexist, racist, fascist, atavist, and a whole lot of other words that meant nothing to Cairo. He thought it was rather good, himself; man's stuff. But he didn't dissent, Marl didn't like that; and anyway, he knew she was down to the last of her tablets. That was why he was getting up so early. The music stopped, and long-haired Thor came up on the screen, lumpishly ranting against Nanny and all of her works. Marl relaxed.

It had taken weeks to get Marl off the heroin. Cairo wasn't sure she'd have made it; but down at the Barn a week or two back, Moses Brandt had told him to try his new drug on her. It came in big yellow tablets, and was really a good one, Moses' best product yet. It had eased her pains, and even, occasionally, made her lively. It was also, to Cairo's relief, considerably cheaper than the smack — though naturally he'd never complained. He secretly believed that Marl had been out robbing oldies and backpackers on what was left of the tube, to support her habit; he knew that the dribs and drabs he made on what messenger work he could get was no way enough.

It had been just about alright when she still got the dole — she'd been jobless for years, and always would be, after foolhardy attempts to unionise the marketing department of a software company where she'd worked — but now the dole had stopped her cheques for co, co, cohab—…something else Cairo couldn't understand. All he understood was it meant he had to find more money. So he'd asked Moses whether he couldn't buy this new stuff in bigger quantities, to sell it on at a mark-up amongst his messenger fraternity. Cairo wasn't really sure whether this was right — but Marl needed her dose, and the rent was due.

Moses said he couldn't carry bulk on him down at the Barn, he could only sell it there for personal use — he didn't say that Ramon would have knifed his face if he'd acted any other way — but he gave Cairo a time and a place for scoring tabs by the hundred. It was across the City; there'd be a man with a walking stick, in an abandoned warehouse.

Cairo edged over Marl's thin body, and into the one foot gap between mattress and wall. There was just enough space to get dressed at the foot of the bed, between the telly and their clothes crate; he hauled on his leathers, teetering against the door, then told her he'd be back, and squeezed out of their bunker of a bedsit and onto the stairway. There was already a queue for the building's one sink, so he didn't bother washing, and went straight on down to the street. As he unchained his bike — painted many bright colours for disguise, after he'd stolen it from under the body of a crash victim — he saw Bludge's graffiti-splattered panda go noisily screeching across the bottom of his road. He wondered what that dangerous woman was up to, with her siren wailing, and her lovely lights all firework and circus; but that was how she usually went to work — how else could she get through the traffic?

In the early light, the first sharp kids were laying out their boxes and their square yards of canvas, displaying for sale what they'd nicked in the night. A cigarette tout, maybe ten years old, tugged at Cairo's sleeve, looking up with wide eyes; Cairo smiled and said no. Dust blew through the bricks and rubble; the neighbourhood cleaners swept litter into stinking piles around the broken lamp-posts. Wheeling his bike away from the railings and off the pavement, Cairo, as he did nearly every day, narrowly avoided stepping into the man-hole from which the metal cover had long been removed; the cavity was slowly filling with rotting vegetables and fruit peel, paper, grimy waxed cartons, and other indeterminate black mire. He looked forward to the day when it would be full, so that he could walk on his pavement without thinking again. Then he kicked the engine over, listened to it growling, and roared off down the street.

The main roads were chaos already, jammed with big low Yankee cars brought over cheap for the auctions — dreadful old heaps, squashy handlers, flopping around corners on fat flat tyres. Tinny little Nippon stuff, rusted all over, zipped in between them; sturdy old Beetles chugged along behind, metal wings flapping as they crunched across the potholes. The odd spanking new Suzuki jeep, or Jag, or BMW, stuck out a mile, the rich-boy driving it studiously invisible behind tightly shut and tinted glass. And then there were the private buses, all shapes and sizes of clanking old Dodges, Volvos and Saviems, painted in crazy colours with hand-scrawled lettering to tell their routes, and bouncing bonnets threatening to eat up the cars jammed in front. Their ticket men hung from the ever-open doors, calling destinations, and stopping the vehicles dead wherever there were passengers willing to be collected. The roads were no place for motorbike boys; Cairo didn't know any other who'd lasted intact for more than a year.

But Cairo had scraped a living for nearly two years this way now; he was a mechanical animal, instinctive with his machine, and knew every hole in the road, every place round the town where the kerb had collapsed and spilt stones across the street. He weaved through the clogged West End, and accelerated through the silence of the empty City. Beyond it lay Wapping, Bethnal Green and Mile End, where the Pakis and the oldies huddled together against the National Front amid debris and never-emptied dustbins. Down by the river, on the City side of security-walled, hi-tech Docklands, where people made TV and computers counted money, Cairo found his warehouse. Glued together with mud, there was a pile of tubes, wire and concrete; the old man crouched behind it with his stick, dripped on from holes in the roof that moaned in the wind like empty milk bottles. Cairo edged the bike up through the entrance and carefully slid, engine ticking, over rotting spools of cable and the black oily earth.

Back in the bunker, Marl shivered under thin blankets, feeling her body grow tired. She longed for another pill, and Cairo's soft coffee skin. On the flickering screen Thor raved, yobbish didactic.

THREE

Thor Thunders said — on a better screen, in a smarter part of town — 'When Nanny spouts on about your bad old days, all she means is any time between now and a hundred years ago, see? 'Cos everything before that was Victorian and perfect, right? But you only got to look at your hiss-tree to see things were totally dead 'orrible for your every Victorian bar your richest — which is just like today. And your sentry in between, when the likes of you and I got a mite better off — she only means that was the bad old days, 'cos them was the days when your so-schlism got listened to. And your cows like Nanny didn't have no clout then, now did they? So use your vote, and be shot of the bitch. Here's a can of brew to victory and the People Party.'

Wally Wasted hated Thor. With his heavy metal and his beer, and his miserable commitment, he debased the fine art of television. So Wally escaped to a news channel, to find fawning pressmen asking planted questions after Nanny's health. 'It's a routine operation,' Nanny smiled; 'I'm having my ears cleaned out' — expectant pause — 'the better to hear the people with — and you can quote me on that.' Polite laughter fussed around the conference room. Behind the leader, broad-shouldered minders shifted watchfully, obscuring the slogans camera-ready on the backdrop; media advisers gently re-positioned them. Wally killed the screen.

You'd have thought, he fumed, with an election imminent, that there'd be at least just a wee bit of noise abroad in the country. But God, was it boring. Soothing as treacle, the common sense of the Money Party oozed from every pore of the media. Every other page of his teletext was a stodgy froth of sweet right reason. Now and then, carefully tailored little success stories chattered on to nudge at the tiller of public opinion; but with the boat so firmly headed in the one direction only, and all so very quiet down there in the steerage, Wally couldn't see how anyone could consider it a contest. As the people had been told for fifteen years and more, so they were told all over again: 'We are doing very well'. The medicine tasted good, spooned out in print and pixels; we've got, people thought, the best we can hope for.

It was, of course, a free country. Distorted faces of the left did get squeezed in now and then — the most prominent among them being Thor's, as the People Party politicians were untelegenic. And this did lend a thin illusion of excitement to proceedings; but little else. Carefully edited between ministerial pronouncements on the great good health of the nation, the lefties jabbered in a brief helpless rage; and abruptly they were gone.

The vote was a foregone conclusion. Only newspaper editors, who had product to sell and knighthoods to earn, got worked up about it. 'Look, guys,' Wally tried on his millions down the cable one night, 'a people without expectations is a people without rights; know what I mean?' That's a laugh, thought the viewers. Old Wally, he's got that Thor impersonation right down to a tee.

But it wasn't just Wally who mimicked the lefties. One of the big software companies had a commercial that took the piss out of the People Party something rotten. The proposition was simple enough, and very familiar: your firm would do better if it employed programs, not people. To demonstrate the disadvantages of people, they showed this real scabby old dustheap of a typing pool, staffed by various luminaries of the left; played by famous comics, they turned the antiquated office into a morass of slapstick bunglings. Hard cut to a natty set of gleamy hi-tech rooms, all light and space, with just a scattering of zecks to weigh up the info and do the deciding. And these offices, natch, were being ceremonially opened by lookalike actors playing government top dogs. Now it just so happened that wherever else it cropped up, this ad was always on halfway through the news shows on every channel in the land. Wally would have laid big money that they got that space free.

But he'd have been cheating. He'd have won the bet, because the girl who wrote the ad had told him just how much space the right got given. Milla Sharply, she was called; and she was something else. Wally fancied her more than the girls in the booze ads, even. Milla was his tenant, living on the floor downstairs with her boyfriend Grief; she worked for Crinkly Crisp and Greenback, the agency which — according to its publicity — gave the people 'the flavour they require'. In a brief and dazzling career, Milla had thrilled the millions with witty, vivid, manic images of masking tape and tampons, toasters and Toyotas, computers and disco dance barns — you name it, she'd written an ad for it.

After the software epic, Milla was awarded the ultimate accolade. She was appointed to write the ads for the Money Party in the coming election. You couldn't, in her line, get more prestigious business; but for Milla, it was like living in a goldfish bowl, with the pressure of everyone waiting to see what she'd come up with, and all the papers interviewing her so the people would look out for her work when it came. So she wasn't around, this morning with a fortnight to go — she'd had a bit of a breakdown.

As it happens, when her mental gears did slip, she'd already turned in what was (by all accounts) a truly knockout string of ads. And, luckily for her sake, she'd done so with two weeks to spare before the Money's big guns were officially due to be shown them. There wasn't another creative team in the building could come up with work that'd match them. So to make everything safe, the agency shoved the ads into research, and Milla on a plane. Loving her to death and paying her accordingly, they packed her off sharpish to a Crinkly Crisp rest home, way away in the Bahamas — they had to have her head clear, when she presented those ads.

But there was more to the breakdown than a bit of pressure.

11

What the agency didn't know about poor Milla Sharply was that, being desperately optimistic as well as unduly imaginative, she was a closet People Party voter. Why, she'd even attended a meeting or two (before she got rich) . . . .

'Healthy, wealthy, and wise. That's the message, and that's the Money.'

'Don't you worry, your Nanny's in charge.'

'There's nowt more nifty than your old Nanny, and nowt more meaty than the Money she runs.' (For Central, Yorkshire, Granada and Tyne Tees).

Breakdown? Wally wouldn't have been surprised to find one day, as he turned on the in-house cameras, that she was slitting her wrists.

And if you're wondering about advertising standards, forget it. By the time of the Last Election, ads were all-powerful. You should have seen the sort of stuff they were putting out for the health insurance companies, like disaster movies, really; Mad Max in towering suburbia. Wally especially loved those ones with the burning people hemmed in by the psychos at the door with their axes, and only saved in the nick by the man from BUPA. Being a cripple, the telly was his only entertainment. And that's why the election was such a terrible disappointment. He put the kettle on, and rolled himself a joint.

FOUR

Milla sat bolt upright in her bed, the sheet soaked right through in a Caribbean sweat. The telly in her beach chalet bleeped; the message flashed, 'Miss Sharply. Plane departure, 09.00. Arrive local time, 17.00. Car to collect in one hour.' Birds croaked in foliage above the sand bar; the sun rose livid orange at the edge of the deep blue sea. Oh God, oh God, she realised, it's London time again.

She had had a terrible dream. She was in Nanny's house — a palace — and in awe of its luxury. She trod lightly through marble corridors, where light curtains softly waved in a faint cooling draught. Magnificent grey stairways rose away up above her. She found a room with a patterned carpet, and plush baroque sofas. There was a videogame console. The

12

program instructed her to make up her characters, with which to play the game. She invented ten people, funny, sweet, distorted people; the program then placed them in a maze. Nanny, smiling, brought her tea in fine china. She played the game, and Nanny watched, approving, comfortably reclined with an eye on her screen. The game involved searching through the maze, to destroy all the characters you'd created.

Milla shook her head, stepped from the bed, and towelled herself down. She felt horribly light — hadn't had a drink the whole week — but at least the pains in her kidneys were gone. It wouldn't last, once she was back. She heard the security man pacing outside, and primly closed the window.

When she cut off the alarm, the agency teletext automatically took over, relaying to her the latest info on her business. There was the issue of the day — what, she yawned, defence *again*? — plus daily polls, updated; and all yesterday's quotable examples of People Party people putting their feet in their mouths. She noted without pleasure that the current tally of cock-ups was especially juicy, from a Money point of view. She pressed graph, and the ratings chart came on. Consistently, the Money showed thirty points ahead nationwide; though she knew the red towns in the north were removed from the equation. Not that they counted.

Outside, chalet doors were opening, and other cases of adland burn-up called to each other, went swimming, or headed up for breakfast. There were ten places on the Crinkly Crisp beach, for the people who'd overdone it on the coke, the booze, the work and the nerves. They were usually full. The agency gave you a week — it wouldn't do to calm the staff down too much. And if a week wasn't enough, too bad; you were out.

Milla doubted her week was enough. She packed, with precision and economy. Would Grief be nice to her? Fingers crossed . . . the car came to take her to the airport. She tipped the guard as she went. Island children on the roadside, fat-bellied with hunger, watched her driven by.

FIVE

Cairo edged his bike over red metal meshes and rotted brick.

All around him lay disintegrated engines and machinery. He circled a vast wooden cable reel; the iron bands that had held it together were all sprung out and buckled, lightly wobbling didgeridoo-style on the breeze. Overhead, choppers thundered on the air into Docklands, and plasterboard flapped off the girders. Water trickled down the pocked iron columns. On the river, executive motorboats buzzed and whined. In the distance the ever-sounding sirens, and the constant grumble of the traffic. As he neared the end of the great echoing hangar, he could see the old man, scratching the mud with his stick.

Suddenly, to one side, there was a clunk of stone on old sheet metal, a hissing little rush of small rocks over concrete, and was that a gasped curse? — or was it just his engine that had missed a beat, exhaust pumping air as he idled and slithered across the oil-slicky ground? He tried to speed up. A mangy cat behind an outcrop of breezeblocks made him jump with its mewing; then spun and fled silently through the razor-edged waste. Dust slipped down stone; crumbs of stone slipped down metal; scales of metal slipped down concrete; and in Cairo's worried mind, flesh cut on all of it.

The old man would not come forward. Cairo nosed right up to him, gripping the handlebars, and kept the engine turning over. 'You're the first, and you're late,' the old man said, face twitching with his worries. 'And you should have been fourth. Where are the others?' Cairo put his hand out to see the goods. Behind the hillock of piping was a gap in the wall; through it, he saw paper-strewn tarmac stretching down to the riverside, split jaggedly where weeds had pushed through.

The old man handed him a polythene bag. He tucked one leather glove into a zippered pocket, and weighed it in his palm; he had roughly counted less than forty tabs by sight, thinking there was maybe two hundred in the sac, when Bludge appeared through the hole in the wall. At her side was a man, more boy than man, grinning in his raincoat, with a gun. The old man grunted feebly and tottered back; Bludge and her man-boy advanced, all smiles. Cairo shovelled the bag into his pocket and heaved his body round, the bike whipping round beneath him with the pull of his shoulders and thighs, and revved the engine wildly, so that the free-spinning back wheel sprayed greasy filth and water all over the two of them.

14

Surprised, they stopped and backed, arms raised, as Cairo hauled the bike out of the gouge the back wheel had made and raced, engine screaming, wheels and body all together sluicing and jerking and bumping and sliding away over the garbage and oil where he'd come.

The man-boy raised his gun, but Bludge knocked it away, saying, 'Don't bother, I know him, he's small fry. Besides, you might hit Dwayne.' She brushed indifferently at the muck on her uniform, thinking that perhaps the next one might fit. Dwayne stepped off the road, walking into the entrance gate as Cairo skidded and skated towards him. He too raised a gun, jugend-blond hair wavily dipping on the breeze above his perfect-toothed smile. And he too saw that his colleagues were in his line of fire; he paused, and then realised that Cairo was nearly on him, face gritted in his helmet with stubborn and desperate determination to be away. He hopped smartly aside, and would have rounded to shoot Cairo in the back; but saw Bludge calling him over — she was thinking, why, oh why, do they second me these posing teenage wankers? — so he casually turned to cross the warehouse without a second thought.

Bludge approached the shivering old man; his dentures clacked in terror. The man-boy went past her, shoved him up against the mossy brick, and shook him down, finding as he went six more bags of the big yellow tablets. 'Now where,' said Bludge, 'did you come by these?'

'They're put through my door,' stuttered the oldie, 'I don't know the source.' Bludge was silent; he whimpered and repeated, 'I don't know the source.'

She took his walking stick from his shaking hands, and slapped it lightly in her own fatty palm. 'I don't believe you,' she said.

'Oh Lord,' he pleaded, 'please believe me, I got letters that said I'd make money this way, it was after I was out of the hospital, I'm on the dole for God's sake, I don't know who it was, they knew my wife was dying, they knew I needed the money, so I never asked who . . . .' Bludge raised the stick. The man rushed on faster, gabbling his words. 'My wife,' he blurted, 'don't you realise the cost of a God-fearing funeral . . .'

'Bollocks,' said Bludge, and smashed his nose open with the blunt end of the stick. Blood spurted; grey cartilage showed through the split skin; he crumpled down the wall slowly, caving in, all the air wheezing out. 'Now let's try it again. What can it be, that we should find an oldie such as you engaged in this unpleasant method of wealth acquisition?'

'Can't you see I'm a Christian,' splashed the gerry through his blood. Bludge turned her face to the sky, thinking it must be some clever kind of bastard, who put up a screen as impenetrable as this wrinkled scumbag was likely to be. Beside her, Dwayne and the man-boy quietly smiled, looking about them with no sign of interest.

A mile away to the west, Cairo sat on his bike in an empty alley, lungs pumping, brain void as he stared dully at the glistening cobbles. The bag of tabs lay safe in his pocket; and so, it eventually occurred to him, did his money. Marl would be pleased. He flexed his cold hand, examining the blue knuckles, and then put his glove back on. Suddenly the radio on his backbox crackled, and he jumped. 'Cairo,' it said, 'you on the road yet? Hey Cairo, it's gone nine, are you out yet?' He settled himself, dimly aware that he'd got more than he could have asked for, and a job already as well. Sometimes, he'd sit outside the bunker with the bike till way past noon; and watching the street while he listened to Marl might be nice, but it didn't rope in ackers. He called in and said he was available. 'OK good,' the radio farted back, 'can you go down to Docklands, yeah? There's a tape waiting now, at 147 HQ.'

'Who's it for?' he called back.

'Quarter-finals for Mr Wasted,' chirruped the staticky voice. That bastard, thought Cairo; but gunned up the engine all the same.

SIX

In Milla's absence, Wally's week had dragged. For a start, watching her take a bath on his monitors was one of the few sexual kicks he got these days. But — to do him justice — it was mainly her company he missed. Evenings, when Grief was out at work down the Barn, he'd be lying in bed, fiddling with his machinery, and she'd come up and sit with him to let off steam about the latest dirty doings down Crinkly Crisp way. Skinny as a bird, she'd perch and be bright, fine head angled forward on her scrawny neck like a heron hunting fish; racked with a twitchy stillness, she'd burst into sudden sharp movements of intensity as she made her violent points. Laughing, he encouraged her to rave at the immoralities of advertising; then he rolled huge joints to get her miserably stoned, and lecherously flirted with no end of lewd suggestion. Because he knew that she and Grief were more or less broken, when it came to sex; it was only a safe routine of argument that held them together, and a terrible fear of loneliness.

At least they had a nice place to live. The past decade had seen whole chunks of the money game up and off to the green and pleasant places, micros tucked under their arms, and the paperwork burnt behind them. Now, with the smokestacks dead, the money went instead to the bit, byte, bug and gene-crazy businessmen-scientists who were plotting tomorrow in the quiet heart of the country; the only other place to put it was abroad, and all you needed for that was a computer to move it.

This left holes all over the City, and no one to fill them. Wally, being a superstar, was stinking rich; so he bought two vacant floors of office space on the top of a tall, tall building. He had the upper himself, with access to a tasty little roof he'd vaguely hoped to cultivate — but then his leg got done in.

Milla and Grief rented the lower floor. It was fairly normal; they'd left some of the partitions up, and, littering different areas with different kinds of expensively chic and lightweight furniture, had turned it into a thoroughly stylish, big-roomed apartment — arty, plush, uncluttered. A central corridor was a kind of hallway, with glass to fence off studies on either side, for each of them to work in. Milla's room was full of bits of kit on which she knocked off rough versions of ideas for ads; a camera, a computerised paintbox, a video and TV, a sound-to-picture mixer, a library of records, cassettes, films, old ads and pop promos; with old posters covering the length of her career all over the walls and glass, so you couldn't see in on her when she was working. Grief's study had a pool table, and video games that had gone out of fashion in the Barn, but which he still liked to play at himself; and there was a micro for counting his money on. A designer friend had painted up the glass with a frantic, erupting pattern of lines, squares, triangles and circles — so that when you looked through, you could only see him in fragments, in black, red and blue.

The corridor opened onto a large central relaxing area, with thick white carpet, and black seating that swallowed you up so you could hide and not be noticed. The TV here was usually on, with the sound always down, and there was a stereo wired to speakers that ran all through the flat. Beyond this on one side was the bedroom and bathroom, and on the other a kitchen, with screens in all these rooms also. And beyond these rooms again was Milla's folly, a crazy room she'd dreamed of all her life, that Grief hadn't been able to dissuade her from building; though he was finally glad that he'd acquiesced, when it became the place that she hid in when they'd argued too severely, and holding each other close didn't make it any better.

One whole wall of this room was a vast screen; the wall opposite was a fish tank. The tank was only a few inches thick; floor to ceiling and corner to corner, it was sealed by thick sheets of glass that magnified the tiny, brilliant fish floating amid leaves and glitter and bubbles. Milla thought she was a fish like that. Two glass handrails extended along the two side walls as far as the screen, so the fish could have a little wander away from their wall now and then; which, again, was about as far away as Milla ever got. The light in this room was dim; the blue of water and electronic images. The floor, ceiling, and side walls were all black; the only furniture was a padded swivel chair in the centre of the room, so she could spin from the film to the fishes and back again, effortlessly.

Wally had hidden mikes and cameras installed in the ceiling of all their rooms, so he could watch this strange girl who so strongly turned him on; but in no room did he like her better than in this last, her blue room. When she span in slow-motion, with her long legs splayed away out in front of her, sipping killer cocktails in the flickering blue light, then she was his; because Wally too was a sea-bed creature.

Older than his tenants, well past forty, and always too stoned to do anything difficult like walking through doors, or living in a closed space, Wally knocked down all the partitions on his floor; now his leg was no good, he lived in his one vast space, rarely moving from his nest of bed and equipment. There was a bog and a bath, sealed off at the far end from the door, and otherwise nothing; just the deep blue carpet, and the heavy blue blinds always closed so light never entered; and the room was the deep murky blue of the bottom of the sea. Thick air, fuggy from the joints that he chain-smoked night and day, hung around the faint electric twinkles from his editing desk; hooded work lights bent over him, and the monitors gave off a static subaqua shimmer of green print, and grey, white and blue pictures. From the doorway, his little huddle of living space looked like a submarine, suspended, with a great weight of water all around, against which the soft coloured lights made no headway. He lay in his bed, in the middle of all his space, with his kit all around him. He did his job, and the messengers came and went bearing the video cassettes that he worked with; and as he worked, she'd come and talk to him.

So too, sometimes, would Grief. This Friday with a fortnight to go, he came up early, at ten in the morning, with that grumpy hunch in his walk; so Wally knew it was a cop shop day. He said, 'Bad luck. You got to see Bludge today?'

Grief nodded yes, and Wally as usual felt sorry for him. Sure, they were all in the control business, one way or another. Grief's problem was just that he felt responsible for those he controlled.

Back when he was starting out, Grief was in film production, mostly for oil companies. That meant a lot of good times whizzing about in helicopters, and clambering up and down on jagged metal structures in weird places with a camera. The oil paid for him then, just like it used to fund all the dole kids, and the growing army of oldies in their hostels and their hospitals. But the oil was running out; so Grief changed horses. It was a brilliant idea, both lucrative and altruistic. If he'd thought a bit harder about the people who were backing him, before he jumped into the agreements on which their backing depended, it could well have been perfect.

Grief had a signal advantage over others of an entre-preneurial bent. His dad was Home Secretary (though since moved on, for screwing too many women like a good Money shouldn't). So Grief went to his dad and spoke two magic words: 'Urban renewal'.

Grief said, 'I've got my eye on a disused warehouse in Bermondsey. You subsidise me every way that you can —

grants, rates, tax relief, that kind of thing — and I can turn it into a palace. It'll have huge bars, and a light show like the kids have never seen; all of them can go there. They'll be happy; and you'll look good.' Never averse to good press, the Money Party jumped at it; so the Dance Barn was born. Imitations sprang up all over the country. They were hugely popular, and highly profitable.

Subsidised bop and booze for the dole kids — who'd have believed it? What Grief had forgotten, was that they were also places where the kids could be watched.

SEVEN

'Will you please stop him bleeding in my car?' The oldie sat in the back between Dwayne and the man-boy; Bludge watched his nose drip in the mirror as she barged through the scattering traffic. Newspaper kids, darting between lanes to hawk their rags at driver-side windows in the jam, skipped aside, making filthy gestures as she passed. Some idiot crazy enough to ride a bicycle teetered and lost control as a Chevy veered from her path and cut him up; he tumbled onto the pavement, plastic exhaust mask falling and breaking, and angrily waved away a bevy of oldies who came clucking to tend him while his spokes pinged out beneath the wheels of a truck. Waving her pass, Bludge took short cuts through cordoned-off streets not yet re-opened after bomb attacks, then came to the barrier at the end of the City Store road.

Armed law stood guard around the entrance, hard eyes on the document salesmen touting for business round the queue of visitors. Bludge nudged her car through the crowd, listening to them crying their wares; bail loans, legal aid, parking fine remissions, prostitution certificates, stamped tax papers and denouncements.... When she made it to the entry post, she fed her plastic to the slot and punched in numbers; the card was spat back and the barrier rose. The guards fended off the queue's faint-hearted surge as she slipped through into the station street. The oldie moaned behind her as the barrier dropped.

All down the side of the street, mechanics tended police vehicles. Bike coppers in shades swopped the time of day in twos and threes while they waited for call-outs, and constable infantry loaded up in vans with steel-meshed windows, visors glinting as they stacked their shields in the back. Bludge concealed her dislike of all the ostentation. She felt that open eyes, and smart questions to the right people, would always get more done; but no one ever listened to Bludge.

She pulled up at the City Store door, and climbed out amid the groups of lawmen striding in and out with their catches and their informers. Behind her, Dwayne and the man-boy bundled out the oldie, who slipped and fell to one knee, tearing the thin cloth of his suit. Suddenly short-tempered, Bludge cursed, and told them for Christ's sake to be careful. There was no need to cause any more hurt than would serve you; though the bugger was understandably in no shape to show gratitude. She ordered the man-boy to put him in a cell and clean him up, enjoying the look of distaste on his face for this nurse's task; and sent Dwayne off to pull out his records, and get back to her with whatever he could find. They hustled off, and Bludge stared sighing at the gleaming City Store sign.

There was a cough at her side; her mechanic stood waiting to ask if her car should be cleaned. She said no, telling him just to park it, then asked how he was, and how the day went. 'See over there?' he pointed, ruefully smiling; down the road was a vast, windowless armoured truck, metal grey-green. It was dented all over, mightily battered, the paintwork ruined, and charred smoke and flame scars rose up its sides. The reinforced glass of the driver's eye-slits was bejewelled with glinting cracks, radiating out from opaque patches where missiles had impacted. The protective metal grilles over the glass were buckled, or torn clean away. 'I don't know why,' her mechanic complained, 'those sods in the north can't mend their own motors, instead of sending them down here all the time. It's not our fault if they can't keep 'em quiet up there.'

'Don't worry, Hal,' Bludge smiled; 'we make a profit on the service.' He nodded, hopping into her car to take it away. She lumbered up the steps into the foyer, elbowing through the bustle. In a side-room, pretty receptionists served coffee to key visitors. Posters advertised burglar alarms, security devices, electronic locks, telecom links for instant police response, bodyguard services, and everything else the City Store had to offer. Bludge pushed through to the staff bulletin screens, and the chattering text flickered by as she called up the flotation details; she found she had a choice of a bonus share option, upon retention of her original allocation for thirty months, or vouchers off the cost of police accommodation, phased across a similar period. The Met was going out on the Stock Exchange. Bludge looked at her watch.

A short walk away, Grief stepped out of the lift onto his apartment's ground floor, punching numbers to let himself out through the bullet-proof glass doors of the reception area's back wall. He nodded hello to the two guards on the desk, gave Wally a mournful wave on the security monitor, then passed out of vision and into the street. Wally used to wonder about that boy, he really did. He'd ask him, how could he be so casual, just strolling down the street? Maybe Wally was paranoid — being stoned all the time can get you that way. All the same, by the time of the Last Election, the bombs didn't hit just the one store, one bandstand, one barracks; they were taking out whole streets. You'd be walking down the road and suddenly whoomph, no road, no you. Sure, it didn't happen every day; but it happened, and it nearly happened to Wally once. That's how he got his legful of metal and glass, and he for one certainly wasn't planning to spend any more time on the wrong side of safe walls. But Grief thought Wally was being extreme. 'Look,' he'd say, 'it's just a quicker way to get about, OK? We got it easy over here. Imagine living across the water.' True, Ulster was a war zone — no cameras, no safety, just uncounted killing behind long-sealed borders. And statistically, Wally conceded, Grief was right. Over here we had more cameras.

When Bludge saw Grief coming, she went into bluff-and-bumbling mode, knowing how well it sat with her physique; so it felt to Grief like he was hardly through the City Store door, before the porker was puffing at his elbow like she seemed to be all his life. He saw her skin chafe in her uniform with the drying muck glistening oily all over it; and her shining face was queasy with mock eagerness. His heart sank; but as he turned, easy in his ancient baggy suit, worn smooth as silk and just as painless, his eyebrows asked, Yes? with overbearing smoothness. You slick shit, Bludge was thinking; but she waved his tip-off record at him, making hearty play of trying to be friendly. 'Well Grief,' she started; 'I see you've not been nicking a lot of those black bastards for me lately.'

'You know something, Bludge? There's days when your sense of humour really makes me puke. How's your mum?'

Grief knew she wasn't as thick as she played it. Taken aback, she blankly replied, 'Hanging on.'

Nastily he continued, 'You'll be glad when you're shot of her, don't tell me. Then you can move house to get vouchers off the rent, and play stag instead of sitting on duff shares. I know you, Bludge.'

If he had something on his mind, she thought, then the morning's negotiation wouldn't be so easy. She wondered if Milla was back yet, and put a lumpy hand on his shoulder, turning to usher him through the jostle to her office; and started reproaching in a coy, part-motherly way. Grief shivered. If there was one thing about Bludge that bugged him especially, it was the ghastly suspicion that the bulk somehow fancied him. But she was saved from the way that he'd thrown her by the arrival of Dwayne, with print-outs on the oldie they'd celled up downstairs. He handed them over, eyes half-closed and wandering, no colour in his face.

Looking down the data, she asked Grief to wait, and said to Dwayne, 'Did you not notice anything strange in these records?' He shook his head no, indifferent. 'Then how old,' she asked, 'would you say that our man of this morning might be?'

Dwayne shrugged, and guessed sixty.

'He's forty-six,' Bludge informed him.

'So he's sick,' Dwayne replied. 'Who gives a fuck?'

EIGHT

Wally had another problem with the coming election. Every way he looked at the numbers, they just didn't add up. Wally loved numbers, and not just the workaday stuff of editing his tapes to the millisecond, or calculating what points were left on the table to see if a snooker was required. When the guards called up that they were letting in Cairo with another cassette, the numbers he was juggling with concerned oil and the oldies.

Cairo padded over through the unclean air, videotape held out with the clipboard for a signature; Wally said hello, and jeeringly asked after the heavy metal brigade. 'Nice to know someone still watches that Thor, eh, Cairo?' he bantered.

'I like his music, Mr Wasted,' Cairo quietly replied.

'Here's an equation, Cairo,' Wally breezily continued, propping himself up to sign for the tape. 'There's thirteen million OAP's, OK? And half a million more of them are eighty plus than was the case a decade previous. Now it costs a lot of money, looking after so many gerries.'

'I didn't know that,' said Cairo.

'Hell,' said Wally, 'I thought there was so many oldies crowding up the pavement out there, you had them falling under your wheels every day.'

Cairo bridled. 'I've never hit no one.'

'Sure, sure, I'm sorry,' Wally hurried, 'but anyway, listen to part two of this equation. Right now, we're pumping maybe half the oil we were used to, even just a little while back. The price is low, 'cos there's too much of it about, and the dollar's dodgy, 'cos no one's paying their debts; so the income on that oil is getting pretty shaky.'

'I'm afraid I wouldn't know.' Cairo wanted to leave.

'What I'm saying, Cairo, is that a lot less income, against a lot more expenditure dole, pension, and health-wise, does not add up to improving hospitals as the Money have promised.'

'I thought you liked the Money,' said Cairo, confused. Marl said Wally was a bastard, because he was rich, took the piss out of Thor, and was therefore pure Money and QED evil. Cairo was content to accept what Marl said. For sure, there wasn't nothing clever about being spiteful; and Wally had plenty of spite, when it came to heavy metal. He said, 'I have to go now, Mr Wasted.'

Wally handed back the clipboard. 'Who's on to win the snooker?' he asked, as Cairo turned away. Cairo was tall; high above him in blue darkness, Wally couldn't see the stolid antipathy restrained on his face. Cairo said that Geoff Geometry would win. 'At least we agree on something. Here,' Wally smiled, and tipped him a lump of good black hash. Dimly, Cairo felt insulted; just as dimly, Wally felt that he did. Why was it, he wondered, that what worked on the telly, made people scorn him face to face?

Cairo had no more work calls on his way back to Marl, which was nothing out of the ordinary; but today he was glad, because the tabs could pay the rent, and all he wanted was a cuddle. Wally made Cairo feel stupid; it wasn't kind to do that. Marl didn't do it. Marl explained things.

There's nothing a lefty likes better than a malleable listener. Marl had met Cairo on the floor of the Barn eighteen months back. He'd just had the best week his bike had ever bought him, and it stretched to two whole rounds, and a line of coke too — a small line, sure, but coke all the same. Marl at the time was on a lesbian kick; it was ideologically sound, though her partner was a bitch and the sex not worth tuppence. Cairo, being half-something — Cairo didn't know what, but it was coffee-coloured anyway — was arguably 'ethnic', and therefore oppressed, and therefore acceptable, his gender notwithstanding. So Cairo and Marl got together.

If it sounds like she used him, it wasn't that bad. She saw he was soft, and generally hopeless, and took over all the things he couldn't manage for himself. She taught him how to read, and how to do battle with the dole to extract the odd allowance, and even came to enjoy cooking for him, on the odd occasions when they could afford decent fresh vegetables. Cairo, of course, could handle boiling up the Taj Mahals; though they'd since switched to Doo-wops, which were cheaper and better. And so they scratched along.

When Cairo got back, he blundered about in the communal kitchen till he'd found what was needed amongst the crumbs and empty packets; then he made tea for Marl, as a coming-back present. He squeezed through their door to find her sleeping, with the telly still on — it was a news channel, with millions of the starving numb beneath the lenses of the world, and commentary telling fibs about the Money's generosity towards this latest 'disaster', as if the hunger was some sudden, isolated event. The undercurrent, naturally, was along the lines of how lucky we are not to be like them (Vote Money). Cairo, distressed, turned back to Thor on 147. He wished they could afford a better telly; somehow snooker wasn't too hot in black and white. The picture was all over the place anyway, and snowed up like Alaska. Still, they wouldn't have one at all if there were still licences to be paid. Ads ran as the black ball went down, images of wealth to pay for Cairo's viewing. Naturally, Marl thought the ads were poison and corruption. Cairo didn't argue.

The door nudging open had brushed her feet at the bed's end, and she stirred, waking. 'Here,' he said, kneeling on their worn blanket and handing her the tea; 'drink it quick, before the plastic melts.'

She murmured thank you, love, pecking at his hand as she took the thin white cup, and asked him how his journey had been. He tossed over the bag; she visibly brightened, and swallowed a tab with her first gulp of tea. 'And,' he said, 'I didn't have to pay for them. Bludge bust the dealer, and I got away without paying.'

'Pig bitch,' said Marl. 'Still, that's brilliant.' She was waking up sharpish now. 'You know,' she smiled, 'I think I should go canvassing, this last fortnight.' Cairo felt happy; she was getting so much better. He thought about getting his clothes off, to snuggle up; but the bike radio, which he'd brought up with him as a matter of habit, crackled and fizzed and suddenly told him he should go to some print shop, to deliver artwork to Crinkly Crisp. What a downer; they hadn't made love for ... he couldn't remember, so it must have been several days.

NINE

'Nice staff you keep,' muttered Grief.

Bludge came clean: 'I can't help it if they give me the scum.' She took him to her office.

The antagonistic fencing between these unlikely associates was by no means based solely on hostility. Grief knew his life could have been a whole lot worse, if it wasn't for Bludge. He could easily have found himself forced to treat with one of the new kind the law had got so keen on: grown-up Dwaynes, snakes fresh-faced and vicious, straight out of gangland, preening white soul boys with sharp shoes and knives. Then there was the military breed, the gun-toting tyros turned out in such numbers by the police colleges, who were shorter on brain but longer on thuggery. Still, that kind was ambitious; he couldn't see any of those boys ending up with a shitty posting like Youth Surveillance. So Grief reckoned he was safe with

Bludge for a good time yet. Ugly and incompetent she might be, but she was willing to give as well as take, and do deals, and tolerate his qualms and reluctance, and his clearly deliberate tendency to finger people she could easily have busted herself; or indeed, people she wouldn't have busted at all — people of her own kind.

Sure, they had their differences, and Bludge bitterly resented the limits of her hold on him; but his connections in the Money gave him a clout that he played to the hilt. He'd way back instilled in her a nagging paranoia that if she pushed him too hard, she'd find herself on riot control up in the red towns as quick as she could blink.

In fact, Grief privately doubted his strings would stretch that far, now his dad was out of office. But then, even if his dad and all his slippery mates had been just the same kind of smooth clubland drug merchant as Grief was, Bludge still couldn't tie him down, and get the info she wanted straight out; because technically, Grief didn't work for her. Technically, to his shame, Grief was a 'research consultant', on permanent contract with the Home Office. You had to pay for your profit in funny ways, those days.

Although Bludge had sounded jokey with her crack about not nicking blacks, she really did have a quota to keep and it exasperated her, that he shopped so few of them. Couldn't he understand her position? All too well he could, far better than she could ever understand his wet liberal desire to protect them. But Grief had had a trendy, well-heeled upbringing on Motown and reggae; Bludge's dumb white working-class xenophobia turned his stomach.

There was naturally more to it. For a start, the black kids were better customers. They were more active, more ingenious, and more keen to flash the cash whenever they could make it; and, when they did so, they rarely got foully drunk in the process. They danced better, and fought less. But more to the point, Grief didn't bust many blacks because they mostly only dealt in grass, and he couldn't see much wrong in that. He dealt in plenty of dope and grass himself, and cocaine too, all of which nicely topped up his retainer from the Home Office, and his money from the Barn.

Wally sometimes abusively demanded that Grief defend these activities, which was out of order, seeing as Wally would have been dopeless if Grief didn't supply him. Grief never took the bait. With an ironic shrug, he argued that the Home Office needed him to keep *au fait* with the rise and fall of prices, and the supply and demand situation — who was giving how much of what to whom. Also (truer Money than the Money themselves) he believed in competition; he liked to make sure that no one got a monopoly on a turf he felt should be as much of a free market as possible. But in the end, what it came down to was — Grief was coining it.

Appeasing himself, he tended to try and turn in only the smack dealers, because he didn't like them, or their drug; and because if he didn't turn them in, no one else would, what with how it suited the law and their leaders to keep the kids junked out, quiet, and quickly dead. Anyway, smack was bad for business — junkies don't do much in the way of dancing. The smack sales force was almost exclusively white; pink and grey faces spawned on the same estates as the likes of Inspector Bludge. So Bludge saw her kith and kin come wheeling in one after the other with Grief's tag on their cuffs, and it wound her up, when he wouldn't nab any niggers for her; especially when she got stick from the sales teams' management, when Grief had a purge, and turned in too many.

All of which added up to Grief knowing his market backwards. His DJ's played soul by the barrowload, with a heavy spicing of the juiciest rub-a-dub, and the crowds came running with oil in their joints and a frenzy to dance. You should have seen Milla's ads for the place, too. By the time of the Last Election, they'd started making out like there wasn't anything in the world you couldn't have, if you'd only sell your soul to the clubmaster. It was different in the early days; but Milla was younger then.

The Barns in the meantime had become great palaces of street fashion, with extensive cottage industries of hairdressing, clothes styling, writing, performing, video-making, games programming, drug dealing and plenty more besides busily backing them up; the apotheosis of the Money's obsession with the service sector. And if Grief wasn't the world's most moral man, he nonetheless felt like a father to the whole huge movement; so the enforced little treacheries, catching friends and acquaintances in his paymasters' net no matter how he tried to avoid it, all rustled in his heart, like the bubbles in your chest the morning after you've smoked too many cigarettes.

One day, he swore, he'd be pushed too far. But then, Milla felt the same about advertising, and said it far more frequently; and they both kept on taking the money all the same. Like a lot of angry people, the first cause of their anger was themselves. Not that Bludge helped, on this morning with a fortnight to go; she roasted him.

TEN

Bludge passed Grief out of the City Store checkpoints, again with that unsettling excess of physical familiarity — but she was well pleased with her morning's haul of names. They stood on the teeming pavement, cringing station suppliants eddying about them, and Grief itched to be gone. 'By the way,' Bludge casually remembered, on the point of leaving him, 'I'm getting news here and there of a new drug on your premises.' She pulled out one of the big yellow tabs from a key-clanking pocket. He shook his head and said sorry, it was a new one on him; he asked what it was.

Bludge said, 'It's synthetic; the labs are on it now, but they can't seem to crack it. Seems to be an upper, but I've only collared three users so far, and I can't really tell. The come-down after use is certainly fatigue, though nothing too drastic.'

'So it's speedy?' Grief suggested.

'I guess,' said Bludge, 'if you took enough; but they seemed more numb than manic. A kind of alert sort of smack, is the best I can make of it.' Grief laughed — that elusive ecstasy kick. 'If you hear anything,' she asked, 'let me know;' and shoved her way back to the barrier.

No chance, thought Grief. He shouldn't let things get to him; too busy worrying about what sort of state Milla might return in, he'd already given away far more this morning than he'd needed to. He walked quickly away.

Turning onto the main street off the City Store approach road, he noticed a figure stepping back out of sight in an alleyway behind him; he ignored it, too busy ducking past a beggar, then leaning back from a surge of oldies retreating in panic from a crossing as the lights changed, and traffic roared. But as he sidled through the whittering mass, head and shoulders above all their grey hair, the corner of his eye again caught the figure, which was pulling out to follow him. Further down the road he looked behind him and saw it in silhouette, rounding the corner after him and shoving past the oldies with mean, jabby little movements. He recognised the gait, and tucked into a video store doorway to wait.

Music bellowed and posters screamed. 'Wally Wasted's One Hundred Greatest Breaks — Snooker At Its Best!' 'Maria Pulls It Off!' 'The Sickening Galactic Evil of Gargoyle the Globe-killer — your guts will run and your flesh will crawl!' 'Snakefucker — New Regions of the Bizarre!' On monitors in the window, men boxed and played cricket, barbarians slaughtered hordes of demon invaders, outer space warriors zapped each other in fountains of gore, a caveman swung across what looked like a missile silo towards a control room in which a mad masked axeman made ready to hack up a screaming pubescent girl, and women wanked ferociously in a variety of imaginative positions.

The shifty figure snuck past, trying to see where he'd gone. He reached out and grabbed him by the collar, hauled him up close, and said, 'Morning, Moses. Now what you doing, running round in my wake?'

He would have said more, being seriously annoyed, but was too surprised by the condition of his friend. Moses was grey and white, skinnier than ever; his skeleton rattled as Grief held him up, and he shivered with the shock of being pounced on. He said, 'Grief, I got to get some help from you.'

Grief sighed. He'd have charity status, if he helped all the people that asked him. He set Moses down, and asked 'What's the problem?'

'Bad,' said Moses, re-adjusting his bones as Grief let him go. 'Ramon shopped my dealer.'

Grief sighed some more. 'Oh Moses, Moses,' he wearily asked, 'why are you dealing yet again? You are simply so bad at it.'

'No,' Moses jabbered, shaking, and beginning to gesticulate with alarming and unnecessary vigour, 'I had a really neat set-up. I laid the arrangements on an oldie who needed the bread, and it was perfect. And the product is magic.'

'Uh-huh,' Grief nodded, who'd heard it all before. 'What is it this time?'

'It's a jacked-up derivative of a painkiller I made for the oldies,' Moses enthused, 'and I tell you, it's electric; sweeter than coke at one-sixtieth the price. It's heaven in the shape of a pill, everyone should have some — here, look;' and he fished out a big yellow tablet.

'Well well well,' chuckled Grief, 'I should have guessed. OK, Moses, listen to me good. Ramon's in Camden tonight, so you can move whatever stock you got left in the Barn while he's away. I will then tell him to leave you alone, because after tonight, you will cease doing this business, and I mean that absolutely; because Ramon is the least of your problems. Bludge is now aware of this product.'

Miserably crestfallen, Moses admitted, 'I reckoned she would be. And it was such a good scam.' Then he giggled, quaking, 'But who'd have thought it, eh? The youth getting high on an oldie painkiller.' Grief wryly suggested that it didn't look like it had killed too much of Moses' pain. Taken aback, Moses jerkily babbled, 'So this morning I took too much of it, I got the shakes, that's all. But inside, boy, I'm rolling on the wind . . . .'

Grief wanted to close the conversation. He said, 'This is the last time that I fish you out of your bungles, OK? I really don't want you moving the results of your dodgy experiments in my Barn any more, not ever again — is that clear?'

Moses grabbed at his sleeve; he whined, 'We could make a mint, Grief, hey.'

'I do make a mint, you jerk. Now will you just naff off out of it and leave me alone?' Grief stomped off, leaving Moses in the video store doorway. A bunch of dole kids knocked him aside, barging past to take back last night's porn and loudly discussing what to swap it for next. 'Bermondsey Ballbreakers — cunnies afire with lust, these dance barn darlings can't get enough cock thrust in all their gaping holes! The sex, the drugs, the music: close-up oral, anal, and hard, hard fucking all night long to a pounding, throbbing beat!'

ELEVEN

Milla had never got used to being important. Customs and

immigration had all been pre-arranged; what was normally an hour at the least of hassle with documents and searches had been, for her, a VIP's five-minute formality. She stood staring round the muted hubbub of the Heathrow concourse; the dusty disrepair of the roped-off Ulster desk preoccupied her. Then she felt the first tug at her sleeve, and remembered she was back. The man beside her — short and unshaven, with a gold chain showing at his open collar — clearly assumed from her random gaze that she was foreign. He showed her a photostat of a badly typed price list, and suggested through yellow teeth, 'Taxi?'

'I'm English,' said Milla distractedly; then angrily added, 'And no way does it cost that much to get into town.'

He began, 'Then for you. . . .'

'I'm flying,' she said, and waved him away; shrugging, he sloped off. A scrawny pair of kids rushed up, holes in the knees of their trousers, barging and scrabbling at each others' faces to try and get to her first. The bigger one won, and stooped to pick up her bag. 'Clear off,' she said, yanking him up by the elbow.

'Then fuck you, missus.'

Milla's skin tingled. The smaller kid stayed, staring up at her hopefully. 'Alright then,' she sighed, 'come on.' He jumped to take her bag and trudged along behind her, the tongues of his too big shoes dusty and flapping. First they went outside to money-changer's alley; Milla's tongue dried as fingers sampled her wisely empty pockets. She span round; in the faceless crowd, it could have been anyone. Dirty men with fistfuls of notes called their rates, eyeing her brashly. No one wanted dollars; the yen was a mile high. The kid waited with her bag; she gestured him back into the concourse, wondering what to do with her money, and stopped to peer up at the jungle of signs. She asked the kid, 'Transit? The helipad?' He stepped ahead and took her there. And when they arrived, and she showed that she only had dollars, he spat, took a fistful before she could move, and was off without a word into the crowd.

The flight to Battersea took no time; and horrors, Crinkly was there to meet her. He'd brought an official Money car, with the little blue bonnet flags bearing the party word, 'Resolute'. As the traffic cleared aside and they slid silently over the bridge, past the clutter of stalls, the racks of digital watches and the smoking grills of barbecued kebab, he handed her a wide, thin, brown paper package. She opened it; inside were three exotic sub-continent travelogue paintings mounted on polyboard. The headlines read, 'Toughen up your taste buds with a Taj Mahal'; 'Tease your tonsils with a Taj Mahal'; and, 'Tickle your tongue with a Taj Mahal'.

'Crap,' said Milla.

Crinkly smiled. 'That's what the client said.' They purred into Chelsea; ferocious teenagers yelled abuse out of black lipstick mouths.

Milla asked, 'What's it got to do with me?'

'You're firefighting, my love. Save us this business, and your rewards will be boundless.' Milla asked who was handling the account; Crinkly pouted, and said, 'Maelstrom,' affecting offhandedness.

Milla groaned. 'I hate him. Anyway, the product's a dodo. Why can't we just sack them? What's the mileage in advertising garbage?'

'My darling, look upon it as a challenge.' Crinkly stroked his velvet waistcoat. 'Sales twenty percent down in the last quarter alone, and still falling. What a coup it would be, to turn it round, don't you think? See if you can't come up with something that would justify the expense of, say, going out on 147; how about it? For me,' he crooned; then said 'Besides,' hardening up, 'we're committed. Trolly's already designed the new packs; they go to photography next week.' His shining lips puckered; she watched his rings flash in the orange light of the fire-eaters performing in Sloane Square.

'This is all very well,' Milla muttered, 'But I thought I was working on the Money Party account.'

'My love,' Crinkly soothed, 'you are, you are. But really, that's all over bar the shouting. The research report's not in till Monday, but already I hear that it's marvellous. We present the finished work in a week; then run it, and bingo. Shall I drop you off at home?'

Milla said, 'No, lend me some sterling and find me a bar.'

They swished through Victoria. Drunken Scotsmen manhandled tourists, and whores showed their thighs in laddered stockings.

TWELVE

Grief took a bus to Bermondsey, and in its crowded, resentful, petrol-smelly silence he worried about Moses. Moses was a bug-eyed, tweed-clad perpetual student type, hopeless in all respects, excepting chemistry. But his tendency to swallow the chemicals he invented was already making him look a great deal older than he actually was. He worked in a state hospital on the urgent business of developing cheaper new drugs to cut the bills and keep the oldies quiet; drugs that could then be sold on at a profit to the private homes. But if what he invented worked, and if he could devise a version of it that kicked, and if it didn't then kill his assortment of test animals — next thing you knew, he'd be flogging it down the Barn. Grief knew how little Moses got paid — a bit more than a cleaner, maybe, but not much — and didn't like to rein him in; but he'd become increasingly keen to do so, especially after certain dicky hallucinogenics had caused a near riot in the toilets. And he was so irresponsible; when you told him to ease up on his consumption, he simply shrugged and said, 'Hell, man. The only way out of this shitheap is up.' Grief wondered how much longer Moses had.

When they got to Bermondsey, he hopped out to bury his worries by spending a day with his sparks; they were adding new toys to his lighting rig. It was a pleasant few hours, but the contentment was naturally marred the minute he got home. He found the answerphone flashing, and played it back to find it was a standard health service recorded announcement. 'Dear Person. We regret to inform you that a relative of yours has been admitted to this hospital. (The address followed.) You will be pleased to know that his/her injuries are not serious. Due to a recent government initiative, the permitted duration of minor injury stays has been extended from three days to six. If you would like to visit, the hours are as follows ....' Bastards, thought Grief; chucking a bone to the sick with an election round the corner. It'd be back down to three, the minute the votes were in. He went upstairs to tell Wally about it.

'So, hardheart' — now that was unfair; but Wally usually was — 'when you going to visit him/her? And who d'you think it is?'

Grief couldn't imagine; surely not his dad. If that man didn't have private cover, Grief was a Cayman; not that he knew, as he hadn't spoken to him in two years. (The last affair and the divorce of his second stepmother were the end, as far as Grief was concerned.) So he guessed it was one of the stepmothers, whose alimonies, he suspected, were pitiful. He said he'd go on Monday; he'd been planning to go away for the weekend with Milla, and he wasn't giving that up.

Wally didn't pursue it, privately pissed off that Milla was going away again, just as soon as she was back; so he rolled a fat joint instead. They sat in the dim murky blue of Wally's whispering sea-bed, Wally in and Grief on the big bed; Nanny's voice boomed and thumped like depth charges from the wide bank of screens. She was giving her last press conference before the operation, with no end of one-liners for the headline writers to play with tomorrow; ear to the ground, hearing no evil, etc etc. Then she switched gears and steered a more familiar course. Red-eyed from dope in the dark, Wally and Grief listened again, numb, to all the claptrap about nerve and resolve, greatness and go-getting, the ghastly sin of a debilitating dependence on the state, socialism is bananas, we are doing very well . . . until the security monitor bipped, and there was Milla, lurching about and kissing the guards in the hallway.

'Oh Lord,' Grief said; 'She's drunk.' And in she bounced, bumping against the doorway, spinning on the spot, holding her arms up high; sparkily grinning like an urchin in a rumble.

'I'm drunk,' she announced. 'And what are you watching the maniac for?' She wrapped one skinny arm round Grief's head as he held her loosely in his big tired arms, nose buried in her sweater where he could smell the spilt alcohol; with her free hand she picked up a stray remote control to zap Nanny and flee to a better channel. But Nanny was on all of them, so she killed the screens dead, gave him her other arm, and shook him about, laughing and coughing; then fell in his lap and gave Wally a wave. 'Hello,' she said, 'all sad and boring here, are we? Hey, aren't I brown? My forearms are burnt, but the rest cooked nicely — wouldn't you say?'

You wouldn't, not really; she was the same wasted white of London that she'd always been, and whiter still against her fountains of jet black hair. Grief asked, how had her holiday

been. 'Lovely,' she cackled, 'hot, exotic, sunny and lovely.'
He tried to unwrap his head from her clenching embrace,
and asked, had she done any work. But of course she
hadn't, darling, not a stroke; what, for Christ's sake, was a
nervous breakdown for? Besides, she rattled on, the big theme
ads she'd done already, they were ace and impeccable, they'd
be bought in seconds, Crinkly himself had said so. As for
the up to the minute, hot off the press stuff for the papers in
the last flying fortnight, well; she'd knock them out later as
and when the need arose. 'After all,' she said, frantically
laughing, 'd'you think I really care? There's more lies in the
crap I'm writing for those people than my conscience dares
count.'

'They'll sack you,' Grief hopefully suggested, always dreaming of the day when they would, and he could have her back to
himself, normal again. 'This hysterical pretence of indifference, you know, this forced cockiness; I'm sure it's not the
attitude that they're looking for.'

'On the contrary,' she bragged, 'They've given me a new
account; so don't you be so patronising. No, they won't sack
me. I've got the common touch, I'm too valuable. Like Wally
here.' She grinned, and gabbled on in a nervous frenzy of
statistics about the eating habits of the nation. The heavy blue
fug of smoke and light washed thickly around them; like lost
divers clinging to a rock, they swayed and slipped about while
she pointed in a million directions, releasing gas from their
cylinders and urgently trying to wave against the dead weight
of the water.

THIRTEEN

Wally's employers did once try to sack him. It was soon after
his leg was damaged; he'd sunk into new regions of bitterness,
and had his first crap-fit. But if his viewers had liked him
enough before, with his sick cynical jokes and his bleary,
giggling, no-hope philosophy, they loved him afterwards,
when he degenerated into denouncing everything straight out
as a huge pile of crap. He was so in tune with the feelings of his
millions, that when it was rumoured that he'd gone too far and
the big push was imminent, a torrent of letters and phone calls

gushed in to support him. They ended by upping his salary to hang onto him.

It had looked very democratic; but what swung it in the end wasn't the viewers, but Nanny. She intervened in his favour after advice from Crinkly Crisp.

They suggested that the huge public boredom of unemployment needed a public expression, if it wasn't to result in more riots; let Wally endorse and appease it, as simply *the way that things had to be.*

Nanny knew a good displacement activity when she saw one; Wally's cackling tirades on the terrible state of the nation became as good a running joke as the England football team — now composed almost entirely of second division players, as the big clubs were staffed exclusively by Danes, Finns, and South Americans. But Nanny's intervention was so secret, not even Milla knew about it; and Wally, knowing her views, most certainly wasn't letting on.

Obviously, Wally Wasted wasn't his real name; but it was how the populace knew him. The *Sun* had dubbed him thus when he first got big. It had stuck all the time he got bigger; and now he was the biggest. On good days, like when the finals of the more spectacular tourneys were running, Wally got audiences touching ten million. In those fragmented, megamedia days, no one reached more people than the whingeing Wally Wasted.

Wally's employer was a cable outfit called Channel 147, which supplied the sleeping multitudes with a twenty-four hour a day diet of non-stop snooker, snooker, snooker. Wally was the star commentator, but in all there were ten of them, working a loose kind of shift system; between them, they had the mass audience targeted, taped, sewn up and sold to the profoundly grateful admen. Every break was filled with extravagantly glossy big-budget commercials for all those high-volume, low-unit-cost essentials that the people just couldn't do without, week in, week out; cornflakes, soap powder, bog paper, chocolate bars, new games for your micro, new movies for your video, tapes, table wine, magazines, milk, bread, eggs, lovely cheap tinned fish, toothpaste, tea, tampons, razor blades, beans, own-label beer — gassy filth, but all other booze bar wine and the subsidised Barn stuff was prohibitively expensive, and advertised instead on

AB channels like the Business Station and Vogue TV to reach the likes of Milla; for the dole mass, other drugs were cheaper. And finally, of course, Nanny and the Money Party, for whom high-volume simply wasn't the word.

So 147 pulled the crowds and shifted the units. To do this, it used front men who shared the tastes and states of mind of the great workless mass, and the great mass of others who worked for a pittance; after heavy research into which, the station had settled on five alkies, two dopeheads, an acid brain, a coke fiend, and a pair of junkies who counted as one because they worked together, to cover the frequent occasions when one or the other was crashed out and inoperative. To top up the certainty that every angle was covered, these stars were also all DJ's, playing pop promos in between the snooker and the ads; or whatever other music suited their chosen styles and chemicals.

Two of the alkies, conformists, reached the oldies and the normals, playing a bland stream of sentimental guff; the bigger of these two was dubbed Silas Smooth, and he performed in a smoking jacket from an armchair, with a magically ever-full glass by his side. For the god squad, there was a wine-soaked vicar with a musty mix of religious and classical musics; and for other oldies, folkies, and general weirdos there was a dazed flowerchild called Tina who played sweetness, light, and obsolete acoustic instrumental stuff. Tina performed under a plastic oak tree, with a huge cask of cider beside her on the astroturf; though when the world was too much for her, she shamefacedly turned to real ale. The fifth alky was Thor Thunders — dry ice and canned lager.

The coke fiend was young, blond, modishly suited and Scottish. He performed leaning against a gleaming chrome and silver bar, a cocktail by his side and flashing lights in the background; he played the very latest in hip-hop, pop, disco and funk. He was electric, and Wally liked him, though not for too long; he found him wearing after a while because he went so fast, and was horribly happy.

The acid head was likewise a laugh in short doses, though if you weren't on his wavelength, you were soon driven to less demanding channels by his strangeness. He rarely managed to follow the games he was commentating on; if he referred to snooker at all, it was usually to wax lyrical about the colours of the balls, the patterns they made (mandalas, leylines, Nazca astronomy), the spiritual qualities of the players, the inner space of the table, and the fascism of the referee for not allowing people to try again when they fluffed tricky shots. Wally considered that his greatest moment was when he intoned an enormously long passage from *Malone Dies* at the height of a climactic game between some unknown whipper-snapper from Dorking, and Rodeo Rodgers the Texas Typhoon. Performing in a darkened room surrounded by candles and alchemy books, the acid brain played psychedelic music and had an unsettling tendency, when he should have been talking to camera about the progress of a match, to edit in instead footage of elephants mating, men on the moon, the minting of money, and war.

The junkies, Thin and White (as in cue and ball, let alone their appearance) were, in Wally's estimation, immeasurably cool. Like him, they performed from their bed, although theirs was rather grubbier. They played bleak dark rock, obscure mournful doom music; except for the really bad days, when they got into stuff like the heavy bits of Verdi's Requiem, or just left the screen blank, or the camera trained on their staring, staring faces. On the other hand, when they both managed to be together simultaneously, they had a nice line in rap. 'Hey Thin?' — 'Hey White?' — 'Let's get together and go down a hole.'

Then there was a fine Rastaman called Style Rotterdam, who played reggae, castigated Babylon, and smoked ganja by the armful in great candlesticks of flame; his favoured setting was a toaster's mixing desk, but he had a bucketload of stamina, and frequently took his show out into the street for noisy, disorganised, and hugely joyful parties.

Wally's show was exactly the opposite. He stayed in bed, stoned stupid and moaning, either in a literary vein or, more often, in a brute-ugly barrage of foul jokes, jeers, and derision. For music, he played soul and jazz, though he had a free hand to veer into whatever pop took his fancy since, with the biggest games and the biggest audiences, he had the widest range of tastes to meet.

The way it worked was simple. 147 supplied their stars with whatever promos they ordered, and then, every other day, sent in a videotape with four hours of mute, unedited snooker on it; and, separately, an hour's worth of the ads that were booked onto that shift. The commentators recorded a voice-track over the actual play, unless it was boring, in which case they just played some music, or rapped about whatever took their fancy; then they edited in the ads, the promos of their choice, and film of themselves talking to camera about the game as it proceeded. They said pretty much anything they felt like, discussing the players, the music, the ads, and life in general, till they'd cobbled together a six hour show.

Wally kept the price of courgettes in front of his public for a fortnight once — and the next week it came down. That was because Milla had complained to him, after having to write ads deliberately designed to make it look like courgettes were thin on the ground when they weren't, so the price could rise. It made her angry, when she knew what the average family budget was; and Wally earned a kiss for helping out. But most of his little campaigns were a sight less constructive; just now, he was conducting a vigorous character assassination on Thor Thunders, after discovering that his viewing figures had gone down the toilet. He knew 147 was keen to be rid of Thor, and suspected that he was only retained to counter pre-election People Party criticisms of media bias. Wally harboured vague hopes that 147 would take on a Paki to replace him, once the voting was over; but sadly, as a race, they weren't really that into the game. Glumly, Wally predicted that the next face on 147 would be a young, female version of Silas, playing soft soul and MOR to pull in more oldies, especially the upmarket ones out in the countryside who still had plenty of cash that the admen hadn't properly laid hands on. Catering for this market, people were opening special oldies' travel agencies, wine bars, hairdressers, health shops and work-out clubs. . . . They needn't have bothered.

FOURTEEN

Wally gave Grief and Milla half an hour to consummate their reunion, before flicking the switches to check in on their conversation. Given her drunkenness, and Grief's fatigue and disinterest, he didn't reckon they'd bother. Still, he let them be for a little while, telling himself he should respect their privacy that far, at least; but remembering also the foul stab of jealousy, the day he'd switched on and found them fucking. When he did tune in, they were clothed as he'd expected, and lying on their bed. Grief was on his back, immobile and expressionless, with Milla straddling him, snuggling and nuzzling; and lecturing, as usual, on the political situation. Grief looked bored.

Milla said she wanted to be 'involved', she wanted to 'do something'. Wally thought, here we go again; and so did Grief. He turned over beneath her, and laid his head on his elbows, staring at the wall.

What you going to do, wondered Wally, when the people have snooker, and dance barns, and ads to make them promises? And, if they don't like it, there's always the news shows, cheerfully pointing out that the banks haven't crashed, and the Russians haven't come, and the price of wine's come down again; he giggled to himself. Milla yapped on, that the people in unison could be stronger than Nanny.

'What people?' Grief asked, 'What unison? Look, when you can get your identity off a peg — the team you follow, the band you like, the snooker player you fancy, the drug you take, the paper you read, the channel you watch — when you can make yourself up out of the media, it doesn't matter any more how poor you are, because you're an individual, right? So you haven't got anything in common with anybody; and lonely babies need a Nanny.'

Milla'd been trying to break in all the time he'd been speaking; now she said, 'So we need an explosion, we need to tell the truth.'

'People need truth,' Grief said, 'like I need weedkiller in my coke.' He pushed her off him, and rolled over to cut two lines on the bedside table. He asked, 'Why can't you rest up?'

'But people get fed crap every day, Grief; and we're accomplices.'

'Look, they like the taste, read your bloody research. Besides, we don't cook it up; we're only the waiters. Here, sniff this.'

'But the place is falling apart,' she howled, head jerking up; the coke buzzed up her nostrils. Fish in the deep sea, they darted up, down, and around each other across the big bed, shimmering in the dimmed light of Wally's screen. 'You should see the lies they're telling this time,' she continued, 'when there's no money left to pay for anything, anything.' The coke had made her frantic. 'We won't be short of hospitals next year, we'll be short of fucking food, don't you see?'

'I see it, I hear it, I'm helpless to change it, and anyway I'm rich.'

Milla rolled off the bed and stamped around. 'That's not good enough,' she gritted, teeth clenched, 'when everything's so shitty for so many people.'

'You say.'

'Yes,' she wailed, 'I say,' flailing, still drunk and high now too, crashing out of the room, tripping on the thick white carpet of the main room, falling and screaming. He was with her in an instant, kneeling beside her just out of Wally's camera vision. He could see his arm around her, and the fingers of his other hand stroking her white cheek, shaking as they did so, yearningly sad. 'What,' she asked, 'if we did know something, if there was a truth to tell?'

'Then,' he promised, 'we'd be able to do something.' But Milla wasn't listening. In the corner of her eye, she watched her boss flouncing up the marble steps of a private hospital, passing policemen, on their silent TV screen.

FIFTEEN

'I'm Nanny's media adviser.' Crinkly preened, showing credentials while security men went through his briefcase, and flashed detectors across his bright soft clothes. When the steel wand discovered his pocket micro, it bleeped, murmured, and twinkled a small red light; Crinkly took it out for an unsmiling guard to open up the back panel. He peered gormlessly at the wafers of silicon. Crinkly quipped, 'The batteries are thermonuclear;' and showed gold fillings.

'That's not funny,' said the guard, thinking, what a woofter; and passed him on into the wedding cake foyer. Crinkly clipped his identiflash to his tailored lime jacket, and studied the modern masters elegantly spaced to touch colour into the clean white walls. The Charm Pharmaceuticals Hospital for the Discerning — you couldn't buy better the whole country over. In a glow of soft lighting from thrilling chandeliers, flowers filled the air; as he left the cool marble of the reception area, red carpet hushed Crinkly's cream stacked shoes. He strolled down a corridor, and the air-conditioning delivered the faintest hint of a breeze.

Waiting for him behind acres of leather-topped mahogany, a surgeon studied discreet, compact grey hardware while it silently shuffled a pack of 3-D graphics of facial contours. He rose to greet Crinkly who sniffed, approving the restraint of his scent. They shook smooth hands, then the surgeon, seated again by his screens, tapped manicured nails on the desk-top and said, 'So that's how she looks at the moment. Now what can we do for you?' He selected a full frontal grid image of Nanny's face, and slowly turned it with touches at a button to demonstrate profiles.

Apologetically, Crinkly said he wasn't too good on a face made of green lines. 'Besides,' he added, 'we're not making structural changes, are we? Can I see the real thing?'

They stepped out into the corridor, letting past a full-breasted blond Nordic with a neat steel trayload of pills, smorgasbord, and what looked to Crinkly like a dry martini. As they followed her, Crinkly asked if he'd seen right, eyeing the curve of her thighs under cotton. 'It's for a pop star,' said the surgeon, disdainfully, and he ever so slightly curled a lip; doing so to hide a smile as the drink was, in fact, for the chairman of a rival ad agency.

They came to a pair of windowed double doors, with polished no-entry signs and a burly man seated beside them, staring at the opposite wall, an old copy of *War Machine* crumpled in his pocket. The surgeon showed a laminated plastic pass, and they went through to another set of doors which opened with a hiss, after a clacking little flurry of number-punching, into a reception area with two more guards. Finally they reached a featureless white tiled room. Nanny lay unconscious, clothed, on a steeply inclined sheet of non-reflective metal. A video camera on a wheeled stand was trained on her face, full frontal; a monitor showed a crisp image of what it saw.

Crinkly peered through the camera, one eye closed, then rolled it around a bit nearer and to her right. 'Lovely,' he said, checking quickly to see his positioning was correct on the monitor screen. 'Now this is her best angle; this is how we set cameras for press conference and speeches. And what's worrying me is her neck.' He pointed at the image. 'See these wrinkles? Can we smooth them out?'

The surgeon went over to the real thing, and lightly stroked the side of Nanny's neck. He asked, 'How smooth are we talking?' wiping his fingers on a tissue which he then discarded. 'If we get over-enthusiastic, the grafting may be visible.' He let Crinkly think about it, then suggested, 'If we just mildly ironed them out, what might be nicer is to increase the size of the earlobe, so it could carry a heavier pendant. That would obscure both the earlobe change, and the worst of the wrinkling. I'd recommend,' and he took another look, 'something circular.'

'Fine,' said Crinkly. 'You're the driver.'

The surgeon winced behind his smile. 'Is there anything else we can tackle while we have her?'

'There certainly is,' Crinkly replied. 'Her knuckles are getting bony. She uses her hands well, we like to go in close up on them now and then. I know you haven't got as much flab to play with there, compared to all that stuff dangling down her neck; but can you manage anything on the fingers?'

'That may be difficult, I'll let you know tomorrow.'

Crinkly rubbed his hands together and said, 'Fine. Otherwise, could you get your gadget to print out an optimum hairstyle to go with the face? We're taking out some of the white at the salon next week, putting in a touch more steel-grey instead; if you could help us get the shape right, that'd be nice. And there's one last thing. Excuse my asking; but how many staff will be involved in this operation?'

The surgeon deliberated, and then said, 'Four, beside myself. Plus one in admin, and one in accounts.'

Crinkly smiled. 'Would you mind arranging for all of them to take two weeks' holiday as of Monday, once you're through? I'm sure you're aware of what journalists can get up to. Send them somewhere nice; and bill the agency, of course.'

The surgeon smiled back. 'I'm told Singapore's very congenial these days.' Crinkly started recommending hotels as they made their way out.

SIXTEEN

The Barn was packed — not because it was Friday night, since the disappearance of work as a major activity amongst its patrons had long ago killed off the weekend syndrome — but simply because it always was. People hung over the railings around the many levels of galleries and bars, looking down onto the seething dancefloor through the harsh multiple flashes and splatters of colour from the great metal, glass, and neon chandelier of the lighting rig. It was an electro-disco night; the sullen beat of the drum machine invaded your body, battering through the walls and floors around you, while a swarming confusion of tiny whistlings, electronic farts and belches, rusty clangings and clatterings, and strangled voices truncated in half-phrase all pounced in and onto and back off the bass beat, echoing away through the hubbub. Here and there along the walls, surrounded by watching tables, flame sprang up from the fire-eaters and snake-charmers; jugglers hurled torches, clubs, balls and machetes up and down, up and down; acrobats span in the air beside them; and clowns bounced and bungled beneath screens silently displaying quick-change pages of textual, graphic, and image information, along with the ads and the videos. Franchised pitch-holders did make-up, cleaned shoes, gave haircuts, took photos, cooked food, and sold clothes, discs, games, tapes and writing. Clusters of the thirsty thronged loosely round the many bars, and hustlers moved past them through the crowd; 'Hello, my friend. Want hash, good sputnik stuff? Cocaine, speed, acid,' or, if you were obviously a tourist, 'girls?'

Standing on the ladder that led up from the DJ's raised cockpit into the entrails of the lighting rig, Grief surveyed his domain. Milla — who'd gone down with Grief so as not to be without him, and so the noise would smother her apprehension about returning to work after the weekend — found Moses loitering by the bog. She leant against the wall beside him, well drunk, trembling with dance in the booming blackness at the back of the Barn; together they looked up at the far figure of Grief, motionless, so high in the air, a figure in ascension over the furnace he'd created. Milla, feeling pissed and Miltonic, turned to make some comment about Satan giving the people a place of their own; but Moses looked so bad, it made her feel sober by comparison. 'Christ, Moses,' she said, 'your hair's gone grey.'

He muttered, 'It matches my face, don't you think?' His head slewed up but not for long. He tried to grin as it fell back down again, then gave up trying. 'But I'm wrecked,' he announced, 'that's all. And every wreck goes grey in time. If you celebrate enough, the edges have to blur.' Milla gave him her drink, and asked what he was celebrating; he slurped inside her glass, choked, gasped, and swore. 'What the fuck is this?'

'Drambuie and Amaretto,' she grinned, 'half and half. A Godfather, so-called because it blows your head off.' In front of them, records segued in the wall of music and green neon took over from red flashes. Moses' face took an accompanying turn for the worse. The new disc had a faster bass, and his body flickered, idling on autopilot, unconsciously responsive. Around them everywhere, dole kids boozed and boogied. The air stank of hash.

'I should be celebrating,' Moses finally managed, 'because of a great moral and chemical achievement. I have eased the pain of many failing oldies. I have discovered a great new painkiller, and it's cheap, cheap, cheap. I have, in short, done what I'm paid for. But really I'm celebrating because I found out today they've been using my drug nationwide for at least a month already; and when I told them I now knew this, they grudgingly gave me a rise. I have saved money for our leaders, and the small change has fallen my way.'

'That's wonderful,' Milla howled above the thundering electrics.

'What's really wonderful,' replied Moses, placing an inhaler in one nostril, snorting in a rumble of mucus, and suddenly lurching forward as an instant alertness burst out into his eyes, 'is it's a really fucking wonderful drug.' He went rigid, eyes locked onto a space across the teeming hangar.

She asked, 'What's up?' touching his shoulder, and worrying about the shakes she could feel in his body.

He spluttered and spat laughter. 'There's an oldie on the dance floor.'

'So?' she replied. 'They're not all crippled or basket cases. They're not all dead.' But Moses was bustling off to go about his business; there were tablets to be sold. His grin was badly dislocated.

Up in the DJ's platform, Grief was dancing, drinking mineral water, and playing coke-addled games with the light show. Beneath him, a profusion of haircuts jiggled, bobbed, bounced and swayed, with strobes, flashes, spots and neons darting back and forth all over them. Milla joined him, fell against him, and asked him how the night was.

'Only three sick so far, no violence, the bars are busy, and all the busboys turned up for once. All that, and you back too.' He looked her up and down; she offered him a winning smile.

'You dreaded it, didn't you?'

He laughed and admitted, 'Yes, a bit.' So she rubbed her drink-wobbly thighs around his hip, leaning her long neck down along his shoulder to nibble at his ear, and remarked, 'Moses is here,' as her body travelled up the rockface of his.

He replied, 'I know, and I ought to say hello; I was foul to him this morning. How does he look?' His arm was around her waist, his hand cupped down between the back of her thighs, pulling her in and around him; he had thought, once, that her embrace was like being tied up in warm dry string.

'Terrible,' she whispered, licking at his neck. 'But he's happy, tonight. He's selling his wonderdrug.'

Grief stared out across the throbbing floor, saying, 'For the last time, too — I tell you, Bludge cottons on to a new drug quicker than it can score its first overdose. So I told him to stop; otherwise, Jesus, can you imagine getting pushed into where you have to bust your own mates? I couldn't ever show my face again.' He looked gaunt at the thought.

'No one,' she said, running a distracting hand down the front of his trousers, 'would ever suspect you. The master of the house.' They turned to face each other, freed in the club from all her jagged anxieties, and put their arms tightly behind each others' backs as their tongues met, hot and wet. He knew that he wanted to make love with her after all, and remembered how they used to, when everything was younger. A couple of kids looked up and pointed. Later, when they danced together, a few even cheered — including Cairo, who liked seeing people look happy; until Marl told him to stop — and a space was cleared for the boss.

On their way back in the car, Milla asked Grief if he'd found Moses, after they'd talked about him. He was concentrating on the road; it was a bad night, they'd been held up at two road-blocks already. Vaguely, he murmured, 'Yeah,' then recalled, 'But by that time, maybe an hour after you saw him, he was way too far gone to sell anything; just slumped at a table, quaking a bit. Annoying — I wanted to ask him about my mysterious relative. He/she is in Moses' hospital. I tell you, anyway, I can't take it, the way he gets those spasms. Don't you think we should maybe take him in, dry him out for a while?' Thinking it might maybe dry her out as well.

She put on a face. 'I'd rather not. It's his carcass, isn't it? I'd rather just us.'

'Hark to that,' he laughed, 'she who cares for the people.' Her head was slumped back on the head rest, face sweaty, neck rolling. He knew she'd overdone the drinking, despite all her promises otherwise, and it spoilt things, made him distant. He waved his pass at another block, and they purred on down the road. In the corner of his eye, he noticed how her head jerked lazily, loose-muscled, every time they hit a pothole. 'Why do you think,' she asked, and the words came slowly now, in a weary haze, 'they didn't tell Moses they were using his drug?'

SEVENTEEN

Workwise, Wally had a big week coming; the final week of the Danegeld Lager Supreme Championship of the Globe. This was the biggest of 147's production line competitions, an annual, megavast knockout in which the top-ranked 256 players in the world fought it out for one million pounds while prominently chaining their way through pint after pint. The prize would then be collected before a special exhibition game held 'for charity' between the finalists in the sealed off, high security tourist colony of Agadir — where you could stand beneath the Coca-Cola hoardings on the viewing platforms, and watch the locals starve beyond the gates.

To promote this enormous exercise in armchair yoga, Milla'd written an ad that got two hundred thousand new subscribers signed on to 147. It opened on an ashtray, fag logo prominent, with a fat-fingered hand crushing out a butt. Cut to a plainly unhealthy great wreck of a man, coughing ferociously. He gets up, downs a mountainous gulp of

Danegeld lager, and lurches unsteadily to a table at which he pulls off a stunning, curving, gravity-defying double plant from a snookered position, potting a hidden red at the far end of the table. Cue roars of canned applause, with voice-over, 'Get ripped on snooker — eight weeks of action with 147.' The success of this ad depressed her for a fortnight.

Naturally, the tourney was neatly timed to coincide with the run up to the election. As viewing figures built up into the last weeks, so too did the frequency of the Money Party ads. The last week of the championship was the penultimate week of the campaign; you couldn't move on the airwaves for messages from the Money pouring out between games. Afterwards, as everyone relaxed from the TV, and maybe even went out a bit, the last few days before polling date would see the country suddenly plastered with Milla's posters and press ads. Then, the night before the vote, with a wondrously coincidental return to big viewing for the prize-giving ceremony, up popped the Money again, with a flurry of steamroller pro-motion. The logic behind dropping out of TV and into the other media during those final days was simple: by that time, the Money'd be on air from start to finish of every news programme anyway. And they didn't want to spoil things with any hints of overkill, now did they?

Wally was working late, wrapping up a special state-of-the-tourney-so-far section to close his latest shift. They were down to the last sixteen players, all set to battle through the weekend for the quarter-final places. Recording himself talking to camera, Wally summed up. 'So there you have it, my dear dole city sump-heads, the last sixteen are out on the grid and the engines are revving. And it only remains to wonder, behind whom do we place our money? Now certain money that's been calling itself smart has, I hear, swung around behind this Thai kid. I'm afraid I'll say, if you bet that way, you've lost your cash; the Thai kid's just a flash on the felt. As ever, my own money is on Geoff Geometry, the Malden Machine. He's not fluffed a big one in years, and I don't see why this one should be any different. But then, dear dole souls, you never ever know. Snooker is the human condition in spherical form; on the table of life, you get knocked about a bit, banged on the head, and dumped down a hole. Speaking of which' — he leant forward and scowled — 'one toad who badly needs dumping in a hole is that fat beery freak of a heavy metal lefty, my so-called colleague Thor Thunders. Can you believe where that moron's been putting his money? Behind Deadbeat Delaney, for Christ's sake; a no-hope old fart if ever I saw one. How crass can you get? I tell you, that guy is so far from reality, he makes his own precious People Party look more put together than IBM. I say, sack the fucker; he's built of crap. Agreements on a postcard to yours truly, Wally Wasted, megadude of the data base, superstar of the sub-routines, hip-hop hero of the 147 CPU.' He flicked a switch to cut the picture from himself, to footage of the last sixteen players leaving the vast underground cavern of a studio after their photocall to a tumult of canned approbation; clay gods, trailed by the high priests of adland bearing thorny crowns of sponsorship, they disappeared up the tunnel in a dirty haze of lager and fag fumes. 'Anyway,' Wally continued, voicing over picture, 'I'll see you the day after tomorrow with the quarter-final previews; in the meantime, here's a great bit of crap to be playing you out with — a group of naked Austrian saxo-phonists, no less. Never say your Wally don't give you the best.'

He flicked at buttons, matching up his final edits, and rolled a giggling joint. On screen, sax players tried expressing themselves without exposing themselves; all Wally's monitors were covered in flesh and brass. But his downstairs mikes were still on, so they picked up Grief and Milla coming in from the Barn. He stopped, considering whether to watch them; but he could hear that she was stumbling drunk, and feared moreover that if they'd had a good night out, they might yet fuck to celebrate her return. He was deciding that he'd rather not watch that, when Grief started talking; it was a low breathy whisper, and kicked off so romantic that Wally knew for good he'd better not watch if he wanted to stay calm. So he lay back to make do with listening, bitterly imagining them stroking, caressing, loving, as the words bubbled up through the changeless, the sunless blue light.

'Shall I tell you what I thought of, while you were away? I thought mostly of your lips, and your shoulders, and your nipples, and your clitoris, and your ankles. I thought of the look on your face, when we undress to make love, or when you lie on the bed and I kneel over you to touch you. I thought of your shoulders, because they're slim and elegant, but broad too, so all the soft and the hard of you is balanced in the line and the weight of them, the unbending grace; you look, when you lie on your back, like there's a last reserve of strength, like there's knowledge that you can only be pushed so far down, and never any further, because there's a secret in your womb, your gender maintains you. Then I thought of your arms, how fine and slender they are, and how delicate the touch of your hands; when you finger my balls, my spine trembles, and when you take my cock in your palm, you stroke it like feathers, it melts my heart, it runs like lava down my thighs. And I thought of your nipples, because I love the way they grow hard between my teeth, and the brown warm ridges build up around them, relief maps of mountains; and I thought of your breasts — you've always been right, when I lay my head there, that I want to be mothered, when things wind me up, and I need to be held onto, so my gears don't grind, so my programmes don't crash. But you're wrong, when I lay my head on your stomach, to think I want mothering then too. I love your stomach, it's an open plain, and I feel when my head's there the desire and biology, and the wanting a child. Before you, all girls were only that, just girls; but my head on your stomach puts an ache in my chest, says I'm close to a mystery, the snug little cave where a child can be built — you used to speak of that — never mind. I thought, anyway, of how, when my head's on your stomach, I can see where the hair starts, and how long your legs are. I thought of your thighs, and when I come into you from above, how you raise them up to encase me, it's gorgeous. And I thought of your ankles, because if anyone ever asked me, what do I see in Milla Sharply, I know that I'd only have to say, well a-here she comes, just a-walking down the street — and did you ever see such a good-looking woman in your life? Did you every see such a tall true lady? I even thought of your feet, hell, I used to think if there was one thing in the world you could be certain of, it was for sure that you'd never see a pair of human feet and think them pretty. I thought, the most beautiful man, the most beautiful woman in the world, they could have everything, but they couldn't possibly have nice feet. Then you came along; and even your feet are sexy, little pointed hard clean feet. How do you come to be made so well? I thought of your sex, your whole sex, and I thought of your clitoris, because I love the way it bobbles between my fingertips, I love its own special metal taste, and the touch of it, the feel of it under my tongue, soft, swollen, such a rich little pad of a thing. All of you there, it's all so finely formed — I always thought cunts were a mess of flesh, really; but then, along you came. Your vagina, the lips are so sweet beneath my fingers; or when I'm inside you, you fit me, just so, like a well-tailored glove. Then, differently, when I go down on you, it feels huge, great wet soft cave of flesh, tunnel soaked in honey, it's lascivious, it's an embrace; and I thought of your arsehole, how prim and proper and tight around my finger when my tongue's diving for pearls in the sea of your juice — I thought of all these things, but most of all, I thought of the way you sit down onto me sometimes, you straddle me and fuck me and it feels like there's not a millimetre more of me left to get inside you, and I can look up and see so much of you, I can hold your breasts, or I can have your clitoris hard over one set of fingers while the other reaches round to clasp the strength of your bum behind you, with your arsehole wet at my fingertips, truly, then, there's all of you in my hands, and when you come it's heaven, you lean forward and your back arches, your breasts fall into my face and fill my mouth, I want to drown in your flesh, and your neck strains up and you shut your eyes and you grip your teeth a tiny bit and smile and give just a little gasp — and then relax, stroke your nipples across my chest, and it's sad and sweet and gentle, and I love you, love you, love you so much.'

Wally lay rubbing at his old grey cock, a dream of Milla laid out beneath his closed eyes. He heard Grief going on, 'And I'm sorry, if it's all just my image, only an image when I know you don't see yourself in the way that I do; but who's to say it's not valid? It might as well be, it's a good way to be seen; if you know I can see you that way, then you can think whenever you're feeling bad or unbeautiful, or sinful, or lonely, or hammered in a hole by the lies we live by, that to me you could always be good and lovely all the same. But forget it if you want, it's only words, I can't blame you for not trusting them any more, the way you have to use them; and my heart, well, don't worry about my heart, if you must fall away, the way that you're falling, it won't break my heart. It's just a hole you climbed into; and if you choose to climb back out, it'll just be a hole all over again, with drawings on the walls. We always were the hollow men.'

Wally'd long stopped wanking; whatever they were doing, they weren't making love. He flicked switches, tuning a monitor to the camera in their bedroom ceiling; Milla was crashed out, still fully clothed, flat on her back on the bed, obviously dead drunk and passed out long ago. Grief sat on a small chair beside her, leant forward with legs apart and his elbows on his knees, wringing his hands and staring at her blankly, while the smoke from a joint in an ashtray at his feet floated up round his face; was it this, that brought the tears to his eyes?

Wally watched him get up and lumber into the sitting room, heavy-footed and bumping through the doorway. He listened to him recording a thick-tongued message on the answerphone — 'Grief and Sharply are away for the weekend, back Monday morning, leave your message after the tone and here it comes (beep)' — and he thought, hey ho, alone again. If his tenants weren't around, who did he have? Retarded motorbike messengers bearing videos, and the sad wads of post every day — endless open-crotch shots of fans who, for reasons that escaped him, wanted his body — and then, thank god, that corrupt little vixen of a groceries boy. Wally did all his shopping by micro; he'd tried every delivery service the teletext had to offer, one after the other, until he'd landed at last on a sassy little blond kid who'd suck him off once a week in return for huge tips.

Then he saw Grief noticing, apparently for the first time, a video cassette that was sticking out of Milla's handbag where it lay dropped on the floor, fallen open where she'd left it. He picked it up and examined it with the slow, distracted movements of a well-stoned man; then stuffed it into the machine, turned on the telly and pressed play. The screen flickered; a picture formed of a naked woman lying openlegged across a snooker table, knees up and fucking herself with the fat end of a cue. Disgusted, Grief killed the picture. Wally laughed, and lay back to sleep with his cock in his hand, one day nearer to the Last Election.

MONDAY

EIGHTEEN

As soon as Grief had dropped Milla back at their apartment to get herself ready for work, he set off for the hospital where the mysterious him/her had been stored. It was still early, but the night-time traffic truce was over already, and it took him an hour to make it to Balham through a heavy, smoggy morning. While the traffic was almost stationary in the High Street the clouds had mercy and it began to rain. The driver in front of Grief wound down his window and thrust his face out into the plashing of the droplets, when suddenly a shabby man stepped off the pavement, with something in his fist. Grief froze, and everything went into slow motion as he saw what it was: a live rat, shrieking with fear. The man heaved it through the open window of the car in front. The driver braked violently, and ducked. The thief tore open the door, coshed him, took his wallet, retrieved the rat — Grief saw then that it was on a thin string — and was gone in a flash. A gang of dancers round a throbbing funkbox broke into applause at the panache of the manoeuvre, while a troop of scavengers, clearly forewarned, fell on the car and began stripping anything that they could loosen and cart away. Panicking, Grief hauled out round the stricken car, regardless of the blaring of horns and screeching of brakes from the cars behind and beside him. In his wing mirror he saw the driver's limp body, head bleeding, bundled out onto the pavement. He was still shaking when he got to the hospital.

Queues of the unwell, clutching bags, staring down without words, waited scratching and coughing outside the main gate; mostly old, many black, all poor. To help them feel extra good, posters advocating private health insurance had been carefully sited all around. The car park was jammed; but Moses had told Grief too many stories of theft from the hospital courtyard, so he parked around the corner instead. His car smelt of money, amongst the older models of the locals.

In the hospital's foyer, kids screamed, blood dripped, people slipped and tripped on the greasy floor, and the oldies swayed in chairs if they were lucky enough to find one, or buckled in corners and down onto the lino tiles if they weren't. Harassed nurses and ancillaries zoomed about, sweating, eyes darting as they tried to pick out who looked worst. No one was 'next'; you just waited until they could deal with you. The stench was strong, and unmistakeable; shit, beneath a thin layer of disinfectant. Some of the many lying all over the floor looked as if they'd been there for days, and one, an old man, had pissed himself. Those who had tried to get a bit of clear space away from the walls, where the dirt and the crowding was worst, were kicked and buffeted as poor-sighted oldies stumbled over them, and scuttling staff in their stained and frayed white coats barged through, too busy to sidestep. Grief grimaced; then, donning his mask of no expression, waded through in his lightly swishing suit to the front desk.

The receptionist had sacs under her eyes like bags of coal; the counter was a mound of untended papers. She wore a joke badge, saying 'Look after yourself. We may not be able to'. A poster behind her requested that people keep away, if they could possibly manage to mend themselves, couching the request in terms of 'have concern for others'. Grief gave his name, and said he had a relative just gone in. The receptionist shrugged and said, 'I can't help you, pal, the computers are down again; could be anywhere, there's thousands in here.' She waved jerkily at the mess all over the desk. Grief fended off an old man who toppled up against him, snot drying in his stubble; ghoulishly, the man planted his arm across the papers to show it was a stump, and garbled something drunk about how, when the hand had fallen off, they'd taken his glove with it, and could he have it back, it'd fetch a few pennies. Under a caking of snot and dirt, his skin was flaking and dry, horribly ancient. Behind him there was a screaming in the doorway as a woman turned and was thrown against a wall by a stretcher rushing in, the body on it bleeding from knife wounds.

Grief hung on to himself and asked through his teeth, 'Would you look under minor injuries?'

The receptionist cackled, 'We haven't updated that file in a fortnight; there were two closures last month, we're over-flowing.' She fobbed him off with a badly statted floor plan,

rosses in the wards where he'd most likely strike
ou'll have to find whoever it is for yourself. In a
:, for all I know.'

ıks a bunch,' said Grief.

joked, 'Roses would be nice,' not looking, as she waved
him away, at the tramp's stump eighteen inches from her
face.

The next day, anonymously, Grief sent roses; he was
thoughtful that way.

NINETEEN

Milla lay against the side of the lift. She was narked by the
mind-elsewhere coldness of Grief's 'see you tonight' when
he'd dropped her off. She also felt terrible; toxins gushed from
every pore as her body seized its chance to flush Friday's
sewage from her system, after a sexless weekend of short-
tempered, mean little battles while he kept her off the drink.
Her face washed over hot and cold; her stomach was hollow,
her limbs weak and trembly. How much better, she thought,
to be cushioned in poison, than this naked, live-wire alertness,
this draining, sharp-sensed, echo-headed immediacy of
contact with all your surroundings. Hurry, hurry, she begged
the lift, and then tumbled out of it to fumble with her plastic
entry card, putting it in the slot the wrong way, then punching
the wrong numbers. The digital display above the punch-keys
printed 'Error. Get it right next time, or I'll call the guards'. She
cursed Grief for his flippant way with machine-stored
messages, stopped, held her breath, and got it right. Then she
was through the door and running, bouncing against the
walls, to the bottle of Drambuie kept hidden in the screen
control panel in her big blue room.

The fish, fat-cheeked, hung drifting up and down in the dim
glass wall. Milla took the bottle by the neck and pulled in a
long, deep slug, shivering as it warmed her. Enough, she
thought; better now. The drink made her feel sexy again; she
slipped out of her weekend clothes, laid out a smart, clean,
zecky outfit to wear to the office, then wrapped herself in a
silk dressing-gown and hopped up the stairs to see Wally,
taking with her the video porn.

56

Wally lay motionless in his nest; above and behind him three screens were alive but silent. On one, panicky oldies sweated under studio lights as they answered questions about disease in the Health and Sickness Quiz (prize, free medical insurance); on another, two Money ministers mouthed smoothly in a news studio; on the third, scantily clad models ate chocolate while hang-gliding. Wally's eyes were open, unblinking, his head void of thought; he was concentrating hard at getting focus on the half-smoked joint in an ashtray set into shelving beneath the near end of his kitchen unit. In the gap between this, and the racked unit behind his pillow where his cassette stock started, he saw Milla's legs swinging through the door, the gown swaying open around them. He mourned the unscarred white flesh, following the flow of the silk on her skin.

She stood over him and grinned; she was wet with the drink, and the prospect of taunting him, and the memory of the images she held in her hand. 'Morning, old pig,' she said, 'how's life in the sty?' He coughed and rolled over, unashamedly peering up her legs. 'So light a joint,' she demanded.

He replied, 'For a bit of thigh.' To his surprise, she stepped lankily forward, placing one leg beyond him on the bed as she leant over to feed the tape into the machine beneath his monitors; so her gown fell open, and there, right before him, was her cunt. He thought to himself, yob at heart as he caught his breath, she's obviously not getting any; aloud, he said, mock prole, 'Cor, darling — you can have a piece of my courgette anytime.'

'You should be so lucky,' she smirked, collecting the remote control and stepping back to a more decent stance. 'You think I'd swap Grief for a wreck like you?'

Brave, thought Wally, so very brave; and asked innocuously how things went between his tenants.

She curtly replied, 'Stagnant but stable.'

Through phlegm and more coughing, Wally said, mock-solicitous, 'You'll have more time with him, when the election's done with;' that was part one of the game. He went on easily to lay down the cards for part two. 'But you can always get your nookie up here, next time you're in dispute.'

She said, 'Fuck you,' and stopped playing. 'Shut up and have a look at this. You'll love it.' She jabbed play, and the screens all filled with the girl and her snooker cue. Wally laughed, lit the joint, and settled in to enjoy himself; under the covers, his free hand snuck around his hard cock. The girl on the screen was joined at the table by another, who sat on her face, and went down between her thighs to lap at her cue-stuffed fanny. The camera moved slowly round the table as they ground away with hips and tongues, then stopped behind them, zooming in on the first girl as she strained up to lick at the cunt of the second. Then cut, and — oh joy, thought Wally — enter Thor Thunders. He watched awhile, in the dumb, disinterested, unactorly way that the porn movie has; then stripped, accompanied by much jeering from Wally at the size of his cock. Thor chalked a cue, and formed a steady bridge with his left hand over the second girl's raised buttocks; then, neatly, as if he were playing a soft little safety to hide behind the pack, he inserted the tip of the cue into her offered anus. There was a close-up of the entry, and then of Thor's stupid, grinning, vacant face. The threesome proceeded mechanically to adopt a variety of positions, with and without cues and other accessories, until Thor finally came, with short high moans, like a child being slapped.

'Took his time,' giggled Wally. Spunk spattered over the blue, chalk-covered breasts of the girls; they mixed it with the chalk, rubbing it into their nipples with looks of deep boredom. Wally said, 'His mortgage must really be biting, if he's fallen to crap like that. But then, with his ratings in the basement the way it's been the last few months, I shouldn't think he's seen a bonus in ages. I'll have him sacked with this in no time. Thanks, love.' The tape ended in a fuzz of white noise; he asked her where she'd got it.

'It was on sale in the Barn, Friday night,' she answered, and he heard a hard crack in the honey-soft hush of her voice. He realized she was crying, and saw, feeling weird and even, by his standards, compassionate, that beneath her gown she'd had a hand between her legs, as sadly as he had himself. Genuinely, he asked if she was alright. 'Oh,' she moaned, then wailed, 'this isn't me; I'm not like this, this isn't me. Sorry,' she gasped, 'sorry, I'll perk up, look, I've got to go;' and, still scattering short, unhappy, incoherent little phrases, she fled the room. He watched her downstairs, packing away more Drambuie while the fish danced around her; then she slipped on the zecky work outfit, and with it, a dry-eyed hard mask of togetherness. Looking fresh and efficient and smart as you please, the manufactured career girl headed off to the office. And that wasn't her, either. Wally thought to himself, if he worked on it, then one of these days, he'd surely get to have her.

TWENTY

Grief knew about the hospitals; he'd talked with Moses, and visited him in the past. He could handle seeing the people in the corridors, the old men and women kitted out like convicts in clothes that weren't their own, sitting or lying where their last energy had left them. He could do the footwork, too, the weaving hop and dance known to the ancillaries as the NHS quickstep; you learnt it soon enough, trekking through the litter of seniles and retards in the shit-smelly hush of the pale green passages. Neither the smell nor the dirt, which got worse as he burrowed deeper into the heart of the huge building, shocked him all that much. Nor did the many smashed windows surprise him, knowing from Moses how sometimes the medication didn't work; how the tough stayed doggedly alert, and got violent in frustration with the forcing upon them of lethargy in pills. He was accustomed too to the look on the faces of those for whom the doping had been effective; he could handle the gaga lolling of the heads, the faint stupid grins that came and went between the dribbling fits. And then there was the muttering and the murmuring, the coughs and the sudden, loud, half-finished sentences that hung on in the air, with no hope of conclusions. . . . And he could live with the sorry begging, when the more conscious among them reached out as he passed for books, newspapers, games, something to do, anything; a fag, or a few coins for tea in the canteen. . . .

But there was a new look now. There was a ubiquitous, quiet, wide-eyed surprise, as if a general announcement of death's imminence had just that minute been made, and they all suddenly knew that it might be tomorrow, or the next day, for all of them together. This look took away a residual feeling that he'd always had before, that no matter how grim the conditions, a hospital was a place where you might hope to be cured. This place was somewhere where you came only to die. And this new look on the wasted faces was far worse than another new feature of the corridors — a distressingly high incidence of people missing limbs. That, he assumed, was just a speciality of the house.

Grief peered into ward after ward, recoiling from one in which two slobbering, wall-eyed retards made gasping love under the admiring gaze of the oldies gathered round them. A passing nurse told him not to worry — they didn't know it, but all the women were on the pill. They had to be, she said, with the beds all squeezed so close together; they were bound to get rampant now and then.

'But they're fucking,' Grief complained.

'Good for them,' she said, bustling away; then called over her shoulder, 'You think I've got time to stop them?'

He wandered on, gradually more numbed, crossing off each ward on the floor plan as he failed to find anyone who was anything to do with him; and finally he knew he was hopelessly lost. So when an ancillary went hurtling past, he asked where he might find Moses. Crashing by like an express train he laughed, 'What, the gene fiend?' and shouted directions as he faded into the ill-lit distance. His trolley-load of trays and bottles rattled and clattered as he steered it round the sleepers.

Grief knocked on Moses' door, waited for a reply, didn't get one, and went in anyway. Moses' lab was dark and still; a musty odour mingled with a stink of chemicals, and the silence was now and then broken by a rustling of small animals over straw. Grief made out his friend, immobile at the far end of the room, with his head on his hands at a workbench covered in cages. He tapped him on the shoulder, and Moses slowly, slowly sat up, his head turning so shakily Grief felt like he could hear it creaking. He seemed to have aged years in a weekend; and his hair really had gone grey. Moses, he recalled, was thirty-four.

Moses said, 'My rabbits are dying.'

'They take as many drugs as you, what d'you expect?'

Moses said, 'No, no; I've not fed them any chemicals in a week.'

Grief peered through the wire of the cages at the small

sluggish bundles of fur; they certainly weren't too lively. He said, 'They look better than you do —' and would have said more.

Moses stopped him, saying, 'It's spooky,' then lurched round in his chair and knocked over a paper cup of coffee. He muttered, 'Oh fuck,' and slumped, groaning. 'It's too early in the morning.'

Grief asked, 'Did you drink as much last night as you did on Friday? 'Cos that was too much, for sure.' He cleaned up, searched around, found a kettle and plastic cups, and made fresh coffee for them both. Moses was nodding off, so he slapped him gently in the face, appalled at how dry his skin felt; even, he shuddered, wrinkly. 'Come on, boy,' he wheedled, 'shape up. Tell us what's wrong with your beasts here.'

Moses half-smiled, weakly saying, 'You know, I really liked these rabbits. Been with me a long time, this lot; we've had a few good trips.'

'I'm surprised they last five minutes, the filth you feed them. What's their problem?'

Moses whispered, 'Age; only age.'

'Is that all? So get a new batch.' Grief was losing interest.

But Moses waved his hands about, feebly, almost whimpering, 'No, but there's something badly wrong here. . . .'

Grief cut in, saying, 'Look, they're dying of natural causes, right? And if all that's wrong is they're getting there early, well frankly, the same applies to you and far more so; and no surprise, considering your consumption. What you need, Moses, is a new batch of rabbits, and a week or two's abstinence. Take a rest, why don't you?'

Moses sighed, 'But there's so much work.' He fumbled in his pockets, eventually finding his yellow tablet container; but it was empty. He swore, and scattered things around on a shelf or two, until he found a bottle of big grey pills instead. 'At least,' he said, 'I invented this. Helps make do, seeing the bastards won't give me an assistant.' Swallowing two, he offered the bottle to Grief, who demurred, watching; it was barely two minutes before Moses was relaxing, and more alert. 'Up again,' he smiled, self-deprecating; and Grief asked what he'd taken now.

Moses shrugged, getting lively. 'It's the megadose version of the original painkiller. They don't normally use this much, unless someone's been run over by a truck.' Then he winced, realising that what he'd said had more significance than Grief knew. Only then did it occur to him, to ask what Grief was doing there in the first place; so Grief told him about the message on the answerphone.

'Uh-huh,' Moses nodded. 'I guess I was hoping you'd not find out. Sorry, but it isn't a relative. It's Fiona James. She was in a car smash; she's broken both her legs.'

Fiona was a ballet dancer. Was. And, before Milla, she'd lived with Grief.

TWENTY-ONE

Milla used the vast glass and silver expanses of the Crinkly Crisp facade for a final raincheck on the booze-fuelled creative zeck mode that she'd logged onto so neatly. She swallowed the last of the mint she'd been chewing to cover the Drambuie. As soon as she was plunged into the building, her own front would need to be as reflective, as mirror-sharp and impermeable as the agency's was. The greetings of the receptionists and security men were all genuine; but sure enough, once beyond them and into the cool, pot-planted jungle of wacky-coloured designer steel railings, she could see them all harshly estimating her roadworthiness behind the smiling metal welcomes.

It didn't surprise her to find the corridor outside her room busy with a mock-casual gaggle of worrying zecks. Their faces pretended only to faint interest; but their eyes darted, and they scratched at their hands as they probed for reassurance. 'Good holiday?' they asked. 'All cool on the Money front?'

'Totally cool,' Milla breezed. Used to believing the opposite of everything they heard, they grew more nervous. She passed through them into her office like a breath of wind through fading flowers. Glad that he was in, she grinned a greeting to Trolly, her art director; he was pensively working his way through a joint, and a bottle of chilled white wine. She asked what he was up to; he was, he told her, developing an appropriate state of mind for the tedious task of taking arty photos of instant curry. The Taj Mahal rescue bid was under way. Milla, posing hard for the non-stop stream of people who were passing by to check her out, lay down on their couch and dozed awhile.

Then there came a flutter beyond the open door, and her eyes blinked up. There was a scattering of little zeckies as Crinkly came, his belly held back by the weight of his theatricality. Listening to the bowing and scraping, and the laughter at his jokes, Milla cringed inwardly and remembered the clean island sun. Back here, the heavy rain fell; through the floor to ceiling windows she could see, between rubber plants, the scurrying of the oldies way below on the pavement as they dodged the sparse, outnumbered youth. A poster she'd devised stared down at them from across the road: 'Pop a Pill and Pelt down the Pistes'. There was a granny on skis; the drug was brand-named, 'Zest'. The poster was mounted on revolving triangular slats; each time the slats shimmered round and re-formed, the granny was further on down the slalom. Milla smiled, recalling the Zest binge she'd had with Moses, when she'd been working on that poster; but it hadn't lasted long. The stuff made you spotty.

Hearing Crinkly at the door, Trolly frantically swept away the ash and litter from his joint, packing his slopping wine glass hurriedly into a drawer. Milla rolled off the sofa and managed to catch the joint before he stubbed it out, then lay back to smoke it. As Crinkly entered, she again shut her eyes.

'Milla, Milla,' he trilled, with a nod to Trolly, who was instantly drawing; 'Good to see you back where you belong.' His jangling wrists came to rest on his hips; gold clunked against gold. 'So, pet,' he then announced, 'the research report is triumphant. Not a soul that we talked to disapproved of your ads.'

Opening her eyes, she wondered again at how such a short, ugly man could come over so flash and cocksure. He was, she thought, the act of compensation made flesh. She said, 'Well that's no surprise, since we only talked to Nanny-lovers.' He laughed. 'You'd prefer it if we talked to the Trots? Anyway, I've just had round some various little people from Money HQ, and they too duly loved them to death. Just a few little touches here and there. . . .'

Milla flared up, 'Whaddya mean, little touches?' and rolled up to sit.

Crinkly held up his hands, and smoothed the air with them. He tenderly explained that it was mere little jiggles of art direction only; Trolly, he said, would shortly be briefed. 'Which only leaves us,' he went on, 'with the formality of presenting it all to Nanny and her lapdogs; they have to chuck in their tuppence, after all. Now I'm afraid that the only time they can fit in for that is the coming Friday evening, so would you keep that clear, please?' He looked hugely pleased with himself; he was dreaming of the catering arrangements.

'So,' said Trolly, 'we run off the posters at the weekend, then slap 'em up all over the country for Monday morning. Neat, huh?'

Milla trod the joint out on the carpet, and asked, 'Have any of the other parties got hold of an agency yet?'

Crinkly smirked. 'No one'll take them, even if they could raise the money to pay them with.' He sat on the sofa beside her, so she stood, and went across to her desk. It was a vast black wooden affair, covered in crumpled paper, tapes and magazines, and samples of various products; a rarely used micro poked up through the debris. 'Don't you ever tidy that thing?' Crinkly asked. His fat jocularity bugged her.

She snapped, 'I'm too creative. And listen,' she asked, longing to puncture him, 'is Nanny really bananas like the People Party say? What were you doing in the Charm Clinic, Friday night? Don't tell me she needs an adman to help her clean out her ears.'

'Client service,' he laughed. 'I gave her flowers, grapes, and a pack of Chanel's Cosmetics for Maturity. And she's fine; but aren't those People people imbeciles? That smear did them a lot more harm than good, we didn't even sink to it. The day it came out, we ran film of her reviewing the troops; she looked as compos as you please.'

Milla asked how old the film was, but he didn't answer. 'OK, OK,' she said, changing the subject and doing her job, 'there's only one thing left that we're weak on, and that's the hospitals. I can see we'll have to do press ads on that, so can you get them to be sensible, and stop closing the things? Otherwise, I don't really see what I can say.'

'Who knows,' Crinkly mused, rising, and stroking podgy fingers on gleaming pink cheeks; 'maybe the People are so dumb that they won't even raise it. But don't worry. Sometime on Wednesday they're sending us a runner with a brief on that. So keep it clear — whatever Maelstrom says. OK?' And chortling, he left.

Milla rooted about on her desk, fishing out rough copies and sketches of all their work for the Money; Nanny gleamed up at her, and the weird make-up her wardrobe crew had taken to using gave her face a crazy glare. Shuddering, Milla ditched the wad of pictures in a drawer, and asked Trolly what he reckoned they should say about the curries.

TWENTY-TWO

Fiona James slept, the lower half of her body cased in a white box of sheets laid over metal tubing. Grief watched, considering tears. It was a while since he'd seen her, but she was pretty as ever, albeit looking a decade older than her twenty-eight; he guessed that wasn't surprising, when you'd had an armoured security truck come careering round a corner and land in your lap. She still had her freckles: they were the best, last touch to a sparky face that was precise in every detail, and sharp, with acid and lightning in the thin blue eyes — before now. She was very different from Milla, to look at, though similarly demanding; she was tiny, breastless, a minute bundle of raggedy grace. They'd been together just past two years, when she left. It was when he was putting the Barn together, and she'd got fed up with the time it took up in his life, leaving too little for her. In desperation, he'd asked her to dance there; it was an insult, and she was out of his flat — Chelsea, in those days — in less than ninety minutes, silent for all of them and coldly packing. Now he could see she'd not be dancing any more. He wasn't surprised to find her in a state hospital; she'd never got much more than three months work in twelve. Art — he snorted bitterly. There wasn't a lot of it about, by the time of the Last Election.

A nurse came through the ward from a small office at the far end, distributing tablets; looking at Fiona, she told him she'd pull through. 'She's a tough little thing.' Grief thought, minor injuries; he complained about the message he'd had, saying who he was. The nurse nodded, acknowledging him, and told him sorry; it was what the young lady had asked. And they only had two tapes to play out anyway — good, or bad. She seemed happy to chat while Grief stood at the bed's end, so, not knowing what to talk about, he told her about the rat trick he'd seen on the road.

'Probably one of ours,' she said. 'We've had so many recently, we don't know what to do about it; we did get some cats in. It's the sewer collapses, I'm sure of it. Just around the back, there's four huge new holes opened up in the road this last month alone.' Grief nodded; he was parked by one of them. She went on, 'I think, myself, when the rats get cleared out of those, where else stinks like shit like this place does? And that's why they come.'

Lamed by her brusqueness, Grief limply responded, 'You'd think they'd do something, wouldn't you?'

'Do what?' she asked. 'There isn't the money, so there can't be the doing.'

He tried, 'There could be the money,' and thought of Milla, and the comfort of their lives.

'Never enough to cope with all these,' she said, with a large harsh gesture round the crowded sleeping oldies in the beds all around. 'They shouldn't be alive, mostly. In a better age they wouldn't be.'

Shocked, he breathed, 'But they must be cared for.'

'So they are, as far as they can be.' Grief looked at the tray she had with her, loaded with little tablet cups filled with tiny grey pills; he noticed that the cup she placed at Fiona's bedside had the larger version that Moses had taken. With a sudden sharpness, the nurse turned back from setting down the cup and asked, 'You're rich. Couldn't you pay for her to be somewhere proper? Or you could at least take her in, and give a nurse a job. There's plenty could use one.'

Grief hated being made to feel guilty. And he thought of his personal life; it was, he decided, a joke. He said, 'We're not related; I've not seen her for months. I don't even know why she asked for me.' But she'd always been a loner.

The nurse brutally said, 'People should care for their own.'

Grief saw the cross hung round her neck, and realised he was dealing with one of the new Christians, the yankee kind. She angered him, he wanted to put her right. 'You got to look at the economics of it. People have small homes, and no money, they don't have the resources to look after themselves, let alone the old. If people had bigger homes — if families were what they were ....' He trailed off as he caught himself saying what Nanny had taught with the one hand, just as she took away with the other. He sullenly concluded, 'I only have one bedroom anyway,' ashamed, not admitting it was half the size of the whole ward.

Unimpressed, the nurse shrugged. 'Well, she's in here now. At least keeping the pain away's got cheaper.'

Grief took a last look at his broken ex-lover, sleeping easily. He saw that the skin of her face was dry, and flaking. She'd lose her freckles ... he left, hollow-hearted. Outside, someone had scored a great jagged scratch all the way down the paintwork on the side of his car. It didn't trouble him; he was in the kind of mood where he felt as if he deserved it.

As he drove away, two dark-skinned men in costly suits and glinting shades stepped away from the black Mercedes they'd been leaning on, got into the big car, and slipped into the traffic behind him.

TWENTY-THREE

'Good afternoon. I'm canvassing on behalf of the People Party.'

But the man who had opened the door to Marl was clearly drunk; dirty shirt open to his paunch, he scratched his chest hair with one meaty paw, turned the own-label beer can around and around in the other, and looked her up and down. Finally he said, 'You wanna fuck?'

Dwayne was bored. The City Store noised with phones, jangled with cuffs, chattered with screens, yelled and moaned with complaints all around him. Bludge was off chasing some stupid idea about oldies. He played with paperclips; then he got up, saw himself in a mirror, considered the light baggy suit and his raincoat hung behind his desk, and decided that the Weimar Republic bit had had its day. He wandered off to Clothing Dep.

'Good afternoon. I'm canvassing on behalf of the People ....'

'No thank you, dear, not today.' Already, the oldie was closing the door.

Marl took a carefully non-aggressive step forward, and said, 'Please, could you not just consider. . . .'

'I'm sorry, dear, my vote's with Nanny. We need a strong leader, don't you see?' And she really would have shut the door; but then she took a closer look at Marl, and kindly said, 'My love, are you alright? Do you need a cup of tea?'

'Well,' said the gay young couturier at the Clothing Dep counter, and examined his nails; 'we could do you up stateside.' Dwayne said no thanks, he wasn't the movie star type. Besides, his eyes weren't so hot — he couldn't handle wearing shades. 'Uh-huh, I see,' span the gay boy on his stool — Dwayne wondered what it'd be like, to mash his face for him — 'how about Hispanic?' Dwayne asked how it looked, so the dresser hopped off to dig out all the items. Returning, he said, 'First you get these nice boots, with lots of lovely zip and buckle, see? Now these do up above the ankle — the caps, by the way, are steel, but not obtrusively so. And into these you then tuck this rather serious pair of olive green trousers, which combines, I think you'll agree, just dreamily with this short-sleeved light khaki little number. And to finish it off, we have a choice of simply splendid leather belts. All in all, rather fetching, and ever so menacing. Oh, and the tin hat's optional; I'd do without, myself, it looks rather silly and spoils the effect. As for weapons, well, let's see — you could go with one of these wonderful old machine guns, they look divine, and I adore the holes in the barrel. But of course they're absolutely useless. Rather ties up your hands, you see, and anyway it'd probably blow your face off if you ever tried to actually use it. So really you're better off with one of these stubby wee pistols; you can stack a few bullets up front on the holster here, which is a touch I'm very fond of. And the truncheon, which of course is a must, well, my my . . . .' You could see him thinking as he caressed it, what a heavenly dildo of an object. Dwayne felt like stuffing it down his throat; but wouldn't have given him the pleasure. He could see why poor fat Bludge didn't get any joy with her uniforms.

'Good afternoon, I'm canvassing on behalf. . . .'

A middle-aged punk, sped half-way to the moon and back. Appalling music thrashed wildly behind him as he quaked on his feet in the doorway. He screamed, 'Don't you know there's the snooker on?' — and slammed the door shut in her face. She watched flakes of paint drop off the woodwork and onto the welcome mat.

Dwayne, feeling better in his new outfit, but still very bored, sauntered off into the street to try out his toecaps on the wheel of a water cannon truck. He did, he had to admit, feel very, very heavy; it was nice. One of the crewcut tyros from the Election Section followed him out, and, when he'd stopped laughing, wiped his eyes dry and said, 'Look, kid, you got nothing to do. We got complaints of someone canvassing in North Ken. Ordinary sort of bird, young, scrawny, light hair. D'you wanna go get her? We're a bit tied up.' Huffy, Dwayne humphed, and said OK.

'Good afternoon, I'm canvassing. . . .'

'Not any more, you're not,' said Dwayne, hand on her shoulder. 'Up against the van.' He searched her, and found three yellow tablets in a polythene coin bag. 'Well well,' he told her, 'you're in the shit.'

'Fascist pig,' said Marl.

In the back of the van as they wailed their way back, Dwayne's heavy-bodied constable assistant looked Marl up and down. He leant forward, and put a finger under her chin to lift her face. Finally he said, 'You wanna fuck?'

Dwayne slapped him off. 'Don't be disgusting.' Then he looked round at Marl; he saw the colour of her face, and the way she was trembling, as if very cold. He said, 'Hey, chuck; you're not in such a good way, are you? Here, have a fag.' She

shook her head no; he said, 'No really, please. It's no problem.'
No one's all bad.

When Cairo got back, the couple in the bunker next door told
him what had happened. He nodded, and shut himself in his
room — his and Marl's room. He sat on the bed, and stared at
the wall, and started to cry.

TWENTY-FOUR

When the phone rang, Grief was on his way out to work at the
barn. Upstairs, Wally heard it too; he stopped sifting through
the quarter-final contestants, and gloating over how to
incorporate the porn to destroy Thor's career, and logged on
to listen. Grief clicked the phone on, hoping it would be Milla,
sober, saying where she was, and was peeved when he heard it
was Bludge. Wally didn't mind; he'd never met Bludge, and
was keen to see if she was as stupid and lumpen as Grief made
out. Given that he had this impression, it struck him as a dead
weird phone call.
  'Hello Grief, Bludge here.'
  'Hiya fatface, how's your mum?'
  'Bad. Could we talk about business, please?'
  'If you make it short. I've got a club to run.'
  'Oh honestly, Grief; you think I wanted to talk about the
weather?' Wally noticed what Grief was used to, a thin
pretence of cloddish familiarity as she approached her subject;
but this time, perhaps, the hesitancy was justified. 'We hear
news,' she said, weighing her words, 'that you've had
sexagenarians down that club of yours.'
  'Who's been reading the dictionary then? Yeah, you're right
though, one or two. So what?' Grief worried at his stubble as
he paced the room, trying not to make faces at the receiver on
the table. He was scared she'd learned more about Moses'
drug, and, after his failure to send on any news of where it
came from, was building up to a really nasty request. If there
was one person he really did not want to finger, it was Moses;
and that was what he thought she was after.
  But all she said was, 'It's odd, don't you think?'

Grief paused, stumped; then tried acting discursive, and sounding more reasonable. 'You're right,' he replied, 'it is a bit strange. But honestly, Bludge, old people dance too. I mean, these people were young when Elvis started; it's sort of nice, really, if a few of them have managed to stick with it all this time.' Then his voice grew harder, as he wondered if she was after something else. 'I hope you're not going to ask me to mess with them — you leave them alone, if they want to bop before they drop, you just let them. It's only fair; it's rather sweet, too.' A strange idea occurred to him; he said, 'Maybe I should start targetting my ads at an older age range; smooth out a little, know what I mean?'

'What,' she laughed, 'and get a barnful of cripples? I don't see it, myself.'

'I dunno, the ones I've got are sprightly enough. There's one couple, some of the kids have more or less adopted them, like mascots. What's it to you?'

'Just ask them what they're doing there, that's all.'

'Oh for fuck's sake, Bludge, they're drinking and they're dancing, what d'you think? I mean, they're hardly dealers, are they? You can't seriously be wanting to go out busting oldies?'

But she insisted, 'I simply want you to find out what they're doing, alright?'

'Yeah, yeah, OK.' Flicking a switch, he cut the connection. So did Wally, and both were thinking, as one, that people were getting altogether too suspicious. But only Grief had an inkling of what the suspicion was about.

An hour or two later, when he spotted the same two young oldies come in for a bop, he nudged through the crowd to their spot beneath the lights, and coolly ran through his welcoming proprietor act. Then he persuaded them to go up with him to a quieter bar on one of the high balconies, festooned with creeping plants, that hung Babylon-style over the dance floor. When he'd bought them a drink, he asked them, carefully, with a lot of 'if they didn't mind him asking', how they came to be there. And the old bloke said, rustling in his worn stuffy jacket, 'You wouldn't believe how nice it is to have a hangover again.'

Grief hummed and hawed, and eventually said, 'That's nice, I'm sure. But don't you find it,' he paused, 'rather tiring?' He found that he really had no idea what to say. He tried, 'Or a trifle noisy, perhaps?'

The old couple exchanged a conspiratorial kind of glance, then the old man leant forward and hesitantly said, 'We were in the beat generation, you know.'

'Indeed, I can tell,' said Grief, 'and I'm William Burroughs. But dancing then is different to dancing now.'

'Not any more,' the woman blurted, 'dancing's easy now.'

Grief realised that he was leaning toward them, peering as if they were a delicate curio; not wishing to insult them, or appear to be patronising, he wrapped his hands round his Perrier and asked, as casually as he could manage, 'Doesn't the music faze you?'

'Oh no,' she replied, 'we watch Wally Wasted all the time. And that nice Scottish boy too.'

Grief was troubled by a lizard quickness in the darting of their eyes, the tapping of their feet, and the speed with which they spoke. 'Do you take drugs?' the old man suddenly asked, leaning forward to make his confession. 'We used to, when we were younger.'

Grief recoiled. 'A bit, yes, but not much. So?' He found he was strangely breathless.

'That's good then,' the bright-staring old man carried on, 'because we wouldn't like to shock you, would we? But we take drugs, just like we used to, when the music was jazz. Here, look.' And he pulled an envelope from out of his pocket; in it, there was a whole heap of the king-size grey tablets.

'Fuck's sake,' gasped Grief, 'where d'you get those?' Visions of a money-hungry Moses trawling round the old folks' homes to flog off his goodies quickly popped up in his coke-buzzy brain.

'Sister, of course,' the old woman replied.

Grief noticed that her legs were faintly trembling. Was that to the beat? Or were they both, just ever so slightly, shaking all over? The more he looked, the older they seemed to be. He pointed at the tablets and said, 'I thought you were only supposed to take a little bit of that? It's a painkiller, right? I mean, those big tabs are for people who've just woken up out of major surgery.' All of a sudden, in the darkness and the noise, he felt weirdly, vulnerably illuminated. 'I mean,' he qualified, 'taking drugs is one thing, but you've got to be a heavy headcase to get into those big grey jobs on any kind of regular basis. My friend's a doctor,' he then hastily, inconsequentially explained.

'We know,' the old man soothed him. 'But you know how it is in the homes. They buy these bigger, stronger, bulk versions, because it's cheaper than buying lots of little baby ones. There's never enough staff to make sure everyone takes what they're supposed to, and we're trusties, so they just give us a scalpel, and expect us to chop it up and share it out. We're ten to a room, you should see it. But,' he said, holding up a hand at Grief's open mouth, 'don't you worry about us, son. We know what we're doing.'

'Come on, admit it,' Grief said, smiling in spite of himself, 'you thought a tenth of a tab was nice, so you reckoned you'd try the whole thing.'

'You betcha,' the woman grinned, 'and it was ten times nicer. I've not been so groovy in years.' She nudged her husband, as if to say, what's the harm if he knows we're a bit wild?

But Grief pressed, 'I still don't see how you've got so many.'

'Sister,' the old woman said, her grin widening uncontrollably, 'I told you.'

Ghastly suspicion dawned on Grief. 'And do you mind my asking what you're doing with so many?'

'Selling them of course,' the old bat beamed, 'how else could we pay the price of your drinks?'

'But they're subsidised,' he howled.

'Not compared to Devon, they're not.'

'But this drug is supposed to make you feel better, not richer. Surely your home will find out?'

'You're a bit square really, aren't you?' Sagely she informed him that Sister was cooking the books. 'Besides, the profit pays for replacements. The more we sell, the more we buy.'

'In our own little way,' the old man smiled, 'we're helping fund the health service. You surely can't mind that.'

'Well, no,' burbled Grief, 'I mean, I won't say a word. But, you know, keep it dark, won't you? And do be careful, for God's sake. I really don't want you flaking out on my dance floor, OK? I'm sure you'll appreciate that.'

'Naturally. Can we go now?'

Bewildered, Grief escorted them back down to the booming floor. No wonder the kids were adopting them. He did wonder dimly, recalling Bludge's sneaky inquiry on Friday, what an OD on this stuff would look like; but half his kids were so ravaged anyway, he couldn't see how a punch-packed pain-killer could be much of a problem, compared to the lorryloads of smack he was fighting off daily. With prudish distaste, he noted how busily the old pair bopped in the wild-haired crowd.

He went to call Bludge at home, and told her the old pair were 'apparently harmless'; just reliving their youth, he said, which was true enough. But Bludge didn't seem as interested as she had before. She muttered some vague sort of response, and then there was a long pause. Grief said, 'Hey, Bludge. You still there?'

Bludge said, 'Do you know what it's like, to share a house with a person that's dying?'

'Oh shit,' said Grief. 'I'm sorry.'

Bludge sighed, and collected herself. She said, 'I'm sorry too, forget I said it. It just gets to you sometimes, that's all.'

TUESDAY

TWENTY-FIVE

In the desert of the Square Mile, dawn came silently; light came down the streets, chased by scraps of litter. Beside the electronic multi-locked doorways of Wally's empty building, the shadows thinned out on the ramp leading down to the basement port where Grief kept his car, revealing as they faded the sly old wreck of a woman who lived in their garbage. Between them, Wally and his tenants threw away more than enough to keep her going; and as it decayed, it also kept her warm — the refuse was only collected once a month, by the time of the Last Election. The pile accumulated in an alcove off the ramp; it shifted and rustled as she stirred amongst the black bags, then slopped back into place as she crawled out, standing to stretch and scratch at her bandages. Across the road, the two dark-skinned men in their black Mercedes lifted their shades to look her over. She eyed them suspiciously as they beckoned her across, but moved fast enough when one of them waved a crisp note. 'This,' said the giver of the note, pointing, 'is where Mr Grief lives.' She nodded. 'Then would you tell him, when you see him, that we should like to talk with him.' She nodded again, taking the money, and they drove off without thanks. She too wandered off, for her day's aimless walkabout; richer, and so, not inquisitive. Above her, an edge of electric grey light from Wally's monitors ran along the bottom of the slats of his heavy blue blinds, waning as the day grew.

Wally was talking to the camera at the foot of his bed. 'I tell you, kidlets and old folks, you're better off jobless. I mean, look at the bags beneath these eyes. I'm completely unpresentable.' Chortling, he lay back in his blue dusty darkness, wreathed in smoke from the ever-present spliff. 'I've worked all night to sew this crap together, and when I'm finished, I'll be carrying straight on with tomorrow's semi-final. Well, the Thai kid plays Dixon — should be a belter. But there's no rest, is there? You don't know how good you've got it, dear vegetable people, crashed out as you are in front of your boxes. But rejoice all the same, for the graceless berk Thunders now joins you in joblessness. A limp cock on a tabletop; that's the last you'll ever see of him. I know you'd all stopped watching him anyway — but it's good to be rid of the oaf all the same. For sure, anyone who reckoned Delaney could win just had to go. Remember this?' Wally replayed the end of the session in which Delaney had been knocked out over the weekend.

Fat Ferdy Niedzwinckli (Double Decker choc bars, Canada) had just bust the reds open to kick off the tenth frame; he'd won all nine so far. Wally jeered dementedly at the wobble of the fat man's gut, then the picture cut to his opponent. 'There you have him,' Wally gloated, 'Dublin's own, the Persil Challenge title-holder. What a heap. What a flabby-fleshed blotchy old scowler. He's shaking so bad he can hardly hold his cue.' Wally'd known all along that Delaney didn't have a dog's chance; he was amazed he'd made it as far as he did. The man's problem was simple. Danegeld made him spit; it was piss, he said, and wouldn't touch it. Delaney was a Guinness man through and through; he poured it down his throat in real life, and his shirt in the soap powder ads, like the nukes'd be hitting tomorrow. But for the duration of Danegeld's tourney, the black nectar, along with all other brands, was banned from the 147 building. By the time the contest was down to the last sixteen, Delaney'd been without for far too long, and, playing Ferdy, he cracked completely. 'Watch this,' Wally hooted, as Ferdy finally stopped rattling them in, and played a safety. Delaney lurched to the baulk end, quivering, and tried to line up the long shot to the far end where the reds were. The camera zoomed in on his trembling hands; he stabbed at the shot and fluffed it, miscueing, going under the white ball, which flew off the table. 'That's it,' said the Irishman. 'I quit.'

'Exit the man,' Wally sneered, 'that Thunders backed. What a jerk.' He cut back to himself, speaking to camera. 'And exit Thunders likewise. See you tomorrow lunchtime, guys.' He stopped the tape; the counter said six nours dead.

Phew, thought Wally, lying back and drawing on his joint, what a week. The last eight players had been sorted out of eight games of six hours each during the weekend. The quarter-finals were running from yesterday through today for twelve hours each; the shift Wally'd just completed was the second half of the last of these, for screening that evening from six to midnight. It involved, to Wally's glee, Fat Ferdy taking his own turn at being ignominiously demolished. The winner was Rattlesnake Rodriguez, the Guatemalan stinger with a whiplash long shot so sweet and true, it was like the ball ran on rails; and he'd be on again, for the first twelve hours of Wednesday, in a semi-final against Geoff Geometry. (Geometry was at that very moment beating Ten Pint Ted, Danegeld's own man from Aberdeen.) This game would be in the hands of the acid-head and the cokefiend; Wally was sad not to be on it himself, as it'd be an intriguing struggle between safety and sensation. But Wally's money stayed firmly on Geometry, so he was happy enough to be allotted the other semi.

This pitted the Thai kid against Flabba Style Dixon, a skinny black bloke from Balham, and a hotly tipped outsider who was coming through nicely. To get there, the two youngsters had taken out, on Monday, two of the game's elder statesmen — Silent Silvester the Peruvian deaf mute, and the Swiss cheese, Karl-Heinz Emmenthal — with some dagger-sharp potting and dazzling fast play. Wally was covering the first half of their contest, going on air from midday to six on Wednesday afternoon, with Silas taking over for the remainder. It was an enticing prospect. From what Wally had seen of it so far, fast-forwarding through the four soundless hours of tape that had arrived with Cairo yesterday lunchtime, the Thai kid had the edge. The surprise of the tourney, he was, to Wally's chagrin, coming on stronger and stronger.

He thought about starting in on it right away, but he was weary, all bile spent on the vicious diatribe he'd recorded against Thor over selected edits of the juiciest tabletop porn. It sat, thought Wally, rather well between frames; more fun than pop promos. He lay back, stubbing out his joint, and stared at a monitor which showed him Milla's fish-walled room, the single swivel-chair still and empty in its centre. As he looked, she slouched in, naked, to get her morning fix of Drambuie. Then, long legs spread, she slumped down in the chair with her head thrown back, seeming to look right up at him. Her fingers flickered over the remote controls in the arm of the chair, and, opposite the fish, the huge screen filled with Nanny, ranting at all poor, small, floating creatures to get up and go getting. Milla stared with eyes of hate at the made-up mouth in its caked environment of powder; she asked it, 'How can the poor, the old, the weak, and the sick ever go get anything?' And she laughed to herself, with a voice all bitterness, 'Real jobs, ha. Vote Money.' The image of her pale lank beauty bore down on Wally in the dimness of his room.

TWENTY-SIX

Four years ago Fiona'd just left Grief, the Barn had just opened, and Milla wasn't yet working for Crinkly Crisp. Grief had invited three agencies to pitch for the business of promoting his new venture on a regular basis, once the government-sponsored launch had died down, and Milla's previous employer was one of the three. She came to the Barn and danced quietly, by herself, diligently considering it 'research', and evaluating the place as best she could. A real fun palace it certainly was; but studying the clientele, she hadn't yet coldly formulated what 'benefits' it had to offer, or how to go about selling them, because you couldn't just say it was vast and cheap, when it was also very glam, and so stylish. A tricky combination of qualities, she thought, and then found herself hurled to the floor by a flying body, as an ugly ruck broke out behind her.

Grief was financially stretched, and gambling on a minimum staff when he opened; so he had to do a lot of his own bouncing in the early days. He was into the rumpus like a man from the movies, smooth, oiled, rockfaced and, as ever, immaculate in one of his cool, old, swishing suits. Impassive, giving out no violence, and unharmed by that which was given to him, he cleared the dispute up in seconds, and, the moment they arrived, had other bouncers sending two drunken rowdies on their way to the door. Still dazed, Milla was sitting on the floor, and wondering whether she could do an ad saying that the Bermondsey Barn had the best bouncers in town, when he put out his hand, and helped her up.

When the Barn opened, Grief was taking too much coke; he was lonely, post-Fiona, and he was in debt to the hilt with a project that could easily have been disastrous. So the idea that a customer had been knocked down on his dancefloor appalled him, especially when the customer looked like Milla.

She was a fire-eater then, as yet unconstrained by success, and the need to look normal to keep the really big clients happy; the straights from the fag and booze companies, the Japanese and Americans, or the fresh-faced paranoids from software land. She had a face as white as alabaster beneath a jet-black explosion of hair gelled violently upwards, and lanced throughout with thin, vivid strokes of pillarbox red that twisted and shone, like fires in the blitz. She wore standard hipster's African ethnic, Ken market stuff, but with less of the garish colours that were trendy at the time, inclining more to black; and she added to the cotton bagginess some odd leather trappings like wristbands, and studded kneecaps twined in thongs that laced up from her soft, floppy velvet and suede boots. A salad of shark's teeth and bone hung down between her breasts; her bare arms were thin, her shoulders wide and bony, and her waist quite desperately slim. She looked taller than she was, but that was the hair, and the thrilling flash in her eyes. Grief had since come to the decision, and so the claim, that he'd fallen in love on the spot. But then, all Grief's happiness went backwards; he classified it retrospectively, like a museum curator.

'Perhaps,' said the putatively love-struck Grief, as he picked her up off the floor, 'if you ate more, you'd not be knocked over so easily.' It was meant as a reassuring sort of joke, but as he said it, it sounded limp and rude; he was trying to smile, but his face felt lopsided. 'Sorry, sorry,' he rushed, then realised he was still holding her hand, and let it go. 'I didn't mean to be insulting.' The crowd swarmed around them; they were close, to be heard through the noise.

'Oh, I eat loads,' she said, with a bright intimacy, laying all the stress on the last word. 'But it doesn't seem to go anywhere.' She spread her hands, mock-weedy. Grief had a broad, craggy face, with the jaw slightly forward; if he'd been a model, she'd have labelled him 'rugged', and used him for shirts, or adventure holidays. He was faintly unshaven, with a casually untidy hairstyle, short on top, and long behind the ears. She preferred taller men, and normally didn't like such wide shoulders — so engulfing — but there was a harassed kindness about him that appealed very much.

'Look,' he said, looking up and then down again, 'are you

alright? Can I get you a drink? Would you like to sit down, maybe?' She was thinking, this is one hell of a courteous bouncer. But then he got her a cocktail, and took her up to the DJ's platform, and told her who he was. 'What about you?'

Discovering that he was her firm's potential client made her nervous. She was still pretty junior then; and anyway, she thought, all clients were supposed to be wankers. She wondered whether to say what she was there for, but couldn't bring herself to do so; she worried he'd go cold on her, and become professionally distant. She'd heard he was a straight, with a conventionally dim view of ad people as greased creepy-crawlies; she didn't want to blow it, when she really rather liked the idea of getting to know him. After all, he looked well smart, in his rich, quiet way; and his business idea, for sure, was a gem. They sat by the record decks, with Grief showing off the tricks he could play with the vast neon and meccano saucers of the lighting rig.

Milla liked the look of him, but that didn't necessarily mean she wanted to bed him; sex didn't interest her, so much as the idea of an important friend. Moreover, she decided, if she found out what sort of bloke he was, she'd be more likely to write the kind of ad that he'd buy. She reckoned she could get away with this, on the grounds that she was too junior to present her own work to prospective clients, a task that was left to the heavy guns, her creative director, and the zecks in suits. She thought she could write the ads, and then, if they won the business, he could find out who'd written them later, and it'd be a nice surprise. She was exhibiting inexperience; she should have told him straight out.

TWENTY-SEVEN

After this meeting, Milla went out with Grief four times in a fortnight. He was attentive and understanding, he drove a nice car, and he gave her cocaine, which in those days she still couldn't afford. Once hooked into the deception, she couldn't find a way to tell him what she did; the more she liked him, the more she realised how cheated he'd feel, and the less she knew how to explain what her business was, without it looking like she was simply a spy. Grief didn't press her — he guessed she was unemployed, and ashamed of it. And her vivacity, the vitesse of her observations and opinions, lifted him up out of worry and weariness and helped him forget the weight of his venture, and the gnawing beginnings of an understanding of where his funding had placed him in relation to the police. So they didn't talk business.

At this time, Milla's ads were not only beginning to shift product, but also to find favour with the trade press; she'd started to pick up the odd award here and there. Her firm, which wasn't in the big league, was anxious to keep her, so they'd upped her income, and given her more responsibility. The morning Grief was due to come in and see the agency, her boss announced that she should present her own work. She gasped, and squirmed.

'What's up, love?' he then slickly grinned; 'you surely can, can't you? You've done it before.'

'Oh but he knows me,' she desperately moaned.

'Well you cunning little vixen,' her boss, surprised, winningly reacted. 'All the better.'

Trapped, she went to sit in the empty boardroom, staring at the ads all around the walls. 'Is this love?' she thought, disbelieving, yet feeling, now she'd probably lost it, that it could well have been. Could she be suddenly ill? Could she cry? Not Milla. So did it matter? Grief's business wasn't such a huge account, after all. But a nice one. And screw losing the business, what was that to losing a kind, cool, smart looker of a friend — with a big wallet in his pocket and a big heart in his chest? She drank too much black coffee, and her hands shook on the glossy surface of the big round table. Steadily, her self-esteem evaporated; she felt base, imbecilic, tiny.

The media director lolloped in from the pub, and passed beery comment on her outfit. 'Fuck you,' she snapped, 'it's a dress, isn't it?'

And as she was snarling, the door opened behind her; in came Grief with her boss, and one other zeck. A secretary followed, with coffee, and designer crockery. Shining with sanitised welcome, like detergent, the boss presented, 'This is our media director, Colin Stares. . . .'

'Does he?' asked Grief.

Milla laughed, too quickly, though she'd heard it plenty often before.

'At TV, all day,' Colin issued as standard reply.

'. . . and Milla I believe you know,' the boss carried on. Grief nodded her a hello from which icicles glinted. 'One of our brightest young writers, her work for the youth magazine *Popstart* is very much in vogue just now, not to mention a sales increase of thirty-seven per cent. . . .'

Inside her head she repeated over and over, 'Please shut up, please shut up'; but the spiel treacled on. Playing the efficient young businessman to the last, Grief was impeccably, eccentrically, understatedly classy beside the bright new Covent Garden suits of the admen around him. His face betrayed nothing. In his heart he was thinking, here is one agency I shall not be working with. He'd long believed that the advertising industry was a swamp of corruption — now he knew. Impassive, he listened to the long wheeling out of the agency credentials, then the media man whipped through statistics designed to prove that they could reach everybody under the age of twenty-eight in Greater London 5.3 times a week for two months at less than two pence a head; and then Milla stood up.

'We've seen that Channel Four and the local cable stations allow us to use advertising's most powerful medium, television, to create instant impact and high visibility amongst our target audience, without too great an expenditure; indeed, that we could achieve our ratings objectives, and still leave enough within the budget to put the ad into trailer packages on perhaps five hundred of the highest turnover films now in video rental. It only remains to outline our proposition, and to give that proposition a creative expression. We believe we should be telling young people who have a nose for fashion and style, but limited resources with which to sniff them out (weasel words, weasel words) that there is now a new sort of club established very much for them. A place with a lot of space, a lot of class, a lot of good music, and prices they can manage. A place that caters for their needs in a town where clubs are either exclusive, for the well-heeled only, or too grotty for words.' Her voice was calm, smooth, knowledgeable. But her stomach boomed and echoed, and she held her fingers pressed to the table to hide their shaking.

'I'd therefore like to suggest that an interesting, effective, and suitably modish vehicle for our message would be this

Chandleresque vignette we've come up with, starring an unemployed bouncer who gruffly growls his tale of woe while a smoky' sax plays in the background.' She tacked up a storyboard on little velcro buttons, and ran through the pictures. 'Frame one, we open on him walking the streets, expressing disappointment that he can't find a club worth working in. Frame two, they're either full of snots who treat him like dirt, or, frame three, they're low-rent, low-budget scumpits he wouldn't be seen dead in. Frame four, times are thin. He's down at heel in a seedy bedsit in Bermondsey when, frame five, he hears sweet soul music, and, frame six, looks out of the window to see where it's coming from. He follows his ears to the Bermondsey Barn, frame seven, and we'd have the logo up big above the foyer here; and his eyes are opened. Frame eight, he goes in, and we see what a hip pad it is, while, frame nine, the bouncer deigns to take a job there. "The Bermondsey Barn. Even the bouncers are style boys." Then, frame ten, we super the entrance price, and the fact that no drink costs more than two pounds fifty, over a freeze-frame on the dancefloor.'

She sat down. She wanted to die. Grief said, from between his hands, 'Oh yeah? And what the fuck is that little Hollywood production going to cost?'

TWENTY-EIGHT

Clear enough, here was one idea that hadn't gone down a whole bundle. 'I'm sure you'll agree,' frothed the boss, stoking manically at the embers of a very chilled meeting, 'this ad has everything we're needing to say. Certainly (faster, faster) production costs are a worry, we can look into that, but it's stylish, it's modern, it's a good little story, it's original . . . .'

'I'll tell you what,' said Milla, looking wearily across the table, 'it's crap. Any agency could give you that; I wouldn't be surprised if someone does. Any copywriter worth tuppence could toss that off between two courses of lunch.' She saw the stone harden in her colleagues' faces, but hurdled over their looks with a businessman's phrase. 'But if we discard it, it's still good that you saw it, if it's something we went through on the way to giving you what you need. You're dead right that it's inappropriately lavish; but it's a great deal more inappropriate than that. Because what we need here is dirty realism.' She was fishing in her handbag for her Walkman, from which, nails rattling on the plastic, she took out a cassette and jammed it into the boardroom stereo. 'The point is, what makes your place different? Why should any of those kids ever go there?' Jacking up the volume, she played Iggy's 'I'm Bored' — totally unhip, but then, she was young, and only thanking heaven she'd had it on her at the time; and luck does come to those who don't maybe always deserve it. Then she told Grief what she felt.

'You know the kind of shitholes these kids are living in, you've told me yourself. So let's show them that you know. Let's take a hand-held camera down the streets, when they're kicking cans past graffiti-littered wall after wall of corrugated iron, sidestepping garbage, tripping over old men sleeping out under cardboard, slipping by the junkies on the concrete staircases, standing still when the coppers drive up, with nowhere to go, no work to do, no money to earn, and no place to spend what they do get; and then we can tell them that no one else might give a fuck, but the Barn sure does. Face it, we're not just providing fun here, right? We're providing a lifeline.' She turned off the music and sat down. Three blank zecks' faces peered round at her, bewildered.

The boss shuffled in his chair, and nervously began to go backwards. 'Within reason,' and you could see him flailing to get a grip, 'I hear what you say, but the Barn, I take it, is not primarily a charity, and social concern never sold . . . .'

Grief stopped him. He said, 'No, that's much more like it. I like the way she thinks.' The zecks unwound visibly in the brittle light. 'I'll make my decision by the start of next week. Please don't bother to show me out.' He hurried away, getting out quickly to be on his own. He needed to believe that she meant it. But he also needed to believe that he hadn't been tricked; and didn't want to give them the business, because he didn't want it to look like he had been.

That night, she wrote to him. She begged forgiveness. She said she'd been an idiot. She explained how she'd not known that she'd have to present the work herself, and how, even if she had known, she'd been worse than stupid anyway; but she'd not wanted the job to be between them. She said she'd understand if he didn't give them the business; that perhaps it'd be better if he didn't, and her ad had been lousy anyway — though he wasn't to tell a soul that she'd said so. She just wanted to go on seeing him, that was all.

It was the best piece of copy she'd ever write in her life, because it was selling the only product she really believed in — herself. And it had the target audience totally taped — she knew what he wanted, though neither of them was anywhere near daring to admit it yet. He wrote back and asked her to marry him.

Enormously relieved, Milla refused. This in turn was a great relief to Grief, who'd asked out of passion, loneliness, and an increasingly conscious desire to be parental; all of which, of course, were states and emotions he couldn't entirely approve of. Besides, he remembered, confused, even as he posted the letter, that he wasn't normally the type to rush things.

He gave Milla's agency the business of selling the Barn, explaining to her when he did so that it was entirely a business decision. Typically, he wasn't lying. Like she'd predicted, another of the agencies in the pitch had indeed produced a Chandleresque vignette, although, without the benefit of inside information, it featured a barman instead of a bouncer. The third he dismissed out of hand, because under the heading 'Proposition' in their presentation document, they'd written the single word, 'grooviness'. They were equally misguided in their praise of the Money Cabinet and all its works, delivered in the erroneous belief that Grief's dad's presence therein was something that gave him pleasure — when all it gave him, was subsidy, and Bludge. Moreover, their coffee was unspeakable. Milla's bunch, Grief reasoned, had at least only talked about the job that needed doing.

As far as that job was concerned, they only saw each other occasionally; otherwise, outside work, they found themselves together every lunchtime they could manage, and every night she could get to the Barn, or he away from it. After three months, they both said what they were thinking, that the Barn was no place to conduct a relationship, and why didn't they live together?

Grief refused the notion that this should be in Chelsea, where, though she'd not left a particle of herself, the flat still smelt to him of Fiona. Milla reckoned anywhere would be fine, because it was bound to be finer than the cupboard she lived in in Clapham. And Grief reckoned anywhere would be fine, because he was learning how demanding she was. With hindsight, he regarded the offer of marriage as a down-payment on a product, which to buy outright would have been altogether too risky a capital outlay. Therefore, another capital outlay he wouldn't make, much to her chagrin, was the buying of their place-to-be. But he said that as they were bound to be nuked any minute, or suffer unspecified social upheaval, or be victims of the ever-threatening bank collapse as global debt grew; so, it followed, money was better liquid, so you could have what you wanted now, rather than tied up and then evaporated, so you couldn't have anything later.

Besides, he happened to know that Wally's lower floor had just come onto the rental market. 147 was taking off at the same time as the Barn, and, with more income, better backers, and less sense than Grief, Wally'd just bought his piece of real estate. Wally knew Grief, because he hadn't yet copped his legful of shrapnel and glass, and he used to go down to the Barn to film any promising new bands that were playing, for screening on his show. Grief gave him free drinks and dope in return for the promotion, and, in return for the material, Wally's bosses ran the club's ads at cut price. Wally liked Grief, so when he said he and Milla were looking for a flat, he snapped them up. Who could have asked for better tenants? Hearts of gold, propped each other up a treat, interesting jobs, great talkers, wonderful cooks, kind as all hell when the bomb took him out, and regular payers to boot.

Wally watched Grief, still asleep in his wide cotton bed, with the image repeated on screen after screen; but it was still the picture of naked leggy Milla that stuck in his mind, a trickle of Drambuie running down her chin as she sprawled in front of Nanny's wall-sized talking head. There were times, by the time of the Last Election, as Wally fell deeper and deeper into lusting after Milla, that he wished he'd never met them. Bloody dissidents.

TWENTY-NINE

'She was canvassing, Bludge; that makes her ours.'

'She was also carrying, and that makes her mine. Look, I'll tell you one more time, it was my boys picked her up, she belongs in my department, and I want her now.' Honestly, she thought, who gives a toss about canvassing? Bludge was in Election Section, and she didn't like it one bit.

The man at the desk looked up at her long and slow, and said, very deliberately, 'Listen, porky. Why don't you just go screw yourself? Why don't you just scuttle back to your pigpen, and your little boy sidekicks, and get on with wet-nursing your youth like you're supposed to? We got better things to worry about, OK?'

That was it. Bludge had a problem. And here was this marine-style crewcut cocky little bastard, with his feet up on his desk in his smart casual trousers and his matt black boring responsible bloody shoes, playing with his gun and leaning back in his chair like he owned the whole wide world; and would he listen to Bludge's problem? Would he fuck.

She leant forward and laid her hands, fingers out, straight-armed, heavily down onto her side of the desk, letting all her considerable weight press down. The desk tipped over her way, pushing his complacent feet suddenly up in the air and throwing him, face all amazement, uncontrollably backwards. He fell to the floor, rolling sideways, and his chair clattered behind him. As he got to one knee, and his shocked, discomposed face appeared up above desk level again, she said, 'Now. One last time. Are you going to give me Marl Foster? Or aren't you?' He was getting back to his feet; she couldn't afford giving him time to get angry, so she reached forward to take him by the collar, and hauled him violently across the desk with her great big hands. 'Because if you aren't,' she continued, 'I'm going to cave your fucking face in. Do you read me, you smart-alec cunt? Or do I print it with a needle and thread on your belly?'

He could see that, at this time, resistance would not be wise. He said, 'She'll be in your office in twenty minutes.' Bludge let him go; as soon as he was a sensible distance away, he added, 'And a report on you will be on my chief's desk in thirty.'

Bludge sneered, 'You scare me shaky.' The way she saw it, she had some crazy drug spilling out all over the market from God knows where, and cells slowly but surely beginning to fill with feverish kids from every bust she made around town;

and the last thing she needed to worry about was new order nancy boys getting uppity about her methods. If she didn't sort out just what was going on, her job was down the tube anyway.

Just as she turned to leave, the man-boy nervously put his head through the doorway to tell her Cairo Jones had turned up. She said, 'OK, come on,' straightened herself out in her uniform as best she could, and strode off; behind her, Crewcut was already filling in some neat official bit of paper with his precious, skinny, neat official writing.

In Bludge's office, Cairo stared stolidly at the wall. He was red-eyed, but doubtless obstinately resistant as well. She knew he was simple, it said so on his file somewhere in the huge database; not that she could ever make head nor tail of how to get into the thing. She looked him over, and said, 'You're not happy, are you?'

He asked, 'How can I be? You've got Marl. But you shouldn't have. Marl's not bad.' He refused to look at her. His leathers creaked as he moved uneasily in his chair. When he'd been told to come, he'd come, because of Marl; but that didn't mean it didn't feel like riding his bike right under a bus, coming to see this woman. She 'only wanted a word', they said. But coppers never 'only' wanted anything.

Bludge wondered how the hell you make a retard relax. 'Look,' she said, 'you're unhappy. Well, me, I'm wound up. I'll tell you what I do, when I'm feeling this way, and things are on top of me. I close my eyes, and I let all this big body flop loose, and I count to one hundred. Will you do that with me?'

Cairo continued to stare. The suggested activity was entirely mysterious to him; besides, he doubted he could count so far, without solid objects in front of him to be counted. Bludge sighed. 'Look,' she tried again, 'I got no sleep last night, and I've had a lousy morning since. It'll do me good, to get a minute's silence, even if it's useless to you. And if it makes you feel any better, I agree. Marl's not bad, for all her silly politics.' Cairo shrugged, closed his eyes, and waited to be told when he could open them again. So the miserable simpleton, and the fat, unlovely copper, sat together breathing, with the City Store hubbub muted beyond the closed door. The man-boy, peering through glass, wondered if his boss was going weird in the head. He studied in a mirror the new outfit that Dwayne had recommended.

'Right,' said Bludge, so Cairo opened his eyes, and stared as before at the same piece of wall. 'Sure, you can have Marl back. But, obviously, there's two sides to every exchange — are you with me?' Cairo nodded. 'So what you have to do in return, is come down to the Barn with me tonight, and find me anyone who's selling these' — she showed a bag of the yellow tablets, and Cairo looked away — 'because I know that you know perfectly well where they come from, right?'

Cairo understood. He asked, 'Does that mean you won't bust me?' She indicated yes, so he went on, 'Moses Brandt. But no one's seen him since Friday.'

'In the circumstances,' Bludge said, 'I'm not surprised.' She didn't know the name; Grief had protected him well. 'Anyway, it's a start. But it doesn't let you off, we're going all the same, for anyone with those pills, or anything like them. And now,' she looked up, 'it's a deal. Here's Marl.'

Marl looked terrible. Her face, which wasn't in the first place the world's greatest piece of architecture, rushing forward at you as it did from her forehead like a ski-slope, was now pale, worn, and grey, with drying skin and wrinkly bags under her eyes. Cairo, whose shoulders at first had visibly lifted, went hastily to hold her, and, turning sullenly, said, 'What have you done to her?'

Bludge shook her head; Marl told him, 'It's OK, Cairo, the pig's alright. Are we going home?' He told her yes, hurrying to leave, but she held him up, asking Bludge, 'I don't suppose I could have my last tabs back?'

'Don't be silly,' Bludge replied wearily, 'I know you've got a whole stack more back at home. But if I were you, I'd leave well alone till we know what they are. Don't you think that would be wise?' Marl, however, half-whimpered that she didn't want to wait until she'd got back; Bludge thought about it, then made a face and tossed her a pill from the bag on her desk. There weren't, she supposed, so many wise people left in the world.

When they'd gone, Bludge called in the man-boy, and asked if Dwayne had been in touch yet. The answer was no; she threw her hands in the air, and cursed how long it took to get anything done. 'It's a long way,' came the nervous suggestion, 'that home he's gone to.'

'So what's he got a siren for? Here, make yourself useful.

Call me up the file on Moses Brandt on that, that —' and she gestured curtly at the office micro. She wanted his work number; the man-boy had it accessed in moments. But when she called the hospital, all they could say was that Moses hadn't answered his phone all day, or yesterday either. Then the vidphone button on her desk panel flashed, so she grunted OK and hung up. Changing connections, fat fingers bumbling over the ridiculously small switches — no one, bloody no one ever designed anything with a thought for fat people — she eventually got the monitor screen to flicker, fuzzing, until an image of Dwayne, sitting in the back of a telecoms van, emerged from the snow. She asked, 'What kept you?'

'I'm sorry, Miss . . . .'

She looked closer at the screen. 'What the fuck's up with you?' Fancy gear notwithstanding, Dwayne looked about as far away from heavy as a boy can be.

'I feel ill, Miss.'

'You what? What's the matter?'

'Well, there's a lot of really sick people over here, Miss. I mean, some of these people just aren't in no shape at all . . . .'

'What d'you mean?'

'Well, I dunno, they're all so old . . . .'

Bludge spat, 'So what did you fucking expect, in an old people's home? Get back here.' She hung up on him, and rolled her eyes to the ceiling in disbelief. The coppers that worked for her were cretins, and the coppers that didn't were bastards. She told the man-boy to mind the shop, and drove down to Moses' hospital. But all she found in his lab were authorised drugs, emptied animal cages, and moulted clumps of rabbit hair.

THIRTY

Dreaming of Milla in the years when she was younger — when she didn't have that sexy edge of decay to spice her — Wally woke with a start to find it was past four in the afternoon. He could see he was going to be working all night again, and tried to swear, but only succeeded in coughing. He leant over to make tea, and built himself a joint. Smoking it, the room swam. He noticed on the monitors that Grief was out of bed, and flicked through to the sitting room, and then to the jagged, angle-shadowed study, where the camera found him working on papers, making calls, and sending messages via the micro in the electronic mail — he was fixing deals, booking bands, and contesting the club's electricity bill. Wally could live without listening to that.

He hauled himself into a sitting position, balanced stiffly as usual on the splayed-out pivot of his still, thin leg. He considered a shower, but decided it could wait; cutting Grief abruptly off his screens, he jammed in the tape of the Thai kid and Dixon. He felt so tired. What music? What ads? He rummaged grumpily behind him for the tapes he'd be needing to fill out the shift, and tried to get on with the work. The Thai kid was rattling round the table like he'd been doing too much speed; he looked orientally wise, and old beyond his years. Every shot was a tense, deliberate little pinprick, and he was leaving the white ball dead, tucked on the cushion, with numbing frequency. Dixon, unruffled, and deceptively lazy, nonetheless found himself in all kinds of trouble. The Thai kid began inexorably to creep ahead. 'You've got to give it to him,' Wally hacked, reluctantly, 'this boy's position play is simply faultless. Still, acupuncture snooker; it isn't half boring. Let the man play, yellow-face.'

The awful looming possibility that he'd be proved wrong about the Thai made him angry. Dixon lost another frame, and Wally cut the tape, deciding he couldn't bear it any longer; he looked at his schedule, to check out what ads were due to be stitched in. Next up was Milla's software epic, and then a chirpy economics 'bulletin' from the Money, going on again about how well we were doing. He watched it through, amazed at the audacity, and hit out sharply at the buttons on the editing console, cutting himself in as the Money spot ended. 'OK gang, crap-fit. This politics stuff, is it, or is it not, an absolute bunch of crap? I mean, there's a lot of crap in the world — snooker, ads, pop videos, all that for a start — but this politics thing really is a turd the size of a baked bean tin, know what I mean?'

He paused, dead-headed, and stared in blank immobility into the lens. His face peered down at him from the screens. The turning tapes hummed; he imagined the nation in grisly suspense, then flailed an arm, and made an indeterminate, drawn-out thinking noise, until something else occurred to him. 'Still,' he suggested, 'at least crap is funny. It's funny, because once it was something good; so naturally people gobbled it up, and down in their bellies they turned it into crap. I think that's a good joke.' He scratched his head, but he was on automatic now; it'd all come out. He went on, 'I won't be sorry though, when the crap's all gone, and it won't be long, either. Some day soon, the last crap'll get voided, and then the world'll just be an empty gut. And there won't be no one left, bar the savage and the psycho, beating up the bowel they have to live in. Maybe soon, who knows, when all the crap's been shat and there's no food left, when the whole world's hungry, maybe then the planet'll just have to eat itself. The whole dirty thing could just go plopf, enzymes bubbling away, and cave in on itself, disappear from space altogether. And I tell you, a stain will be removed from the universe on that glorious day, the weight of crap will be lifted from our heads; we'll float up free. The only thing that isn't crap is empty space — yeah, space is the right stuff, y'know? Why, oh why, was I not an astronaut?'

Wally slumped back. He'd said it all often before, giggling and jeering, sure that the end of the world was coming, shaking beneath the stare of the camera and screaming, 'I want to be a spaceman.' (One of his fans sent him a space helmet — but it didn't fit.) He replayed the rant, and laughed at his image, his sweat-sheeny face looming out of the murk of his room, like a cross between Francis Bacon and Velasquez. But that, he thought, is what the punters buy. More than anything else, it was crap-fits that had marked Wally's rise to the top. At first, they were rare, maybe monthly; but towards the end they came weekly at least. 'Everything's crap,' he'd say, red-eyed to camera, hunched over one knee while the other stuck out like a rotted plank of pine. He'd see a wildly brilliant shot, or a tremendous new band, or a crazy new ad, and he'd praise it, praise it like it was water after days in the desert, which often it was. And then he'd say, 'But it doesn't help us, does it? It doesn't make us richer. It doesn't buy a fine meal, or a fancy car. And if we did have a fine meal, or a fancy car, would we be richer then? Nothing lasts — still, so what? Neither will you, come to that, or me, so nothing matters either. Fuck it, anyway, here's some more crap. Today we have the Bolivian refugee, Enrico Pasta, to tackle our very own dour doughty scouse, Expressionless Ed, who, let me tell you, is as much fun to watch as laundry on the line on a rainy day. Never mind, when it's over I got some ace music crap....'

Wally was, for Nanny, a godsend; the people's painkiller. Ten days ago, he'd officially become the Jimmy Young of the Last Election — she used his show to announce said election in an hour-long interview. It was a stroke of PR genius, with the added bonus that his leg gave her a juicy chance to slag off the bombers. Wally was the stooge, the feed. Even by forgiving them, he played into her hands; the noble, generous victim. What he meant was, he really didn't blame them — they were fighting a war, after all, not sneaking around and ducking the issues the way that he did. But by then it was too late; there she was, breathing fire. All he could think, watching her rave, was, 'Shit, the woman's demented.'

Everything being crap the way it was, he was told what questions to ask, and she then replied by rote. It ended with an invitation to sum up the current state of things, and out it came: 'We are doing very well.' Twice she said it, ritually, with this really crazy gleam in her eye. But Wally didn't reckon in the end that the woman was any kind of fool. He reckoned the gleam was laughter, because she and her mates *were* doing very well — very well indeed. Shame about everyone else.

After she was off camera, and getting out of his stale smelly room as fast as her minder would let her, Wally turned to the lens, and simply couldn't think of a single thing to say. 'Well, people,' he finally, lamely managed, 'I'm glad I'm not a Russian, with that lady to deal with.'

What with the Yankees invading Mexico to get their money back that day, the Russians were the last thing on anyone's minds. Milla was disgusted with him, for his crawling performance. But Wally knew he was jobless without Nanny; and anyway, fuck it. By the time of the Last Election, everything was crap, right?

THIRTY-ONE

Wally tried to go on working, but the relentlessness of the Thai was too wearisome for words. He could see cracks opening up in Dixon's play; he didn't have the machismo of Rodriguez, he was too young to hang on in there. The Thai had come this far with more open play, generally speaking; but now the tourney was into the home straight, his eyes were glazing over, and the strategy was getting fanatical. At least, Wally consoled himself, there was Geoff Geometry to sort him out.

He was whacked, and his leg hurt. Lack of sleep, too much dope, and the fear of Milla finally going bananas before he found his chance with her, all combined to make him feel almost trippy. He stopped work, deciding he'd go back to it in the night; besieged, bewildered by memories, he lay back and listened instead to Grief at his deals.

When they'd first moved in, Wally had been very much like Grief; he went clubbing with the gang, he was in and out of fashions and bands, he was pleased as punch to be famous, he was liberal and generous, he was really a nice guy. Now, he laughed. What a bunch of crap that had been.

Wally revelled in his deterioration, never fighting back the way Milla did, on the grounds that all you managed that way was to tear yourself apart. Oh no, said Wally; accept, accept. He got into likening his decline to that of the nation, instead — invisible, mostly, at first, and for a long time decorously gradual; so English. But this train of thought seemed so interesting, that he put the tape back on, and, as fazed as the acid-head had ever been, he mused aloud while the Thai kid and Dixon cracked away, uncommented on.

'The direction of the play here, jobless,' he said to the mike, 'is depressingly obvious. I feel, don't you, that you deserve an additional layer of stimulation to spice up this shift. So allow me, if you will, to consider the notion of deterioration.' In between games, he started editing in all manner of apposite material — police recruitment ads, close-up wildlife footage of insects devouring each other, old Ulster stuff from before the borders were closed, nukes, starving Africans. 'Most deteriorations are, I'd say, initially invisible. Not in themselves — there's frantic signals pouring out every second, if you think about it — but in that no one around them can see them. It's a problem of perception. No one else can see them, because they're all so busy deteriorating themselves; so they're just not looking. Consider as well the notion of "form". There's a nice wall of pleasantries, built on the foundations of day to day behaviour, and if you can stand up straight on top of this wall, you're in a position of strength. You can negotiate. You can recognise all the things you're used to, and you can deal with them. But when it comes to all the things you see and hear that you're not used to, and that you maybe also don't like too much either, well, you miss them; you block them out. They seem few and far between, after all, and they're more often than not pretty distant, like spies on the horizon. So you don't take notice.' Dixon lost another frame; Wally dropped in the next scheduled ads, for shares in public transport, and frozen pizza. 'And then,' he continued, 'suddenly, whoomph; it's the wood of Dunsinane all over, come knocking at the door when you least expected it. "The person downstairs is having a breakdown." "The country's fallen apart." Well, fuck me — who'd have thought it?'

He paused, and took a deep breath; then thought, come on, let's go for it. 'Take unemployment, dear jobless. We're long past the point, are we not, when we first started acting like it simply wasn't there. Like it didn't matter, like there were more important things. Though I'd like like hell to know what. And while we ignore it, it just keeps on growing.' He put on a parrot voice to say, 'But I'm afraid it's only to be expected. World conditions. Time of change. Technological upheaval. Back on our feet. Doing very well. Real jobs. Tomorrow . . . . Anyway, it's not getting really massively worse, is it? For a start, demographically speaking, there's fewer kids. They go on the dole, sure, but the oldies are so busy flooding off of it and onto the pensions, you don't really notice. What you do notice is the clogged roads, and the holes in them, and the rats under the pavements, and all the closed places, and the old people, and the mess and the grot and the dust and the fag-ends, and the overflowing bins, and the dirty trains, and the lousy TV, and the non-stop Americana, and the thrown-away leaflets, and the stench and the lies and the fever to enjoy yourself, dancing in the coffin while the lid creaks shut. Put it another way, we are pelting down the piste like nobody's business. England is a toilet, and they've run out of Harpic. So they've knocked out the sit-down, and turned it into a squat-hole instead. And it might not be going there visibly, but you can sure as shit *smell* the place that this country's headed for.'

Wally lay back and played some really dirty dancefloor

funk. The Thai kid's scores mounted up; Dixon was way out of it. When the frame was over, Wally rewound and listened through his chat. Milla, he thought, would love it. His masters, on the other hand, wouldn't like it one bit. In the execution of his brief, he was steering altogether too close to the wind here. Still, fuck 'em. They couldn't change it; he'd not be finished with more than an hour or two to spare before it was due to be screened. But . . . fearful, he equivocated, and added this addendum: 'So what can we do, gang, with the state of play as it is? I say, drop the white at the baulk end and play safe. Leave out the flash stuff. Obey the boss, and keep your heads down.' He laughed, long and loud, and chewed at his nails.

THIRTY-TWO

Grief dozed, with a music paper in his lap and Yankee football on the box. Then Milla zoomed in, and he stirred himself awake, glumly seeing (as did Wally, watching) that it had taken just the two days back at work, to get her straight back to abnormal again. It was booze all day, laced with pressure, deadlines, Trolly's joints, and the horrible stimulus of strange, isolated facts from the research boys. By evening, she was a pocket of frenzy, unnaturally high on the veneer of her daytime's excitements. Bedtimes, she didn't go to sleep; it was more like she just ran into a wall, and stopped dead. She didn't give Grief anything but the curtest hello until she'd fixed herself a drink; then, ice clunking, she pounced into his lap, crumpling the paper before he could remove it, and forced him to listen to her.

'Did you know,' she laughed, 'why housewives like take-aways? It's because, if the menfolk get pissed, and then buy a chinese on the way home, that means they've paid for the night's eating with money of their own; so there's more left in the housekeeping, for the wives to spend on themselves.'

'Gee,' said Grief. 'And how much does a research whizz get paid, to find out this common sense?'

'You know something else?' she continued, unhearing. 'There are now five times as many Indian take-aways as there are fish and chip shops. Mornings, there has to be a lot of sore arseholes in this country. And also, did you know,' she hooted, abruptly changing gear, 'that nine per cent of people now say unprompted that Nanny is a fascist? At least there's some thinking souls we'll never convert.'

To Grief, it sounded like the kind of thinking that wasn't really thinking at all; just Nanny-rant, reversed. Where, he wondered, had all the sensible people gone? But he had a far bigger worry. He said, 'You're drinking too much again.' It got so she'd leave half-empty glasses all around the flat, scummy where the ice had melted, smeared with lipstick, and dotted with little islands of ash that floated awhile before sinking into sediment. Grief hated sloppiness.

'The bottle doesn't criticise. It knows how to pay me attention.' She fingered his cheeks, mock-reproving.

'That's not funny. Now listen. Trolly called, this afternoon. He asked if you were OK; he said he was worried about you.'

'Traitor,' she snapped. 'Why can't he tell me that himself?'

'He said he does, and you tell him not to be daft. Me, I think he's right.'

'And where was I, when this confab occurred?' She smiled sweetly, her false plastic smile, deliberate because she knew he disliked it.

'Getting pissed with your boss.' A slight downturn of his lips indicated distaste; jealousy, he refused to hint at.

'That's right, I remember,' she yelped, leaping up, and padding about with larger steps than was natural for her, stabbing the air, 'that's right. I told him I hated doing the Money ads.'

'Good. Maybe now he'll sack you.' Hope springs eternal, thought Wally.

'Why should he?' she replied. 'They're good ads. Besides, as he reminded me, they're a drop in the ocean. Why should I worry, when they get a quarter-hour's free advertising up the front of every news bulletin? In the haystack of publicity, I'm a mere needle.' But, thought Wally, a very sharp one. 'I told him I hated that, too,' she vaguely added.

'God, you're a mess,' said Grief, heavily, slowly landing his forehead in his palm, his elbow on the arm of the chair. 'Six in the evening, and you can't even remember what you were doing at lunchtime.' He sat still, watching her wander, cold-eyed.

She whined, 'Oh but I can, baby, really I can. It's just been very exciting today, that's all. You want to know who I'm presenting to on Friday night?' As she asked, she spread her hands wide, not noticing drink splash out onto the white carpet. It soaked in quickly, staining faint brown. 'Not just Nanny, but the whole top half of the Cabinet. Famous, huh?'

'I thought you hated them,' Grief complained, stymied again by the rapidity of her inconsistence. 'Monkeys, you said. Trained to go through hoops in the dark for the rest of their lives by a crazy ringmaster in a long-closed circus, I quote. Very graphic.'

'I do hate them, I think they're evil. But don't you see, it's exciting, it's exciting for me. It makes me feel important.' She regretted saying this, knowing how hard Grief tried to make her feel just that.

'You're just looking forward to being in the same room as them, and finding out you're cleverer. Honestly, lover, please resign. It's killing you, pretending.' He got up.

She ran over for a hug, seeing in the slight dropping down of his shoulders that he was leaving, running away to his work. 'Should I resign?' she asked. 'But what would I do?'

'You'd slow down, be happy, and live with me. Hell, I could sell the Barn, I'd be a millionaire. We could go ... I dunno, there isn't a hot place left in the world where they don't have a war.'

She clung to him. 'So we could go to a cold place. And tonight, we could go to a restaurant. Please?'

'You're too drunk, and I've got Bludge on my back. She's been hassling me again, about Moses' drug, and the oldies; I got to see what's happening. You go get stoned with Wally, he calms you down better than I can.' It was said in sadness, and again, without jealousy. Wally rubbed his hands together, gleeful.

Still she clung to him. 'You're not interested in me any more. Fuck me, won't you? Fuck me now.' But he pushed her away. 'You know what I should do?' she called after him. 'I should take a bomb to that bloody meeting on Friday night. I should blow all those bastards into pieces.'

Grief turned in the doorway, and stared. 'That,' he said, 'is the stupidest, the most grotesque thing I've heard from you yet.'

Right, thought Wally, watching her cry. That's the kind of

thing you really do not want to be doing. He started rolling a joint for her, knowing she'd be with him soon.

THIRTY-THREE

'He doesn't love me any more, Wally.'

Wally made a big act of laying the Thai kid and Dixon aside, beckoned her over, made false fatherly noises like, you listen to your old chum Wally; and proceeded to fill her full of dope. She cried and cried, tucked into his shoulder; he cradled her, and carefully said a lot of right things. 'Listen, love,' he offered, aided in invention by the mock-philosophising of his day at the edit desk, 'when I first met you, you were a finely drawn person, an unfinished sketch of a thing, you were light on the page. And Grief thought so too, he thought new lines could be slipped in anywhere, thought you could profitably be expanded in a multitude of directions. Filling you out, making the most of you, it was a good job, a big job, and he wanted it. And then you went and let your work do it instead.'

'You're telling me I'm a lousy manager of my own life,' she said, trying to laugh. 'But,' she snuffled, 'I'm incapable of delegating.'

She was, thought Wally, wretchedly resilient. The last thing he wanted right now was to see her get happier, and start making jokes. 'Grief doesn't not love you,' he said, 'he just thinks your job is a disaster.' Dope lent him wings. 'On the huge page of time, my sweet, you were, like I said, this loose little bundle of lines, just faintly etched at the centre. The strokes to make you whole should have been long and loving, certain and fluid. But ads, well, there's a life that goes too fast, like a game of squash, it's all quick and jerky, when you should have been a swimmer. I mean, every new achievement in that career of yours, it's just a short stubby line, each unconnected to the last or the next, and thickly pencilled in without thought or attention — this week curries. computers the next, with an airline to look forward to and a chocolate bar to look back on and be proud of — so you've turned into this jagged seething fuzz, a buzzing swarm in the middle of the page, with vast white space just hissing and empty all around, and no way to reach the edge and look out on things. Which is no way to be.'

Wally wondered where his eloquence was taking him, then saw that she'd fallen asleep. He looked back on the road she'd taken, a road on which, he knew, he was merely a bus-stop, where she sheltered when it rained. At first, Crinkly Crisp had been sunny skies, making her an offer, soon after she'd moved in downstairs, that she couldn't refuse — big league blue-chip products to work on, and twice the salary for doing so. Her credit with Crinkly was good from the start, because naturally the business of selling the Barn moved with her. (Even here, though, Grief couldn't claim her to himself. There was a beer-bellied marketing man from the north, who'd been trying to bed her for months; he too moved his business to Crinkly Crisp when she went there — though he moved it straight out again, when they told him it wasn't important enough for Milla to be working on it.)

At first, it seemed the new agency was nothing but good. Crinkly straightened her out; he gave her a bonus to buy new clothes with, and said things like, 'You'll have to scotch that hair-cut, pet, if you're going to let us bring you on.' But again, Grief resented it, that another man was moulding her; especially a fat failed actor of a rightist chairman who spent all his time proclaiming he had "the voice of the people". 'How can he?' Grief complained. 'He drips with gold, he drives a Roller, and he lives on the river. What the hell's populist about that?'

'Everything,' said Milla. 'He's got everything they dream of.'

Money. 'Making the world go round,' said one of her ads. And, writing them, she'd cracked. For four quick years she'd been running up a dunghill. She looked down as she neared the airless summit, and far in the distance, knocking aside the bits of shit that fell upon them as her natty zeck shoes kicked along on the crumbling path, was a mass of tired lined faces; blurred, indistinct, old, and, ridiculously, cheering.

'Do you know,' Milla murmured, suddenly stirring, 'that I went to a People Party meeting?' Wally pricked up his ears. 'But it was a waste of time. There was this scrawny junkie there, name like mine, face like a ramp, kept on going on about the working class. What sort of a working class is it, when they don't work any more, or own their own homes if they do? No, you got to be more serious about it than that, if you want to take out this government.' She levered her body upright against him, sleepy-eyed, arms floundering. She dropped the joint that he passed her, burning a hole in his bedcover, picked it up, and demanded music. Wally, stretching out, hoped at least for a glimpse of thigh to make the evening worthwhile.

'I'll tell you,' she said, 'where the downturn came, for me and Grief. It was when the ads for the Barn changed.' After two years of the original gritty realism, the crowds were beginning to thin; Crinkly Crisp did some research. 'This social concern bit,' said a smooth young zeck to Grief at the next meeting, 'I realise it's close to your heart, but frankly, as your professional advisers here, we'd like to suggest that you dump it. It's older hat than a school cap and blazer. Like a Latin motto on a frayed peak, it's sweet, but no one understands it. They know now that you "care" about them; all they want to do is dance.'

Grief was furious, and would have sacked the agency there and then; but Milla agreed with what was said. She started writing ads that were pure exploitation — wild parties, endless boogie, sexual healing. Grief, dead-hearted, all businessman now, gave up, and went along with it. When Moses complained, he just said, 'I'm sorry, mate, it happens. You get far enough into your thirties, and then you're very, very tired.'

'It was about that time,' said Milla, 'that he stopped asking me to marry him.'

THIRTY-FOUR

She talked about advertising all bloody night. It got to the point where Wally couldn't wait to be shot of her. He plugged her with dope and sympathy, and got no nearer to her knickers than he was to liking Thor. She'd have to be got more desperate yet; tonight, she was almost happy again. 'I can't see the faces,' she declaimed, lurching to her feet and toppling about, 'just the ABC1C2DE's; just the "ninety per cent of housewives believe", and the "fresh food is generally felt", and the "Heinz is preferred to own-label whenever the budget can stretch to it". I know what they've bought, and I know what they'll buy next, but what they *want* is a mystery. I'll lay money it isn't Taj Mahals; anyhow. But choice is determined by the moving image; I'll sell 'em somehow. And on that note, sweet prince,' she cried, 'good night.' It was nearly one in the morning. Glumly frustrated, Wally turned back to the Thai kid and Dixon.

Milla slept without dreams, after evenings spent with Wally. She'd be so full of dope that going down the stairs, it felt like there was concrete in her knees; she'd fall into bed with no power left in her muscles, limbs like tree trunks. 'How can such a thin thing feel so heavy,' she grinned to herself, staring at her body where it lay, incapable of moving it. She often couldn't be bothered to undress when she'd got there; or simply couldn't manage, though she knew it'd make her angry in the morning, when she'd wake up feeling dirty, and have to spend that much more time tarting up for the day's zecky sleekness.

This night, unsurprisingly, she failed to undress, and Grief, when he came in, was unusually rough in the way that he jolted her awake. When he heard Grief coming in, Wally was mumbling curses and incantations in the vain hope that if Dixon couldn't bring down the Thai, maybe voodoo would. He was surprised at how late Grief was back. Now the Barn was just another business, and now he was so worried about Milla, he left it to his staff on more and more nights, coming home early to keep her from drinking, and see she got better sleep. He didn't, Wally thought, seem too worried about her sleeping tonight.

He was saying, 'You slobby mutt, you passed out again. What am I going to do with you?'

Weird, thought Wally. Was he drunk? It wasn't like him, to stare that way, so hard-eyed, while she moaned, turning over, and tried to stay asleep. He jogged her some more, and she muttered dull swearwords. He suddenly said, 'Every day you come back from that crystal ant-palace you call work, and you lay all your booze and dislikes and excitement on the carpet in front of me. So maybe for once you should sit up one night and listen to the shit I have to spar with. Just maybe for once.'

Frankly, Wally couldn't see any way she was going to make it. The pact was broken, their confessional a prison. But she rose to it, big heart bigger than the drugs and the fatigue, and she rolled up, rocking on the way like there wasn't the strength in her back to get her all the way up; then she stood, chin on her chest, and shuffled over to embrace him, hanging arms round his neck, cooing, hands pecking and stroking at his head and his back, cheek on his shoulder and whispering, 'Tell Milla, tell, she's sorry, and she loves you.'

The stiffness went out of Grief, though the more general fury was still steel in his voice as he clung to her body. 'They busted my oldies. Bludge in her own fucking person came down to my club with that idiot bikeboy, and the bikeboy fingered my oldies.'

'Poor baby.'

He took a deep breath. 'You think we should free them from the media. So sure, yeah, they get fed lies, and crap. But they got an on-off button for all that stuff. What you cook up isn't so bad, they're not forced to eat it. But you try freeing them from coppers, that's all. That's where the fucking state is, angel, it's right on the doorstep, and when those people want to fuck you around, you can't turn them off like the fucking TV, no way. When those boys want to come down on you, that's a jammed fucking set, and you strapped in front of it.'

She reassured him, 'There's nothing we can do, there's nothing we can do,' rubbing against him, half-asleep, warm, telling truth late at night. He undressed them, himself efficiently, and her carefully as she stood, hands dangling, not moving, until they got into bed, and lay huddled together. Wally watched them sleeping for ages, not that he was going to learn anything. He watched, because it was good to know there's worse ways to get crippled than glass in your leg.

THIRTY-FIVE

Cairo Jones was a well-pleased boy. He'd done what was asked, and it hadn't been difficult. Bludge had promised that Marl and he would be left alone — and he'd even been given a neat little plastic pass card, that allowed him to get home without molestation on the way. Naturally, he had no clue why Bludge should have wanted him to do the thing that he had; but now it was done, it seemed a remarkably slight payment, for such a considerable let-off. Still, Cairo was the last man to ask any questions. The ways of the law would forever be a mystery. There were bigger, dirtier things in the world than his soft, lonely mind could take in.

His bike muttered softly through the darkness, the garish colours of the tank flashing as he passed the rare street lamp that still worked. He let himself drift round the potholes and the pools of broken glass, dumbly giving himself to the pleasure of motion. The buckled lamp-posts and broken-topped bollards stood still and reproachful, half-undressed in fly-posters whose corners flapped where the cheap paste was weakening, until the image was torn away, or another plastered over it. As he chained up his bike, Cairo looked at one, grimy and faded, that fluttered on the flaked, mossy cream post at the foot of the steps of his building. He recognised the word 'Premier'. Premier were short, stubby cigarettes that flared and crackled, and were quickly smoked, rasping. Marl would pop out to buy one or two off the street kids, when they were down to last pennies. Cairo didn't like them; they made the room smell, and the tiny window that looked into the building's dank well didn't open properly, to clean the air.

When he got back he found the door of their warren open an inch or two. No one had ever bothered to mend the lock; there was nothing in the building to steal. He found Marl, long and naked, in bed but awake. She looked drained of colour, as before, but bright-eyed, with a strange combination of peace and alertness. She stared, with this livid good humour, at the ceiling, and then him. 'Well,' she asked, in a hidden voice that seemed many, many miles away, 'how did it go?'

'I found two oldies,' Cairo told her, 'and Bludge took them. That was all.'

'We have been so very lucky,' she smiled. 'But I take it I'm banned from canvassing.' He nodded. She said, 'Those bastards' — but oddly, without the normal bile of her politics; she seemed washed up and bleached, on a far away shore, bones white in the sun — 'those bastards have cooked the whole thing so it rises their way. D'you know what that Nanny lapdog Wasted did this evening? He destroyed Thor Thunders. The last voice of the left on television has been crudely blown away.'

She might as well have been saying happy birthday. Cairo wondered how she could be smiling; the news made him furious. Thor was Cairo's hero. He played good music, simple and forthright, music Cairo could understand; not just trendy junk for wimps. Wasted, he thought, was too pleased with himself, too bloody cocky, too sure he knew what was good and what wasn't. Why couldn't Cairo listen to the music Thor played? And still Marl was smiling. He said, 'Why you so happy?'

'Oh love,' she murmured, 'don't be angry. We've had a let-off, let's be content, at least for tonight.' Without shame she admitted, 'I took four of the tablets to celebrate, I'm in the sky. Try some, let's just lie here with the snooker; let's not let anything hurt.' She was, he realised, all over softly trembling, with insect sensitivity. His dull anger fused with desire. Her bare thin shoulders had sharp tiny bones. Her scraggy neck quivered, dry-skinned. He wanted to be wrapped in her lightness, they'd not made love for so long. He ripped his body from out of the bike clothes, and threw himself in beside her. She said, 'Be careful, I'm terribly frail; I'm terribly tired.'

The voice wouldn't come any closer, though it came skin to skin from right beneath his chest. She was at the far side of the world from him. She stared at the ceiling, and lightly shook. Rising to touch him, her hand was skeletal, grey, beginning to wrinkle; bone showed through, in shape and colour. Stupidly he cried, 'Come here, where have you gone? Marl, come closer.' He rolled to squat above her, his knees between hers. He wanted her, she was all he had.

She whispered, 'Don't,' and dreamily thought, men; it was virtually rape, always, no matter how tender. She said again, 'Don't,' and fear rose in her. Her body felt so weak, so light, not up to it, birdsong in the sky, shards and pieces. His clumsy hands fumbled with her slightness; she felt like stale crustless bread, easily crumbled. Panic grew, fighting the drug as it insolently insisted that she continue to be happy. Once more, finally, she pleaded, 'Don't.' But Cairo's erection was un-manageable, his lust and confusion hungered for relief, and how else could he be close to her, when he didn't know the words, and touch didn't work? He reached down, hands taking her by the inside of the knees, his strength thrusting her thighs wide apart.

Then, as he scrambled back gagging from the fountaining blood, Marl, dying, said, 'It's alright, it doesn't hurt.'

WEDNESDAY

THIRTY-SIX

'I'm telling you,' Bludge sighingly told him, 'they could have kicked an elephant half-way to heaven, the amount of that stuff they had on them.' It was nine in the morning; but when she'd called him to tell him what had happened, he was out of bed and round to the Store in a flash.

Now she was trying to excuse herself. Oddly, this new, strange event, of which neither had any experience, had brought Grief closer to her, just at a time when he was primed to hate her the most. It was like two people meeting as strangers before a high wall; it didn't matter whether they liked each other, they had to co-operate, if they were going to get over.

'Look,' she went on, clutching his arm — and he didn't shake her off, his head was too busy to feel any revulsion — 'I'm not a monster. I've always wanted you to like me, actually, I'm human. This gives me as bad a feeling as it does you, really it does.'

Grief was inclined to believe her. He remembered, some time last year, how Dwayne had greenly tried to excuse his chief, when Grief was furious at one of her less sensitive intrusions; the kid had quietly mentioned to him, without details, all the raps Bludge had taken, when she might have climbed higher. Now he looked about him, he understood why Bludge had always seemed so ill-fitting. They were in the downstairs, the dungeons, a place he'd not seen before; and with its bare barred cells, it looked so American. There was a mournful howling of slogans from the People activists, and so much banging and clanking and rattling, and such dull paint, such an infinity of corridors and the light so grey — it was straight from a Hollywood prison movie.

The images clicked in Grief's mind, taking him back to the spanking new, paper-crowded, computer-busy, open-plan upstairs, and he suddenly knew it just wasn't British. They'd pumped so much money into law and order, and they'd obeyed so slavishly the advice of our sponsors across the water, that their gleaming new stations weren't stations at all. They were television sets. The men wore shirtsleeves, and drank coffee from polystyrene mugs, and the young bucks all carried guns; they even sported shoulder holsters. With something horribly close to affection, Grief realised that he'd never seen Bludge with a gun. How out of place she was, with her brutish joviality, her excess of fat; how poor and English.

Then Grief recalled, getting it in perspective, how Bludge liked her violence English too; close, unsmiling, sweaty, workerly. She liked the arm's length immediacy of the truncheon; she'd have got no kick from the glamorous dropping of a villain with a bullet in the back from a block away. No wonder the only job she could pull was watching over the kids. It was the TV that did it — not just the Yankee shows all over the cable, but the news, and the way the journalists went in onto crime stories like flies onto shit, tiny cameras buzzing on their shoulders. And, when the police image was so vital, of course they wouldn't dream of having pink porker Bludge on the sort of job that got filmed. Poor fat Bludge — the world was gone past her.

Grief felt seriously uncomfortable, with the shouted slogans and the hammering of metal noises all around him, and the thin paint on rough brickwork only weakly casting back the blank, weightless light. There was no air. In the cell before him, the two oldies lay painlessly dead on narrow foam mattresses, benched up a foot off the floor, with a yard of space between them.

Bludge was nervous beside him. This wasn't the sort of death she was used to. Bloody ones, drunken ones, deliberate ones, OK, but this was outside her range. 'I'm telling you,' she tried again.

'You told me,' Grief said. 'But you didn't tell me why you picked them up in the first place. I thought I told you to leave them alone.'

'I picked them up because there's something really bad going on with this drug. I have kids coming in here that look like ghosts, Grief. And the home these oldies were in, Dwayne half spilt his guts at the state some of those people were in.'

That seemed pretty lame to Grief. It wasn't news, that there were private homes you wouldn't keep a rat in. He asked her how they'd died.

'We got them in here, maybe two-thirty in the morning. We took all their stuff off them, asked a couple of questions, you know what we do' — all too well, he knew — 'then we gave them the cell. Came back six hours later, there they were. Doesn't look like it hurt much, does it? They just went. What I don't like is, they look wrinklier than they did last night. See? More grey? I mean, they're only early sixties. I got a guy down the block, he looks that way and he's forty-six.'

Grief peered in. The bodies were smiling. He couldn't tell how old they looked, or whether it was different. Briskly, he asked, 'What are you trying to tell me?' He didn't see what she could tell him; she was plainly foxed.

'Well,' she said, fingering her collar, 'it's like they died of old age.'

'Oh big deal,' Grief spat, suddenly too pissed off with the whole foul thing. 'So they burnt out. There's people doing that everywhere. More likely shock killed these two, fatty; the shock of meeting you just when they were beginning to enjoy themselves.' He was on his way out, but Bludge hung onto his elbow, clearly hurt and frightened, pleading for understanding. He regretted his harshness, and asked what she'd meant.

She said, 'It's like, what should have taken six years, took six hours.'

'OK, Bludge, you're always on my back for information, so try this little nugget for size. That drug is being given to every oldie, in every hospital, in every town in this country. Shit, I'll bet your copper welfare's even pouring it down your mother. And like you keep complaining, it isn't killing *her*.' It was only then that he remembered Fiona.

THIRTY-SEVEN

Grief got through the crowd milling round the City Store gates, and then stood, slowed by the brightness of the light, with his ears shut to the mewling of a queue of oldies lined up for their pensions at a post office. The sky was hot, but they were still closed up in their cheap woolly coats, that funny, checked sort of man-made, with white hairs sprouting raggedly all over it, and the white not quite white, the black not quite black; nothing sharp, all faded. He felt complaint bitten back in the withered effort to stay upright, and wondered how many of them had made it onto Moses' drug.

Would all of these, too, suddenly flake out and keel over? You're in there all your life, paying your taxes, and then gratitude comes pill-shaped. Grief had been confirmed, at public school, and God then had seemed a huge, wet, fresh-washed peach of an idea. Then, as he grew, it had shrunk to a dried banana chip, too small to hang onto, something he'd lost under a sofa cushion when he'd put his feet up after the hollow business of the passing days. But now, as the queue turned their watery eyes onto the light radiation of his unimpeachable ease and wealth, the dried fruit grew soft again, the notion expanded in the drip-drip of their sorrows. God was there — a big beggarly hope.

He resisted the impulse to dish out money, angered to see how, in a street too near a cop shop so the beggars couldn't sit there, the ordinary people were now brought so low as to look at you just the way beggars would. And would the Lord lift them up? He could imagine Fiona's nurse, asking who else has the strength? The whole human race had abandoned its responsibilities to the glib release of the free market truisms; they plopped into his scared head, like stones into wet mud. Why does the shit fall on the people at the bottom? Gravity. What do you do if you don't like it? Buy a rope. And climb like a toad into the cistern. He wondered how the poor, with their plaintive slanted glances at the cut of his cloth, could suffer so long, when the fat cats like his father raised hell with their worries, fighting like maniacs to hang on to their slice. But fill a cage with rats, it's the fat ones get frantic, because it's them that feels the squeeze. And the thin ones just jostle, crowded out into corners.

An image of the smiling dead oldies swam behind his eyes as they hurt in the light; then, like a tune recalled, a hearse floated by, the engine quiet with the greased assurance of an adman's sales pitch. 'Let us handle it, we know what's wanted.' Comfortable deaths. The hearse nagged at him, he felt like he'd been seeing more and more of them. What was it about hearses that bugged him?

He remembered how he'd been sitting at the wheel on the way to see Fiona, gnawing at his nails, and seen two at least on that trip alone. In all that jam, you still didn't exactly mind, and anyway there was no point minding, if you had to squeeze out of the way for a copper, or an ambulance, or a fire engine, seeing as how they did, maybe, have something vital to be getting on with. Though in the copper's case he doubted, mostly; he knew Bludge used her cherry-top and siren just to do the shopping, or get home to give tea to her mum — or even just to play racing drivers. She was, he realised, just a kid, really.

But why pull aside for hearses? Everybody did it, shame-facedly, pretending respect, and why? When the world still had things to do, why hold it up for a corpse? Bodies didn't have meetings to make, deadlines to meet, forms to fill, clubs to run, ex-girlfriends in hospital — or, he thought, current girlfriends as near as dammit likewise. So what was the hurry, to hop in the fire? He remembered, on Monday, seeing a third hearse pulling out of the hospital itself, right under the noses of the feverish, the broken-limbed, the bleeding queue. Indecently indiscreet; what, he couldn't shake from his mind, was the rush to be shot of them?

Thirty-eight years. He was worn down, sure, but physically well; no aches, no bruises, still supple from exercise in a fairly clean body. Grim, he thought, how he couldn't see himself, or anyone else, being granted another thirty-eight.

He shook his head and strode out, assuming stone-faced purposefulness as he plunged through the bent-backed scrummage with their up-rolling eyes; but death was now solidly anchored. In his head he begged them not to stare at him so. Death. Even the kids knew all about it — his kids. Passing the video store, he noticed how the dance barn porn vogue was still in all the windows, and it angered him, because he knew how his kids weren't ever into sex; in four years, he'd not seen so much as one sneaky blow-job. They came to dance, to drink, to drug it up in the best clothes they had, and be seen, clean, untouched, keeping their balance. They knew that sex only ended up with more kids — and there wasn't enough to go round for the ones there already were.

THIRTY-EIGHT

Grief hovered outside the breakproof glass of their huge front doorway. He considered copping out, going up to Wally's for a thick head in the dope smoke, not admitting the awful possibilities — but only for an instant. He knew why he'd sympathised with the policewoman; she'd spoken of the oldies with that same fuddled, bemused little slump in her shoulders that Moses had had, when he'd talked about his rabbits. Before, that was, he'd jacked himself up on the drug. The drug that was greying his hair, drying his skin, wasting him away. Was that what it was doing? Was it doing the same to Fiona? It hadn't looked that way; but the rank heavy smell of paranoia was rising in his nostrils, like ozone before thunder.

Still he hovered, then jumped, as the old woman suddenly popped up from the garbage down on the ramp. 'Grief?' she cackled, 'there's people been looking for you. All manner of people.' And back she dipped, chewing on a bone, in amongst the bags. Behind him, he heard a car purring closer in the empty street, and turned to see a black Mercedes pulling up. Through the tinted windscreen he saw two dark faces, and sunglasses, and smart suit jackets. He prayed it wasn't him that they wanted; heavy people was the last thing he needed. Pushed into action, he ducked down the ramp, reaching into his pocket for his car-keys as he went.

In the darkness of the space beneath the building, his mind buzzed and clattered; his hands riffled shakily through the tinkling keyring. Out on the road he heard the Mercedes' engine switch off; doors opened, and feet stepped out onto the tarmac. Incongruously, it popped into his head to wonder what had happened to 'Sister' at the oldies' home. He heard the car doors shutting, and footsteps beginning to cross the road. Fumbling, squinting in the dark, he couldn't find the key to his own car door. He held the ring up in the air, his back to the ramp. That, he thought, brain whirring insanely fast, is one Sister who's out of a job. He couldn't shake off the intimations of higher authority behind Bludge's shuffling, side-stepping, confused explanations — who was putting her up to it, to move so fast? He wondered if government agents drove Mercedes these days, now that Rover was gone. The soft footsteps behind him changed tone as they stepped up across the pavement, crossing the kerb to the corner of the ramp; they seemed titanically loud, booming in his skull. He found his key, and leant forward. Something cold, heavy and metallic thudded into the back of his neck. He grunted, and fell against his car, sliding down the side of it, threads of his suit catching where the paintwork had been gouged by vandals two days earlier. Another body, disgustingly smelly, toppled forward over his own, dropping something as it fell with a liquid clunk on the concrete.

Thor Thunders, who'd been waiting in the darkness, was as always foully drunk, and mad now with rage at his exposure on the screens of the nation the night before. The force of his blow had nearly up-ended him; his weapon, a full, chilled can of Special Brew, had been knocked from his hand, and it rolled away, clinking across the uneven floor. Grief lay stunned, the back of his head throbbing horribly, his face turned up into the light from the ramp. Up at the top of the dip, he saw smart shiny shoes that had stopped on hearing the noise of the attack; they started to walk again now, creeping silently down the slope past the garbage. As they descended, the trousers came into view; Grief noted, dimly, that they too looked pricey, like the shoes.

Above him, Thunders had righted himself. Festooned in the tattered badges and logos of a whole host of dud rock bands, his shabby denim flopped about his paunch as he swayed on his feet. His filthy hair hung down around his spots and his stubble. 'Are these,' he blurred, 'the keys into your building?' He had Grief's keyring; he rattled it, demanding which ones let him in through each of the doors, and which got the lift to work, and which let him through onto Wally's floor.

'Why?' coughed Grief, groaning, shifting on the rough, oily floor. In the corner of his eye, he watched the two very expensive suits slinking around behind Thor off the bottom of the ramp.

'Because I'm going to kill the bastard,' Thunders yelled, 'he's destroyed my whole life. And if you don't tell me how to get in, I'm going to kill you too.'

Wearily, Grief noticed the superiority of Thor's accent to that which he'd deployed on the TV. Another middle-class wanker posing as a man of the people. 'Look,' he muttered, 'it's hopeless. All the doors have punchcards, there's guards in the foyer, and anyway Wally has a security monitor. Even if you went in with me, he'd know you were coming.'

Thor lurched about a bit, swigging at another beercan in his confusion at these difficulties. A smooth, clipped, well-educated Arabic voice asked, 'Is this unpleasant man giving you some trouble, Mr Grief?'

Grief breathed out in relief — they had worried him far more than Thor, who was spinning round, stumbling to one side as he did so. Grief heard the faint pfut of a silenced handgun, and his relief evaporated as quickly as it had arrived. Jesus, he thought, Jesus Christ, as Thor was knocked backwards two yards by the impact of the bullet. The Arabs stepped forward, one retrieving Grief's keys, the other helping him up. As he did so, he calmly inquired, 'Mr Grief, would you talk with us, please? We have business that we believe you will be really most interested in — if what we see and hear of you is true.'

Grief steadied himself on his feet and unlocked his car, trying to grasp in his pounding head just exactly what was happening. Then he remembered why he'd wanted to use the car. 'Guys,' he said, 'I'm sure I'm very grateful' — though he was sick with shock — 'but would you mind if we left out the talking till tonight? Is that OK? I mean, a friend of mine may be very ill, I have to go to the hospital now. Can we talk in my club, this evening?'

Obviously, he'd said the right thing. The Arab in front of him smiled; Grief saw white teeth in the darkness. The other man, the one who'd given him his keys back, stood further away, waiting. The first man said, 'You must go to the hospital. That is good. I understand perfectly.' If a voice could wink, then this voice was winking. Grief wondered what he meant.

'At the club, tonight then,' he repeated, numbly. He was determined not to be seen shaking. 'And we'll have a look at what business we might be able to do.' Still smiling, the Arab answered that this was fine. Silkily, he insinuated that Grief was now bound to the meeting; and that they were people who took their business seriously. You're not joking, Grief thought. And they would be perfectly happy, in the meantime, to dispose of the pornographer's body — so they knew their onions — while Grief, ah, visited his friend. 'No, really,' Grief insisted, 'that's what I'm going to do.' What did they think he was going to do?

Grief needed to get away badly. He climbed into his car, thanking them nervously, and screeched off, his hands shaking heavily on the wheel. The Arabs went back up the ramp to bring down their car for Thor's body, giving the crazy old woman another note on the way. It was Ramadan. The old woman didn't know that, but she was loving it anyway.

THIRTY-NINE

Unaware that a potential, if drunkenly ill-conceived attempt on his life had just been so neatly aborted, Wally lay before his camera in a state of terminally trippy exhaustion. He'd been up all night; there were two minutes of the shift left to fill. He was saying, 'My room is the blue of the seabed, the deep heavy blue where life must scuttle on an uneven surface, cased in shells, a welter of feelers thrown out all around in slow-motion, frond-swaying terror. You stumble upon hot rock, or are blown aside by sudden rumbling eruptions of gas, crushed down all the while by the great deep weight of the blueness. Action is anathema, and survival the only business, when every movement is the hauling of ton upon ton of reluctant dead flesh without spirit across the eternal gougings of the coral.' There was a long, long pause. 'Can you dig it?' he then sarcastically giggled.

He played the speech back, timing it out at seventy seconds, and was proud of it as he listened. He liked the lead in his voice, and the look of weight where his shoulders hung in, with that faintest occasional twitch upward at the lens, the eye, the mirror. He looked nailed, pinned, ugly butterfly. It was exactly right, exactly how he felt, dragging himself into the final stretch of the Championship of the Globe. With, to make it worse, an election all around, spoiling the ad breaks with chirpily earnest bursts of Money *fol-de-rol* about how well we were doing.

One of Milla's bright ideas was a kind of Money Party problem spot. Every afternoon and evening, all the biggest channels carried ten-second trailers announcing the issue of the day. The whole of the evening's final ad break was then bought out by one of a long list of companies as a token of their esteem — a thank you for massive machine-made profits which were, of course, invested abroad. And in the space thus graciously provided, the Money killed each issue dead, like they were putting down old dogs.

114

Foreign policy was like the weather reports, considerately explained by a man waving a tapered stick over brightly coloured maps. 'In this yellow area, including as it does such exotic and primitive nations as Chad and the Sudan, nations, I might add, whose wild desert beauty and warm friendly welcome to the westerner makes them ideal locations for the more adventurous holiday-makers among you (cut to a series of picture postcard slides) many people today are starving. Your government, mindful of its responsibilities, provides very condiserable funding at extremely favourable rates of interest, to aid development and alleviate such problems. (Cut to presenter's ingenuous young face.) There are those who taunt us for these enlightened aid policies, suggesting instead that we should simply give the money away, or that we are somehow courting disaster by being firm with our clients. I must confess, I cannot see how such charges add up. (Cut to green map demonstrating US military achievements in Central America.) On the contrary, it is only by maintaining a firm grasp of the difficult world economic situation, that the free nations can ensure stability in those parts of the world where communist rabble-rousers and papist instigators would otherwise use our generously loaned resources directly against us.'

But Wally's favourite was law and order, which had a very sexy mix indeed. Stern, parental speeches from good, solid, authoritarian desks were interlaced with thrillingly directed live action material, in which the minister arrived at the scene of the subversive terrorist or industrial activity — the man of action taking charge. A few undesirables would then be efficiently blown away by glamorous men with blacked faces — 'men who have seen action in defence of freedom all around the globe'. Back at his desk, the minister would then let us know that 'your government will not cease in its perseverance. We are ever on our guard, unbendingly vigilant at all times in the name of security and the free right of passage. A virgin in a white robe with a child in one hand and a bag of gold in the other must be able to walk without fear of let or hindrance from one end of the land to the other.'

The law and order slots were directed by Laz Stones, the best live action man around. Laz and Grief had learnt their trade together on the rigs; but Laz had stayed with it, and moved to higher things by virtue not only of an ability to consume vast quantities of cocaine, but also, more significantly, an ability to dish it out to the right kind of people in quantities even vaster, and looking all the while like it didn't cost him a penny. The result of these abilities, by the time of the Last Election, was clips of shoot-outs and strike-breaking that had more pace than a cat with its tail on fire, shot on budgets that ranged from the merely generous to the simply outlandish. Grief didn't see much of Laz any more — apart from the fact that he handed out too much coke, and then flirted with Milla, all he had to talk about was how many ways you could kill people in front of a camera.

Tonight's issue was defence, another Stones speciality — he'd moved more jump-jets and old missiles round the third world buyers than the Malvinas war. Wally stitched in the trailer — 'Tonight, the defence of the realm. How the Money has more muscle — at eleven thirty' — voiced over slow-motion film of a missile slicing up through the surface of the sea. And then, much to his delight, he found that he had a People diatribe he could sew in next. He lay back to roll a joint and make more tea, then settled back to enjoy it — the People couldn't afford too much in the way of ads, so when they came, you really had to savour them. It was the usual homemade stuff, fronted by some bearded militant maniac delivering a rabid attack on Crinkly Crisp and Greenback. 'Perhaps,' he howled, 'we'd be nearer the mark if we said Crinkly Crisp and Goebbels.' Obviously not used to TV lighting, the man was sweating rivers. Cheap tacky slides tried to show how rich Crinkly was — hardly top of mind with your average voter. 'If you want the truth, read our leaflets.' Trouble was, you'd be hard pushed to find one; most people who did just used them as doorstops. The faithful were arrested for giving them away (disturbance of the peace). And that was their thirty seconds.

Closing the shift, Wally tacked on a ten-second freeze-frame of the Thai kid at the table, using his caption generator to print on how many frames the kid was ahead. Looking at him closely now the image was stilled, Wally realised for the first time just how ill he looked; but it could hardly be said to be interfering with the deadliness of his play, so he didn't dwell on it. He said to the mike, 'That's me done for now, jobless, so it's over to Silas. I'll see you with the final on Friday.' Then he called for a bike to collect the finished tape, and tried to ring Silas to find out what happened in the game's second half. He got no answer, which was odd; so he left a message in the micro. Glad it was all nearly over, he finished his joint, put on some music, and was soon fast asleep.

FORTY

Cairo Jones dreamt that he felt a pain in his side. He lifted his shirt, and saw a blackhead, below his ribs and above his hip. He popped it, but it didn't spit out the blob of pus he'd expected. A rubbery length of something off-white, flesh but not flesh, spindled out, waving; he pulled at it, and out and out it came, growing thicker and thicker, and the hole in his side also grew as the alien plant slid out of him. Eventually, an inch and a half round, and a foot and a half long, it had all curled out of him — it had roots, like a spring onion. He looked into the hole in his body, into the round cavity within him, and there were soft white tuberous bulbs growing off his flesh, with round pulpy heads swaying on fronds like anemone heads. He wrenched them out in handfuls, screaming.

He woke, sweating, and shaking, as all of England now seemed to him to be shaking. He had seen them, in doorways in the night, the teenagers trembling as their hair grew thin and their skin grew dry; and they were only the beginning.

He was in tramp alley. The rain of the early hours that had cooled his panic, pouring down his face in streams that made him blink at lights blurred misty, or broken into prism, was now stopped; it had become instead rivers in the gutter, with rafts of litter bouncing this way and that on the black-surfaced water. At the end of the tunnel, in the morning light where the shadow of the bridge stopped, he saw the boots of the law splashing into this water, come to clear away the dross for the day, so the richies who worked in government buildings along the river could park there. Hastily he threw off the sheets of cardboard he'd wrested from a frailer, very much older man in the night, and stood to look busy, which was the only way they left you alone. The first stalls were up; he hurried away to one on which he saw the pots were already bubbling, and bought a spiced boiled potato, to indicate he was only there in passing. The policemen kicked and heaved the old men and women in their ragged coats and blankets up off their carrier bags, their beds of milk bottle crates, of waxy garbage moulded to the shape of their bodies, of hard paving stones. Coughs and choking moans of pain echoed under the iron girders of the bridge, which shuddered and shrieked as a train passed overhead. Cairo kicked the engine of his bike over, and zipped away to a safer street, riding with his breakfast tucked between his knees on the tank. Once away from the police, he stopped, turned off the bike, and ate the food; it was pasty, old and overcooked.

And Cairo Jones, who had left school at thirteen with not an R to his name, now counted his last pennies. His particular brand of stupidity was not impractical. He had learnt street basics, trawling the cafés to pay his mother's rent by selling government lottery tickets; and when she'd died, he'd learnt to get by. No one seemed interested in harming him, since he was big, and harmless himself. The chicklettes of the street had protected him because he was useful, gentle, and clumsily awe-struck by their pale tough bodies between sheets, or, more often, in alleyways. He knew now — with the horror no longer visible or concrete once the rain had washed the blood off, and therefore receding in the short span of his memory — that he had, whatever he thought, got by before Marl, who had left him strangely, and then died. He knew too that the world was incomparably more foul than he'd ever been able to suspect; that from now on, he should be as hard as the road. And after he'd scrambled into the street and his engine had batted howling around the empty town, and he'd hurled himself, broken-winged bird, against all the walls of the sealed box of London, mouth open in a scream without a voice, he knew that, foolishly, he'd wasted precious petrol. But he didn't know where any of this left him, or where it would lead him next.

He started walking, pushing the bike on the long trek to the near side of Hackney. It would take him, he knew, well past lunchtime to get there; but if a job was called through, he needed the petrol. Of his friends from orphan teenage, only one had a job, and so money to lend him to see him through until pay-day, now the pills were unsaleable. Others, he knew, girls especially, might kindly find room to put him up, or even stretch to feeding him a day or two — but the thought of girls and their bodies, known or unknown, took him back to his dream, and the locked space in his mind, locked as the bunker was now locked, where he'd left behind what had happened to Marl. Cairo wouldn't think of it, wouldn't consider complications, until he had a loan from his one working friend, Davey Haynes.

He pushed the bike away from the blackened brick bridges of Waterloo, over the river and into Parliament Square. A screaming crowd of women was assembled there, with placards that named them, 'The Mothers of the Market'. They were demonstrating because the government wanted them all moved off the street to a specially designated covered area, away from the shops. But, they said, no one would come to buy from them, if they were hidden away in this covered place; and then their children would starve. They advanced, chanting. The ring of police moved in; water cannons threw women to the ground, and truncheons came down on their heads, splitting skin and pulling out blood. The newspapers tomorrow would describe these women as socialist subversives.

Twenty-four hours ago, Cairo would have whimpered in sympathetic panic. Now, he looked the other way. Cairo Jones was a new man. What the new man was, or what he would do, he didn't yet know. But he knew it would be terrible.

FORTY-ONE

Milla lay lead-headed in her chair, aching brain cradled in her arms amid the mess of papers on her desk. Why, oh why, she was thinking, must I get so out of it every night? Then she thought, if I just stopped thinking, if I just took my money, if I could just stop worrying...her head nodded over the cooling plate of runny curry slapped onto the desk five minutes ago by her tea-lady.

'Message from Mr Maelstrom,' this worthy had sourly snapped. 'Where's the brilliant idea, he says. Millions, he says, are simply slavering for a meal like this. And are we going to let them know about it on primetime TV, or aren't we?' Milla gave no sign of hearing. The tea-lady leant forward, chucking her under her chin, feeling with her fat finger the gauzy white skin over sharp, fragile bone. 'Milla, sweet,' she sympathised, changing her tone, 'you need a cheer-up. He's a stroppy bugger, everyone knows it, but never you mind all his tetchies, you hear me? Here, I'll tell you a secret. See this goo they call a curry? Me, darling, I wouldn't eat it if it was shat from God's own arsehole. And, do you know, Mr Maelstrom knows that too?'

'How d'you know, Bessie?' Milla used her elbows to push the rest of her body stringily backwards off the desktop, her legs falling out from under her chair to flop away in front of her. Her head nearly fell straight on back over the back of the seat, trajectory continuing; but she managed to hold it steady, before the momentum was too great, and stared up, glazed, at the gossipy minion.

'I read all Mr Maelstrom's memos, didn't I? He reckons nine months it'll take, inside that company, just for them to sort themselves out and approve a new budget for this muck. And, he says, product quality's got to be totally rethought.' Milla poked at the yellowy mush on the plate; a thin film of grease shone over the sauce, and the rice grew dull, faintly brown.

Trolly chipped in, 'Too right. I wouldn't feed this filth to the tiger that wanted my leg.' He was bent over a light-box covered in colour transparencies, photos that made the same meal look like it had been cooked up in the Ritz. A glowing basket of peaches and grapes, and a full glass of white wine frosted with chilly beads of mist and running water, lay behind the faintly steaming plate on a fine lacy tablecloth. Silver cutlery gleamed. Trolly said, 'You take these photographs, you know, you spend two days of your life and fuck knows how much money taking these photographs till it looks like a seventeenth century still life — and then you have to put fucking "Serving Suggestion" on it. That's what kills me.'

'If they up the quality,' said Milla, 'then they have to up the price. So still nobody buys it. The product's a dinosaur. And still the crud Maelstrom wants his ads by next week. Tell, Bessie, what for is he hassling me? Sit, O fount of wisdom, smoke a fag and tell us all.'

'Don't mind if I do,' said Bessie. She was a violet-haired and lavishly built old bruiser; plonking herself down on the office sofa, she adjusted her weight, and shoved aside a mountain of ridiculously expensive artwork. Milla gave her a coffee from the filter machine on the floor by the window. From one of her nylon coat pockets, she took a small bottle of tablets, and popped one down with the first gulp of coffee. Then she settled back, shifting on her bum, and said, 'The way it is, chuck, is our Mr Maelstrom reckons that the company that makes this muck need to be made more interested in their own rotten product. You got to do ads to sell them their own curry, see? Before they give over and whatsit, you know — discontinue the line, that's it.'

Milla snorted, 'What a waste of time. If they don't like their own product any more, what sort of an ad is going to change their minds? They're not idiots. Honestly, you'd think we didn't have enough to do.'

'He does think you don't have enough to do. He also thinks, even if you didn't have anything else to do at all, you'd still not do enough for him. And he thinks, if you knew the way it is with this curry, you wouldn't do anything for him, full stop.'

'He thinks right.'

'Milla, chuck,' said the cleaner, leaning forward, 'he wants you sacked.'

'I warned you,' said Trolly. 'It'll only take a few more suits getting peeved with the work we're giving them to sell, and we're out.'

'They'll change their tune,' Milla commented grimly, 'when the votes are counted. Tell me, Bessie, what's those new tabs you've been taking?'

'What, these, dear?' She cheerily waved the bottle at her. 'Oh they're a blessing. Kills the pain in me veins something lovely. Cheap as Smarties, too. My doctor won't hear of a soul going without.'

Milla was on the brink of asking for one, when Crinkly zoomed in, rubbing his hands. 'Come on Bessie,' he chortled, 'let's not have you distracting the horny-handed.'

Milla muttered, 'Heavy-headed, more like.'

'Heavy handed you will not be, my own precious one, when you hear of the goodies the Money have come up with now.' He was clearly excited; his tie, normally fastidiously pinned down, waggled playfully round his belly. 'They've got a present for the oldies'll pull more votes than nuking Libya.

The runner's coming in to brief us in half an hour; would you be ready to come and play creative for us then?'

'Sure,' she replied, standing to ask, 'but what is it? Have they cracked the health problem? Is there money for the sick?'

He paused, then said, 'In a way, in a way, you certainly could say that.' And he scuttled off cheerfully, humming to himself.

FORTY-TWO

Over the river, Kennington lay beggar-packed and sweating in the smoggy heat haze. A woman pressed a scrawled note to Grief's windscreen, to tell him how many children she had. Before he could react she'd been jostled away by an eddy in the shuffling crowd. He stared into the rows of little holes in the wall which used to be shops, where Asians as dust-coloured as their shelves and their old cardboard boxes sold cartons of soap powder and fizzy drinks off the top of rickety ladders.

A few yards further on, the pavement widened in front of a white and silver supermart, gleaming behind its obstacle course of chrome railings. The doormen loitered, mean, bored, guns heavy on their belts. Customers nervously emerged, clutching their brown paper sacks with both hands, taking deep breaths of worry before diving into hoped-for anonymity in the mob. Like the oldies, they halted and spun round to present their backs whenever a gang of youth jostled by. The wider pavement allowed space for clearings where ragged men and kids laid out bits of canvas or plastic on which to display sun-glasses, socks, teapots, digital watches, paper-back books, batteries or whatever else they'd been able to scrape together as stock. Teams of bike coppers, shades glinting, edged through the jam or hugged the kerbside, invisible eyes scanning the throng.

Suddenly one of the bike police smashed on his siren and mounted the kerb, screeching in to where an old woman had fallen. Grief saw a gangling white kid slither his way out through a gap in the crowd, clutching the woman's tattered handbag, and vanish between the stop-start cars. As he went he knocked a little girl of maybe ten or twelve off the wooden crate from which she'd been selling loose cigarettes, sending her wares flying.

The child scrabbled frantically to recover her cigarettes, but the pack was on her, shoulders shoving and fingers raking as she whirled on her haunches among the thieves. When she realised that all her stock was stolen she stood up, head bowed, hands loose by her sides, and started to cry. The tears ran through dirt on her face. She was, Grief saw, wondrously pretty; his chest filled at her pain, and he too wanted to cry. He wound down the window, shouting, hey, and when she looked up, tossed her a five pound coin. She caught it effortlessly, and scampered up, staring round-eyed through the window. He leant over from the wheel, shocked by the child's stained beauty. He said, 'Get in. I'll give you a job for the morning, how's that?' She was into the car in an instant, primly sitting herself in the exact middle of the passenger seat. Her legs looked pathetically matchstick against the expanse of seat on either side of them; her feet barely touched the car's floor. She leant forward on the dash, and peered shyly forward.

Grief had forgotten to close the window. A brown hand, flashing rings, slapped down on the metal of the door by her head. The girl leapt away from it, and Grief freaked, suddenly remembering the rat trick; his hand fired down for the window switch, but, looking up at the same time, he saw a grinning Hispanic face, with black moustache and yellow-brown teeth, bending into view.

'Wan' some sheet, maan,' said the teeth, hardly moving; mocking their own accent, and viciously amused at Grief's reaction.

'Ramon,' said Grief, breathing out relief. Ramon — an ex-death squad Salvadorean runaway, from a family sufficiently landed for the Money to let him in when his life had looked shaky; a man with six passports, and, these days, more grass than the Rif.

'You're a dumb fuck,' hissed the teeth, 'with your window open. I hear you walk about a lot too. You just don't care, do you?'

'I'm careless, yeah.'

'But not carefree, eh? You shouldn't be, either, friend; it'll be a long, long summer. When they's in with five more years to play with, they — will — come — down — like — whips — cracking.' He drew out each word to lay weight on it; though it seemed he didn't mind much himself.

'It's the way, Ramon, we all know what's coming. How's business?' Sly, Grief added, 'Moses out your way?'

As the car crept forward, the dealer walked alongside. He said, 'So no one sees Moses, these last few days. But still, the people don't buy so much grass any more.' Grief said he didn't know, he'd been too busy to deal. Ramon told him, 'It'll make you sad, when you're back to it, to see them all so tired. These cloud-head dumb-happy painkillers they get into now — it's sure a good way to keep the kids down, no, to turn them into oldies?'

Ears prickling, Grief probed, 'How d'you mean?' His suit jacket lay on the back seat, but sweat still ran in droplets down his chest.

'Everyone thinks they speeding up,' laughed Ramon, 'and all they doing is slowing down. Still,' he shrugged, 'fads are fads. A few more die, makes no difference. What you up to, down this way? Got business? There's Arabs been around, I mark them down for hash merchants, been asking after you. You got something going?'

'I've seen them,' Grief told him, 'and they kill without blinking. That's all I know. But that's not what I'm into now; I'm seeing a friend down the hospital.' And after what Ramon had said, he wanted to get there badly. He wanted the air-conditioning . . . . until he remembered that the hospitals couldn't afford it anymore. He'd heard of people, now the heat was coming on, who'd try to get into the supermarts just to stand in the cool air; people who'd buy some tiny thing, a choc bar, a lemon, five fags, just to buy ten minutes of freshness.

Ramon said, 'I sure hope your friend's well, Grief;' and before Grief could ask any more, he was gone, squinty eyes peering through the snarl-up for the quickest way to get on. Everywhere around him, Grief heard the stifling murmur of the street welling up through the window. He wound it up hurriedly, and edged on through the traffic.

The girl asked, 'What job you want me to do for you, mister?'

Crinkly strode the corridors of his quietly humming empire, and the staff with their files, their videos and their papers stepped aside as he passed. Behind glass partitions men and women in casual clothes chewed pencils, drank coffee, drew, wrote, and chatted with their feet up. Round a corner, down stairs and onto the next floor, everyone now was in suits, leaning back with phones cradled on their shoulders, or huddled together round glossy tables with wine and snacks, examining photos, watching television, talking numbers. Secretaries darted with drinks and messages, trailing subtle scents through the jungle of plants around the wide walkways. Milla, straggling, struggled to keep up with his boisterous pace. Her legs ached — too much lead in her knees left over from the night before.

'What,' she panted, 'is this dead good giveaway? What have they got for the oldies?'

'You'll see,' beamed the boss, 'you'll see. A brilliant notion, quite brilliant, and thoughtful too.'

Milla hinted, 'A discovery? A new drug?'

He looked at her quizzically, but replied, 'Oh no, dear, no, nothing merely pharmaceutical. Although I do understand there's been splendid advances in that field as well. But no, no, this is altogether more immediately useful. And very, shall we say, voter-friendly.' He laughed at his little quip. She knew he thought of consumers as zeroes in a binary code, to be switched to a positive one by the program of advertising — load image, and run — and she wondered what the vote-winner could be.

Crinkly's office was a treasure chest of goblets and lanterns, rugs and low tables. All the necessary tools were tastefully tucked aside in one corner; desk, micro, TV and video, stereo cassette-radio, and a mountain of magazines and research reports. In another corner, a fine table, red and black Japanese lacquer, nestled intimately between cushions, beneath shelf upon shelf of lustrous knick-knacks. Here, you were comfy and yet dominated, as you had to look up if Crinkly was standing, doing one of his performance art sales speils; or you could sit cosily round the table, like kids at teatime, so that planning the expenditure of terrifying sums became painlessly playful. At this table, clients parted company with monstrously extravagant budgets, and went away feeling like auntie had just given them an extra eclair.

Milla approached the man sitting at the table with hand extended, and served him up a wide warm smile as she contemptuously thought, this runner's such a creep. He wore standard quiet pinstripe, with the white-collared, light blue and white-striped shirt and red tie; the whole effect spoilt by a grotesquely large rosette. Regulation shoes and haircut, both dark and shiny, completed the feeling he gave you, that you were looking into a garishly labelled vacuum.

'Hi,' said Milla, sitting. Crinkly buzzed at the intercom for tea, which was instantly with them in the hands of a nubile Texan, constructed apparently from the same rounded and slightly yielding material as the cushions on which Crinkly now joined them. 'So,' Milla continued, jumping right in, 'I hear you're onto a good thing?'

'Indeed we are, Miss Sharply.' He placed his hands together on the table before him, fingers pointing towards her, and studied them carefully before looking up. 'A great concession to those with troubles, I think you'll agree. And it's not only generous, but also, publicity-wise, ah, it's a cracker.' He smiled with faint embarrassment at this uncharacteristic, though considered, little gush of enthusiasm. He was, thought Milla, like a puppy dog surprised at the size of its own shit.

She nodded, 'Great, great. Let's hear it.'

He studied his hands some more — did he have eczema? Milla's brain was all over the place — and, speaking before he looked up this time, announced, 'Free cremation.' By the time his eyes were upon her, she was laughing helplessly.

'I love it,' she cried, 'I love it. How the hell am I ever supposed to sell that?'

His voice went one hundred per cent formal. 'I don't think you're quite aware, Miss Sharply, of just how expensive death has become. Proper funerals and burials are quite simply out of the reach of the ordinary run of the people nowadays, and the alternative, cremation, is not greatly cheaper. Government death grants are quite inadequate to meet such expenses; the figure was decided upon in the dark ages, frankly, and it goes no distance towards helping any more. It's an archaic anachronism that's long been a source of complaint.'

'So you're going to burn them on the state. Marvellous.'

'I assure you,' he ploughed on, 'the cost of death is a very real worry for our senior citizens. We should like to be seen to be acting on this issue. You will of course present it as a service, one more service offered by an increasingly efficient NHS. We should use it, we feel, to distract attention from any undue concentration on other, ah, shall we say, weaker aspects of our record in this difficult field.' He looked pleased with the tactful precision of his brief; and then, politic, added, 'Aspects, I may say, which you will find are also being remedied at this moment.'

Milla was still stumped, trying against hope to think of a tasteful, not to mention plausible method of promoting the government as undertakers. 'What exactly are you offering?' she asked.

'You may perhaps have heard recent reports that a not inconsiderable number of people now die unclaimed in hospitals, and the majority of the poorer hostels as well. The state already handles the cremations in such cases. However, we suspect that many of these patients are in fact known to their relatives; but that these relatives drop out of sight at the end, to avoid bearing the costs. We should prefer it, and doubtless so would they, if people were able to attend their departed's last service. So, if they sign the form that we shall provide, they shall be allowed, without charge, to attend such a service and cremation at the time appointed; and all handling of the body will be managed by the state.'

'Very kind. Everyone that pops off, it's out of the bed so someone else can get in, then into the coffin, down to the furnace, and the relatives can meet it there. Am I right?'

'Your way with words is vivid, Miss Sharply, but yes. That is the general idea.'

'So they don't actually get to see the body?'

'We shall have to make that clear, yes, before death has occurred, at the time of the form's being signed. You must understand, in the interests of administrative efficiency . . . there is no alternative.'

'Your job,' said Grief, 'is to mind my car — it got scratched, last time I was down here. You can handle that? 'Cos it may be a while, I don't know yet.' She nodded, and said it was fine. He told her, 'You get two more fivers for it. Deal?' She nodded again, grinning widely. Charity, thought Grief. Anybody else wants a go at this car, this waif's not going to scare them off. He thought he should ask, 'Now you're sure you've not got other things you ought to be doing?' He could see there was no point suggesting school; she couldn't afford shoes, let alone books. Instead, he tried mentioning, 'Parents?' So she told him a story.

She was an only child. Her mother was ill, her father in jail; but, she said, he wasn't a bad man. He'd worked on a machine that arranged cans to be put into boxes; his job was to hold up each box, to take each grid-held stack as the machine spat it out, and then transfer the filled box to the fork-lift. But then the supermarts had complained to the company that sold them these cans in their cardboard boxes. Big, edge-of-town stores, these supermarts stayed open late, to catch the uptown workers on their way out to their rural idylls (with the electric fencing among the flowers). And that meant they had to pay the shop-girls to stay even later, to re-stock the shelves for early opening the next day. Now if the cans arrived in cardboard boxes, then either the supermarts put up with the girls just tipping out the boxes into huge wire bins, in the interests of haste — but that looked messy, damaged some of the cans, and was an inefficient use of space — or the girls had to unpack and re-stack, one by one, the contents of each box. And that took ages, and ages means wages. So, under this pressure, the little girl's father's company spent eight million pounds on a new machine, which laid cans by the two-dozen onto cardboard trays, then shrink-wrapped them, so all the girls in the store had to do was take off the polythene and stack them tray by tray; and all the little girl's father had to do, was sweet nothing, because the machine also came with a conveyor belt that took its neat pellets of cans all the way to the waiting lorry. He was redundant. Not unreasonably, he pointed out that he was cheaper than eight million pounds. No one listened. So, perhaps less reasonably — but his wife was ill

— he blew the new machine right up. And the little girl clapped. Grief was liking her more and more.

He parked in the hospital car park, thinking she might be more of a put-off to thieves than to motiveless vandals. Stepping out, he told her to do likewise and wait for him there, which she obediently did. Then he crossed the tarmac, across which, he noted, the trailing queue seemed rather smaller. As before, many sat; a couple played cards, while a mangy cat loped around them, then slunk off through the bowed legs. Looking back, he saw the child sitting neatly, palms down, legs straight out, on his bonnet. She gave him a little wave.

When he got into the reception area, the coolness of the air instantly struck him, drying sweat, and making breath easier. He stopped to relish it, then thought bitterly, what a blatant scam, to turn on the air conditioning *now*. Funny how, in the weeks before the vote, everything gets that little bit better.

His roses had arrived, and were plonked unarranged in a vase at reception. He caught the scent of them, as he approached the girl who sat beside them. She looked better, like she'd had a night's sleep, and, to his surprise, remembered him. There was still a crowd, sitting in the tatty, ripped-up chairs, or milling round the desk; but there seemed to be a few more nurses to organise them, and fewer people haphazardly crashed on the floor. The girl asked him, 'Did you find your relative? So you know where to go? Good. Computer's up again, that's all — I could maybe have helped you, today.' He was about to tell her, Fiona wasn't a relative, actually; but she was already turning away to the next thing, running smoother, maybe, but still plenty busy.

He went round the desk and off along the first corridor. As he went, he realised that the fresh scent of roses didn't die in his nostrils; the shit smell was gone. And he thought, boy, they're really laying it on. Air-conditioning, the works. There's not a trick those people won't pull. But the changes ran deeper, and soon his fear began to grow that there was worse than vote-catching going on all around him. That is, everything was the same; but there was less of it. He walked quicker and quicker, petrified of what he might find, and it was easy to do so, because there were fewer people to step over; and most of them in cleaner clothes, too. Nor were the ancillaries hurtling about in quite such a panic of harassment; he even saw a couple walking, almost slowly. Disbelieving, he began to spot the occasional empty bed. But worse, how much worse, was the flesh-crawly feeling that the bin was a cripple farm; everywhere, all around, were people missing limbs. And all of them gazed at the ceiling, faintly fluttering all over, and vegetable happy . . . .

At last he made it to Fiona's ward, and sat by her bed with a huge unwinding of relief. She looked fine, sitting up smiling, slow-headed and slightly nodding. She said, dreaming, a million miles away, 'Minor injuries, huh? Good joke.'

It hit him like a hammer in the belly. The cage of tubes and sheets was gone. His lungs, his chest, his heart solidified, he couldn't find breath. She saw him staring, and said, 'I guess they went. No more dancing. But that's OK. I am, as they say, doing very well. I'll do very well, as long as I last.' And still she was smiling.

He gasped for air, let alone words. She told him — and as he turned, he saw her once so fine-edged little face, that was now translucent, dried to shining paper — 'You got to keep together, boy. There's a room down somewhere in the basement, authorised personnel only, you know the score. Get on down there, the war starts there. Moses is holed up, waiting, he reckoned you'd come again — when you learnt.'

He whispered, 'What war? Learnt what?' He couldn't believe her voice, it was halfway to heaven, singsong, leisurely up and down with melody in a terrible distance.

'Old friend,' she said, 'at least it doesn't hurt.' The voice was waving to him, laughing across space from another planet; and yet, it was a roaring in his ears. Her eyes rested in his; maybe seeing, maybe happy, maybe not. Inconsequentially, she said, 'You know, the food's got better. Sometimes, now, it comes hot.' He realised she was trembling all over, like cinders from a fire blown high in the stratosphere, and bouncing now, lightly but uncontrollably, on hidden but tremendous winds. His fear sprouted sorrow, as he saw, on her lovely, drained, pixie-bright face, that her freckles were gone.

He seized her hand, demanding with a frozen urgency to know what was happening. Too late, she told him, with wondrous indifference, not to touch her. Beneath his fingers he felt dry skin rustle, snap, split, peeling back like the stretched coat of an over-ripe plum. Warm liquid ran into his

130

hands. He looked down, close to vomiting as he saw how, as his love and terror pressed so tightly, the flesh across the back of her fingers was parting. Her hand fell apart in his. He screamed for a nurse, as the cuffs of his suit stained pink and purple.

FORTY-FIVE

Milla leant forward across the table, blinking against the smug glow of the Money man's self-infatuated, regulation face. She said, 'May I ask how you plan to afford this? As you are aware' — she realised, when she'd meant to mock his tone, that its insidious smoothness, its bland harmonious rhythm had in fact ambushed and depersonalised her own way of expression; so she compensated, and overdid it — 'there isn't enough cash in the coffers to feed and house the living, let alone to burn the dead.'

The runner bridled, sitting up in his chair and looking holy. Milla wondered if he was one of the new Christians; the Money Party crawled with them. (Armageddon as prophesied, coming soon, probably in the Middle East — but if you're one of the elect, that's fine, you can go to heaven after). She tried to imagine the runner at the wheel of his car, when the engine suddenly stops, and the radio suddenly dies, and the huge flash suddenly rises in silence before his eyes over the town just ahead. Then, she thought, when he knows he's got seconds before the firestorm comes to fry him, will he praise the Lord? Will he gladly prepare to be raptured, to be whisked into the sky in a sea of white light? Or will he just shit his pants? Junior versions of these guys were so obedient, so sure the boss was right — you could ride them till they dropped.

Crinkly knew of Milla's tendency to bewilder the runners with her quick sharp sallies of non-conformism; to say things the thought behind which was so impenetrably alien to their own way of thinking that they were stunned, like fish just caught, and the fisherman banging their heads on a post. Her motive was, it got more out of them than simple humble questions. So he tried to butt in and stop her, saying something soothing about resource management; but the runner had already patiently started, as if to a child.

'This new service,' he told her, 'can be provided at minimal expense. The facilities exist, and it is felt to be only right and proper that we should use them more productively. The option I have just outlined is considerably more cost-effective than the alternative, of raising the death grant. But it achieves the same objective — dignity in death.' Milla snorted, so he was spurred to give her more. 'Futhermore, Miss Sharply, you will soon find that prudent management of resources in the health service will be bearing fruit, as we have always maintained. Our drugs bill, for example, has of late been sizeably cut back upon, due to certain long-awaited break-throughs in the development of better, cheaper variants of the standard drugs for mass consumption; so the coffers won't be quite as empty as you fear.' Again he looked pleased, to be so neatly back in control.

Milla was all ears, silently begging for more, more, to let her get closer to whatever was really going on; but he'd gone as far as he was going to go. 'OK,' she said, 'you got it. Free death. I have to hand it to you guys, that's really a wheeze.'

Crinkly hurried to steer things into a more businesslike dialogue, asking, 'When would you like this to run, and in what format?'

On happier ground, the runner answered promptly, 'We feel we should give this some weight. If it could be put together as one of our issue-of-the-day items, for one of the full break slots at the end of the evening, that would be most welcome. We'd like a lot of people to hear this news. Then we'll give it to the press the next day.'

Milla knew she'd got everything out she was going to. She re-entered zeck mode, and crisply pronounced, 'I could run something off for approval by this evening, we could shoot it tomorrow, and we could air it on Friday. All you have to do is fax me over the relevant fact sheets, as soon as you're back in your office.' The runner nodded. Milla supposed that death would, at least, be more fun than curries.

'Well,' smiled Crinkly, 'that's perfect. As you know, we present the final week's posters and press to the Cabinet on Friday evening. So we could sit down to a light dinner here, then run through the presentation, and sit back to see this announcement go out on air when we're through.' He was thinking, feed 'em first, and flog it to 'em after.

Ruffling through papers, Milla found a 147 schedule. She said, 'Late Friday would be dreamy. We could go out right in amongst the last frames of the snooker final. Wally Wasted could deliver eleven million that night, on one single channel. On the other hand,' she remembered, 'we were supposed to be doing law and order then.'

'I think we can all agree,' Crinkly rushed to say, 'that we've won the law and order debate hands down. Health's the problem. Any kind of improvement on that front should be cried to the hills, wouldn't you say?' He was thinking that since the law and order clip was already made and paid for, he was a lot more interested in getting paid again to make a new one to replace it.

'I expect so,' the runner admitted, 'I'm sure you're right.' Not in a position to make any decisions, he was keen to leave the room before he found himself railroaded into one despite himself. 'I'll recommend all this, and get back to you later, as soon as it's agreed.'

'We'll hear from you then, and in the meantime we'll get cracking,' Crinkly blathered, heartily scooping the man up from out of his cushions, and seeing him off through the door to reception. Milla heard him asking the runner who he thought was on for the snooker final; the runner wasn't a fan of the game. 'Myself, I back the Thai kid to surprise us all,' she heard Crinkly advise, with a positive orgasm of come-this-way matiness; then his voice faded, and she gladly missed the rest. When he came back, he rubbed his hands together greedily and said, 'Still here? I thought you'd be dying to write that one, ha ha.'

Still sitting, and scratching her head with irritable vagueness, Milla complained that it was gross. 'But if they've got better drugs,' she pondered, 'why can't they sell that instead?'

'Milla my love, you know what it's like with drugs. Always the teething problems, the odd complication, uncertainties, side-effects; best to talk about what you can't be tripped up on, eh? Wouldn't want to find ourselves having a bad trip, would we, ha ha. Besides, nothing like telling the people you're saving them money. Go to it, I say.'

She asked, 'What sort of side-effects?'

'How should I know? Clear off, will you, chuck, there's an election to be won.' He plopped into his chair, and stretched for the phone. With horrid clarity, Milla saw his belly shifting under the shirt; so she left.

FORTY-SIX

Hearing Grief's yells, the brisk Christian nurse came zooming out of her office at the end of the ward, saying, 'Lord, Lord, it isn't the end of the world yet.' And then she clamped her hand over Grief's open mouth. Amazed, his eyes widened wildly as he struggled to be free from her grip. 'If you promise to be quiet,' she told him firmly, 'I'll let you go.' He nodded frantically, and heaved in a breath as her hand came away. Fiona was looking down beatifically at her disintegrating hand, and the spreading ruby stain on the sheets. Grief noted, madly clear-headed, how much cleaner these were than you would normally have expected.

'Like I said,' Fiona told him, 'not nice — but really, it doesn't hurt at all.'

'Your fucking fingers are falling off,' Grief howled, part horror, but a greater part fury by now.

This earned him a ferociously stern glare from the nurse, who was busily bandaging. 'I'm afraid,' she told him, 'that this is an unpleasant eventuality some of these new cancer victims have to face. She'll probably lose the arm.'

'Cancer, bollocks,' Grief snarled, 'since when's she had cancer? And as for losing the arm, well bollocks to that too. Why not take 'em both, you could chop off the full fucking set. It's that drug, isn't it? Oh Jesus,' and he heard himself begging, 'people don't just fall apart, do they?'

'Don't blaspheme. And I'm sorry,' she breezily continued, 'but yes they do. Not pretty, I'll admit, but it's as the Lord will have it.' Grief choked; she was preparing a needle, and as he asked what she was doing, it sank into Fiona's arm. 'I'm putting her out. We have to move quickly, when the rupture's this abrupt. We'll operate today.' He saw skin and flesh loosen and split around the puncture. Fiona slumped; still, impossibly, smiling. 'If you worked here, Mr Grief,' the nurse then turned to him, and went on, 'you'd realise that more sick people, and especially a great deal more old people, means more dead people. And more dead people means more ways of dying.

Now I'm afraid we must have a serious talk.' She took his arm, leading him irresistibly up the watching ward to where her poky little office was tucked between hardboard partitions.

Grief was half-hysterical. 'You mean, he babbled, 'we haven't said anything serious yet? People's fingers falling off isn't serious? This is run of the mill, this is ordinary dying? What are you telling me?'

'It's ordinary dying, Mr Grief.' She sat behind her desk, rummaging through files for a sheaf of small white card forms, which she tapped together into a neat wad between her hands on the desktop, and then looked up. 'Now, Mr Grief, I realise how upsetting this is, but I'm afraid I'm an administrator and a nurse, not a counselling service. However, thanks to a government initiative just recently put in practice, there is one service I can offer you which may be of help at this difficult time. First, we must accept the reality that your relative, I'm sorry, your friend, will soon be dead.'

'Him fucking her,' Grief said through clenched teeth, 'know what I mean? Just another body, isn't it? You don't give a monkey's fuck, do you?'

The nurse put down the stiff white cards, and stared at him. He felt that she considered dealing with him more vile than what had happened in the ward outside. She said, 'Mr Grief, I will explain this slowly, and I will assume as I do so that you are a tolerant and reasonable human being. What I am telling you is for your own benefit. First, at your age, you will not be aware of the cost of a funeral, and the burial or cremation to follow. It is, however, considerable. If you so wish, we are authorised to take full responsibility in all such matters for you, absolutely gratis, and thereby ease the strain, both emotional and financial, at this time of your bereavement. The procedure is simple. We would advise you in due course of the time of death, and when and where you should be present to observe the funeral service. So if you'd just like to look over this form . . . .'

Grief had been mouthing silently, rising panic and hot tears of disgust in his eyes. He leapt to his feet. The chair flew out from under him, and smashed back into a rattling tin cabinet. He shrieked above the noise of it, 'You wanna sell me a fucking car while you're at it?' Then he fled through the ward. Already, Fiona was gone. He thundered down and down staircases, until, pushing violently past ancillaries shouting, hey, you can't go there, down deep in the building, in a foully hot room, he found Moses.

The floor was deep red brick. The tiling was warm through his light soft shoes, and smeared with a matt black grime, unwashed in years. The walls had once been glossy yellow tiles, varnished, but these had long gone stained and dank, faded to the sick yellow-orange of retched-up phlegm; and then they'd been covered almost everywhere in a feathery charcoal blanket of black, so that the browning yellow showed through only here and there, like cracks of tooth in a smoker's mouth. Four blackened steel plates with heavy rusting hinges and big round bolts all around the rim hung over four squares in the wall, clanking, creakily swinging just a little bit open now and then, at each distant rush of hot air; and then the whispering you could hear from far away, the quiet conversation of the floor with the walls, briefly grew louder, as a hushed, steady rumble. From high up above in the ceiling, a handful of bare, weak red bulbs dropped down into the blackness a thick dim mist of huddling, dark red light. A sweet smell clung to the air. Grief looked through the darkness at Moses.

FORTY-SEVEN

Davey Haynes was more lucky than he knew, to have the job he had; and it is reasonable to assume that, in the brave new England now being prepared, the skills acquired by Davey Haynes at his work may well place him in healthy demand for years and years to come. Perhaps, on his retirement, they will give him, not a clock, but a golden knife — for Davey Haynes worked in an abattoir.

Cairo Jones, with his leather jacket locked in the backbox of his bike, was nonetheless profusely sweating, when at last he arrived at the gates of Davey's workplace. His ragged sleeveless T-shirt — 'Thor Thunders: Lightning in a Dark Age' — was drenched. Unshaven, his face was darker than was already natural, with the dirt and grime of the city attached amid the stubble to the glue of his sweat. He only thanked heaven that the bike he had stolen was a mere 125; otherwise, the heavy sky was a clouded evil murk, and dully he swore at it, for depositing on his shoulders such a weight of muggy heat. His arms ached angrily, his legs were heavy as tyres, and his breath came slowly, falling out in bursts like the exhaust of an ill-governed engine.

And how can it be asked of Cairo Jones — as it is so often asked of his kind by the Money — that he should believe he is, relatively, well off? Difficult world conditions . . . the heat, even, would not be so, had the Brazilians and others like them not been forced, by hunger and debt, and the need to be developed (as England, now, has so perfectly become) to hack down their rain forests, and make the world slowly airless. What could Cairo Jones know of that? He knew only what he saw. And Cairo Jones had seen . . . .

Cairo Jones had built inside him, in the heat of the day, a heart of ice. All the faces that had been mere blurs between North Ken and his places of pick-up and delivery — all the faces that had been faces like his own, in the days of his orphanage, faces that had faded from view behind the blanket of Marl, and faded too, in that time, with the advent occasionally of the odd bit of money, maybe his pay, or her dole, or even, sometimes, in the form of gifts — for Marl was a graduate, yes, and not entirely disowned — all those faces were back now, and with a terrible vengeance. As he walked along the kerb, they stared up, amassed one by one into a number greater than the stars you could no longer see in the smogged-over sky, a number infinitely beyond Cairo's capacity to count; but not beyond his capacity to feel. They were the weary faces of squatted women, babies strapped in shawls to their backs, selling biscuits, ices, sweets and rolls; the grubby faces of children, scouring the streets for pennies and food, all innocence lost behind the steel wall of need; the hopeful faces of the beggars and the old, with their deep-lined seized-up claws stuck permanently out, and signs hung around their necks to tell their sad stories, now the words were all forgotten; the glinting faces of the thieves, hooded spying eyes darting round for victims, a baggy pocket here, a loose watch there; and the faces of the rich, unmarked, hidden behind tinted glass, unseeing — but not, thought Cairo in his freezing heart, unseen. For Cairo Jones had seen them, he saw them absolutely, and Cairo Jones had today seen things . . . and began to see too, what the new man would be.

And he found, when the guard at the gate would not let him in, that this day he had acquired a new skill. He knew how to lie. He told a story, on the basis of which it was imperative he saw Davey Haynes; and soon enough, Davey came to the gate. He laughed to see him, and took him in, discussing the weather. They passed through the killing room, where cattle lowed, and jolted as they died. The veins were cut, and the blood rushed out. The heads were severed, and hooks went into the bodies to lift them up and carry them away. Skinned, the raw, screaming dead faces of the severed heads passed on a chain above Cairo, then were lowered to a place where they went by at chest height, and one man sliced off the horns, another gouged out the eyes, another slashed out the tongue. And, thus raped, the screaming faces passed on. Cairo stared, and Davey laughed beside him. They passed a rack where men ripped organs from the hanging carcasses, and threw them down one or other of a series of chutes. 'Don't mind it,' said Davey, patting him on the arm, 'that's your lunch. Come on downstairs, my coat's where I work. I'm on hearts, this week.'

They went down to a room beneath the chutes, into which the organs came spilling down into trays for sorting and packing on gleaming stainless steel slopes. They left as they fell a host of fast-running droplets, ruby red, perfectly defined on the immaculate shining surface as they slid and rolled and scampered down behind livers, kidneys, tripe and offal. As Davey leant beneath his sorting tray for the wallet in his jacket, Cairo gazed at the still thumping, pumping, pulsing grey-red heap of hearts in the wide white plastic bucket. He thought of what he had done to Marl — for was it not his own big hands, thrusting her apart by her light slim knees, that had done that thing? — and he knew then what the new man would be, and do. The new Cairo Jones was a murderer.

His radio, which he'd carried down with him, automatic as a machine in the mindless continuing of his life, now crackled and spat to give him a job. 'Cairo Jones? There's a tape of the final ready at 147 for delivery to Wally Wasted.' And the new man said, without expression, that that would be just fine.

138

Moses sat at a thin wooden table with metal legs, on an outdoor café kind of plastic chair, with a mound of black liner bags heaped up behind him. Dully they gleamed, red on black. Whenever a plate clanked heavily open in the wall, a threatening flicker of faraway red-orange flamelight quickly flared around the opening. Moses was plugged into a Walkman, head down over two-pack patience; as the kings went down, so the aces went up. On the table beside him sat an ice-bucket, a carton of orange juice, and a bottle each of mezcal and grenadine. By his left hand, a topped-up tequila sunrise in a highball glass matched the colours of the furnace; a joint in an ashtray fired thin threads of smoke towards the dim red bulbs high above.

Grief went to stand over the table and said, 'This, I take it, is the Barn of tomorrow.' Moses neither saw nor heard him. Grief caught the tiny voice of the headset's phones above the distant rumble of burning, like a cheap transistor heard from a beach as you're driving past; he watched Moses' head bobbing to the beat. Then he rapped on the table to get himself noticed, and, reaching forward to pull off the headset, began again, 'I said, nice kind of a nightclub. . . .'

The Moses whose head rose up with a quavering strain, a palsied bobbling, was well past fifty, shattered by a rushing on of age. Grief stepped back, but Moses grinned wickedly, the light of red fire in his bloodshot eyes. 'I have led you,' he cackled, 'to the promised land.' He swigged hugely at his drink, picked up the joint, and fell forward to go on, abruptly changing channels as he did so to a flat and weary despair. 'But it seems I've smashed my way through a sight too many tablets en route. And I may not make it, to see what it looks like when we get there — to a land free of the ill and the old, a nation unencumbered by the economically unproductive. Because that's what this government has decided to go for.' He laughed, viciously, looking up. 'You ready to gun 'em down, big boy?'

Before Grief could ask what he meant, the door slammed open behind him, and a trolley came in with two men in green coats. It was loaded with a pile of black bodybags. They wheeled it clattering to the row of metal traps, hooked one open, and slung the sacks into the suddenly blazing square of firelight. Grief made out an angled chute of blackened stone, and the bags buckling and creasing as they rushed down and disappeared. The men closed the trap, and pushed off their unburdened trolley with a higher-pitched squeaking of wheels, the door booming shut behind them.

Grief thought he might be sick. Weak-legged, he held himself together enough to ask wrinkled, mole-sprouting, ragged-eyebrowed Moses how many a day were going through the traps.

'Many,' said Moses, winking sagely, 'many, many. But of course that's not all. There's my rabbits too. As a matter of fact, I still have three bags full to burn. Baa baa black sheep, eh? Having a rabbit bonfire.' Surges of the drug in his system forced incongruously contented little smiles onto his withered face; muscles twitched, as he tried to disown his own facial expressions.

Grief gestured, not looking. 'And what's in the other bags?'

'Oh, all sorts. Arms, legs, cocks, tits, heads, just bits.'

'People's heads fall off?' The words hardly made it from his throat.

'Sometimes, yeah, a few, now and then. Mostly afterwards, when they're handling the corpses. Never in public, or at least, not yet. I think, don't you, it'd cause a bit of a stir.' Moses was crying, Grief now noticed; the tears slid past his ridiculous smile. Cards fell from his hands and he slumped forwards, head into arms, sobbing, 'For fuck's sake get me out of here.' Grief stepped round to him, lifted him from his chair, just a sack of dry bones, fearfully light; he was about to shoulder-lift him out, but suddenly panicked at the idea of his friend falling apart at the waist all over him. So he held him out at arm's length, and found he was shuddering as much with fright as Moses was with age. 'It's OK,' Moses then helplessly grinned, 'there's an antidote to the disintegration, if not to the ageing. I discovered that too. You get pretty smart, when you're that frightened.' Unbelieving, Grief gasped, 'So why don't they use it?'

'Why d'you think, man? It's too fucking expensive, is why. Fuck it, what shape do you have to be in to be burnt anyway?' He was snivelling like a kid, dribbling and shaking and smiling all the while up in painkiller heaven.

Grief agreed, 'No shape.' He thought of Fiona's infinitely arousing, sparky little frame, dismembered, and dancing in the fire.

Over in Hackney, Cairo finally got away from Davey Haynes. Davey, increasingly nervous at Cairo's uncharacteristically silent and purposeful demeanour, was beginning to think he'd not get his money back. He tried to get some reassuring response, matily reeling off a string of horror stories about life in the abattoir; they were supposed to be funny, but Cairo, normally an acquiescent listener, stayed stony and unamused. He kicked over his engine, and, shaking the bike from side to side, listened to the petrol sloshing in the tank; he reckoned he'd enough to get to Docklands, and he'd buy some there. Just now, the prone waiting body of Wally Wasted was more top of mind than petrol, or money, or anything. Cairo knew, being simpler than Grief, what you did when the world went bad. You took out the sinners.

FORTY-NINE

Milla pressed print, and the daisy wheel chattered. Then she buzzed for a secretary, and, when one came, she handed over the word-processed sheaf, saying, 'Tart up this script, can you? And don't laugh when you're doing it.' But she laughed herself, trying to say, 'Really, it's not funny, it's deadly serious. Free death — the offer of a lifetime.' Her laughter grew louder, and the secretary scurried out, uneasy. There wasn't a typist in the house that Milla didn't make deeply nervous; she was a difficult woman to work for.

Meanwhile, Trolly had settled up final details on the new Taj Mahal pack with the man from the artshop, and the job had gone off for a lay-out to be set. And then he'd got so stoned, he could hardly sit upright. 'How about, "Burn out your bum with an Indian blowtorch"?' He sniggered, fumbling though a forest of pens and pencils for his Rizla papers. 'Share a spliff with your co-pilot, lover. Let's shut up shop for the day.' She'd not talked to him for an hour, rattling away at her box of tricks.

Once more, Milla pressed print, and the cremation announcement transferred again from floppy disc to hole-edged paper. She said, 'Fuck curries,' and stepped over to pull wine from their fridge while the printer zipped back and forth, indifferent and flawless. She poured herself a glass, slopping cold clear liquid over the rim as she filled it full, and said, 'Arrange shooting this with production tomorrow, before you make that spliff.' She held the glass out in front of her, bending her lips to the edge to suck the level down to where she could walk without spilling any; then went back to her desk to tear the finished words from their dinky plastic womb, and handed them over.

Reading it, Trolly's eyes widened. 'Boy,' he said, 'no wonder you came back so quiet. That really is a weird, weird thing.' Some of the phrasing made him laugh; he thought he ought to suggest a little toning down here and there, but decided he couldn't be bothered. Instead, he said, 'I can't arrange production till it's approved, can I?'

Milla curtly replied, 'They want this out so quick, they'd approve it if I'd written it in Russian.' She took over rolling the joint from him, as he was staring at the script with an amused kind of vacancy. 'Just call production,' she told him. 'It's got to be done tomorrow, or there'll be no time to edit and be ready on Friday.'

Trolly hummed and hawed, scratching at his curly blond hair. He sat back, taking a sip of cold coffee as he went, and spilling a dribble down his immaculate paisley pattern shirt. She dabbed it off for him with a hankie in one hand; tobacco from a stripped cigarette rested on stuck-together papers in the other. He stared at the ceiling, and she stared at him, and finally he managed, 'I dunno. Fucking boring, really.'

She snickered, 'It's for oldies — what you want, coffins in racing cars? Undertakers in bikinis? Funerals on roller skates?'

He nodded forlornly OK, and called production to get them to fix with the runner an hour in a hospital, and an hour in a cremation chapel for a good-looking funeral; then he booked two hours in the basement studio. 'And,' he added, 'I want the most boring talking head you can get me.' Milla was thinking vaguely they'd get everything they asked for — that runner came over like a wimp, but there was something about the speed with which he got things done, all the same, that she didn't trust an inch. Trolly'd nearly put the phone down, when he remembered to ask for an hour on the paintbox as well. 'At least,' he muttered, 'the graphics could be natty. And if they give me that camera crew that's always sped out, I'll kill them. Last time I had them, everything came out green.'

'Not my problem,' said Milla, 'I'm not going near what it'll look like.'

'Dangerous', he agreed. 'You'd put Messaien on the sound-track, and dress the front-man in death's hooded cape with a sickle. I know you.' They both laughed, and she poured more wine, then lit the joint. Trolly idly drew a cartoon of a man running down the street with the seat of his trousers on fire, the Taj Mahal logo chasing him like a dragon. The secretary came back with clean copies of the script on headed paper, and asked what should be done with them. Milla commanded, with increasing pauses as the dope settled in, that two copies go to production, one for the crew, and one for the artist who'd be talking to camera; then three copies to the Money, so the runner and his mates could faff about with the words — which was inevitable — and one to Crinkly. The secretary told her Crinkly'd gone out, and no one knew where.

'Typical,' said Milla. 'Fat fucker's never around when you want him.'

'That, no doubt,' said Maelstrom in a featureless suit from the doorway, 'is how you refer to all of us who actually do the work around here.'

'The very man,' Milla cried, and snatched Trolly's doodle. 'See here, Maelstrom, your problems are over.' She stumbled round her desk to plonk down in her chair, facing him, then arranged her feet on the tabletop to show him a vast expanse of thigh. The secretary didn't know where to put herself. Maelstrom seemed somehow both to back off, and peer forward, as she held up the cartoon. 'The headline,' she giggled, 'is simple. "The Bum Burner".' Maelstrom looked daggers, but before he could speak, she lifted her skirt and said, 'Or alternatively, how about, "Eat me"?'

The secretary blushed beetroot. Maelstrom said, 'I want an ad by tomorrow evening, or you're dead,' and left.

'Who's he kidding? If I'm stuck in here all Friday night with those Cabinet monkeys, then I'm taking tomorrow off. And that's final.'

'Well fuck you,' Trolly told her, as the secretary shrank away through the door, 'You fucking cow. I'm here all Friday night too. How come I always get to do the shitty work on my own?'

In Bethnal Green, a preoccupied Cairo Jones failed to notice that a set of junction lights weren't working. He went straight across without looking, and narrowly missed death beneath the wheels of a MacDonalds delivery lorry. Heart pounding, he pulled up on the far side of the crossroads, and told himself to keep his mind on the road.

FIFTY

Wally's internal time-clock had long been out of synch with the ordinary turning of night and day. His waking and sleeping were organised entirely according to the constant requirement to be at least a shift or two ahead of the TV schedule; so his head would wake him up with unpredictable irregularity. Today, conveniently, it woke him at six, just as Silas was due to take over on the air. Watching the end of his own shift put it, as always, in perspective. When preoccupied with the nuts and bolts of sewing his programmes together, he had time to take each element out of context; but when it played back to him seamlessly down the cable, he could see how items like the Money's trailers were so perfect for their on-screen environment. Snooker, advertising, politics; everything a fluid, relaxing whole. On his monitors the missile, impressive, magnificent, burst leisurely through the surface of the sea. The voice teased you, told you to hang on and stay up for more. And, as ever, Wally wanted to know. Show us your muscle, Money.

The election, he felt, was beginning to hot up, certainly as far as pretending to be a contest was concerned. From that angle, it was as good as the soaps, with all the fascination, the evil glee at the relentless tormenting by the vilain of an opponent who can't even see any more where the punches are swinging from.

144

The People Party, by now, was a goose well-cooked. Every night, the red hot knife of the Money's media clout came slashing down for another slice of fatty breast. They'd hold it up to the viewer, jeering, 'Look at the rottenness of this sorry beast; I wouldn't eat this garbage if I was starving.' Then they'd toss the meat to the fly-buzzing bucket of the papers, for consumption the next morning by fat-bellied bingo magnates.

When the Money Party turned on the hostility, the nuts really came loose. One night, they edited the People's bearded, sweaty huffer-puffer to make him sound like he thought the Russians were really terrific. Then they asked, 'Do you want this fathead in the Foreign Office? Come on now, really? Let us tell you what the Russians are like.' Cut to a quick-moving sequence of grainy black and white slides, with SFX shutter noise to give documentary urgency. The slides show Afghan children burning, and 'great thinkers' tubed up and taped down like so many lab animals in their hospital beds. 'As a party of peace, we will talk to such people. But respect them or trust them, we cannot do.'

When they weren't setting out to make you angry, they could instead get you proud against all your better instincts. It would be the splendour of our guns, or new Korean factories for the blackspots, or the football team's triumphs in Eastern Europe, or the royal family, or the worldwide sales of nancy boy pop groups. The nation marches forward, nukes in one hand, pop videos in the other. And on the personality front, there was an absolute barrowload of Nanny mixing with the great. Leaders from every capital you care to name dropped into town to protect their investments with a grin for the camera — until, by sheer weight of repetition, they'd helped to create the 'woman in charge'. And all she was doing was having lunch with her mates, the lot of them as senile as she was.

In amongst it, Crinkly Crisp did a grand job, flying the flag — as their house publicity said — of Great British 'creativity', as against the growing pile-up of hideous American hard-sell commercials. These involved, one after the other, famous people clambering into your living rooms to tell you, 'you really need this product, it's great — heck, I use it'. Not that sly Crinkly was averse to a bit of that himself, if it helped — and the last eight in the snooker tourney had all duly taken their turn to endorse Nanny. Like Fat Ferdy said, Double Decker melting in his mountainous paw, 'you really need her, she's great — heck, I'd vote Money.'

Wally bumped that noxious image out of his head as his shift wrapped up on the screen, and quickly hopped over to a news channel for the hourly round-up. Smoothly, the regulation non-person announced, 'The government said today that the long period of effort and adjustment will begin to pay off in the current financial year. Prudent finance, the efficient management of resources, and the determined programme of privatisation now nearing its completion have together resulted in the achievement of the Cabinet's primary objective — a real-terms cut in public expenditure. Ministers are reported as delightedly announcing that over the next twelve months, a significant reduction in public spending will be effected without any adverse consequence for the provision of public services. On the contrary, it is being made clear that the provision of health care in particular can be expected to improve quite dramatically in the very near future. With me now is Dr Jeremy Jarvis, chief health finance administrator. Dr Jarvis, could you tell us exactly how these improvements will come through, and why now?'

Leaning forward, hands clasped on the newsdesk, with his huge specs glinting and his beaky nose bouncing beneath them, Jarvis smiled sweetly as his voice slid out into the nation's homes. 'Well,' he said, 'we always knew they would, of course. But if you're asking me specifically about the health service, what we're seeing at the moment is a major demographic change, namely that for some time now we've been feeling the effects of the so-called geriatric explosion; but now, you see, this is coming to an end, and the strain imposed on the service by a high proportion of old people in the population will be seen from now on to decrease quite quickly. In effect, you understand, there'll be a bit more in the kitty per head, as it were. . . .'

Blimey, thought Wally. That's a bit blunt.

And Cairo sat waiting for his heart to slow down. An old woman, bent beneath the sack on her back, asked him if he wanted to buy any fruit. 'I've got some lovely bananas.' She was, he noticed, all over faintly trembling; her smile was beatifically calm.

'You're dead,' said Cairo Jones, and kicked his engine over. It whined as he revved it, and she watched him race off, grinning through grey fumes from the poorly baffled exhaust.

FIFTYONE

Grief helped Moses through the hospital foyer, and, propping him up as they walked, eased him past the shrinking queue in the forecourt. Moses told him it wasn't necessary, he could manage walking quite easily if you gave him time; but Grief held him up anyway, not wanting any strain to pull him apart, flesh from bone. When she saw them coming, the urchin on his bonnet hopped off onto the tarmac and scooted across the yard to help, taking peculiar, uneven steps out of some private superstition about not stepping on white parking lines (or the alligators will get you). They carefully packed Moses down along the back seat like a pile of precious material, then Grief drove them out, past the hope-eyed waiting sick, and into traffic. Silent, the girl sat beside him.

It wasn't long before he decided he couldn't handle the driving. He pulled up onto the pavement outside a café, and, cutting the engine, put his head slowly down on the steering wheel. Against the wall, opposite where they'd stopped, a woman laid a pair of bathroom scales down on the broken paving stones, and propped up a card saying how much you paid her to use them.

The touch of the little girl's hand on Grief's was light as a leaf off a tree. She said, 'Mister? Is your friend very ill?'

'Yeah,' Grief told her, not moving his head, 'he's pretty ill.' He waited a while, thinking about it, and the street grumbled and muttered all about them. Then he picked himself up, and lay back against the headrest, explaining, 'But he's not the friend I came to see. The friend I came to see is dead.' Salt drops fell down his cheek, fatigue as much as emotion; he wiped them dry and suggested, 'Come on, little thing. Let's go get us a drink.'

They elbowed through pedestrians to a table on the edge of

the pavement, and he ordered rum and coke — his rum, and her coke. Putting fingers round the thimble of a glass, he stared out at his car, the road, the people, the heat; he listened, at the table beside theirs, to a man bowed forwards toward a woman over spillages of beer, and whining at her with a strange, vivid, childish intensity. Without turning his head, Grief asked the girl, 'What's your name, kid?'

'Suzie.' From somewhere beneath her grubby cotton shirt, from some primitive form of money-belt, she pulled out a gold ring — genuine, but miserably thin. She turned it round between her fingers, and Grief looked at her now, to see what she was doing. He asked where the ring came from. Suzie told him, 'It's me mum's. I'm to sell it, when things get bad. But I'm not going to. It's me mum you want to talk about, right?'

'You're bright, aren't you?' She nodded, and he smiled. She was lovely, with long black hair falling straight around a fine, dark-skinned face, and big brown eyes; her smile was small and quick, but she wasn't using it now. There was a thin, straight scar down one side of her nose, where a cheap tin popper on her shirt had scratched as she'd pulled it over her head. He gritted his teeth and asked, 'So tell me what's wrong with your mum.'

'They say she's got cancer, mister. She's in that hospital we was just at. Has to be, living round here. It's the only one left.'

'They say cancer, do they?' Grief's knuckles whitened around his glass; then he realised how cheap and thin it was, and loosened up. He said, 'You see her much?'

'They don't let me, not since Friday. Say she's always sleeping.'

'I'm so sorry, honey.' He put his hand on hers, carefully not the one in which she held the ring; her deep eyes looked up from under a ragged fringe. But before he could tell her, she told him herself that she knew her mother was, or would be, dead. The street was beginning to talk — there was a disease, it said, and the whisper had reached her. He wondered how long she'd been out there, hardening up. She told him, as if reading his thoughts in his kind open face, that she got by. In his car, he saw Moses' head trying to lift itself up in the rear window, then slumping back down. People passing took sneaky looks at the expensive leather interior, then looked away again, very quickly. He realised she was quietly crying, and gave her his handkerchief, faintly damp from his own inadequate mourning; it was too big, and her face disappeared in it. As she rummaged and snuffled in his soft clean cotton, his heart felt the frailty of her arms, and pitied the graining of filth into the lines on the backs of her fingers. His fingertips lifted to touch her knuckles, and he said, 'Look, hey . . . if you want looking after a while — you can come stay over with me.' She stared up at him from the crumpled handkerchief.

A street musician in waxy sackcloth trousers came to the front of the café. There was still a bit of colour left, yellow and gold here and there, in what must once have been a gorgeously embroidered waistcoat. Beneath it, his open shirt was torn and stained. For time, he beat a small soft drum; and he blew a soft tune on a five-barrelled pan pipe. The sound was sadder, darker, fuller than a flute, the only thing Grief thought he could compare it to. A tiny child bounced in around the tables, his face fixed in a simian grin; the bells on the buttons of his breeches cobbled together a melancholy tinkling as he danced. Suzie said, 'OK, mister. But no sex.'

Grief turned to her sharply from the music. Beside their table, the people walked or shuffled by, drying up in the rays of the hidden sun in the sheet-metal sky. He said, beneath the song and the bells, 'But you're only a child. Are you — aren't you still a virgin?'

'Out there? You must be joking.' She held up the ring, and told him she didn't mean to lose it. 'And anyway, it's not so bad.' She pulled her shirt down tight enough to show him her buds of breasts. 'I'm thirteen, I'm old enough to stick it. The men like us small, these days.' Appalled, Grief promised her no sex. She said, 'Thanks, mister. I didn't think you was one like that.'

'You can stop calling me mister, OK? The name's Grief.' Bringer home of dying men and orphans — Milla was going to love him for this. He put money into the dancing boy's cap, standing up from his chair and onto the pavement, wrinkling his nose against the smell of sewage. The traffic was beginning to clear away.

The whining man at the table beside him stopped whining, and suddenly, savagely, struck the woman he was sat with five times, full in the face, clumsily but clench-fisted. Blood burst out of her nostrils; she made no sound, nor did she raise her arms, but simply cowered away from the blows. Then the man got up and shoved Grief aside, swaying out onto the pavement and looking about him with a bizarre, surprised kind of absolute misery. Two women from other tables quickly moved over with sympathy for the trouble and cloths for the blood. Mysteriously, Grief heard one of them offering, as consolation, 'He knows, what could he do, if you were dead? What could he do then?' With a terrible inappropriateness, a street vendor approached the tender, murmuring group, not knowing what had happened so quickly, and attempted to sell the women hacksaws, handsaws, hammers and knives. The women took their bleeding sister away into the café, and a child little different from Suzie, moving among the tables with two opened packets of cigarettes, came nervously to look at the blood on the table and the floor. A waiter shooed her away, spreading sawdust with a straw-brushed broom. The whining man, unsteady on his feet, was randomly gesturing at cars, as if all of them were buses, or as if someone, somewhere, might take him home; he took a step backwards, half fell, and lurched into Grief again. Disgusted, Grief span him round and brutally broke his nose; he collapsed to the pavement, moaning and clutching at his face. Then a bus screeched its brakes, and the ticket collector, hanging out from the rattling tatty doors, emitted a piercing whistle from between tongue and two fingertips to warn off a car that was backing into their path. Grief winced, and remembered that the traffic was worst when it began to go faster, and everyone tried to get home before dark. Suzie took his hand, and led him towards his car.

North of the river and away to the east, Cairo ran out of petrol just a quarter of a mile from the Docklands gates. He swore blind for two minutes, heaving bits of brick through the broken windows of empty warehouses in a fury; then, when he'd worked it off, he reverted to his previous grim purposefulness, and started pushing the bike down the last stretch of road.

FIFTY-TWO

The hourly round-up turned out to be nothing of the kind.

Jarvis was a special feature, and he talked for an age. Set questions gave him opportunities to wax optimistic about better hospitals, better social security, better roads, better transport, bigger investment in the infrastructure, more teachers, more nurses, more jobs, more training . . . the cleanest he came was to say, 'clearly, the general effect on the public borrowing requirement of less old people will be positive.' But the significance of this and similar remarks was obscured behind a cloud of rosy futures.

Wally thought the whole performance both tasteless and tedious, but was fixed in the grip of an amused fascination — it was, after all, the numbers problem solved, albeit with the predictable propagandist exaggeration. He watched the lot; then a light flicked on to alert him to someone arriving downstairs. He cut to a camera in the hallway beneath him, and the monitor showed him Grief helping a very wrecked Moses towards the bedroom. Flicking through the apartment's other rooms, he found a grubby little urchin whirling round the flat in a fever of hyper-activity, picking things up and putting them down, and staring around her in awe at the luxury — Suzie'd thought Grief had merely offered a roof, and was over the moon at finding that the roof was on top of a palace. Somewhat surprised, Wally followed her round until she went to help Moses into bed. On the dim fuzzy screen, the chemist looked awful. And Wally thought, magic. He'd had a sick bet, when attempting to cheer up Grief in Milla's absence, that Moses would go down the pan for good long before she did. He started to calculate his winnings, but his attention was diverted by the replacement at last of Jarvis' vast nose and spectacles on the news screen with a bleary still of Silas Smooth's pocky, cratered face. Moses getting wasted was no news to Wally; but what the announcer had to say was news indeed.

He intoned, 'And now the rest of the day's headlines. Silas Smooth, the perennially popular snooker commentator who was second only to Wally Wasted in the viewers' hearts, minds and ratings chart, died suddenly today of a heart attack. He was fifty-nine. The worlds of sport and show business were united in shock and sorrow on hearing the tragic news, and messages of condolence were this evening pouring in to his wife and family.' A brief obituary followed. Wally thought, too right, I'm shocked and sorrowed. Why hadn't anybody told him?

On the other monitor he heard Grief muttering, 'Heart attack my arse,' as he watched the same show in his living room downstairs. The urchin sat a yard in front of the television, bug-eyed, attempting to nod in serious agreement; but she was far too excited by the unprecedented enormousness of the screen. Mysteriously, Grief added, 'I'll bet he fell apart too.' He was pacing about and taking chunks out of his nails; then he cut the picture, and the girl complained loudly. But she scampered after him promptly enough, when he turned to stomp out the door. Hastily, Wally closed down the in-house camera circuits, and looked back to the news.

The announcer was winding up, 'Boisterous, boozy Silas Smooth always believed that the show must go on. As a tribute to his irrepressible joyousness, his wit, wisdom, and knowledge of the game, 147 are now screening his last shift as scheduled, just as he'd left it before he so sadly passed away.'

Wally thought, 'You what? They're surely not going to have him just die on the air? Shit, that's evil. He'll get better ratings than me, with an act like that.'

Crashing through the door, Grief said far too loudly, as Wally was trying to concentrate, 'Wally, there's something terrible going on.'

Suzie stood in renewed amazement in the doorway behind him, staring with eyes wide enough to burst at the country's foremost television personality; then she screamed, 'Wally Wasted, yeah, Wally Wasted,' and bounced like a ball past Grief and onto the edge of the bed, peering up at him in wonder and joy.

Wally waved them both abruptly to be quiet, bustling about in his bed to make tea while the newsreader dispassionately continued, 'Still on the subject of snooker commentators, topically enough in this, the last week of the Danegeld Lager Championship of the Globe — Thor Thunders, struggling in the ratings, and now exposed as a purveyor of pornography by Wally Wasted last night, has since disappeared. A police search is currently under way.'

Grief moaned, spinning on the spot with his hand slapped to his forehead, 'And that's another thing . . . .' He flopped himself down onto the floor, somewhere out in the heavy blue darkness beyond the circle of the monitors' watery light. Wally squinted out over the top of the teapot, but could only just make him out; he shrugged, uninterested in what he assumed was just another bad day with Bludge. Besides, he was deep in TV land, where everything is better.

'Hey,' said Suzie, quite transformed in this fairyland of glittering equipment, 'it's great to meet you, Mr Wasted.'

'Informed observers have indicated,' the announcer was saying, 'that Wasted's part in exposing the vicious double life this prominent public figure and People Party supporter was leading, may well contribute to his finding a place on the forthcoming Honours List.'

'Yay!' screamed Wally, waving his hands about in the air and jiggling limply up and down in his bed, 'Yay-ay-ay! Nanny loves me!' And, he thought, well she might.

'Yay!' screamed Suzie, mimicking him perfectly and leaping about likewise. As she bounced on the bedclothes, her ring fell unnoticed from the still-open pouch beneath her shirt, and disappeared among the blankets.

Wally called into the gloom, 'Hey, Grief, d'you hear that? Fuck it, man, cheer up, come over here and have some tea. Tell us the story of your day. Oh, and while we're on the subject of fame and fortune, there's Arabs been hanging round the front door looking for you. Guys want to talk to you, Grief.'

Suzie said, 'Cor, it's non-stop when you're famous, isn't it, Mr Grief?'

'I've met them,' Grief sighed, 'don't you worry, I've met them. I have to meet them again, and they're no fun at all.'

Again he was ready to go on, and say what he'd learnt, as Wally seemed at last to be free from TV — which was now running ads — but Wally beat him to it, cheerfully informing him, 'Far as I could gather, chief, from what they hinted on the intercom, they want to do some business with you; that's the impression they left with me, anyhow. Import-export, that's my guess.' He gestured at him to stop looking grumpy and come over to get his tea; sipping at his own with an OBE smile. Wally loved a cup of tea; when you've been smoking too much spliff, it descales you something lovely. He shook the cup, and gazed dreamily at the ringlets rippling on the drink's brown surface. In his head he was working out the profit margins on the bulk purchase of Moroccan hash. Suzie gazed at him; the great man drinking tea. 'Tell me,' the great man wondered, 'are you into a big deal at this time?'

Grief asked himself, how do you explain geriatricide to a useless oaf like this? He tried, slowly and carefully. 'Wally. There's something going on you should know about. You have to listen, and you have to understand. The government is killing all the oldies, you hear me? Now Moses is downstairs dying, if you just take a look, you'll see . . . .'

Uneasily Wally asked, 'How can I take a look?'

That was it. On the bank of screens, a man promoting a cigar drove a car into a ditch, and smiled. 'You get off your butt for once,' shouted Grief, 'I mean, Jesus, if you can get to the loo, you can certainly get downstairs, and then you could see, you could realise just for once' (a woman selling washing-up liquid presented a whole warehouse full of gleaming crockery) 'you whining, mercenary little creep, that the world is no longer so easily shrugged about.' Wally was making slow-down gestures, but Grief, once started, was going all the way. 'You know that drug Moses made,' Grief pressed on, 'well, it flicks switches in your genes, right? You start ageing, just like that, and you die, right? If the dosage is heavy, you crash straight out. And if it's a drip-drip dosage, it takes longer, you could last for months.' (Aliens exploded all over the screens, demonstrating a new video game. Suzie was entranced.) 'And, if you're lucky, as it pulls you apart cell by cell, you get the added bonus of bits of you falling off along the way. Nice, huh? It was cheap, so they rushed in and used it, then they found out what it does, and they thought, "Great, let's keep on going, let's empty the beds, let's phase out oldies. Hell, they're not economically viable, are they?" Give them a year, they should have that little strata of society nicely thinned out. I tell you, Wally, large numbers of people are dying as a direct result of a Money government policy decision . . . .'

Well that, of course, was completely ridiculous. Had Grief not heard on TV that a demographic change was occurring? Wally said, 'I suppose, Mr Paranoid, that this is like all those funny little post-colonial wars your Milla keeps telling me are deliberate? Or is it more straightforwardly commercial? Kill an oldie, win a Metro, that sort of thing? I never heard such a bunch of crap in my life, it's worse than your girlfriend. Take a holiday.' He thought, God's sake, who needs it? I've hardly woken up.

154

'No no no,' said Suzie sweetly, rather disappointed in the very great man, 'it's true, Mr Wasted. And we got to do something.'

'And who the fuck is this, anyhow?' screamed Wally.

A couple of miles away, Cairo pulled his bike up onto its stand at the first barrier on the Docklands entry road. He said hello to the guards, who joshed him about his running out of petrol. But, knowing him, they were friendly enough. When he'd passed in through the gates, they gave him permission to fill his tank at the executive pumps, gleaming where the first row of offices began. Davey's money rustled in his pocket, and the uniformed attendant fed him his four-star.

FIFTY-THREE

Downstairs, Moses couldn't sleep. He lay, face on one side on the pillow, and felt the slow separation of his body into its constituent elements. He supposed, at some basic level, he'd never asked for less. From the sitting room he heard the fractured, momentary sounds of advertising on the television. Grief had put the set on hold, and, after five minutes without further commands, it had automatically switched itself on again. Cheerful music distantly backed a voice informing you of the benefits of joining a health club. The drug forced Moses to smile.

His body between the sheets felt paper-thin; his limbs floated, as separate entities. Beyond the curtains, the dying evening grew murky. Slowly, sharing the pressure out evenly across his body, he turned himself over. His dry lips were beginning to crack from all the stupid grinning, and white flakes of skin lay like dandruff all around him; he noticed where it was beginning to split across the backs of his fingers, leaving thin crusts of hardened blood. Pulling himself up to sit, he felt one knee was damp, and, pushing aside the top sheet, saw that the skin was giving way there too. A trickle of blood stained the bedclothes. He itched at the waist, and found moulted grey hair, rough like horse-hair, scratching at his hips on the pillow. That it should happen to him was, he considered, only justice; but the only way he could kill the relentless, ridiculous smiles of the drug as he died of it was to know, in purest anger, that the accident he'd caused was now an instrument of economic policy. And he'd thought England was a civilised country; a nation of reasonable people.

Moses Brandt had left his native Germany years back, too nervous there because the Bavarian maniacs in power shouted so stridently at the Russians — in the unlikely event of the inevitable war being limited, it was Germany that was first on the list for flash-frying. And, with the revanchists and the new fascists fighting it out in the street with the greens, the country was re-running its history. So Moses slipped away to England. They'd let him in because his abilities offered to the health service a chance to save money — and he'd saved them money with a vengeance. Whether or not he was permanently drugged half-way to heaven and back, Moses had always retained some Germanic sense of certainty; where there was evil of this magnitude, you fought it. So Grief's bewildered inability to see immediately that reprisal, and if at all possible violent reprisal, was necessary, enraged him. And where was he, anyway?

The only sound in the flat was the greased offerings of the TV. Moses fumbled in his clothes for the antidote tablets, to stock up the dose in his system so he'd stay together a few more days yet. They did the job, these tabs, but they weren't any fun — you didn't feel any higher for taking them; just, maybe, a bit tighter and tenser as they worked on you like glue — and Moses needed to be high, he needed artificial energy, if he was going to be involved in any kind of action. At least, he knew, if Grief wasn't up to it, then Milla would know what to do. He toppled off the bed in slow-motion, and knelt on the floor, bloodless, weak and shivering. It took him an age to get his clothes back on — that little girl who'd so gently helped him to bed, before flying off squeaking round the flat again in the jerky trajectory of her explorations, had neatly folded them; shaking them out to put them on was dangerously muscular. Then, pushing himself up off the floor with both hands on the bedside table, he stood, and wobbled precariously on his feet. The slight remainder of his weight on the table as he'd risen had been enough to tip it over towards him, just a bit; the top drawer had slid an inch or two open. Looking down, Moses smiled, but this time genuinely — he had discovered, by accident, Grief's supply of bedside coke. He eased himself down to sit on the edge of the bed, and, taking out and unwrapping a surgical scalpel from its foil sachet — ever optimistic, he kept a supply of blades always handy, because you never know when rich friends might be generous — he cut himself up an enormous line. He felt no qualms at snaffling some of Grief's expensive store. Grief, he thought, viciously, had been too long grown old and boring, acquiescent and retreating into ease. Besides, if you got to go, go out in style. Germans don't do things by halves.

Moses wasn't to know that in forty-eight hours, his going out would be the most pyrotechnically stylish on record. The only pyrotechnics he knew now was the electric rush of the coke to his brain, the disappearance of his last frail weight, as the energy lifted his vellum bones and parchment muscles into the joyous thrill of chemically powered movement. Wrinkled as a raisin, dying Moses bounced around the bedroom thinking, Kill, kill, kill the Money. Then he heard the main door open.

Milla toppled into the flat, loudly drunk. She heard the television on, and lurched, sliding off the walls, into the empty living room. She tried to speak, calling for Grief, but only croaked, and her tongue smeared lipstick as it shifted dry spittle round her mouth. Then she tried again, and cried, 'Hey Grief. You'll never believe what they're gonna do now. When you die — no, listen to me — when you die,' she went on, failing to control the breaking of her laughter, 'they'll burn you for nothing. What a fantastic fucking country, eh? Shits all over you all your life, and soon as you're dead, can't wait to be doing you a favour.' She slipped sideways against the wall where she was leaning, and pushed herself off it to wander off down the further corridor to her blue room. Beneath the control panel, her Drambuie was nearly empty. She drained the last swig, and went back to sway in the doorway. 'Hey, clubmaster, have we got any more Drambuie?' Behind her, the fish blew bubbles, open-mouthed.

Moses bounced like a jack-in-the-box out of the bedroom and into the corridor in front of her. She put her hands to her face and screamed, then retreated to her swivel chair, crawling up the back of it in suddenly sober horror as he loped and lolloped, half-running, towards her, with his fire-filled chinese lantern limbs flopping all about him like so much loose baggage. Eyes wide, Milla held her hands over her open mouth and followed him round the room as he circled, grinning and gesticulating. He said, 'Listen, angel,' whirling past the fish like a torpedo without a target, 'they don't just burn you for nothing. First, they kill you for nothing too.'

Moses didn't mind in the least being screamed at, and as he explained a little more lucidly what was happening, she grew calm, then cold; and her idea of the previous night came back to her. It was at this point that the enraged Grief left Wally, dragging confused Suzie in tow. Wally immediately switched to the flat below, and this is what he heard.

'You can make a bomb, can't you, Moses? And you radio-track your animals, right? You could fix a detonator to blow it from a distance, couldn't you?' Moses nodded, grinning, then stopped, as he felt skin weakening round his neck. He held himself still, gazing at her in admiration. 'So I'll take it to my Cabinet presentation on Friday night, and we'll blow fuck out of the lot of them.'

Moses would have rushed to kiss her, if he hadn't heard the door opening at the flat's other end. He just said, 'You're wonderful,' and felt his smile endlessly growing as the skin of his face stretched away and quietly split and peeled, like sunburn. 'Better not tell Grief though.'

Milla agreed, 'No way. But I've got an idea to rope him in with, too.'

Well, thought Wally. She really thinks she's going to do it. Then, seeing the look on her face, he thought, she's really going to do it, full stop. Shifting back across his bed, he found Suzie's ring among the blankets; he looked at it, surprised, then laid it down beside the teapot.

In Docklands, Cairo pulled up on his newly-fuelled bike outside the shining steel and glass of the 147 building.

FIFTY-FOUR

Deep in the soft-lit pink and grey interior of the 147 studios,

Crinkly watched again Wally's crap-fit, and the deterioration rap that followed it. When it had turned up on the air, they'd called him over to look at it, because it was definitely way too near the knuckle. He nodded to the worried team of directors and producers, and said, 'I agree. And the campaign situation, as it happens, is altogether too sensitive for that sort of material to be running on this station. Let's rein him in. Give me paper.' A subordinate stepped forward into the light of the monitor screens from the cushioned darkness at the back of the edit suite. He profered paper, and asked if Mr Crinkly would like a drink. The reply was no; Crinkly was efficiently writing already, in his neat, manicured hand.

The note said, 'Wasted. Your miserable little tirade this afternoon was a mile too close for comfort. If you don't go easy, sunshine, you won't be on the Honours List — you'll be on the dole. Do you get my drift?' Then Crinkly handed over the note to a waiting lackey, and said, 'Get that typed, and get Randall to sign it. He is, after all, the Programme Controller.' Polite laughter chimed on cue, chasing in the wake of this subtle little quip.

Officially, and as far as pretty well everybody knew, Randall Foyle — ex-TV commercials actor, the face behind a thousand products, the voice behind a million sales — was Programme Controller at 147. In reality, his role was simply to promote the station both to the public, and to the ad agencies, aiming thereby at continued viewing, and continued purchase of space to be viewed. However, being by far the largest buyer of that space, the real boss was, of course, Crinkly, it being only right that he should have the largest say in the material that surrounded what he bought. Besides, when suggestions had been canvassed as to how best to privatise the BBC, it was Crinkly who had thought up the whole thing in the first place. Naturally, very few people — people like Wally Wasted — knew anything about this. But you know it makes sense.

One of the directors had cut the screens back to Silas' show, which was now well under way on the air. The Thai kid continued to pull steadily away from the floundering Style Dixon. Crinkly, his face illuminated green in the light of the tabletop felt off the monitors, scratched his cheek, and allowed himself to look worried. 'I think,' he suggested, 'that we may cause a few eruptions tonight.'

Behind him, the Money Party runner stood up from out of a voluminous sofa. He was drinking Pepsi — all the others were on whisky. But he looked the hardest in the room for all that. Stripped of the meek suit with which he presented himself outside of the centre circle, he was sharp and sinister in a black leather jacket. He asked the TV team to leave the room, then said, 'There's a danger, Crinkly, if the death rate keeps on rising, that this could get way, way out of hand. And this story on the Thai kid doesn't begin to be a solution. We're looking to you to come up with a miracle. And soon.'

Crinkly fluttered. 'My Milla will pull it off, once we know how to play it. You saw what a splendid little job she made of the cremations.'

'Your Milla,' said the runner, 'is exactly what I'm worried about. That script had its tongue in its cheek from top to bottom.'

Limply, Crinkly fenced. 'Everything good creative people do will always need a little ironing out. Overall, it was just what was needed.' He didn't like feeling under this snide kind of pressure, especially from a mere bankers' rep. A secretary came in with his note for Wally typed up on headed paper, and Randall Foyle's florid, illegible signature rounded off hugely all across the base of it. Crinkly asked whether the tape of the final's last shift had been collected yet, and she told him no, the messenger had been delayed on the road. 'Good,' he replied, 'then this can go over with the cassette right now.' The secretary made to take the note off him, but he stood, grabbing the chance to go down to the foyer to deliver it himself, and get away from the Money man. Even Crinkly bristled a bit, when the runner was out of the closet and doing his gestapo number.

Downstairs, Cairo was perfunctorily searched at the outer and inner entry gates, then lumped in his bike gear across the yielding carpet, beneath the soft light, to the gleaming chrome and heavy matt black of the reception counter. He bumped his shin on a low table strewn with glossy media magazines, and stupidly cursed. Zecks waiting to buy and sell space smiled discreetly; from the glittery alcove of the neon-lit, US-style, jukebox-noisy beer bar to one side, technicians and editors laughed less kindly. From deeper in the building came the constant hum of tapes turning, and the eerie sound of disembodied snippets of voices being matched to images of the products they'd sell. The post-production department at 147 worked twenty-four hours a day. Cairo heard a sniggering sound engineer at the far end of a dim corridor, littered with little signs saying this way and that for all the rooms full of tech and tape, saying, 'I think, you know, we should make that explosion louder, when the beer can comes out of the mountain.' Cairo wanted to kill them all. But, one at a time; one at a time.

Crinkly stepped, belly shuffling under his shirt, from a silver lift, just as the perfect-toothed blonde at the desk was freeing herself from the winking flurry of switchboard lights. With a 'Will you hold, please, will you hold just a moment,' she dropped her headset down around her neck, and turned behind her to fish out the cassette from the pile that awaited collection. 'Wait a minute,' Crinkly said, 'stick this letter in with that cassette.' Cairo signed for it — and remembered how Marl had taught him to, where before he'd had to pretend, throwing down a line of hieroglyphics — and Crinkly checked that he was the one who was delivering to Wally.

Cairo turned and said, 'Sure fatface.' Crinkly blinked, amazed. He couldn't remember the last time someone had had the nerve to be that rude to him. As Cairo thumped heavily away, dimly grinning, and zecks hid more smiles behind their hands, Crinkly filed a mental note to have that messenger sacked.

Luckily for Cairo, Crinkly would be dead before he found the time to make the mental note actual.

FIFTY-FIVE

'You know what they'll do, don't you?' Milla smiled, brain well cleared now, after a medicinal little sniff of coke had cut through the alcohol. 'They'll wait until the votes are in, they'll shift in their seats and get settled for the next five years, and they'll casually reveal that 'the government has averted a major catastrophe in the health service'. They'll fire a few administrators, and they'll sack the minister, with, naturally, appropriate under-the-counter compensation — and they'll make Moses the scapegoat, for inadequate testing and general

161

incompetence. They'll whip up a hate against the boy, and then, if he's still alive, they'll have a special branch stooge dress up as a crazy and do a Lee Harvey Oswald; they'll shoot the poor fucker on the way into court. Outrage appeased, drug withdrawn, everything rosy. Meanwhile, amid much triumphant hoo-ha about the new-found health of the economy, anyone who's had even one little tablet, their switches are flicked, and they go right on accelerating to the grave.' She got up and poured herself some wine, looking sourly at Grief, whom she blamed, rather unfairly, for the drying up of the Drambuie supply.

Suzie watched her in a new access of awe — she'd never seen, she thought, such a good-looking, such a put-together lady. Moses squatted, melting down in a corner, admiring her equally and treasuring their secret. And Grief, looking at her as she drifted in and out of the kitchen, feeling sharply somehow that everyone saw things much more clearly than he did, asked quietly, 'So where shall we go?'

Milla was thinking, head bowed over her drink, which she held up under her chin in both hands to breathe in the smell. 'Go?' she asked suddenly, looking up. 'What d'you mean, go?'

'Away,' he said, weakly, 'What d'you think?'

'I thought you promised,' she then slowly told him, 'that if ever we had a chance to do something, we'd do it.' She stared at him, akimbo in front of the TV, which silently threw the livid, instant-whip colours of its commercials up the sides of her body. 'Because now,' she added, 'we have the chance.'

'And what on earth,' he wearily asked her, 'can we possibly do?'

She said, almost spat, 'I'm disgusted. There's this going on, and you want to cop out, you want to run off and play Daddy.' She managed to stop herself from glowering at Suzie, who looked at her feet and felt badly assaulted.

Bemused, Grief let himself fall into a chair. He shook his head; he held his hands wide apart, and his mouth hung open. 'It's too late. The drug is out, the oldies are on it, the country's a funeral parlour. There's nothing we can do, and I want out.'

She cried, 'You're so obtuse,' voice rising in frustration, 'it's obvious what we do. They want to announce the cremations in front of eleven million people on Friday night, right? To do it, they have to go out on Wally's show. So we make an alternative, telling the truth, and get Wally to edit that into his programme instead. Bingo. Shock and horror across the nation, and no more Money.'

'That,' breathed Moses, 'is absolutely brilliant.'

Grief looked at her in amazement. 'Who the hell says Wally will ever buy that?'

Watching, Wally thought, who indeed? 'He'll buy it,' Milla said grimly, keeping to herself a nasty idea of what getting him to buy might involve.

'OK,' Grief continued, 'just what's in this alternative ad? Just how do we make it so instantly?'

Milla ground her teeth, saying, 'Sometimes you are really a moron. I've got a camera, haven't I? Tomorrow we go back to the hospital and we film what's happening. And you go back and sign that form, the one about Fiona's cremation.'

Grief choked. 'What the fuck for? I'm not doing that, that's sick.'

Milla jeered, 'The man hardened by four years of nightclub violence eh? Look, you, this isn't tacky little drug salesmen hacking each other up in your toilets, OK? This is the government, doing it to the people, publicly. So you got to show your bollocks for once, right? We have to film this cremation act, we have to know what's in that coffin — because whatever it is, it sure as shit won't be your precious ex-girlfriend.'

Grief recalled how, once, Fiona had danced in a white T-shirt and trousers in ultra-violet light, so her whole tiny body darted and glowed, an angel in fire all over the dark floor. The image merged with the thought of her flesh, boiling in the flames. Dreamily, away on another planet, Moses volunteered, 'I wonder how Bludge's mother is?'

Grief snorted, jolted from his nightmare. He said, 'You're demented. What you're thinking of is impossible.'

'Right,' said Milla furiously, 'you come with me.' She stalked sharply across the floor, seizing him by the elbow and hauling him out of his chair and into the bedroom so she could talk to him alone. And then she said, in a different voice altogether that yearned and pleaded, with honest affection, 'Listen, my love. Whatever has happened between us, there's one thing I'll never forget. You remember last Friday, the night I came back? And you made love to me with words, because I was so drunk I couldn't move? But I wasn't asleep, I heard what you said, I cherished those words, I believed in them, so very much. Look at the situation now. Don't you see that we have to take responsibility, we have to act? When it's over, we can go, we can find the sun in a quiet place, we can have children, whatever you want — but first, we have a duty . . . .'

Grief understood those words — responsibility, duty — but the change in her voice had been too big, and , grown far too far away from her now, all he heard was manipulation. Horribly cold, he said, 'This relationship has been one long advertisement. But I don't care how good your copy is this time, you're way out of line and I'm just not buying.' He stared, hating himself for the hurt he'd caused as, appalled, she collapsed onto the bed and began to cry. He fled, heart pounding in fear and misery, and grabbed Suzie as he swept through the living room, saying, bitterly, 'Come on, you, let's get out of this bedlam. Give me company, we're going dancing.' He reasoned that even the Arabs wouldn't shoot him in front of a little girl, if he failed to give them what they wanted. Which he was bound to do, seeing as failing people, just now, was something he seemed to be good at.

And in the lift as they descended, Suzie tentatively said, 'Your girlfriend, Mr Grief. You ought to listen to her, she's really neat.'

And Grief buckled, saying, 'I know, I know.'

FIFTY-SIX

Nearby, Cairo accelerated as he left the rubbly waste of the East End, and his wheels moved smoother on the better roads of the silent City. The engine pounded between his legs; he whipped through the settling darkness, and pulled up outside the big glass doors of Wally's block with his teeth showing white and yellow through the dirt on his face. His eyes flashed in the electric light thrown out from the foyer.

Upstairs, Wally was still savouring the aftermath of Grief's departure on the taut air of the apartment beneath him; Moses comforted Milla ineffectually, saying, 'He'll come round, he'll come round.' But Milla said they were on their own now. Then the security buzzer lit up and burred at him —

it is, after all, non-stop when you're famous. He cut to the foyer camera, and the monitor showed him a guard who was saying that they had Cairo Jones waiting with a tape. Cairo slouched into the picture, and spoke into the guard's mike — an unusually precocious thing for him to do — to announce, 'It's your last tape, Mr Wasted.' The words, for Cairo, spoke volumes. Wally peered at the screen to examine him, this huge, greasy-leathered thug, black-haired and unshaven, his skin dark with dirt around a grin of quite remarkably concentrated vacancy — and he shivered with distaste.

But he said, 'Great, hop on up,' and rubbed his hands, preparing to be jocular. Cairo blundered through glass door-ways as they whispered, sliding open before him, and waited for the lift. When it came, Grief and Suzie strode out past him, Grief not even noticing him, and turned into the road to go down for Grief's car. Cairo stepped into the lift, and Wally heard it whirring him up through the building. He wondered how fit he was; he hoped, if he pushed it, to knock off that final shift tonight. It would be good to have the whole thing over and finally done with. He pressed buttons, preparing the edit console, and then heard Cairo's squeaking leathers, the noise preceding him as he came through the last set of landing doors; his booted feet thumped on the floor as he approached Wally's nest. Friendly, Wally chimed, 'So, the Thai kid gets his come-uppance at the hands of our Geometry, eh?'

Cairo looked, Wally thought, intensely happy. He wondered if he was high, and peered back up at him, grinning. Cairo threw the jiffy-bagged package down on the bed and said, 'There's more than one come-uppance in these hands tonight, you clever-clever bastard.'

Confounded, Wally said, 'You what?'

Cairo told him, 'What you did to Thor makes me sick.'

'Of course,' Wally replied, remembering Cairo's dubious tastes. 'You're a heavy metal fan, aren't you?' He couldn't help smiling, really he couldn't. 'Are you into porn as well? Or socialism, maybe?'

'You shithead,' muttered Cairo, enjoying to the full the single-minded focusing at last of his horror and his hatred. He leant down, stepping forward, and his hands reached out for Wally's head. Wally saw the grime on the thick, curled fingers, and the rings of sweat built up around knuckles cased for too long in heavy riding gloves. He was still smiling his perennially cynical, indifferent smile, as Cairo hauled him by the neck from out of his bed and his nest, and onto the open floor beyond it, where he threw him down onto his back and said, 'I'm going to rip you apart, you mean-minded cunt.' And he meant it, literally.

Wally desperately tried to squirm away as what was happening to him sank in. But Cairo caught him by the ankles and wrenched his legs apart; shoots of pain flew up Wally's side as his bad leg was yanked around at the hip, and he screamed as Cairo pulled harder. Cairo was a little disappointed not to achieve, as he had with Marl, an instant and spectacular effect. He lurched up between Wally's splayed legs and shoved even more fiercely as he tried to tear the thighs apart. Again Wally screamed, as his bad leg ground round in its socket, and he howled in horror as well, 'Help me, Jesus, what you want to do?' Cairo heaved again, and Wally thought, in agony and panic, as the stiff, unused muscles of his groin stretched and shrieked, for God's sake, I'm going to be buggered by a bike boy . . . .

Outside, Grief's car screeched up the ramp past the cackling old garbage woman, for whom the day's comings and goings were a seemingly endless entertainment. As he span out onto the road, Suzie suddenly cried, 'My ring, I've lost my ring,' hand inside her shirt, and terrible anxiousness on her face. Grief slammed on the brakes, cursing ferociously, and turned to look at her. Too worried to be apologetic, she said, 'It must have fallen out on Wally's bed.' Before he could say anything, she was out of the car and sprinting up the steps to bang on the doors so the guards would let her back in. She ran for the lift, and it sped her up through the building to Wally's floor.

The minute the doors began to open, she was squeezing out between them and hurtling through to find, to her amazement, Cairo straddling Wally on the floor, with his hands around his throat, muttering, 'Die, you bastard, die.' Wally was choking and gasping and flailing about beneath Cairo's great weight, as Cairo put all his frustration at finding he wasn't even good at murder into an almighty clamp round Wally's white, mottled neck. Suzie scuttled silently across the room behind him, picked up the teapot, and smashed it against his crash helmet as hard as she could. Brown china, cold stewed tea and soggy tealeaves sprayed all over Wally as Cairo, stunned, grunted and slumped sideways down onto the floor.

'The alarm,' spluttered Wally, struggling and coughing for breath that wouldn't come, his face blue and his neck livid with bruises; he desperately tried and failed to pick himself up, his bad leg stabbing pains right through his pelvis, and again he wheezed, 'For fuck's sake, the alarm, first button on the left, top row, second panel from the right.' Cairo moaned and shook his head, pushing himself up off the floor, elbows trembling. Frantically, Wally wriggled crab-wise away from him as Suzie wildly pressed buttons, and the screens above her burst into a chaos of football, snooker, pop music, politicians, game shows, soap operas, ads, war movies, porn films, wildlife, local news, global news, thrillers, while Cairo lurched to his feet and stumbled about groaning, clutching his head in his helmet. Lopsided like a lobster, Wally hauled himself away across the deep blue carpet, as Suzie punched every button she could see and, unheard, he screamed instructions. The speakers went haywire, bawling out, 'It's Johnston on the byeline, that's a lovely cross, MY BABY'S GOT A BRAND NEW CADILLAC, I think young slant-eye's on for the black here, JACKPOT IRENE, YOU'VE WON TEN THOUSAND, the naked mole rat is a peculiarly ugly little mammal, DAKKA DAKKA DAKKA KABOOOM, a cut in public spending has always been our goal, FUCK ME, FUCK ME, RIGHT UP MY BLACKWALL TUNNEL WITH YOUR GORGEOUS POLISH SAUSAGE, countries in North Africa are planning new initiatives to tackle the population problem, THIS DIRT SAYS HOT, THE LABEL SAYS NOT . . . .'

Cairo stopped falling about and headed unsteadily back towards a panic-stricken Wally. Grief, who had grown tired of waiting and come up to help find the ring, span him round and smashed him viciously, flat-handed, with the base of his palm in the chest. Cairo's shoulders fell forwards as the wind rushed out of him, breath whistling away faster than he could hang onto it. Then Grief pushed Suzie aside and punched the alarm button. Eyes ablaze with fright and excitement, Suzie shouted over the babel of the screens, 'You see, that's twice now you've done it, when you've wanted to.'

As the guards rushed in to cuff Cairo, then dragged him away and down to the foyer to call the City Store, Grief looked down into the thrilling brightness of her eyes. She picked up the ring from where she'd seen it by the teapot, and held it up, shaking still, but smiling too. He was almost persuaded; then he saw how much the child was like Milla. 'If you think you can persuade me to be a party to the risking of all of our lives, then you're very much mistaken.' Couldn't they see that they'd never get away with it?

When he left, this time, Suzie didn't come with him — it had been a tiring day. For Grief, however, as no result had been achieved, there was still plenty of extra time to be played.

FIFTY-SEVEN

'Well bugger me blind, Johnny boy. There's a nice-looking piece of equipment.'

'What's that, Jimmy boy? The stereo? Or the bint?'

Mary turned on her knees from tending the cuts and bruises on her six year old son's face — the kid was always fighting — and examined the two hulking frames in the doorway of her Peckham bedsit. She'd known this was coming. The building she lived in was ex-council stock, crumbling away at the bad end of a corrugated iron and graffiti street that stopped being a street where her building stood, and started being a grey concrete smack estate. And, because of the smack estate, the building was unsalable. So the landlord had been bound to bomb it out sooner or later, for the insurance. The men in the doorway were both big, with labourer's physiques in too-tight white T-shirts that showed the fat of their paunches and the muscles of their tattooed arms. Whereas Mary was scrawny. She asked them, 'How did you get into my room?'

'With the key, darling, with the key.' And the man who had spoken held it up to show her.

She nodded. 'And how long have I got to get out?'

'Ten minutes, darling, ten minutes.'

'Shame,' she sneered. 'Doesn't leave any time for a rape, does it?' And it really was a shame, too. It wasn't a bad room, and she'd had it for just over six months. She should, she supposed, have moved out earlier with the others, as the building gradually emptied under threat. But she was a part-time junkie, so adjoining the smack estate was too perfect a location — when she had spare money, she could treat herself any time of the day or night just by popping across the road. The dealers sat in their cars outside the high rises, waiting with unsmiling patience as the kids came down regularly, one by one. The police didn't bother coming any more, hadn't bothered in years, and the stuff was good. But Mary was diligent. She worked four nights out of seven every week — the maximum Grief allowed to any of his waitresses, preferring to employ as many as possible, rather than just a small number who'd each get very rich — and she made better than reasonable money for doing so. The money went first on the kid, second to the hire purchase on the stereo, her pride and joy, and only third on the smack. She said, 'You can have what you want, but not the stereo. It's all I've got.'

With a considerable access of bile, one of the waiting men told her, 'You, darling, have got a job.' Men, she thought, real men — coarse vicious blockheads — and they couldn't get work for love nor money. But then women worked better. And the lump-brains were reduced to doing the evictions. She didn't feel in the least bit sorry for them. She got up, and began unplugging wires, then pulled down the hi-fi's cardboard box off the top of the wardrobe to pack it away. 'Nice,' the bigger man said, and advanced towards the stereo. 'You're even packing it up for us.'

Mary span round, pulling her flick-knife from the belt of her trousers. The blade clicked out, and she stabbed it towards his belly. He stopped, stepped back, and smiled. The other man made to move towards her son; bright, he darted sideways to his mother's side, hands on hips in brave support of their only worldly possession. 'Time ticks by,' the nearer man said, and looked at the clock by her bed. 'Seven minutes, darling, and the place is in flames.'

Mary told him, 'Tough shit.' The blade felt deliciously light in her fingers; she'd used it before, and would love, on this occasion, to use it again. Something in her eyes told them so, too. 'Pack the record player, Zeke,' she ordered the boy, 'any old how, but carefully, and quickly.' The men looked stupid, and angry, unable to go forward. Zeke put deck, amp, and both speakers neatly away in the big brown box. 'And don't forget the headphones. Can you carry it?' He lifted it up, comically — it was as big as he was — but could just about manage. 'OK, fuckface, back off.' She advanced, thinly smiling, on the nearer of the two gross stomachs. Zeke slid out of the door behind her, and Mary thanked God they lived on the ground floor. She called, 'Wait for me,' and circled the two flummoxed men to pull clothes from the wardrobe into another cardboard box. Thinking she was distracted — and, fumbling to make sure with her free hand that the clothes she saved included enough for Zeke, she was — one of the men suddenly lumbered towards her, reaching for the knife hand. His other hand made straight for her flat little breasts. Without a second thought she dug the knife half-way up the blade into his belly — lovely. It was a lover's kiss. Briefly, the faint resistance of skin before the parting, and then the quick warm rush as the metal slipped inside his body. She wrenched the knife sideways, and the blood spewed out. She asked the other man, 'You too?' Amazed and moaning, the wounded man fell heavily back, thick arse landing on the bed in a crash of springs.

The second man retreated as she quickly stepped towards him. Cornering him with his fear, she was free to use her eyes, in quick sideways glances to make sure she got shoes, socks, pants and tights out of drawers and into the clothes box. She saw by the clock there were two minutes left. The cornered man saw it too, and made a run for the door. She met him there, thrusting the blade into his stomach to the hilt. She tried to wrench it through his fat from side to side, but her arms were too weak, it was like cutting up a tyre with a razor blade; so she hauled the knife back out, and stabbed him repeatedly. He began to crumple, his huge arms knocking her about like a puppet, drawing blood from her lips. Head throbbing, she forced herself in close to him, to where the blood was gushing, so his blows couldn't hurt, and kept on piercing his belly until he fell to his knees. The other man was struggling to his feet. She stuck the blade into his neck as he rose, shoved her tapes into the box on top of her clothes, heaved it, grunting, up and under one arm, then ran into the hallway and out the front door.

Zeke was waiting fifty yards away, surrounded by grey junkie adolescents on the grey broken concrete, the stereo on the ground by his side.

The word was out, and the kids were waiting for the bonfire.

Behind her as she ran across the open treeless space, the incendiary bomb went up. And, she thought, serve the fuckers right, as their last high-pitched screams rushed outwards from the windows amid the shattering glass. The building was a pyre in no time. Lethargically, teenagers applauded.

Zeke told her, 'It'd be a whole lot easier if you'd just insure the bloody stereo.'

'You think, clever clogs, that your mum can afford that kind of premium?'

He then suggested that maybe they should go into the property game. 'I'm sick of sleeping in that noisy bloody club of yours every time we have to move house.'

She told him, 'Come on, Zeke, someone'll put us up.' But he'd heard that one before. His spiky ginger hair, short on top, and curling down his back behind, shone in the lamplight. Beside him, Mary's waist showed white between pink trousers and grey T-shirt; behind him, he heard some kid passing a lewd comment on his mother's skinny, sexy little frame. He turned round, and smashed him one in the mouth.

FIFTY-EIGHT

Wally lay waiting for the worst of the pains to go. The babel of the screens continued, firing rainbow colour into the fear-sweaty darkness, and tealeaves dried in clumps across his chest. Eventually, when his breath was more regular, the pain receded to big dull aches, and the terror converted into a conceptual horror that was possibly worse. He dragged himself up, and inch by inch to the bathroom. He lay in warm water and trembled, drained, with the advent of relief. Then he towelled himself down ineffectively, and, shivering, managed to get back to bed. There, he sorted out the jumble of TV, and left just three screens busy. On one, Silas smirked on about the Thai Kid and Dixon. On another, Milla and Moses dourly plotted in the blue room; and on the third Cairo bawled and stomped, locked up in a wordless animal rage under the steady guns of the house security.

Still shivering uncontrollably as he watched, Wally saw gleaming Dwayne turn up in an extraordinary white cotton and gold brocade outfit of casual shirt and long shorts —

sixties Hong Kong, Clothing Dep had assured him, with ill-suppressed laughter — to take Cairo away. Wally hastily made a connection, and jeered down the intercom, 'I hear, these days, you're a police stooge, Jones. I hope you look forward to what Bludge has to say to you now.' Dwayne looked around, surprised; Cairo just carried on yelling inarticulately. Revolted, Wally killed the picture, and stared into darkness with the memory of his terror. Still, his hand refused to stop shaking; he fumbled pathetically to roll a calming joint, but hash and tobacco kept spilling out of the papers and all over the blankets. He couldn't even gum up the Rizlas properly. When he tried to drink the leftovers in his teacup, it rattled violently against the saucer; he couldn't hold it steady to his lips, it spilt down his chin, and he thought, shit, if this is the deep blue sea, then the boat right now is under heavy weather. Then he told himself, come on, boy, who sits at the captain's table around here? And gradually, he got himself together. That, he told himself, is just the way it is, when someone tries to kill you.

So he tried to forget about it, opening his package and sticking the mute master tape of the final's last session down into the edit box. The tape ran, showing the two contestants side by side at the top of the table, waiting to begin. Amazed, and suddenly much happier, Wally saw that next to Geometry it wasn't the Thai kid, but Dixon after all. He whooped and cheered, massively relieved to have something unexpected take charge in his mind. He realised that the second half of the semi-final must, in that case, be a blinder. How could Dixon possibly have turned the game around, when he'd fallen so badly behind? He chuckled to himself, lucky old Silas — no wonder he'd had a heart attack. Eager for distraction, he thought it'd be a laugh to see, or at least hear, old Silas keeling over; he had, after all, been creeping uncomfortably close in the ratings. Looking back to the screen that carried 147 live, where the Thai kid crept ever further ahead, he listened to the mellifluous, phlegmy mumblings of Silas' last performance. The old man was praising the Thai's play with indolent condescension, as if to say, 'not bad, for a gook'. Wally muttered, 'So homely, weren't you, Silas?' Then he grinned and yelped, 'Go for it, Style.' He was safe again, back in TV.

His hand brushed over the jiffy bag the tape had arrived in, and he fished out the ad schedule to see what was due to go in. Attached to it was the note signed by Randall Foyle. And, as Wally read it, all the worst of his panic and terror galloped neighing back at him in a thunder of blood in his ears and hooves in his heart. To be sacked by Crinkly meant never to see a cent in your life again. Joblessness — Wally knew all about it, he had a drawerful of dossiers describing the lives of his audience in every nasty, means-tested detail. And how many more Cairos were waiting for him, down in the street? Who would protect him, when he couldn't afford security? How would he live, when the dole gave no allowances just because a leg didn't work? He would be pushing himself on a wheeled wooden trolley down the pavement for the rest of what would surely, then, be a very short life. And, he cursed himself, he could have been in clover with his leaders for months — had he not just given them the left's last mass-market spokesman on a plate? — and he'd gone and blown it right away with one stupid onset of too much tired, stoned honesty. He'd have to redeem himself with an A-plus performance, to be out of the fire this time round.

On the middle screen, Milla was saying, 'So the ad would run at eleven-thirty. I'd have to leave the room at, say, eleven twenty-eight. And you'd press the button maybe three minutes later. We'll have to work this out really dead carefully....' Her eyes were re-ignited with the thrill of her idea, and glowed up onto the monitor, beautiful with life. Moses was nodding and grinning. The fish swam around them, sealed in their tank; mute on the huge screen before them, Nanny was reviewing the troops again.

Wally considered the thing he was about to do. Terrorism, he reassured himself, is an unacceptable method of influencing a democratically elected government's actions. And then, he thought, who gives a fuck, if all the people at the edge are beginning to fall off? The world might go plopf in the huge void of space — but not, if he could help it, the bit of it that he was parked on. He called Crinkly on his private, reach-you-anywhere radiophone number, and told him what Milla was planning, and everything that she and Grief were up to.

And Crinkly said, 'Bless her, that's fabulous.'

Wally spluttered, 'What d'you mean? She wants to blow your head off.'

'It's fabulous,' said Crinkly, 'because she's giving us just the sensation we badly need right now.' He lay back, the soft leather of the back seat of his Roller absorbing the folds of his flesh, and was envisioning already some beautiful, beautiful images. He told Wally, 'Do everything she asks you to.'

'What?'

'I said, dope-brain, do everything she asks you to.'

'OK,' said Wally, stunned. 'But you listen, no more threats to my job, alright? And not a soul to know it was me that shopped them, either. I've only this minute had some moron try to kill me just for shopping Thor — and there's plenty more love Milla and Grief than ever loved that loathsome berk.'

Crinkly smiled, 'You poor thing,' as the Roller purred past the vanguard of the private armies guarding the mansions of Chiswick. 'You'll have all the protection you need.' He hung up, and sipped his Perrier. Bubbles fizzed round a juicy wedge of lime. Then he picked up the phone again, snarling at his driver as he braked too abruptly before bumping across a sleeping policeman; and he called Laz Stones. 'Laz,' said Crinkly, 'I have a beautiful job for you.' And then, as they say in the trade, he threw some balls up in the air, and waited to see where they'd land. Laz, as he'd expected, caught the lot.

In between two lines of cocaine, he replied, 'I love it, Crinkly. But it's awful difficult. You're talking millions, to pull off a job like this, in that little time.' Never sound too enthusiastic, that's the trick.

'Anything inside five, and it's yours.' Laz smiled and sniffed — he reckoned he could do it for three and a half, ballpark. He said nothing. Crinkly told him, 'But the work starts now. I need your best crew rolling film in half an hour, and I'll tell you where.' Laz listened, and said that was fine. And yes, of course — completely confidential.

Back in the City, Wally shrugged. Sure, he'd do what she asked, if that was what Crinkly wanted. But at a price. You got to take your chances, after all — they only come once.

FIFTY-NINE

Inside the Barn, it was still early. Not many people were dancing yet. Grief wondered how many of them were on the same road as Moses. The two Arabs sat at a far table, tucked in an alcove; in keeping with their style, they had a clear view of the nearest exit. One of them nodded, and beckoned him over unobtrusively. Grief really didn't want to know, but steeled himself to cross the floor, acting casual, and asking a waitress to bring him a drink on the way. He hoped they wouldn't want to become his close personal friends. Since the honest brutality of the white-boy criminal fraternity had been superseded by the too great weight of American and other imports, the ways you had to do business had got a sight more sneaky than Grief really liked.

Both Arabs rose as he approached, and shook his hand politely. The one who'd done the talking at their encounter in the car park was young, fat, with smooth skin, a sleek, bushy moustache, and a slow, cool air about him. The other was taller and older, slightly spotty round his chin; he had wide eyes, and an uncertain grin of anticipation. Clearly more nervous, he wasn't the important one. The fat one was the cat; the other was merely a rat-in-waiting. The cat spoke, again politely. 'You are a businessman, Mr Grief.'

Grief took this to be a reference to his being used to deaths on his doorstep, but he didn't follow it up. He said, 'I do business, yes.' He hoped it wasn't going to take too long; he thought he'd hurry it up and get it out in the open. 'You like cocaine?' They nodded, lazily, so he cut three lines on the table, which were quickly and efficiently consumed. 'Now,' he said, sniffing to hold up the last crumbs in his nose, 'what's your commodity?'

Over-alert, uncool and buzzed up, the ratty one was pulling out papers and dope. 'You like hashish?' he grinned, leaning forward, head nodding. The other one waved him quiet as Grief's drink arrived.

'Excuse my drinking,' Grief said, tactfully careful; he'd seen that they were both on coffee and mineral water. Of course — it was Ramadan.

'*Ça ne fait rien,*' the fat one said, with an untroubled gesture.

175

He then went on, 'I am a law student, an honest man. I do business only to live; I have a family at home.'

'Wonderful,' Grief said. 'You're not a criminal. May I guess you're Moroccan?'

'Quite,' he smiled. 'You will like to know that I regularly drive to Kitama. The police along the way are friends of mine.' The smile expanded, just a tiny bit.

'Best, best quality, best quality,' the rat then blurted, insisting on it as he waved the joint he was building. 'From the Rif, direct. We only deal with Europeans.'

Grief pressed them, 'How much do you want to import?' He couldn't see there being much demand for hash, if all the kids were suddenly ninety, and dead.

The cat's face held no expression. Calmly, voice fluid, he said, 'We do not want your money, Mr Grief. We should be friends. Men who smoke together can see things in a certain light. I understand, like me, that you think of more in your life than merely business. You like, perhaps, to think, and to read. Hashish helps you concentrate, to see things clearly, in a tunnel of precision. . . .'

'Cut the sales crap, I've heard it before. What do you want, if you don't want money?'

The Arab was not in the least disturbed. He said, 'From our observations, Mr Grief, aside from your business in this magnificent club, we see that you visit the hospital. But you are not unwell. We notice also that many in your club have these' — he brought out from his pocket a bottle of Moses' tablets — 'and we have reason to believe that you could help us to acquire them for distribution in our own country.'

Appalled, Grief still had to laugh, both at the misunderstanding, and its implications. 'You've got the wrong end of the stick,' he told them; but the expression was too idiomatic, and left them blank. The rat lit the joint, and fillings gleamed as he smiled stupidly forward through the smoke.

Before he could rephrase it, however, the cat had continued. 'Mr Grief, we are perfectly serious. Would you supply us with an agreed quantity of this drug, in exchange for a reliable supply of finest hashish?'

'That's the deal, is it?' He wondered how he could be shot of them.

'We would also require a European car, which your people

would bring to our country as a part of the exchange. It would facilitate transportation of the merchandise. I like also to drive your European cars. The Mercedes you have seen is hired; a car like that would be most welcome in my country. Such vehicles are not, at home, so easy to acquire.'

Grief struggled not to register his sighting of Bludge across the room. Mercifully, she was in plain clothes; but he noticed that she was standing beside one of the Barn's in-house cameras, cameras that filmed the best action on the floor, and replayed it on the screens around the walls. Only this camera was pointed right at where he sat, and there was no replay of what it was filming on any screen that he could see. Nor could he remember having authorised the siting of a camera on that spot. He tried to stay calm, asking the Arabs, 'Why do you want these pills? How do you know about them?' As soon as he'd found out, he'd leave them as politely as he could; he was terrified that they'd see themselves being taped.

'Do not play games, Mr Grief,' the cat said smoothly. 'You must surely know.'

He saw that the man running the camera wasn't a Barn employee. But it was too late; the man knew he'd been spotted, and was hastily packing to leave. The growing crowd milled in through the door and all around him. Bludge stood staring blankly over the floor, not noticing the man at her side kitting up and leaving. Trying not to rush, Grief said, 'I don't know a thing, really, and I'm not going to be able to help you. How come these pills are in North Africa?'

'You are disappointing me, Mr Grief.' The fat little man's face was impenetrable as ever. 'I am most surprised if you are not aware that these tablets are everywhere. My country buys them from the French hospitals. They ease the pain for our old people, and, I believe, have proved most useful also in placating our more troublesome prisoners and dissidents. But as they leak out, so obviously there grows a great demand among the young of our cities and, what do you say, bidonvilles. We should like to be in a position to meet that demand. And I believe,' he added chillingly, 'that you owe us a favour.' His smile was greased ice.

Countries in North Africa, Grief remembered, were planning new initiatives to tackle the population problem. Shaken, he stood up; stepping back, and speaking louder over the music, which had grown noisier as the club filled up, he said, trying to look compliant, 'You wait here, and I'll see what I can do.'

Bludge hadn't moved, but the cameraman beside her was gone. Holding down anger, Grief shoved his way across the floor towards her. Against the crazed variety of clothes and hair all around her, she looked conspicuously drab. He pushed off the dance floor, and up a couple of steps to beneath where she stood, gazing blindly out, her hands on the rail that stretched around the level above the throng on the floor. Grief could feel the Arabs watching him. He thanked heaven she was looking so far from being a copper, and hissed, 'Two questions, answers now. One, what were you doing with that cameraman in here?'

She peered owlishly down at him, pudgy mits gripping the rail. 'What cameraman? The one that was here? Wasn't he one of yours? Or a tourist?' Then she leant towards him, her face a wobbling caricature of urgency. 'Grief, I found out what's happening.'

Grief stared at her, and came to a decision very easily. 'Look, Bludge, I don't absolutely dislike you, OK? But I've no time to trust you, you're law. Second question. Have you got men in here, and are they armed?'

She told him: 'They're not my men, I'm not running this show any more; I'm halfway certain to be losing my job. And what does it matter when they're killing all the old people? Don't you know that it's happening? Aren't you going to *do* something?'

Trying not to let her meaning reach him, he said, 'Bludge, you're the last person I'd tell what I was going to do, and anyway I've a more immediate problem just now. I don't much care whose men it is that are armed in here, but you see those two Arabs? They're dealing in hash, and the painkillers too. Get them arrested, and be careful — they're killers.'

'Is that all you want?' she scowled. 'And what about the oldies?' He felt his guilt blossom in astonishment at her anger, and snarled at her to do her job, slipping away in confusion. The Arabs watched him cross to the far side of the floor. He climbed the steps into the starship's bridge, the space-age pulpit of the DJ's platform, and was suddenly — to their eyes mysteriously — out of sight.

The back of the platform was rack upon rack of records and

decks; the front was the control console for the lighting rig. The console projected back towards the records from the metal sheeting of the structure's façade, and beneath it was a couple of square metres of concealed space into which Grief had ducked. In the middle of the platform was a trapdoor onto a ladder which went down inside the structure to his office and the store-rooms in the basement. Grief sat on the floor of the platform, feet dangling through the trap, head down beneath the underside of the lighting desk, and stared miserably from an empty face into the cold dark iron on which his forehead rested. The first he knew of anyone joining him on the platform was a foot in a worn suede desert boot giving him a nudge. He looked up the length of a pair of faded pink trousers to see Mary, and Zeke beside her, wolfishly grinning. In the firestorm of the rig's neon explosions, their matching ginger hairstyles, cropped on top and straying wildly long behind, flashed like orange tinsel. Mary squatted down beside him and asked, 'What the fuck is the matter with you?'

'He said, 'I'm losing my bottle, is what. What are you doing here, you're not working tonight. You haven't been evicted again?'

Mary nodded. 'Usual thing. People'll look after your stuff, but no one's got floor space for your body.'

Homelessness was so common that Grief kept folding beds in the soft drinks store for any of his staff who were suffering it. 'OK,' he told her. 'You know where you can sleep.'

Zeke was hopping around the platform, looking down at the floor first on one side, then on the other. 'Hey,' he said. 'There's two guys being arrested. See, Mum — over the other side.'

'Looks like they're Arabs,' said Mary; then, when she saw Grief beginning to stand up, with relief on his face, 'Was it them you were hiding from?' And wearily he nodded.

Mary and Zeke followed him down onto the floor, where he fetched up suddenly against a seething, wet-eyed Bludge. 'You limp-wristed bastard,' she spat. 'You wait and see what a good copper can do.' And she was off, barging her way through the dancers, before he could answer.

Mary laughed. 'What on earth's up with that? I mean, that's a monster.'

Grief said, 'She's playing Laertes to my Hamlet.' But the reference was lost on her.

'Bit of a ponce, aren't you?' Zeke grinned.

SIXTY

'Fuck me,' said Wally.

'Is that it?' asked Milla. 'Is that the price I pay to an old cripple to persuade him to do something he ought to want to do anyway? You filthy old pig. You miserable, disgusting old bastard.'

Wally repeated, 'I'll edit your ad, and I'll stick it in my show — if you fuck me. Sure, oldies dying bothers me. But the end of the world I predicted an age ago, and not getting fucked in the meantime bothers me more. You got to take your chances.' He only hoped Cairo'd left him strong enough to take this on.

'When this is over,' she told him, beginning to strip, 'we're moving out. And I won't ever have to see your filthy pig bastard face again. And if you tell Grief I'll kill you.'

She undressed to the accompaniment of Silas' voice on the speakers; the Thai kid, baffling Wally, was still increasing his lead. With less than three hours of play left to go, how could Dixon ever pull it back? He watched her body as it came out of the clothes; in the dark blue room, the green of the snooker washed off the screens and over her flesh. She had on suspenders; his cock twitched and rose. She said, 'Lie back, slob, you'll get it how it's given.' She was thinking, grimly, she'd make sure that he'd do what he'd said. The delicious skinniness of her frame made her seem enormously tall; small firm breasts jiggled as she stepped out of her knickers, and her bush was a thick mound around the entrance to the slender cave of her stomach. For years now he'd thought of this, staring at the screens, dreaming, with the crackling, stoned little lights in his eyes just flickering, flickering away on the seabed, an angling fish with his electric bait. His body shifted on the ocean floor; hers floated above him, light and drifting like a bubble through the murky fug.

She threw aside the sheets and pulled him out of his pyjamas, roughly shoving at the atrophied leg. He winced, but was too excited to complain. His body was sallow, white, flabby. Sparse black hair looked weak and patchy on his chest and stomach. The old grey cock strained up, unaccustomed to being this stiff. Standing above him, she turned, emptying her head — easy enough, with the anaesthetic gallons of wine that she'd got through, knowing, after all, that this was coming — and then she ducked rapidly down to kneel, one long thin boy's thigh on either side of Wally's head. She went down on her elbows, and a hot thrill went through him as she cradled his balls and sank his cock deep into her mouth. Her cunt was dry. It diminished him, her strength and efficiency. She pressed herself down on his face, smothering, saying through her foully full mouth, 'Eat that, and I hope you choke on it.' She rubbed herself on his chin until his jaw ached, and each was unaware of the other's relief as she finally managed to get herself wet.

Helpless, Wally wondered if that was what the sudden illusion of power could do to you. He wondered if Nanny got this way, feeling the people held down hard beneath her. Hell, he thought, but uneasily, it's my treat. He soaked his thumb in her juice and pushed it up her arsehole, heat rushing up his thighs at the sight of the tight brown flesh resisting and giving. Her buttocks were tiny peaches, soft, firm, meatless. He gripped them, shoving them down so his mouth and nose could get out for air. She misunderstood, pushed herself up, pivoted round, clambered over his cock, and sank herself onto it with a look of pure violence. He came almost immediately.

'Pathetic,' she said, and strode quickly to the bathroom to clean herself up. And when she came back, she said simply, 'Now let's talk timetables.'

She was refusing him a victory. Admiring her, he realised that all memory of pleasure had already been stolen from him. She'd made pure business of the use of her body. Struggling to score a point back, he said, 'Not yet, lover.' He grinned, without shame. 'I've got a snooker game to watch first.' She turned on him furiously, but he held up his hand. 'If you want to save your precious people from the monsters of the Money,' he snidely suggested, 'you got to make the odd sacrifice, know what I mean?'

'Alright,' she gritted, restraining herself; she couldn't look at him, he was smugness incarnate. She felt filthy, and relieved,

Wally saw it. She forced herself again to think business, business, the business in hand; she sat down, still naked, on the bed beside him.

'Tomorrow,' said Wally, putting an arm around her to enjoy the way it made her shrink and shiver, 'I will put together the last shift of the final. On Friday morning, 147 will whip round the thing your Trolly is shooting to replace the official law and order slot. And I won't put it in, because tomorrow night we'll have sewn something up out of whatever you've shot instead. Then I'll tell them my edit box had gremlins, but not to worry, I've ironed them out, and the finished shift will be with them by five. So they don't get time to look it over. How's that for a timetable?'

With the volume down, Silas' voice came distant and faint. She looked at the screen, then nodded, resigned, and demanded a joint. The paleness of his skin that had revolted her so was, she realised, little different to the colour of her own. And the flopping about of his loose old belly was, after all, soft and cushiony; she lay on it, and found it comfortable. Now the job was done, his unhealthiness began to fascinate her; tired, she nestled down into it, and asked, 'What's on 147 tomorrow?'

'Tomorrow,' Wally told her, wriggling with pleasure, 'is Ladies' Day. There's the junkies, Tina, the God squad, and the bozo that's taken over from Thor, all doing shifts on a sudden death women's tourney. Then at midnight through to six on Friday morning, the acidhead's on with a suitably deranged recap of the championship's finest moments. The final starts at six with whoever's supposed to be replacing Silas, then the Scottish kid's on from noon, and it's me to finish. Here, pass me the remote, will you. I want to hear Silas die.'

She murmured, 'You're an evil piece of shit, aren't you?' He pressed volume, and Silas' voice grew louder. The Thai kid was running another big break; it was up in the seventies, and certainly another frame-winner. 'You don't know your snooker, either, do you? I thought you said the Thai kid was nowhere. Then he puts out the Peruvian, and look at him now.'

'Everyone makes mistakes,' said Wally, holding her to him with a horrid imitation of affection, distorted by the complacency of finally having had her.

Silas was blurring on about the Thai kid's strange, jerky style. 'Kung Fu snooker,' he chortled, 'these funny little yellow people, who knows what they'll come up with next? Robots, I don't doubt.' His voice was a rolling wheel of smoothness, oiled with rum and brandy, deep and warm. Dixon fluffed a long shot, leaving the white awkwardly tucked up on a red near the side cushion; but another red was on for the Thai, parked nicely over a centre pocket if he could just get the white cleanly away. 'Don't think he'll have much trouble with that,' Silas gurgled, 'the way he's playing tonight. They've got fingers of rubber, these orientals. Must be all that yoga.'

The picture cut away from the position on the table to the waiting Thai. Flat-faced and squash-nosed, he was standing beside his chair, gazing at the table from afar as if in a dream. Silas cheerfully encouraged him. 'That's it, boy, you have a think about it. He's meditating, my friends,' he continued, while the camera closed in on the expressionless slanted eyes. They rolled up, the whites showing briefly; then he darted like an insect to the table, bending over the felt at the end of his sudden fluid run.

'Shit,' Milla blurted, woken up from a private consideration of whether being in Wally's bed was really so bad. 'I thought you said he was a kid. He's a midget, maybe, but if he's a day, he's forty.'

'He's probably got eczema, honey, Bangkok is hardly the globe's most savoury town. Did you know, it's the only place where the junkies come top in 147's foreign charts? But I promise, he's only nineteen.' Wally thought he looked older, too; he'd thought so for days.

The camera closed in on the kid forming a bridge over the red ball. The fingers craned up, pressed down and bent, with the index held up off the green for the cue, which rested on it and angled just a touch as the kid sought his line. The picture cut to his face, dry, worn-out, not giving away anything as the huge-pupilled eyes flickered; then the mouth slowly opened in a dazed sort of smile, and the eyes went still, looking down, fixed on the hand. The camera tracked back down to follow his stare, and found the skin of the three fingers that were pressed onto the felt splitting across the front of the knuckles where it was stretched the most. Flesh and blood dribbled out onto the immaculate surface of the table. Milla gagged. 'Good Lord,' Silas belched, then groaned in sudden pain; he cut hastily to a Val Doonican video, but you could hear through the crooning the chokes and gasps as he died.

Wally yelped, 'What the fuck did they show that for?'

'I think,' said Grief, who had silently come in and now stared at naked Milla, 'they're worried that it's getting out of hand. So maybe they're taking a new approach. And you, Milla Sharply — I see the same goes for you.' She saw the dull pain in his face, and didn't know where to hide. But he only shook his head, and went out of the room, out of the flat, out of the building. Millions are dying, he thought, and my girlfriend is fucking a snooker commentator. Sure, he wanted blood. But it wasn't the blood of the Cabinet he wanted. Over Milla's shoulder, he'd seen that same nasty old smile on Wally's face.

SIXTY-ONE

Cairo curled in a damp stone corner, trying to pretend that his cellmates didn't exist. None of them was friendly, and two of them were dying. These last, a pair of senile teenage girls, weren't friendly, because they weren't really there. As Marl had done, they stared smiling into the darkness, ignoring the stench, the noise of chains and metal bars, the echo of iron-heeled footsteps, and the wailing of useless class war slogans. Idly they twirled their thumbs, and lived out the end of their lives in a cotton wool heaven. Cairo couldn't bear to go near them, for fear they'd fall into pieces and spray more blood all over him.

One of the other two had seemed friendly at first, approaching Cairo and asking if he'd like a bit of fun. Then he'd taken out his cock, and made appalling suggestions. Cairo'd split his lip for him; he'd beetled back, whimpering, and now stared acidly from the far corner of the cell, plotting vengeance with dried blood on his chin. He was whispering with another of those thuggish white T-shirt unemployables, a man who was in, because, idiotically, he'd broken the skulls of rich Pakis instead of poor ones. The gay and the NF yob made strange conspirators, but they'd come to agreement in adversity after sharing the same space behind bars for four months. Technically, this was a waiting cell; you waited in it for a trial. You might as well have waited for Godot.

Cairo looked round as one of the girls dreamily muttered, 'You know, I think it might be time soon.' She was peering intently at cracking skin on her elbows, both arms held out and turned over in front of her.

The other girl smiled and said, 'It'll be nice, won't it?'

Please God, thought Cairo, don't fall apart while I'm here. Who was responsible for all this? The foul hurtful hours spent jeered at and shoved about by policemen — all of whom wanted to take a turn at him, for attempting the murder of a popular entertainer — and now the long slow hours of this clanking, stinking room, with its devils and dead people for occupants, had broadened immeasurably the range and scope of his desire to murder. Cairo wanted to cause explosions, to see uniformed bits and pieces of the state's representatives flung skywards in muddy great eruptions of blood and shattered bone.

Dwayne, it was true, had tried to help. He'd tried to keep him safely stowed for Bludge to talk to whenever she might get back. But Bludge by now counted for very little. From the Election Section right through to Traffic Control, they'd been forming queues to fuck him around. He was bruised all over.

The white T-shirt came lumping across, and tapped him on the shoulder. 'My friend,' he then oafishly grinned, 'is really upset you won't play with him.' Cairo sighed. He stood up to face the blotchy great moron from his corner; they were about the same height, and Cairo was probably fitter, but he'd been knocked about enough, and was in no kind of mood to be fighting. The other man, however, was just dying for it.

'Hey, peace and love,' giggled one of the girls.

The yob told her, 'Shut your gob, dead-head.'

He jabbed Cairo in the chest with a sharp hard finger, and Cairo fell slightly back against the dirty grey wall. Again, the yob told him, sneering, that his friend would have liked to play ball.

Here goes, thought Cairo. But why me? What did I ever do to anyone, ever? The thug raised a fist — then there was a massive rattling of keys behind them, and the door banged open.

'Come on, you,' said Bludge to Cairo. 'Come and tell me what you thought you were doing.'

She led him away past another cell, where the two Arabs

185

were waiting, not for a trial, but for a lawyer. They didn't know it, but by the time of the Last Election, they were as likely to find one in an English jail, as they would have been back home.

SIXTY-TWO

Grief lay on the couch of his sound-proofed office in the basement of the Barn. He hadn't slept. Perhaps the noise upstairs might have been more sheltering than the padded silence in which he'd hid himself, watching numbers count minutes on a digital display above his desk — but he couldn't bear to see the people dancing. Beneath the display there was a picture of Milla; and a golden arrow she'd been awarded for the early Barn commercials at some European adfest in Cannes. Predictably, the citation had described them as 'right on target'. The Americans present had jibbed at the award, not understanding the way the ads worked, finding them distasteful, and offended that political or social comment should have stained in any way the purity of their art. Client and writer had laughed at their umbrage, and gone down to the beach, playing boules on the way with a ragged gang of kids who had, naturally, demanded money — and who had, on that occasion, naturally, been given some. He remembered she had worn all white that day, and her black hair had shone like a panther's coat.

At first, as he'd lain on the couch, his side growing cold against the bare brick wall, and his face pale in the one dim striplight, people had come down from the bars and the stalls to ask what he had to sell that night, or whether there was anything he was keen to buy. Monosyllabically, he'd put them off, until he'd thought to lock the door, and pretend he wasn't there. He'd spent half an hour mechanically running a stock check, for no good reason; and the hour after that just watching the screen as it clacked its way through the flurry of green digits, the computerised tills upstairs neatly knocking each unit of sale off the central store files. He made a note to get the bar manager to order more white wine and Pernod; there was, at the time of the Last Election, a big vogue running for Death in the Afternoon — in Grief's opinion, a singularly hideous drink. Then, suddenly aware of his boredom, he yanked out the floppy discs that ledgered all the bar business, and stuffed in some games instead. He played Missile Command; but defending the earth was always, finally, impossible against the ever faster waves of incoming warheads, and the cities of the world were repeatedly obliterated in little white mushroom clouds of static. He headed off across the galaxies in game after game, zapping alien warships, strange phoenix birds, chattering monsters and cosmic guerrillas. Then he played map adventures. 'You are at a crossroads. There is a wood to the north, desert to the west and south, and a high cliff rising in the east'. He printed, Go north. The screen told him, 'Three trolls leap out from behind a tree and hack you to death with their axes'. Uh-huh. So he played El Presidente instead, and successfully ran the economy of a small Central American state for twenty-four years. But sooner or later the pollution always got you; foreign industry got rapacious, the tourism dried up, the people got hungry, and off you went yet again to the plaza to be beheaded. He retreated to the simplicities of Hamburger, in which he played a chef, dropping buns onto salad and beef, and chased all the while by animated fried eggs and red peppers. As the game got harder, gherkins joined the hunt; it was always the gherkins that nabbed him. The chef lay down on his back, little brown legs sticking up in the air from out of his neat white coat, pathetically wiggling, while all around him devilishly triumphant green slices of pickle oscillated horribly. Grief gave up and played the racing driver game, zooming endlessly through the night past shimmering little cactus graphics. The photo of Milla stared down at him. He looked at it one time too many, and lay back down on the couch, stretching his fingers back to crack the knuckles; inside his clothes, he felt the sweat of a night without sleep.

The clock on the wall said five-thirty. The club would have been empty for maybe an hour now. He stepped out into the concrete basement and slowly made his way, hand on red rails, down the dirty grey corridors, past dressing rooms, storerooms, cupboards and crates. Red paint flaked on the brickwork of warm, ill-lit passageways; the building's old boilers hummed and rumbled behind the walls. Heavily he clambered up the rusty iron ladder to the trap in the base of the DJ's platform; he unlocked it and slipped through, then stood to survey his kingdom. But what power has a king, when his queen is full of serpents, and unfaithful?

All the lights were on, and the detritus of the night's massed pleasures littered the floor and tables, illuminated white in ugly sharp-edged detail. Broken glass, cigarette ends and roaches, crumbs of pastry and burger, half-finished drinks, lost notes and coins, stains on the carpet, used needles, blunted razor blades, pools of candlewax, spent matches, mislaid lighters, empty rolling beer cans and bottles, ash, tobacco, ticket stubs, tablets, an audio cassette from which the tape had unspooled and spilt away off a table's edge, its magnetic shine dulled where it lay in a drying smear of frothy black liquid, a dirty playing card that showed a woman wincing as she fucked herself with a whip handle, a ripped old pair of espadrilles, a couple of handbags emptied out and then dropped by thieves, bits of paper with boys' and girls' addresses, lost now for ever, combs, lipsticks, dried out scent bottles, a shattered hand mirror, a passport photo of a loved one, half-torn ... the old women cleaners in their nylon coats moved among the tables with dustpans, linerbags, and vacuum cleaners.

Grief passed among them, distributing fivers as an 'election bonus'. The skin beneath his eyes felt tight and heavy. His clothes, he noticed, were crumpled — uncool. He'd have to go home and change. Home. He stood in the middle of the empty dance floor, and peered up into the twisted chaos of bulbs, strips and neons in the mighty lighting rig. You could see, in the houselights, how dusty it was. Would have to do something about that ... then he heard soft laughter from near the bar that ran round behind the railings above the varnished wooden floor. He walked up to the bar front, some part of him still pleased at the gleam of the chrome, the polished cleanliness of the tiled floor and the shining pumps, the tidy full stocking up of new bottles on the cold shelves — he had good barmen, they left their work stations immaculate every night. He heard the laughter again. It was coming from behind the white door of a soft drinks storeroom, and he recognised Mary's light voice.

He hopped backwards off the floor and onto the bar top, swung his legs over, and dropped to the tiles on the other side, quiet in his soft shoes. Then he opened the storeroom door, still making no noise — not meaning to sneak up, but it just happened that way. Mary was on an empty lime-green lemonade crate, with her back to the door. She still had on her sleeveless grey T-shirt; he saw a trickle of blood running down one white arm where she'd obviously just fixed up. A knotted leather strap lay on the floor by her feet. Just that minute put down, a ruby-stained hypo rolled slowly back and forth across the top of a cardboard case of mineral water. Beside it, lying on its side, was an empty medicine bottle. A couple of Moses' big tablets were spilled out at the bottle's neck. Mary turned, faintly shaking with the soft desperation of her laughter, her eyes shrunk to pin-points. In her lap lay the body of her son. She gestured at the empty bottle and said, 'He must have got up and found them some time when I was sleeping. And thought they were sweets. They do taste nice, too.' She stared at him, not seeing, smiling, cradling her dead boy in her bony lap. Their ginger hair looked flat and pale in the bright white light. The blood dried on her arm, and her veins showed violent blue. She asked him, 'Who will look after me now?'

Grief thought, when life isn't worth anything, there's no harm in risking it.

THURSDAY

SIXTY-THREE

Quickly awake in her lonely bed, Milla said, 'I promise you, really, that I hated every minute. But it had to be done.'

'Don't talk about it. It's quarter past six. Get up and get your camera ready, you —' he stared at her as if she was a stranger, a spy on a ridge; then walked out of the bedroom to where Moses, woken up when he'd come in, was waiting with Suzie in front of the TV. The screen showed Nanny dismounting from a helicopter; eager junior officers helped her down, and her hairdo wobbled in the wind of the blades. Behind them, Mary lay pin-eyed and semi-conscious on the sofa, sipping gin to perfect her isolation, and studying with frightening detachment a polaroid of Zeke's body. The body itself, pockets full of bricks, rested now on the bed of the Thames.

Grief asked, 'Moses, you fit?'

Moses hobbled himself up onto his feet and coughed, 'I'm game.' Then Milla whipped through the room towards her study, resplendent in crisply zecky black, white and gold. Grief winced at her beauty. Halfway through, she did a double-take at prone Mary, and turned on him to demand how many more outcasts and junkies he planned on housing in her sitting room.

'It's my sitting room,' he told her. 'And better a junkie in it than a whore.' They stared each other out; to his surprise, he won. She shrugged, and went to get her camera. Grief locked up his cash and valuables in his safe — the trusting type — and told Suzie on the way out, 'Make yourself at home, the fridge is full.' As an afterthought, he added, absurdly, 'And don't let Mary get you out of it.'

Milla looked at him, this time sadly. 'You think everyone with tits is an alkie now, don't you?' Thinking of the smack in Mary's pocket, it wasn't what he'd meant, and he ignored her. She was last out, and Suzie stared after her in admiration. Then she ran a bath, because she wanted to grow up like Milla, and that meant clean and smart. And on the way out Milla had indeed been, all of a sudden, brimming over — she was getting her way, no matter how or why, or with what amount of loss.

The drive to the hospital was reasonably quick; few cars were out this early, though the dawn was already sharp and hot. The gates hadn't yet been opened, and a handful still queued on the pavement outside. The more mobile among them perked up and made a bid to get in as Moses fed his plastic ident into the slot provided, punched numbers, and the gates slid open. But the security men had them quickly thrown out again.

Grief parked, and, quaking and light-footed, scrawny Moses led Milla from the car into the brightly lit foyer. The building's windows still glowed, animal eyes in the dry first light. Striding across the tarmac, she looked great, super-confident, a dragon-killer. The video pack hanging by her side was seemingly weightless — she had, of course, the latest compact model. She wore a loud badge proclaiming 'Money Publicity', and carried in her pockets a stack of accreditations.

Grief felt nothing. He sat in the car awhile, then, screwing up courage, he headed up the stairs and into the buildings after them. Passing the front desk, he muttered the name of the nurse he had to see, then moved silently down virtually empty corridors. Oldies were beginning to totter out of bed to find their way to the canteen, or coming back already from the early sitting. Hugging the sides of the passages, those still equipped with arms brushed spilt food off their faces as they shuffled back to bed, and their trembling nails flaked little rockslides of dried green paint off the walls as they went. When he found the ward he wanted, Grief saw that Fiona's bed was occupied by an old man, sleeping. There was no bump in the sheets, where his feet should have been.

In the nurse's office, Grief stood shifting from foot to foot while she briskly finished off a busy burst of form-filling and chart-marking, then loaded little cups with batches of capsules. The first dose of the day — he saw again that every cup included the painkiller, though only, now, in its weakest version. Little by little, he thought, little by little.

'So, Mr Grief,' said the nurse, looking up at last. 'It's taken you a while to come back, now hasn't it? It's a good thing we're understaffed, or I'd not have been in for an hour yet. Still, we mustn't complain, must we? And it's getting better every day. Anyway, I hope you're feeling better yourself. What can I do for you?'

'Yeah, look, I'm really sorry. . . .' He wasn't acting. He didn't feel angry, just numb.

She pressed him, 'I quite understand, it must have been very upsetting for you. Now how can I help you?'

He stated flatly, 'It's that form you mentioned.'

'Good,' she jabbed, unanswerably conclusive. She fished out the little white cards, laid her pen ready, and said, 'Setting aside yesterday's little performance, I believe you said you weren't very close to the young lady. Is that so?'

'Yes.' He felt himself wilting, and wished there was a chair; perhaps, the day before, he'd broken the only one.

'Well, I must tell you straightforwardly that she is, sadly, no longer with us. I'm afraid she didn't have the strength to get through the operation.' What operation? Rip it off, bandage it up, chuck it in the fire . . . she'd picked up her pen and was ready to write, but he didn't offer any response. She explained, 'It was the road accident that killed her. She declined unusually quickly, compared to the norm in these cases.'

Without emotion, he said, 'That's OK then, isn't it?'

'Please Mr Grief. I realise that the death of a friend is not a happy thing, but we'll all be best off in the circumstances if we accept it, and help things to run along as smoothly as we can. Do you agree?' He nodded, mutely. 'If you would like,' she went on, 'we can arrange a cremation for three pm today. Would that suit you? You understand, the service has only just been introduced. I suspect that in a week or two we'll be rather heavily subscribed, as people come to realise what we can do for them. So it's best to move now, wouldn't you say, Mr Grief?'

'Three this afternoon is fine. Where do we go?' She told him, handing over a crisp white appointment card with the time and place filled in in a clear, hard hand. He said, 'It's just like going to the dentist really, isn't it?'

She looked up and smiled after him as he left, thinking to herself that the Lord was indeed that efficient.

SIXTY-FOUR

Grief sat tucked down in the driver's seat. Once, a plain white van came; he watched as it hummed quietly, waiting, until a full set of body bags had been ferried out and into it. Then the yard was empty again. He looked away, and turned on the radio.

The stock markets were booming. From the information centres in Docklands, Swindon and Aberdeen, reactions to the latest monetary forecasts were universally and joyfully optimistic. Interviewed by radiophone as they prowled from deal to deal down country lanes in their Jags, brokers enthused about the economic prospects. Pension fund managers were particularly cheerful — Grief thought, all that money, and no one left for them to share it out with. On the money markets, the pound was soaring against the whole basket of currencies, even, which was unheard of, the yen. All the world's plum holiday locations were busily preparing for an unprecedented influx of suddenly monied English pop stars, football players, television technicians and genetic engineers. The advertising people, Grief bitterly smiled, will no longer be able to feel so exclusive.

Pundits made strange projections about property investors being better able to serve the market in young married and single parents. (There you go, Mary, they'll give you a luxury self-contained.) And a predicted up-rating in social security benefits might well, they suggested, herald a rise in the number of clubs, cafés, and other meeting places catering for the young — we could all look forward to seeing the streets less crowded and more stylish. Hurray. And, thought Grief, that's me out of business. At least his pounds in the Swiss bank account would be clocking up growth like — insects mutating under radiation.

There had been, it seemed, sporadic civil disturbances in the red towns of the north. (So what else is new?) A previously unknown group of hard-core Trotskyists calling themselves the 'Friends of the Sick' had been 'contained'. The situation was well under control. Grief extrapolated. The Friends of the Sick had been truncheoned witless, and the red towns sealed off by the military (again). The point of this item was that

People spokesmen had refused to condemn the violence, attacking instead what they called (disdainful pause) 'police brutality'. Their poll ratings had consequently hit an all-time low. Money voices were then wheeled on to announce major programmes of public works. And artists were to be sponsored to paint 'uplifting' murals in deprived areas. The Money polls were sky-high. There was brief mention of isolated outbreaks of an unknown new disease in two or three hospitals — apparently, government scientists suspected the virus was sourced in the Far East, and were naturally working flat out to identify it. In the sports news — with no connection being made overtly — it was suggested that the Thai kid, a 'hopeless drug addict', had been 'sick for weeks'.

Grief contemplated other possible futures. The sherry market was in for a terminal decline, that was certain. He wondered what kind of problems that might cause in Andalucia. But doubtless some Hispanic equivalent of Milla was already writing up the blurb for wonderful new Facil-Dormir with some appropriate cultural slant like 'it respects your old folk'. Then a late news flash told him that, following the discovery of subversive literature on their premises, both Help The Aged and Age Concern had been closed down until such time as the DPP had evaluated their cases. Grief switched off the radio.

Milla and Moses came running towards the car through the growing heat. Milla's run was long and light, unencumbered by her equipment. Moses struggled to keep up, shaking through the whole length of his body as each foot hit the ground; he had a pathetic look of eagerness, fighting to overcome the effort that showed in his face. They tumbled into the car, and Milla's breathing behind him seemed quick and small, sexually excited. Moses collapsed onto the front seat beside him, lacking the strength even to cough, and his breath only just made it out through the wall of phlegm in his throat. He fumbled in a pocket with what seemed to Grief exaggerated care, or even secretiveness — but then, the pockets were all crammed with bits and pieces of chemicals and electrics for the bomb — and, after swallowing a fistful of the antidote, said, 'I was, frankly, scared to death.'

'But I inspired you,' Milla announced, 'and you were wonderful.' She sounded to Grief exactly like the radio. He punched the ignition, the engine clicked up and turned, and he slid it into gear and rolled off, grimly wordless. After a while, Milla curtly asked him, 'Don't you want to know what we got?' He stared ahead for potholes, not answering.

She told him anyway, 'We got the lot. There were these wards, right, whole wards full of people missing limbs, arms, legs, the works — you're not supposed to go into those, but Moses sorted it out. He told so many brilliant stories, I began to wonder whether we shouldn't let him write the ad. Public information film, that's what he said we were doing. Too true. Then we did the furnace room. We kept quiet in a corner till we got good shots of a body going down, then we ripped open a few of the bags, and out spilt all these bits, shit, Grief, unbelievable, tits, heads, fingers, fucking bits of rabbit even, and rats, there's even rats in those bags, boy, it was the grossest.'

Moses chipped in, 'You know what? They're laying down my drug for the rats.' He laughed wildly, and then shook uncontrollably. As soon as he could speak again, he croaked, 'Get me back, I'm loose all over.'

Grief continued to drive in silence. Piqued, Milla pressed at him. 'Don't you think it sounds good? Great material, right?'

Without turning round Grief quietly said, 'You're sick as they are. You think the whole bloody world only happens on TV. And you're just wet between the legs about it, aren't you? It really turns you on, doesn't it?'

She screamed, 'Of course, you jerk. Because it's the most valuable, the best fucking ad I'll ever make. Show this to the people and bob's your uncle, riots and revolution, no more Money.'

'For fuck's sake,' Grief then spat, suddenly furious, 'ads do not bring down governments. Can you never get anything you do in perspective?' But both Milla and Moses just quietly smiled, and he felt locked out, little better than a chauffeur. Doing, he thought bitterly, his duty. Stone-faced, he listened to them, like children, excitedly discussing their morning's work.

And Crinkly said on the phone to the hospital administrator, 'Did you let her get everything she wanted?' When the voice replied yes, he said, 'I hope at least you made the silly little bitch work for it.'

SIXTY-FIVE

'Cut,' screamed Laz, forced to do so by the cretin in front of the camera one time too many for his volatile, coke-fuelled temper. Tripping over cables in his haste, he stormed across the studio past smirking chippies and lighting men to where Nanny sat brightly lit in a mock-up of a cozy living room. He put one hand down on the chintzy arm of her chair, and, leaning over her with bulging eyes, pronounced through gritted teeth that 'This is not just another we-are-doing-very-well, OK? This is an EVENT. Will you please put just a little bit of FEELING into it.'

'Oh dear,' said Nanny, which, unscripted, was about all she could manage, by the time of the Last Election. She hesitantly suggested, 'But the words aren't much different from the usual,' and looked up at him hopefully. Laz rolled his eyes to the ceiling; he consoled himself by thinking of the size of the invoice he'd be issuing come Saturday.

In the glass-panelled office overlooking the studio floor, Crinkly smiled. Behind him, the runner was playing games with a calculator. Events, thought Crinkly, had overtaken the boy; he had taken to wearing his black leather in public. The runner looked up nervously from his thin card of buttons and silicon, and told him, 'The census people tell me we've 1,508,000 women and 661,000 men above the age of eighty. So if we conservatively estimate a quarter of those to be one way or another directly in our care, that's 542,250 geriatrics the state should shortly be relieved of. Now, taking the admittedly meaningless mean cost of a state bed at £200 a day, we find an overall daily saving of nearly £110,000,000.' He looked anxiously triumphant, and added, 'That figure obviously doesn't include savings on social security to all those disgusting drug addict teenagers we've eliminated, or indeed the terminally ill and the hopelessly injured. Not to mention that percentage of pensioners whom we got to with GP prescriptions.'

Crinkly turned to reply, 'I can only say thank god you people put a stop to that. It's a close enough thing as it is, without having to explain to a few million more people how come their limbs are falling off, when all they're suffering is arthritis and the common cold.'

The runner reassured himself by repeating, '£110,000,000 a day.'

'Should be able to make a lot of jobs with that sort of money.' Crinkly clung to this straw as the proportions of the problem grew more alarming by the day. If it could only all have happened a little more slowly. . . .

With uncharacteristic vulgarity, the runner spat out, 'Screw jobs. We've got a missile programme to pay for.'

Crinkly sighed, 'You people just don't know the meaning of the word promise, do you?' Then he snidely pointed out, 'Better write off the cost of all those cremations, before you go buying yourself any more of your pointy-tipped virility symbols.'

The runner snapped back, 'And the outrageous cost of all this extra promotional work.'

Oh dear, as Nanny might say — the tensions at the top.

Laz, who was making a considerable contribution to the above-mentioned expenses, came crashing in, no mean feat with a door padded for sound-proofing, and wailed, 'She's hopeless. I can't do anything with the wretched bloody woman. She can't act to save her life.'

Crinkly soothed, 'Calm down, Laz, calm down. She's not meant to act, she's that way naturally. I mean, I know she's not as good as she used to be; but just tell her a few stories about commies eating children, and pervert lefties getting grants off the state to bugger each other in public and call it art, and you'll see — you'll soon get the fire in her eyes. By the way, nice idea of yours, that sideline on Grief and the girl.' A little flattery, he could see, was in order at this difficult time.

'Fuck that,' said Laz, slumping in a chair and cutting up an enormous line on the mirror-topped coffee table. The runner stared in disgust, and then made to knock the precious powder off the table. Laz smashed him full-fisted in the chest, yelling, 'What the fuck is the matter with you?' and the runner fell back wheezing. Crinkly scurried over, explaining that Laz was an artist. The artist muttered, as his eyes wildly widened, 'Roll on the live stuff. This studio lark is pure claustrophobia.'

Then he banged off back down to have another bash at Nanny.

She said, 'Good evening to you. Now the persons we have just mentioned. . . .' And she seemed, this time, to be getting some guts into the business.

Crinkly, pleased, looked back from the window overlooking the studio to the runner, who was pretending not to wring his hands, and told him happily, 'You're wetting yourself, aren't you?' Little sod asks for a miracle, and when you give him one, what does he do? He pisses his pants. Silly, really — none of the people who mattered would now be going to the meeting, except for himself. And for himself, well, you just had to put your faith in the technicians and their gizmos, didn't you? Otherwise, in the modern world, where would you be? The thing that bothered Crinkly the most was whether Laz meant it, when he said he didn't mind directing the death of an old friend. And, of course, the budget, which was indeed absolutely outrageous.

SIXTY-SIX

'Dying forests.'
'Poisoned farmland.'
'Crumbling stonework.'
'Noxious rivers.'
'Acid rain,'
'Sewage on the seashore.'
'Bugs in the bathroom.'
'Lowered crop yields.'
'Tuberculosis, bronchitis, pneumoconiosis.'
'Vision defects in children.'
'Digestive ailments.'
'Skin afflictions.'
'. . . Fuck, there goes Grief.'

Miles Greenback and his partner Milo sat parked in a car down the street from Wally's block. They were considering the state of the nation, pollution-wise, in a frenzy of speed-induced angst, when they looked up to see the object of their vigil halfway up the steps with Milla and Moses, and through the front door already — so they'd missed their chance. Despondent, Miles leant forward over the dash and sniffed a pre-cut line of white powder up a banknote into mucus-runny nostrils. Sneezing ferociously as a few more capillaries burst and the sulphate seared up the ravaged passages, he slumped back; then he clenched the steering wheel, and stared forward down the empty street with a seething intensity. He told his white-faced partner, 'This is the stupidest job we ever got sent on.'

'Better sitting here doing fuck all than trawling round some stenchy hospital with that hashbrain Trolly.' Milo was enormously relieved not to be filming cremations. He rammed some dangerously up-tempo dance music into the car stereo, and writhed to the beat in the passenger seat.

Miles and Milo were almost certainly Crinkly Crisp's least productive employees, but, being sole son and heir of the late and greatly missed Jason Greenback, Miles had to be kept on a wage to prevent him from screwing around with his holding. He was in fact too busy screwing around with his body to worry about his shares; but the board wasn't to know that. Only production knew it, who were well used to re-shooting just about everything that Miles and Milo ever did. Their pictures kept coming back tinged with unexpected reds and greens, or partially obliterated by patches of flare, so that faces lurched in and out of vision round huge glowing sunspots; or the sound would be so bad that all you could hear, during what was supposed to be voxpop street talk, was Milo muttering paranoically about carbon monoxide over a heavy grumbling of the dying traffic. Right now, as the only spare crew left — all the good ones being busy setting up for far more important locations — Laz had despatched them to the City to try, on the offchance, for a little extra dirt. And none was forthcoming.

Miles couldn't take the pace of the music. He hurled open the driver's door and hip-hopped out onto the pavement, wriggling in the hot air, and kneading obsessively at the bags beneath his eyes in the bright light. Then he did a funky rooster round the front of the car, stiff-legged and straight-backed and strutting to the bass, which thumped out so loud the car was shaking. (Laz had begged them, look inconspicuous.) When he got round to his partner's window, he leant down, clenching white knuckles round the door handle, and said, 'We won't get sod all pictures, just sitting here like a pair of coppers — let's go poke about.' Milo, whose freedom to dance while parked on his bum in the car was severely restricted, was happy to agree. He transferred the tape to his Walkman, strapped himself into the phones, and hopped wild-eyed down the pavement behind his leader, looking about him like a soldier moving down a sniper-riddled street.

Up in the flat, Grief watched and listened while Moses, exhausted, collapsed into sleep, and Milla, compensating in advance in case the picture quality of what she'd shot turned out to be poor, justified her mouth off at him. 'Wobbly hand-held stuff, fuzzy picture, dodgy colour — but we won't be short on meat, whatever it looks like.' Even when she'd gone up to Wally's to play it back, to see what she could use, what the edit machine could do with it, and how she could write a script that'd work with the serviceable pictures, the flat wasn't free of the crackle of her nerves on the air. Miserably, Grief realised he still had four hours to kill before they went, he shuddered, 'on location' again.

Mary lay catatonic in front of the wildlife channel. To the sound of saw-toothed mandibles crunching brittle carapace, large mutant insects on irradiated Pacific atolls ate each other in dripping slo-mo close-up. Suzie kept her back to the screen; Grief studied the torn filthiness of her shirt and skirt, and, keen to get out, asked her, 'You need new clothes. You want to go shopping?' She nodded yes, and asked him where Milla bought hers. Half-smiling, Grief groaned, and headed for the lift; Suzie followed, grinning in anticipation. While they'd been out, she'd examined Milla's underwear, and her head was awash with dreams of lace and silk. Mary smiled behind them, and a fist-sized beetle sliced into the dead flesh of a seabird.

Giving off a static field of wariness you could have seen from half a mile off, Miles tap-footed past the building's gleaming front glass, then stopped to peer down the ramp into the car port. At his shoulder, quaking to the beat, Milo slapped his microphone arhythmically against his thigh; he nodded manically and muttered, 'Moody, yeah, I like it.' As they gazed into the shadows, there came behind them the windy swish of oiled doors opening; footsteps hit the stairs out and into the road, and Grief's voice coolly suggested to Suzie that there were better role models in the world than Milla.

Stuck a metre or two down the ramp, Miles looked about

him, speedily gaping and whispering in a panic, 'Where can we hide?' Oblivious in his headset, Milo jigged, jogged, and bobbled to the beat.

Spying another handout, the crazy old woman popped up like a jack-in-the-box in bandages from her bed amid the garbage; Miles jumped out of his skin. She told him, cackling, 'You can hide in here.' Grimacing with distaste, Miles grabbed Milo by the elbow and hauled him into the stinking alcove, hastily re-arranging the ramparts of refuse behind them as he went. Then he poked out the camera's snout between bags, and, squinting, just managed to get Grief and Suzie holding hands as they turned onto the top of the ramp, silhouetted against the daylight. He followed them down as they walked past together, nice and close.

Grief was ribbing Suzie, saying, 'Really, chuck, I don't think I want to be seen buying you exotic lingerie, OK? Would you try to be just a little bit more practical?'

Miles pursed his lips, eyebrows up, and whistled through his blood-gummed teeth. As Grief's car roared up past them, he turned to Milo and asked, 'How about that then? Did you tape what he just said?'

But Milo was bursting out of the rubbish dump and screaming, 'Pollution, fuck, jesus, pollution.' Where he'd squatted down bopping on his haunches beside the giggling crone, the battery back on his waist had slashed open a linerbag; old salad, cereal and coleslaw had spewed out all over his lap. Grains of rice and strips of white sticky cabbage were spattered all over the mike. Miles imagined his fab six second tracking shot of Grief and Suzie backed by the sound of an avalanche of health food. Milo frantically flicked raisins off his flies.

Like a backward native on an island suddenly invaded by tourists, the old woman waved her withered palms in Miles' face, expecting money. Ungraciously he snarled, 'What the fuck's up with you?' He pushed his way out of the refuse mountain and zoomed back to the car, wrenching off Milo's headset and yelling, 'You drive.'

Flailing about on the pavement as he struggled to get the mayonnaise and muesli off his trousers, Milo yelped, 'Where to?'

Miles told him, 'After Grief, of course. Because maybe,' he

then explained, 'if they're window shopping, backs to the road, we could drive past and get a shot of them stood outside a sex shop. Or something.' He chucked the video camera onto the back seat, screaming at his partner to get a bloody move on, and, still letting off little high-pitched miaows of disgust, Milo flew suddenly into the driver's seat, spraying chunks of apple and walnut all about him; he gunned up the engine, jammed on the music again, and the car twitch-bodied off, belting out nervous drums into the quiet road.

Up in the flat, finding Grief gone, Milla rubbed cocaine round Moses' gums to wake him, then told him to get to work. Separately, he measured by weight and ground to fine powder the necessary ratio of weedkiller to sugar; then he blended them carefully on a bed of thin wire wool — a Brillo pad, washed and torn apart. Connecting a battery to a radio-triggered switch, he wired it to the sharp wool, packed the lot down tight into a tin box, and taped the box down solid to the inside of Milla's briefcase. Then he told her for fuck's sake not to drop it; to put it in the fridge the moment she got to work the next day; and to keep it there until the last possible minute before the meeting. Milla gingerly hid the bomb in the bottom of the freezer.

SIXTY-SEVEN

Cairo said quietly, 'You got to know, there's a whole lot of people in the world who are just completely out of it.'

Gagging, Bludge bundled back out the door and down the rickety bare wood stairs, knocking aside two black kids who were waiting outside the loo. Holding down the acid in her throat, she threw her weight against the door and easily busted open the flimsy bolt. Surprised on the brink of fixing up, a teenage girl sitting back knock-kneed on the bogseat jerked up her head in terror, then, whimpering, began begging not to be arrested. Bludge surged past her and vomited copiously into the sink. Even as she was doing so, she was thinking, wierdly lucid, 'How miserable, queueing for your own loo.' She emptied her guts. The girl watched in amazement, needle still poised over her forearm. When she'd finished and got her breath back, Bludge said — the first and last time she'd be nice to a negro — 'Don't you worry, love.' Then she managed a smile, and patted her on the shoulder, saying, 'There's plenty worse you can do than that stuff.' She assumed, as, naturally, did the girl, that 'that stuff' was heroin. Actually, it was fifty per cent baking powder. Bludge went back up to Cairo's bunker.

Cairo stared in silence at the flies settling on Marl's corpse. The huge dried bloodstain down the lower half of the sheets had come from the rupturing of arteries where the thighs had split inside; but far more horrible were the bloodless entrails, where the whole of her belly had burst in half, tearing upwards from the groin and spilling across the bed her white, withered, bulbous organs. Holding the words back carefully on the bitter base of her tongue, Bludge told him, 'I'm not surprised you thought you were a killer. Not your fault. Come on, let's get out.'

With the same absolute calm, Cairo asked as they stepped into the road whose fault it was, then. Bludge breathed with relief the hot air of the noontime street — it smelt of urine, and dead fires. Checking out the vendors, she saw gratefully a young woman boiling water, watched by the staring baby in the rucksack on her back. The primitive gas burner flared orange, as the cracked saucepan dripped. She waddled over and asked for a coffee — Camp, but that was better than nothing. Cairo followed, waiting on an answer. She asked if he'd like coffee too, and he nodded yes. The baby yowled at them as they drank. Next to the coffee lady, an old woman sitting on a bucket waited without optimism for a spot of custom. Five rolls of toilet paper were laid out across a grubby carrier bag at her feet. Someone would come, sooner or later, who'd picked up diarrhoea that day. Too many Taj Mahals, perhaps; or just someone who'd lost the daily game of russian roulette with the tapwater, by cleaning their teeth in it. (The rich used Evian, or bought into household filtration systems from the privatised Water Authorities.) Either way, the old woman would stuff a tin coin in her pocket, and ring up sale — with the likely total of the day's business completed, her budget might well then stretch to a pair of tomatoes. But no one, thought Bludge, is better off dead. She said, 'It'll take one fuck of a lot of public works, sorting out this little lot.' And Cairo asked, what was that to do with whose fault it was?

Giving back their mugs, they walked down the street towards Bludge's cottage. Dogs barked, and the hard sky murmured with distant helicopters. Bludge explained, 'If there's only so much to go round, and some people start taking more of it than others can get, then sooner or later they end up finding they've taken everything. And then the other people have nothing, so they die. Now who's supposed to care for the people? The government. So whose fault is it, if the people who have nothing all conveniently die? Nanny's. Because who the hell else ever takes any decisions around here?' Having been created by television, this conclusion, albeit erroneous, was simple enough for Cairo to understand. It was also simple enough for Bludge to have decided accordingly that the killing of Nanny would set everything right. Cairo, albeit very keen, thought this extravagantly ambitious.

But Bludge only asked, 'Have you ever ridden an 800cc?' No, but he was eager for the time when he would. 'That time,' Bludge told him, 'is tomorrow.' They got into her cottage, and Cairo settled patiently into the tiny sitting room where he'd slept long and well after she'd brought him home. It was funny, Bludge turning out to be a friend, especially when all this time he'd been daubing rude words on the side of her car. (Marl had told him what to put.) He listened to her making phone calls. First, she informed Election Section of a political killing — exactly so — in a bedsit in North Ken. (And thought, Here's Marl Foster, boys. Hope you choke on it.) She called Dwayne, and told him to wangle a bike copper's uniform out of Clothing Dep for a man — she poked her head round the door, and looked Cairo up and down — about six foot three, broad shoulders, big arms. Dwayne demanded a metric translation, and she roundly cursed him. Then she called Hal, and asked him sweetly to 'borrow' a bike. He told her rumours of her dismissal grew louder by the hour, and the tyros were gloating. Bludge wasn't bothered. With what she had in mind, she didn't see herself being around much longer, whether in a uniform or out of one. And they'd never fitted anyway.

She went into her mother's bedroom. The old woman was as old now as a Russian mountain peasant, centuries old; but still, resolutely, alive. Bludge proudly thought, 'Built of iron, my old love.' She was strong as the history of her people, and their labour in the docks and the warehouses, on the doorsteps and down the markets. She lay smiling at Ladies' Day on 147, smiling from her sunken face of lines and dried skin, and her shroud of white hair, waxed crisp. Tina swayed on the astroturf beside her plastic tree, and dreamily asked over the sound of canned birdsong if all of you nice people were doing OK. 'We're doing fine,' thought Bludge, 'and dying in our own time.' And then she thought, harder, 'Ain't no one gonna make a split linerbag out of my mother.' She smothered the old woman beneath her pillow; there was no resistance, which made her sad. Tina downed more scrumpy, and cut to yokels morris dancing. Bludge sat down by the body and cried.

Later, in the sitting room, she told Cairo, 'This is a hand grenade, and this is a handgun. Now the noise down the City Store is, tomorrow night, there'll be much fuss and bother and running about on account of some gang of terrorists or other. So there will be confusion, and eyes elsewhere. Let me tell you what this should enable us to do. . . .'

SIXTY-EIGHT

In clipped gay tones, the vicar called, 'Larry? Where are you, Larry? The afternoon's first mourners will soon be here.' Larry thought, fucking ponce. Why, he wondered, could they not have got in proper vicars to do this job?

In the government cremation centre, Fat Larry was finishing his lunch. All morning, he'd been spraying flowers, wiping seats, oiling wheels on the coffin trolley, straightening kinks in the runners and even in the rails — they hadn't half made a rush job of it all. And as if that wasn't wearing enough, there was the whole grisly chore of waving out every fifteen minutes one bunch of weepies, only to usher in the next, production-line style.

Now he sat back on his chair in the workshop — the room from where the coffin made its appearance — and chewed on his tomato sandwich. He looked at his watch; it said a quarter to three. Must be slow.

Through the little waist-high archway where the trolley rolled out to meet each new batch of mourners, he could see the cheap altar, with the four corners of plain white cloth hanging down around its sides. The rails went on across the platform, past the altar, and through another little archway, with curtains hung across the entrance. As the brief service finished, the coffin would wheel itself off through these, and into a room where a loudspeaker softly played the sound of flames, and subtle red and orange spotlights and filters faintly suggested a distant flickering of fire. When the mourners were out, it'd be quickly wheeled back to where he sat, and the rigmarole would start again. He thought, good thing it was empty; he'd hate to be paying the 'tricity bills, if they was moving the thing here and there all day with a body in it.

Canned music washed sloppily into the workshop from the spartan little chapel. He leaned forward on his wooden crate to try and see the tits in his *Sun* by the dull orange bulb in the ceiling. Then the bulb failed, and he cursed in the darkness. Rummaging on his workbench, he found a new one. By the light thrown in through the archway, he made out where the dud was hanging up above the waiting trolley; he couldn't get his chair to it, so he opened the lid and climbed up into the coffin instead, sandwich in one hand, bulb in the other, and the trolley rickety beneath him. He stuffed the sandwich in his mouth, the good bulb in his pocket, and reached up for the bad one; then the trolley jolted, and started to move towards the archway. A subdued electric humming noise blended neatly with the blurred, soap-sudsy music.

Larry nearly fell foward out of the coffin, but steadied himself by dropping to one knee inside it. He realised, looking behind him, that the trolley was nearly into the archway; he didn't have time to stop it and get out. Trying not to laugh, he hurriedly turned on his knee and lay down, pulling the lid shut over himself just as the trolley emerged into the light of the barren chapel. In the snug darkness, he shifted to get comfortable, squeezed his hand up to get his sandwich out of his mouth, and took a bite as he did so. Tomato dribbled down his chin; but he couldn't help that.

In the front row, prim as daisies, sat Grief and Milla. No one else was present. The vicar came on, and as he began to speak, the coffin rolled onto the platform. 'Big coffin,' Grief whispered, 'for the limbless torso of a very small person.' Mentioning the dearly departed, Fiona James, the vicar gave the trolley a gesture of welcome. As soon as it was in the open,

Milla whipped her camera out of her bag, and Grief dived forward to vault over the mock-shiny gold rails and rip off the lid of the box. Milla tracked this movement, then stood and walked quickly towards the platform, stepping over the railing and pushing the camera right close in on the amazed Fat Larry, red juice and seeds dribbling down his cheek, the light bulb fallen from his pocket and rolling around beneath his neck. She was saying, as she panned hungrily down the length of Larry's body, 'Brilliant, this is brilliant.'

Grief stated, 'Some fucking ballet dancer.'

Mystified, Larry said, 'Sorry mate,' and shrugged.

Milla turned to film the vicar rushing up to stop them; but Grief knocked him brutally aside, so he fell helplessly back across the railings, which caught him in the back of the knees. There was a nasty crunch as his skull hit the flagstones. Grief ran to the end of the rails, tearing down the curtains to reveal the empty, falsely flame-lit room, and yelling, 'Come on, come on, film this too. Get your bloody money's worth.'

Milla ran round, filming as she went, while Larry sat up in the coffin, still munching, wondering what was happening. As soon as she'd got everything, they ran for the door; he watched them leave, owl-eyed and blank, then looked down at the vicar, who was lying very still.

Grief said over and over as he screeched off into the road, 'Fucking marvellous.' He wrenched round the gears and barged through the jam. Then he gritted, 'I have to admit what you're doing is right.'

Milla span round on her seat and kissed him; in the back where she'd been waiting, Suzie applauded tumultuously. Milla wondered whether now, maybe, she should tell him what she and Moses had planned; but decided, better not to.

SIXTY-NINE

Vicious rape and genital mutilation. Chainsaws slashing through flesh; hammers crushing skulls. Bodies of children mown down and smashed in motor accidents; victims of abominable gangs torched at stakes in hillbilly country. Corpses on meathooks, priests skewered by lightning conductors, women eaten by insects, babies eaten by cannibals, men fed to mincing machines, zombies chewing on human limbs; Milla had raided Wally's library of horror movies for the intro sequence of her revelations.

The caption 'Free Death' cropped up across the images. Then came the voice of Wally, for the use of which talent Milla had found herself presented with a headed sheet of his personal business paper. It was an invoice, billing her for another fuck as the price of his services in his capacity as a voice-over artist. Being a star, he didn't come cheap. (She managed to negotiate an agreement stipulating that the payment was a one-off studio fee, and that she wouldn't incur repeat fees.) So Wally's unmistakeably cynical voice announced, 'Free Death. Yes, my sump city dole souls, the Money Party can now offer you a quick, painless, free death — that's absolutely free, gratis, with no charges of any kind — all you have to do is die, and the state picks up the bill.'

The caption fades as we mix to a grisly close-up on Moses' bobbling head. Before Milla had fired the camera in his face, she'd jammed him full of coke; the flaps of his dry skin judder as his unseen body shakes. 'Feeling tired?' sighs Wally. 'Feeling like Moses here, like you've really had enough?'

Cut to picture of the coffin emerging. 'Then end it all. Get your free death from the Money Party now.'

Cut to picture of hospital queue. 'Simply apply at your nearest hospital.'

Cut to Moses, who speaks to camera. 'This is a true story. I am a chemist, and I work for the health service. My name is Moses Brandt, and I'm thirty-four years old. But I don't look thirty-four because I'm the first victim of a drug that the government is now giving to all the old people in all the hospitals all over the country. I'm the first one who took the drug, because I'm the one who developed it. And I know that it kills people, because it's killing me. The government also knows that it kills people, but they're keeping right on and using it, because killing people saves money. You know how pleased we all are about that cut in public spending? Here's how they managed it.'

Cut to the wards. 'You go in here.'

Cut to Moses' tablets, close up in his shrivelled, trembling hand. 'They give you these.'

Cut to wards full of the limbless. 'You begin to grow old, and then you fall apart; your body just disintegrates under the pressures of accelerated ageing. These people will all be dead within a month or two, or three, depending on their luck.'

Cut to the furnace room. 'Then they bring you down here and they burn you. This room is in the basement of the hospital where I work.' Two men come in and tip a body down the chute.

Cut to close-up of hands ripping open a linerbag; limbs, organs, and rodents spill out. 'They prefer to burn you whole. If, however, you fall apart, burning you in bits is just as easy.'

Cut back to the coffin, seen trundling further into the cremation centre's chapel, as before. 'Then they offer you this wonderful new service — free cremation. But, you ask' — Grief rushes into the frame towards the coffin — 'if they've already burnt you, what's in the coffin where you're supposed to be?'

The camera rises, and wobbles towards the coffin as Grief rips up the lid. When Milla steps over the rail, she loses focus, and the camera slews down wildly towards the floor — but this is left in, for documentary realism — then she steadies herself, and rapidly tracks back up to Fat Larry. He sits up, smeared like Dracula, and stares about him wide-eyed in comic bubble-cheeked confusion. Grief runs down the trolley rails — and here, a jump in the picture, where she's crudely chopped out his attack on the vicar — and reveals the lights and speakers in the mock burning room. Moses continues, 'It's the same coffin. It goes back and forth, pretending to be everybody's mother and father, one after the other — until there's no more old mothers and fathers left. The workman has his lunch in it.'

Cut to Wally, grinning in his bed. He speaks to camera, 'This really, dear vegetables, really is a true, true story. Over the next year, a lot of people will die, even if the drug is withdrawn tomorrow. So if you're taking it' — cut to a reminder shot of what the tablets look like — 'stop taking it now, and you might last longer. Next, make sure everybody around you stops taking it. And once you're not taking it, if you're strong and angry, get out in the street and riot your ass off. And that applies to all you coppers too — we're all in this boat together.' The camera moves in on the world-famous grin. 'Free cremations indeed. A cut in public spending indeed. If you don't fight them now, they'll find out it's quicker just to come round and shoot you.'

The screen flickers and dies.

Grief returned from the Barn. He had arranged for the masterpiece to be screened live by the DJ on all the screens around the building. When he'd picked her up from Crinkly Crisp, they would seek safety in the enraged numbers of his following. He now watched it through, and thought, Trolly would have words to say about that. She pushed him, 'Not bad for a rush job, huh? And punchy, right?'

Grief said, 'You fucked him again, didn't you?'

Milla took an early night. Suzie shared the big bed with her, and Grief took Suzie's mattress, sleeping in the living room. Moses shivered on the sofa. Mary lay in the bath, watching sheepdog trials. And Wally watched her, breasts hidden by foam like an actress in a soap, while she grew tense and worried about her smack running out.

GOOD TELEVISION

The ad trade rag, *Harpoon*, yells out with a banner, 'Crinkly nets more £000's in Money mega blitz health ad bid bonanza.'

Grief walks the streets where the thinning crowds scurry; he sees the headline, and is troubled. Elsewhere, Cairo is not; he adoringly strokes the gleaming paintwork of an 800cc police motorbike.

Moses is troubled, and shows it. He swivels jerkily from side to side in the chair in Milla's blue room. Geeing himself up, he watches war movies on the big screen; he fingers anxiously the detonator switch in his pocket. Down the road from the flat, Bludge cheerfully clears up her desk in the City Store.

Crinkly is also troubled, watching technicians install a small matt black box with a winking green light in the boardroom; they fiddle with wire and switches, slips of silicon, and a transistor radio. Also watching, the runner is worse than troubled, pasty-faced and badly sweating. But Milla is a buzzball, arriving jubilant at work like a brand new day, fire-red as the dawn in red skirt, red jacket, and French tart's red cap and scarf. The vision cheers Crinkly, who quips, 'Really, pet, we're selling policies, not pudenda.' He notes the feverish industry with which she slaves her way through the day, and smiles. He tells himself he'd got his little Milla sussed out many moons ago; he knows what she's thinking.

Milla thinks, I'm going to blow your bollocks off.

Trolly's troubled, because Milla is acting strangely, and has put her briefcase in the fridge. She tackles the curry problem with uncharacteristic fervour, and turns down drinks. And he's troubled, because he'd worked past midnight with an amateur freelance film crew he hadn't found till midday, because every other crew in town seemed suddenly, inexplicably tied up. He'd wrapped the shoot and, heroically, the edit too, for an ad on cremations that everybody said was vital; and now, with it done, there's not a soul in sight seems interested. He thinks, it'll run, and, as usual, he'll not get an ounce of the credit. But Maelstrom isn't troubled in the least, because come the end of the day, Milla turns in a pure mountain of saleable concepts for instant curries.

Laz is pretty troubled, because the firm he's hiring special lenses from let him down last time, and if they let him down this time, he'll lose some wonderful shots.

Suzie's under a different kind of pressure. Mary is getting irritable, and almost violent, snapping at her, fidgeting, stomping about, rummaging without shame in all Grief's drawers and cupboards for money or drugs (but mostly, they're locked) and generally looking hourly more off-white, pinched, and peeved. She doesn't go to work, because who is there left to earn money for? She watches hyenas pick off the starving in Africa on the wildlife channel, and barks at Suzie if she pleads for light relief.

And Wally is troubled as hell, because who knows what on earth might happen next?

But perhaps they're all suffering from some kind of mass collective stage fright. The nation slumbers in peace before the artistry of Geoff Geometry, who is finding Style Dixon easy meat indeed. Fires burn in the red towns — so what else is news?

The night comes down, and the streets grow quiet. The Crinkly Crisp offices empty out into the evening, and the first police come round to check the place over. Hired waiters and caterers arrive, bustling in a reverent hush through thick-carpeted corridors as they prepare the food. In the boardroom, Crinkly adjusts the dimmer switch just a touch, for that exactly welcoming golden glow of soft electric light. The street is taped off, and Laz Stones' outside broadcast control van creeps up between security checks.

From their room overlooking the street on the floor above the boardroom, Milla and Trolly watch the preparations for Nanny's arrival. The glow of the boardroom's lights beneath them spills out and illuminates the small busy figures in the silent wide road; newsmen poke and jostle next to policemen, and crowd in little clumps round the lamplight spaces. Behind the watching creative team, unnoticed on TV, Nanny winds up her press conference with the usual pernicious humbug; when Milla hears the voice, she feels dry heat in her bones. Her thighs are warm, and her belly roasts in the light red skirt.

The leaders of the Money arrive. Milla exults, seeing all the stars have managed to make it, the whole loathsome crew of gibbering yes-men. Crinkly sees Milla exult, and feels pity — you give them a glimpse, and they think they know everything.

The regular body of aides and advisers is not present. In another room, generals, bankers, and the men who make television wait over their drinks for things to go their way.

In the boardroom, there is much hushed standing around beside seats. With Trolly padding quietly behind her, Milla strolls in, tingling from tip to toe, skin alive, gleaming, eyes flashing welcome, smile slight and knowing and endlessly, endlessly charming. She gently sets her briefcase down by the leg of a chair, and stays close to it, unobtrusively rubbing her palm warm after the cold of the handle, while fat, faintly sweaty ministers ogle her secretly. Nanny enters, and Crinkly leads her to a seat. Restrained pleasantries ensue; the presentation commences. Milla's posters win admiring appreciation. 'Peace of mind with the Money Party' (young married couple stepping into newly-bought house — old person clutching fistful of notes outside national savings office — Nanny propped upright next to a missile tip straining skywards from a barren rocky shore). And many many more — new factories and hospitals, police parades, Nanny on holiday with her mates on the continent, Nanny in the countryside, picture postcard shots of the Houses of Parliament, Buck House, Faslane, Greenham Common. Dig those silos; and the concrete gantries stain the sky.

Milla begins to wonder if it isn't all going a bit too well. As if on cue, when she moves on to put forward the press versions, and hands out photocopies of the text, ministers begin to engage in long pointless haggling over copy details. Milla reacts professionally, trying not to let them lie too outrageously when it comes to points of fact. Once she says, 'Keep it general. You mustn't let on too much, must you?' She barely suppresses a laugh, and sees the runner throw her a vicious, nervous glance. He looks, she thinks, like he has a cold, and is absurdly swathed in a leather jacket.

Dinner comes — light, crisp avocado mousses and curried chicken supremes, cold meats and dainties with salads and fruit, and delicate white wine chilled in misty glasses. Milla's briefcase rests against her calf. At eleven fifteen, the heat is too much. As they sip at coffee and brandy, she excuses herself, thighs burning together. The fatness of their cheeks, the pink shine as they eat, makes her thrilled and queasy all at once.

'It's nearly time,' shouts Suzie, stamping her feet in front of the quivering Mary. Mary clutches her belly, and feels the sweat prickle in her polka-dot headband. She registers the green blur of the video clock, and nods shortly for the channel to be changed. Suzie finds 147, where Wally is egging on Style Dixon as he stages a rigged last-gasp comeback. (*Build* that excitement.)

Bludge watches camera crews make their final checks at sites up and down the street, and chats idly with loitering constables. Cairo waits calmly beyond the first cordon, smiling in uniform on his big shiny bike.

Milla hurries to the toilet. Through the corridor windows she sees the street outside guarded and waiting, glistening with electric light and shade. Wide of either side of the building, white tapes seal off the approaches. She laughs at their precautions, rushing into the cold white agency wash-room with its mirrors and fancy sinks. (Oh, the days we took cocaine in here. The days our noses bled on the porcelain.) Before she's even halfway into a cubicle, her hands are wrenching up her skirt around her thighs. She slumps down on the seat and feels herself, soaking wet, quickly coming with a shock that bangs her knees apart against the walls.

On her way back, breathing quick and fast, she peers far out of the window, and sees Grief's car approaching the white tapes. His elbow rests leisurely out of his window as he shows his pass. She longs to be beside him. It is eleven twenty-six. In the boardroom, Crinkly turns on the television.

Grief explains to yet another copper who he is, crawling in first gear towards the last cordon, saying, 'Yes, I know, I'm picking up one of the people at that very meeting.' He watches them fussing over his ID card. Moses sits beside him, shrivelling up, shoulders tiny in his now far too big jacket. Grey hairs lie on the shoulderpads.

Awkwardly, he holds one arm up crooked under the seat belt to keep his hand steady round the detonator in his pocket. His face is grim with concentration as he struggles to keep his fingers still. Grief wonders why Moses is staring so, as he nudges the bonnet up close to the tape. Law stands loose and wary-eyed around the limo for Nanny at the agency's main entrance. Across the street, ten yards from where he's pulling up, a van says 'Laz Stones Live TV'. Grief feels the wheels of his car bumping over camera cables. Peering into a monitor in the van's computerised interior, Laz says to himself, 'Just about there, Grief, that'll do nicely.' Grief cuts the engine.

A tiny flatscreen TV on the dash flickers in his face. Wally is wrapping up his intro for the last three frames of the final, which will be, naturally, a cliffhanger. He says, 'Well, people, nearly home and dry now; three to play, and everything to play for. But, I hear you cry, where are the ads? What have the Money been cooking up tonight? So, before we hit the ultimate shoot-out for the Championship of the Globe, let's hear it for the Money.' In the City, Wally watches the 147 logo pop up on the screen, heralding the commercial break, and he thinks, here we go. Suzie grabs Mary's hand, and is slapped away for her pains.

Grief wonders what Laz is doing outside the meeting. There is, he realises, a camera right up close behind his car. He looks away from security men to the screen on the dash, and sees his own face. A smooth voice announces, 'This man is called Grief. He is the son of a former Home Secretary, and a successful club-owner in the fashionable heart of London.' Grief snorts. Fashionable? Bermondsey? But he supposes he'd made it so. His face is replaced by Milla's. 'This is his girlfriend, Milla Sharply. A highly successful copywriter in the fast-moving world of advertising, she is responsible for the origination of much of the Money Party's own advertising and publicity material.'

Grief jeers, 'Come on, come on, what you leading up to?'

Moses' face replaces Milla's on the screen; it's an old photo, and shows him young and healthy. 'And this is Moses Brandt, a senior research chemist working for the health service on the urgent task of developing new and more effective pharmaceuticals.'

Cut to Nanny in a cozy drawing-room. Studs gleam in the arm of her chintzy little chair. She says to camera, 'Good evening to you. Now the persons we have just mentioned may appear to you to be fine examples of today's go-getting breed in today's successful go-getting GB. But let me assure you,' and her voice grows chill and low, 'that these three people

were terrorists and criminals of the basest and most evil kind
— the kind of vermin that we must work together to eradicate
for ever from our Great British shores.'

Grief notes the word 'were'. Moses asks, 'What am I going to
do?'

'About what?' snarls Grief.

Nanny says, 'My government can announce today that after
an intensive undercover police operation, these callous
monsters are paying the price of their sins.'

Listening to a simultaneous broadcast on a cop car radio
down the street, Bludge fingers the gun in her holster, and
wonders what on earth is going on. She makes her way slowly
nearer the agency front, blandly grinning at other policemen.
'You know, I was Grief's case officer once,' she eagerly relates,
'but of course it's in higher hands now'.

The tyros nod superciliously and think, bloated tub. They
pay her no notice.

Moses whimpers again, 'What am I going to do?' The
detonator burns in his pocket. The TV tells how he had abused
his position of responsibility to unleash a devastating killer
drug on our old people in the hospitals, the terrorist gang
hoping thereby to bring down the government by blaming the
spreading death on them. The government has of course
identified and withdrawn the drug. Moses explains to Grief,
'We can still get them. There's a bomb in the boardroom. And
a trigger in my pocket. But Milla. . . .' Grief, half listening, sees
the picture cut to film of himself talking to the Arabs in the
Barn. The voice explains how he'd planned to raise money for
further terrorist crimes by exporting the drug to other left
wing death merchants abroad. A heavily doctored and con-
vincingly dubbed soundtrack, involving a rather different
conversation from the one he'd actually had, is matched to the
pictures of his meeting with the dealers; it was, apparently,
'recorded in situ with the latest police spy microphones'.

Then Grief understands what Moses had just told him. He
turns with delight and amazement; but Moses' head has fallen
down into his free hand. He weeps at their failure, thin back
jerking against the passenger seat, body bouncing limply
beneath the seatbelt as he shakes with his tears. Grief tells
him, 'Just give me the detonator.'

'But Milla,' whines Moses, 'What about Milla?'

Grief grabs Moses' arm, hauling him round in his seat and trying to pull out his hand from his pocket. Moses gasps, 'Don't.' Leaning over, Grief's hip crushes Moses' fist in the pocket, and he feels a series of squishy crunching snaps. Frantically he pulls back, jabbing his hand down into the sopping cloth, dragging out the detonator, spilling bits of finger as it comes. He wipes off the blood to see how it works, and presses the button.

Nothing happens.

Mary rampages round Grief's apartment, howling, 'Bastards, bastards.' Suzie sobs soundlessly in front of the screen as it details the criminal histories of her idols. Wally grins. In the control van, Laz does a final check round the pictures he's getting from the cameras in the street, then snaps into his headset, 'OK gang, we're ready to go live. Announcer ready? Do it.'

A news announcer bursts onto the screen in mid-report, and raps excitedly, 'We have to interrupt the Money broadcast at this point, to go over live to a dramatic development in the heart of London. One member of the gang has been cornered attempting to assassinate our leader and her cabinet at a campaign meeting in the West End. Milla Sharply is sealed into a conference room and threatening to explode an unspecified device. Security forces surround her now as. . . .'

Laz cuts from a long shot of the empty street, dotted in the distance with policemen and their cars, to a camera on the far pavement angled up to show the agency's façade. It zooms in to focus on the long rectangle of the boardroom's lit windows high above. Laz says, sniffy and nervous, 'Come on, come on.' It's eleven thirty-four.

Milla asks, 'How ever could you dare to have a bomb in the same room as the cabinet?' In her heart she is admiring Crinkly's bold and masterful command of the medium.

Relieved like nothing on earth that the notional time of the explosion has been and gone, the runner nastily tells her, 'This room's got a radio jammer in it so powerful, you couldn't set off your bomb in here if you were firing Jodrell Bank at it from arm's length.' He points to the black cube with its tiny, imperceptibly winking green light, sitting like an ioniser on the drinks cabinet by the door. She thinks, that's so simple; then, as the TV closes in on the window, she realises her life is over, and the room seems to vanish around her. She is suddenly, terribly alone, without eyes in a fearful blackness.

Crinkly's voice comes distantly through the fog, saying, 'It wasn't, my pet, by any means a bad attempt.'

Milla stands as the runner comes towards her. She is frozen cold, gut hollow. He takes her by the arm, and leads her to the broad window seat. Seeing on TV the room from outside, Trolly watches their shapes against the light of the windows. The ministers round the table lick their lips, smile, and enjoy the show. Trolly backs off in horror towards the door as he begins to suspect what the runner wants. Milla feels the air wash in from the street, and sees tarmac swim wildly as the runner, with the help of a minder, picks her up and stands her on the ledge.

The announcer jabbers orgasmically, like a sports commentator, 'And I think she's coming to the window.... I can't quite make out what's happening up there. . . .' Grief sees Milla appear at the window's edge on TV, and looks up to see her thin fine frame in real life, backlit way up above the hard road. He slowly puts the detonator back in Moses' blood-soaked pocket. Behind him, cameras pan round, seeking the best angle on his car. Laz positions them, checking them off one by one on the monitors, then tells them to stand ready.

The runner says, 'Now, Miss Sharply, if you could just smile for the good men of the press here....' She turns on the ledge to see a clutch of hired photographers. The ministers clear aside from the table to the walls to allow them a clear set of shots. The flashes start popping as she turns, and she takes a step back, nearly falling. She realises that the minder has put a gun in her hand. She doubts, somehow, that it is loaded, but hopes it'll look good in the papers all the same. The runner smiles, 'That's right. If you could jump, please, it makes a better story. But we can always push you, if you prefer it that way.'

Milla says, 'Don't bother,' and steps out into the cool air. She watches the road rush up into her face. In the control room, Laz appreciates the skill with which one of his best men tracks her trajectory perfectly.

Grief sees the flashes in the window as the cameras fire off. He turns to the screen to follow Milla's body through the air. You get a clearer picture on TV. The commentator raves at the drama of it all. The image bounces once as she hits the ground, then steadies into crisp focus on the unnatural splayed angles of her frail shattered frame. It is, thinks Grief, a kind of apotheosis.

Cut to the camera with the special zoom lens. Laz claps his hands to see the thing is working; no flare, no distortion. Incredible close-up; the screen fills with lusting sexual images of parts of Milla's body. Slowly the lens tracks over her curves like a pair of hands, passionately caressing. Blood runs like oil from her ear; her broken head lies in a deep red pool. Suzie wails in outrage. Mary stares, appalled. Tragic, thinks Wally, just tragic.

Bludge walkie-talkies to Cairo that it's safe to move in closer. She asks, 'How's your throwing arm?'

Grief bangs his head slowly and repeatedly on the steering wheel. The horn blares regularly and mournfully as his forehead falls on it. His heart sounds vast in the hollow caverns of his chest. He thinks, I'm going to kill that bastard Stones.

The commentator's voice is cracking at the pitch of climax. Laz hopes he can keep it up. They've hardly started yet.

In the boardroom, as the ministers applaud the screen, Trolly bumps, backing, into the drinks cabinet by the door. No one is looking at him. He reaches down and wrenches out wiring from the back of the black box; the little green light begins to fade. He stumbles from the room, barging away past security by explaining merely, 'You think I want to be in there with a terrorist?' But the detonator sits quite forgotten in Moses' pocket.

At Grief's car window, a disinterested youth in jeans tells him Laz Stones would like a word; he gestures lazily in the direction of the control van. Grief throws open his door and storms across the road. Cut to a camera following him over the street to the van's back door. The commentator pauses for breath and checks his script. 'And now ... yes ... I'm hearing that the police have surrounded Grief ... he's in a car ... no ... no, that's Grief there, running towards, my God, he's making for the news team's broadcast unit ... trained marksmen are on the scene (Laz quickly drops in a second or two of the Met's library footage of men with rifles in flak jackets) ... we don't know if he's armed, no one knows ... but the response of the security forces here has been amazing. ...'

Grief hurls open the back door of the van. Piling up the steps into the electric-lit cable-packed button-bedecked interior, he is immediately seized by two huge burly men in bomber jackets. He sees on the monitors many cameras all anxiously scanning the isolated van in the empty street. Laz cuts from one to another, showing different angles across the eerie waste of tape and tarmac, while cop car roof lights turn and flare at a careful distance. The commentator whispers, 'And now Grief's in the van . . . we can't see what's happening. . . .'

Grief is pinioned between the two guards. Laz puts his face right close up to Grief's, and says, 'You got time to listen once, so listen good,' then he sniffs abruptly in a sudden outbreak of nervous tics. 'I don't like what the Money script has lined up for you, nor am I in business to kill my old friends. For Milla, there was nothing I could do. But for you, if you go to the Barn like you're supposed to — they'll kill you on any other road, you're only alive as long as you're giving good pictures — and if you can get down to your office before they've shot you, then there's keys to my speedboat in the bottom drawer of your desk, and my signed authorisation for you to get into the dock to get to it. Good luck, keep your head down, and stay in the crowd.'

Grief asks, 'Why are you doing this?'

Laz explains, 'It's a better movie if you get away. Now go for it.'

Grief jumps from the van and runs back to the car, keeping low. The commentator's voice rises an octave as all the van's technicians and other occupants bundle out behind him, hands over their heads in a terrible pushing and shoving panic. What looks like the last one out seems desperately to swing the door shut behind him as he hurls himself down the metal steps and gallops away. There is a muffled thud in the sealed van; the door blows open and hangs off its hinges, smoke rushing out, and a stuntman staggers screaming from out of the fiery murk, flames burning on his back.

Mary hisses, 'Yeah, you kill the bastards.' Suzie yells and claps her hands.

Bludge tells Cairo to watch and wait. She is now pretty close to Nanny's limo.

The commentator gags and gasps, 'That's awful, that's awful . . .' The picture goes dead as the van explodes, and his voice babbles hysterically over a static crash of white noise. Then the image returns, flickering over itself a few times, sliding to the bottom right, and finally lurching into focus as Laz scrambles into the back-up control unit and takes charge again. Crinkly and Wally both gaze in awe at the director's craftsmanship.

Cut from the burning van to brave policemen stampeding towards Grief's car. He jams into gear, races leaping back in reverse, spinning around on the way to knock out the camera behind him, and on the dash sees himself on TV, action man, initiating the obligatory car chase. He veers off screeching through the scattering policemen, bouncing over plastic red cones and carving through white tape. At the main cordon, a row of wooden trestles seals the street. There is a convenient gateway for him to drive through. Another stuntman waits in this gateway, legs apart, hunched down, both arms straight out in front of him, holding a revolver. Calmly he takes aim as Grief accelerates towards him. He fires a few blanks with rocksteady calm, then leaps at the last minute from the path of the onrushing car, and catapults away into a balsawood trestle that spectacularly splinters up all about him into pieces. Cameras follow siren-screaming police cars as they give chase into the distance.

Bludge thinks, neat. That's cleared the decks a bit.

Crinkly and the runner are too busy shepherding all the ministers from the boardroom, to notice that the little green light no longer winks as it is wont. On TV, the getaway sequence winds up, and Laz cuts to the studio where 'hastily assembled experts' discuss the night's events. (You got to give your audience a breather now and then.) Links with the Friends of the Sick are suggested. Obviously, there are connections in all this matter, given the political circles in which Miss Sharply moved, that reach to alarmingly high levels within the People Party. . . .

Grief drives like a maniac, eyes glazed and unblinking, knuckles white on the wheel. Inside eight minutes, for which Laz loudly applauds him, as the studio discussion is quickly wearing thin on meat and thick on prejudice, he pulls into view of the first camera on the Barn's approach road. It's going well. Laz thanks the lord he won't have to fall back on the crap that Miles and Milo shot.

A man with a clipboard rushes onto the studio floor in mid-debate, and whispers into the moderator's ear. He stops his guests abruptly, and turns to camera to say, 'We have more live news coming in. 147 cameras have caught up with the runaway terrorist leader Grief at his nightclub in Bermondsey. Let's get over there right away.'

Grief correctly assumes that entry to the Barn is only possible at the main entrance, where the cameras will have enough light to pick him out clearly. He sprints through the foyer, and barges across the crowded dance floor. Everyone is milling about in a hushed, bewildered buzz of chatter before the huge video screens that have now begun to show them themselves, as cameras in the Barn pan wildly about searching for Grief. He sees himself as he pushes through, ducking and weaving, with Moses straggling and bleeding in his wake. The commentator is chanting a litany of their sins, with an equal measure of praise for the law and order; the creamy voice paints them up as the most bestial, the most drug-crazed and perverted, the worst. . . . 'But the police have got them sealed up now.'

Grief rushes into the DJ's box with Moses in feeble tow. He smashes wildly at the lighting rig controls, and raises up a sudden blinding clamour of neon, strobe, and multi-coloured pulsing bulbs. Moses screams, pointing at the waiting marksmen sited round the upper balconies; they are thrown by the lights, and squinting through their sights at their suddenly refracted and dazzling target. Grief ducks down beneath the controls and frantically fumbles to unlock the trap to the basement ladder. The DJ looks down at him, hands out, mouthing for an explanation. A camera filming the platform full frontal shows Grief disappear from view. Laz mutters urgently, 'That's it, come on, come on.' Moses, eyes on the glinting guns, panics, and begins scrabbling with his last strength spider-wise, one-handed, up the metal ladder and into the entrails of the lighting rig. The gunmen, re-oriented against the tumult of electric lightning, open fire just as Grief is throwing his legs through the trap, and heaving his body in after them. The first bullet hits the DJ in the top of the shoulder, hurling the upper half of his body around, and spinning his arm against the record deck; the microphone falls from his hand with an awful thudding crackle. The way his hand lands on the deck activates the playing arm; dance music begins to thump and boom. The DJ's head, flung round with his body as he falls back against the amplifiers, lands on his wounded shoulder, so he can see how the bullet has split open flesh and cloth; flakes and slivers of bloodied bone splay out in the wake of its passing. Then three in a row catch him across the stomach, buckling him up in a screaming agony at the weight of the blows, until the pain goes out with the last bullet that punches through his skull, and sprays his brains all over the record racks. Rattling down the ladder inside the metal turret, Grief hears the thunderous hammering of the bullets as they crash into and through the structure above and around him. He hears too the slinky beat and sliding bass of his favourite song pounding reverberations through the rungs in his hands. 'Sing me forget-me-nots — help me to remember . . . .' comes the high black voice. The screaming crowd do not dance. They are flung all over the floor in terror.

Mildly smiling, Nanny watches the show in the foyer while they wait for the law to say the street is clear. Her car ticks over at the kerb. Bludge stands nearby; she tells Cairo down at the cordon to turn on his engine and be ready. The runner, watching the foyer screen with his hands on the back of Nanny's chair, curses viciously. Laz has sent an elevated camera high on a robot arm swinging round the wall of the Barn, almost into the line of fire; it gets on a level with the DJ's platform, with a perfect side view, and shows the DJ's body, but no Grief.

Suzie urges, 'Please get away, Grief, please get away.'

The runner demands to know, 'Where the fuck's he gone?'

Crinkly sighs. He's had a tiring two days. He watches bullets still ripping sporadically into the platform, scattering shards of vinyl. But most of the marksmen now are trying to make out where Moses has climbed to. The runner again demands to know why Grief isn't dead where he's supposed to be. Crinkly says, 'Look, boy. In the real world, nothing goes perfectly. We've just won you more votes, and dug you out of a bigger bloody hole, than you could ever manage on your own in a month of Sundays. So stop complaining.' He strides off back up to the boardroom to catch the rest of the show in peace. Milla's briefcase lies amid proofs of ads where she'd left it.

Moses clambers across girders in the heart of the lighting rig. Bullets bounce and whine off the metal all about him, smashing bulbs and ricocheting off around the ceiling. Laz is loving it, cutting from camera to camera in time with the beat. Great bars and blocks of sudden colour dance, dart and turn all over Moses' body. He slips, keening for breath, and falls into the on-off flash of a revolving orange torch. Prisms of light from inverted, spinning pyramidical mirrors flow fantastically up and down his body where he lies, shaking like a tree in an earthquake, all strength gone, across two great slats of metal in the meccano mayhem at the centre of the upper saucer. The next salvo shreds him limb from limb. Bits of Moses rain down in a fine spray of blood and chips of brittle bone onto the prone and frightened dole kids beneath the rig. Severed, his lower half falls from out of his jacket; the legs land on either side of a crossbar covered in strobes, and in weird slow motion they rip apart, and tumble down separately. The rest of him then falls in a baggy lump through the multitude of neons, lit and then dark, lit and then dark as they pulse and flash; and as his torso hits the dancefloor in between wailing bodies, the detonator switch is turned in his pocket. The radio signal jumps across the town.

Crinkly rests, leaning forward, with his palms down on the window ledge; he looks out across the street at the burning van, and down at the roof of the waiting black cars. Behind him, the battery connects, and turns the wire wool instantly red hot. There is a massive thump, and bits of briefcase fly everywhere in a huge yellow flash. Crinkly is blown clean out of the window in a terrible shower of razor sharp glass.

Laz sees it happen on a monitor and yells, 'Did we get that taped? Leave the Barn, we're all finished down there, play that bomb back instead. Where's the commentator? What's happening?'

In the foyer, the runner jumps at the whump of the bomb. He sees Crinkly in a rainbow of tinsel reflections fall with a soggy thunk to the tarmac near Milla. He jolts Nanny and says, 'Come on you, we better get out of the building.' He rushes her as fast as she can manage through the glossy front doors.

Amazed and hysterically grinning, Nanny tentatively suggests, 'Isn't that something of a disaster?'

But the runner merely snarls, 'There's plenty more where he came from.'

Bludge sees Nanny emerge, and calls to Cairo to go. He throws the hand-grenade as far as he can behind him towards a knot of coppers on bikes around a car, then clunks sweetly into gear and glides towards Nanny's waiting limo at the kerb fifty yards in front of him. The bike is beautiful, the power of it effortless. Behind him comes a tremendous explosion, and grinding shrieks of metal and people straight after it. Cairo smiles to himself.

Laz freaks. He yells, 'Get a camera on that,' but when he sees the carnage on the monitors he changes his mind and gasps, 'Jesus, fuck, no, don't.' Plumes of smoke and flame rise up from the fiercely burning police car. Torched bodies litter the road amid bits of motorbike. On air, the commentator is desperately ad libbing over the playback of Crinkly's body spinning out through the cascade of shining glass; he gabbles something about a 'controlled explosion'. Cursing, Laz cuts him off and runs with great reluctance a tape held back in case of mishap. It announces that now Moses, Milla and Grief have met their deserved ends, the 147 news team has hastily assembled background information on these heinous villains.

A pundit declares, 'Grief and Sharply were certainly lovers, but what else these degenerates got up to we really don't begin to know. We do however know for a fact that Grief had illicit relations with children. We've found some secret police film here where he's out with one of his concubines...' Cut from announcer to Miles' shot of Grief hand in hand with Suzie on the ramp. The image is lividly green, and the left top corner has burnt out completely. Laz grunts with disgust at the amateur picture quality, but the import is clear enough.

Neatly edited, Grief's voice says as his mouth moves, 'I want to be buying you exotic lingerie.' Then the soundtrack spills out a ghastly, slushy, collapsing sound of tumbling rice and rotten vegetables.

A distant voice yelps, 'Pollution....'

Laz has the studio team ready; he cuts, and cues them in. They take over smoothly, and launch some rabid anti-pinko rant. Then he races out of the van to see what's happening live. Policemen are sprinting away towards the scene of the explosion. Nanny, halfway across the pavement when the grenade went off, is being bundled into the back of the limo by the runner. Bludge moves swiftly towards the car. Cairo slides up from across the street, pulls up by the driver's window, yanks out his gun, and shoots the driver dead.

Bludge screams, 'After that bike.' Police are all over the place, running in the wrong direction, and Cairo is already a hundred yards away, all but coming in his pants at the surge of the machine's acceleration. Other bikes spin on their wheels, whip round, and hare off after him. Bludge hauls the body of the driver from his seat and steps in in his place.

Voice cracking, the runner screams from the pavement, 'Get her away.'

Bludge turns in her tight pinching uniform and says, 'Don't worry, everything's under control.' She slips into gear and slides off.

The runner chases over the road to Laz and howls, 'What the hell is going on? This isn't in the script.'

The studio crew are anatomising Milla's alcoholism, and proclaiming that Grief sold heroin to infants. Suzie wails; Mary swears revenge. Her body is a pin cushion of irritable need. She gulps hungrily at wine; it goes down the wrong way, and she hacks, spluttering, as her stomach contracts, and retches up runny yellow phlegm. Suzie, thinking it might help, tells her where the cocaine is. She fixes up a massive shot, and starts crawling up the walls, bug-eyed. The television sneers and drones.

In the basement of the Barn, Grief dons an orange wig in the artists' dressing room. Laz Stones' keys and idents rattle in the pocket of his sequinned glitzy jacket. He considers adding a choker, country and western style, to top off his outfit; but it'd probably disappear in the frills and flounces of his blouse. Above him, a massive hammering starts up as policemen find the locked metal trap by the DJ's body. He hastily applies foundation, powder, blusher, some crude thick splashes of eyeshadow, and two unsteady lines of kohl on his lower lids. Then, absurdly meticulous, he checks his stockings aren't laddered, and canters awkwardly down the booming corridor to the refuse yard. The pencil leather skirt makes his knees crash painfully together. He smashes down the metal bar, and the double doors fly open. A waiting policeman asks him, 'Where you going, darling?'

He rushes over, miming panic, and screams, 'They're shooting people, help me, help me.' He flings himself into the amazed embrace of the constable, who steps back, thinking, he's onto a good thing here. Then he crumples in agony as Grief knees him savagely in the groin. As he writhes on the ground, Grief takes his gun, and knocks him out with the butt of it. Then he opens the wooden gates of the refuse yard just a fraction, feet slipping on slimy waste and fruit peel, and peeks out across the main car park. His car is close, up by the main entrance. Policemen are running away from it back towards their own cars, and, sirens bawling, hurtling off into the darkness — the runner's called them back to Crinkly Crisp. The whole area in front of the Barn teems with panicky youth, weeping in shock or merely stunned, and their wild tribal hair and clothes all bob and bounce in the TV lights and the cop car chaos.

Behind him, Grief hears heavy footsteps thundering down the basement corridor. With flat palms he smoothes down the creases of his skirt across his thighs, and steps in among the cave children in their wigs and warpaint to slip across the tarmac to his car. No one notices him climbing into it; he kicks off his awkward shoes, clicks on the engine, backs down a side exit, and sneaks away through backstreets towards the City. No one, that is, bar a sharp-eyed cameraman who picks him out in the milling bright-lit throng, and follows him mincing in his skirt through the crush, orange hair like a beacon flashing in the spinning cop car lights. He tracks the car's getaway; Laz watches this sequence coming in down the wire, and plays it back, pleased. He calls to the cameraman on his radiophone, 'Lovely job, we'll use that in a minute.'

Nanny mutters fearfully, 'Where are we, where are we?'

Bludge nudges the black limo over rotten cable and rusted metal and oily greasy earth towards the far end of the abandoned warehouse a mile or two out from the City. Cairo waits, out of uniform now and, sadly, back on his 125. When she's got as near as she can, she cuts the motor, and steps out to tell him, 'You did a grand job, Cairo Jones.' He grins, and pulls up beside the car to watch her finish it off.

Bludge takes out her gun, checks it over lovingly, spins the chamber, and turns to the car's back door. Cairo leans over to open it for her, saying to Nanny as his grin expands, 'Hello, cuntface.' Bludge pumps all six bullets into the old woman's body, and watches her thinly bleed; brains drip down the soft leather.

Cairo, appeased, makes himself scarce, slipping and sliding away across the rubble and muck. Bludge leans against the car by the open back door, and stares relaxed and happy up at murky cloud and the odd weak star. Beside her, Nanny's body slowly falls out and onto the filthy wet earth. Bludge is at peace, and all that mars her satisfaction is that she had underestimated Milla and Grief. She is impressed by the courage and daring of their plan. She climbs into the front seat to switch on the radio, and finds that the night's events are doing the Money no end of good in the polls. She laughs. Fat lot of good, she thinks, that'll do them now. Security forces, she is told, have everything in hand; on 147, the first of the last three frames of the tourney have, apparently, made it at last onto the air now that events are dying down.

About time too, thinks Wally. Talk about over the top.

At Crinkly Crisp, the runner repeats nervously on the phone to Downing Street that he hasn't a clue where Nanny is.

Grief cannons out of the lift onto his landing. He forgets about the skirt in his hurry, and falls flat on his face; he struggles up, and punches his way through the numbers to get into the flat, ripping off clothes and the wig as he goes. He finds Mary white as death and dancing manically to guitar music. Suzie runs mewing with relief from the news channel, where Laz's cameras are panning round the tidied up Crinkly Crisp street while announcers run fawning obituaries on Crinkly, 'martyred in the struggle against terrorism'. Grief gives her a hug and orders her without explanation to get on the warmest clothes she can find. He grabs documents from his safe, thick sweaters, a coat and a scarf from the wardrobe, and then dresses as himself again. In the bathroom, he half succeeds in washing the make-up off his face. Suzie, tense and smiling, waits on her feet in the hall; in the living room, oblivious, Mary whirls to the crashing chords, nose numb, belly aching, body a mass of scratches. As Grief hurtles out past her again, she calls, mock-noble, from the dregs of her last false energy, 'Anyone you want sorting out while you're gone?'

He hears how she wants to please him. He gives her a peck goodbye, thinking, poor baby, and tells her, 'That bastard upstairs for a start.' The memory of that adulterous smile... as he passes down the hall, he sticks a bit of paper in her jacket pocket.

He leaves her fading as the record finishes. In the empty room she jerks across the thick carpet, battered marionette, still faintly dancing to the echo of the last tune. She longs to draw blood to the music. The vanishing buzz of the cocaine makes her need for heroin sharper. Her throat is dry, her headband drenched. She asks herself, 'What's Wally got to do with anything?' On the television, cameras watch Milla's body wrapped up and taken away. Grief and Suzie race down empty roads toward the docks.

Sitting in wasteland, Bludge flicks through radio channels. As one, they are singing the praises of the government's togetherness in the face of such evil, such fanatical criminals, who'd go to any length.... How, Bludge wonders, how on earth had the poor rich fools allowed themselves to be so comprehensively outsmarted? And then she finds a station that is breathlessly announcing a scoop exclusive. (Because the runner'd thought it best to let this one filter out slowly — one station first, and the rest of the media can pick up on it as they go along.) 'It is rumoured,' babbles the voice in excitement, 'that the police were first alerted to Grief and Sharply's plans by none other than Wally Wasted, already an honours list contender since....'

So that, thinks Bludge, is how. She feels suddenly chilled, and cold as ice. Her mind goes thin and sharp. She throws Nanny's corpse clear of the car, into the black mud and the stacked metal debris; she shuts the back door, and reverses towards the road. She has not, she now realises, yet finished the job. And then she smiles, because Cairo had been right all along.

Elsewhere, Cairo performs his last task, anonymously calling the law from the first working phone booth he can find to let them know where Nanny can be collected. 'And,' he tells them, 'suck on that.'

Laz has a scout posted on the dock's approach road. As Grief and Suzie roar past, he calls in to announce their arrival. Laz rings round his waiting camera teams and actors, then cues in the commentator, who's been standing by, and getting his breath back from the last lot. On 147, the second of the last three frames is abruptly interrupted by his frantic face as he raps out, 'We have to break now for some more hot news. We've got film coming in (cut to Grief in drag in the car park of the Barn) of the terrorist leader Grief, who we assumed had been killed, escaping with wicked cunning. . . .'

Wally yells, 'Oh for fuck's sake what now? How much more are you going to mess my programme about?'

Grief's car is seen slipping away from the Barn. The commentator reappears, thrilled to announce that a 147 news team who'd been out 'investigating Grief's business affairs' has spotted him in dockland with his concubine. 'We'll have pictures for you just as soon as we can. In the meantime, we're told that the police are racing to the scene. . . .'

In the back of the van, the runner furiously demands of Laz what this sudden postscript is all about. 'I thought we'd had everything. I thought we were done. What's he doing still alive?'

Laz spins round from a fat line of coke and snaps, pushed too far, 'Listen, you snotty little scumbag, d'you want good television, or don't you?'

The announcer is handed a teleprinted sheet of yellow paper. Clearly surprised, he looks up, mystified, and says, 'Well, while we're waiting for our link with the docks . . . you know, I'm not sure I believe this one myself, but . . . it seems there's a local radio station now claiming that the law's prime source of information on the terrorist gang is none other than Wally Wasted.'

Wally's heart bangs like a drum. He grabs the phone and calls 147. It doesn't take much infuriated shouting to get him put through to the control unit, and he immediately screams at the runner, 'You bastards, you've killed me — don't you realise there's an army of kids out there who'll slaughter me the first chance they can get?'

Downstairs, Mary, burnt out, stirs sluggishly in front of the screen. She pushes herself to her feet, and staggers about looking for a weapon, shaking with a fever and wheezing badly. Bludge pulls up outside the building.

The runner hisses down the phone, 'We've had a close-run thing down here, and some minor mishaps thrown in, and every martyr we can get'll come in handy. Get my drift?' The runner believes Wally should never have been allowed on television in the first place. It's easier to keep the people quiet with guns, than it is with pap.

Wally breathes, 'But Crinkly promised me protection.'

'And you believed that? Fuck's sake, Wasted, the man was in advertising.' The runner hangs up. A policeman bounds into the van to whisper in his ear that Nanny's dead. He stares, appalled, and thumps his palm against his forehead; then scampers off in a panic to where his sponsors are in conference to break the news. The generals are calculating the kind of defence budget they can look to, now the oldies are dead. The way they see it, they reckon if they can play the never-again-shall-terrorism-claim-so-many-helpless-victims line, they should be free to go a bundle on every weapons system their hearts desire. Impotent cocks stir at the dreamy prospect.

Wally puts down the buzzing phone and stares in terror through his deep blue sea. The foyer buzzer burrs and lights up; Bludge appears on the monitor. 'Wasted?' she asks, looking up into the lens. 'Let me in. I have to go over Grief's apartment.'

A copper in the house, thinks Wally, would be just the thing at a time like this. The night watchman sleepily waves her on towards the lift.

Mary trips on the thick carpet, and falls limply to the floor. She lies there, feeling sick, because she can't find a weapon for love nor money. Grief had locked her knife away, fearing suicide.

Grief and Suzie pull up at the waterfront. As they jump from the car, a flood of TV lights bursts out and blares down on them. Blinded, they can just make out a ring of men in police uniforms huddled behind sandbags under the lights. Grief curses Laz for a traitor, and frantically hauls out the gun he'd collected at the Barn. He fires at random into the light; behind him, Suzie scrambles down the ladder to the speedboat. It has the name 'Nose Candy' painted on its prow. Shots ring out from the men encircling them round the dockside.

Laz cuts to the live action. The commentator has more orgasms about the terrorist getting away. Laz fervently hopes Grief won't hit any of those actors he's put down there — the insurance costs would be horrendous. Hell, Equity would black him for life. All the same, that fusillade of blanks they're firing at Grief and the girl really does look splendid on the screen. Little jets of smoke and flame spurt out all around the ring, real Custer stuff, with Grief pinned behind his car and running out of ammunition. He is beginning to realise that not a bullet has come near him; maybe Laz, he thinks, is honest after all. (But who, by now, could begin to tell?) Beneath him, Suzie cries, 'Come on, come ON.' She stamps her feet in the bottom of the boat, nearly losing her balance as it bobs on the outgoing tide. Grief has no bullets left. He hurls himself down the ladder, jams the ignition key into the speedboat's dash, winds up the engine until the revving is a high-pitched shriek, cuts into gear and leaps forward across the river towards the sea. On screen, cameras are following the uniformed actors as they scuttle dramatically, crouching, in twos and threes towards the waterside. Searchlights fan out across the water; shots are fired after the disappearing boat as it weaves in and out of the beams.

The people who run the country are interrupted from reassuring the runner about the election proceeding famously, and the problem with Nanny being perfectly manageable, by this new, finest, and last of Laz's inventions for the evening. The runner calls him to complain a whole lot more about Grief getting away, and Laz spits out, 'Shit, you just don't give up, do you? Listen, pal,' he then lies, 'don't blame me if your coppers can't shoot straight.' Then he hangs up.

Bludge steps out of the lift and stands staring, face hard as stone, into Wally's fuggy gloom. Nervously he tells her, 'Grief got away.'

She flatly replies, 'No thanks to you.' Then she systematically takes a crowbar to each vast window, one by one, down both sides of the long dark room. She tears down the blinds and smashes through the glass; beneath her, Mary hears the shattering and the crashing of her blows, and topples to a window to watch the glittering cascade tumble past her to the street. She smiles against her pains, and walks carefully, trembling, towards the stairs up to Wally's floor.

A banker, deciding to himself that the boy is becoming unreliable and should soon be got rid of, asks the runner to calm down; he is staring in a rage at the phone Laz had cut off. The banker says, after all, that if Grief is on the continent, then every time something goes wrong in the future, they've got a ready-made monster to pin the blame on. The generals begin to consider what sort of weaponry the acquisition of which might be justified by the posing of such a shadowy threat.

There are no limits to the possibilities. 'Besides,' chips in the cabinet's communications manager — Crinkly's chief — 'this is, you realise, tremendous television.' On screen, Grief's boat leaves a phosphorescent wake through the river's pollution as it vanishes into the distance. Actors run about looking purposeful on the dockside. They shout at each other on walkie talkies, while others rush off in their circus-bright siren-screaming vehicles — straight back, of course, to the props department, from where they will all fade away again into the usual long spells of unemployment, after a performance for which not one of them will ever get a credit. But the pay was good; and Laz had promised it in cash.

Mary stands regaining her breath at the top of the stairs, queasy and faint from the effort of mounting them. Then she slides along the wall to Wally's doorway. She sees Wally staring about him in panic as Bludge puts the crowbar with enormous force through one piece of expensive equipment after another. Then she picks him out of the bed and dumps him heavily, stomach down, arse up, onto the jagged remains of his video console. She drags him back and forth across the sharp tin ruins. She is, she realises, beneath the brutality of her determination, very close to crying. Wally such a foul thing, and Grief such a fine one. She steps back and studies the quivering body with disgust.

What Mary would give for a fix of smack . . . she makes it across the big room and stands next to Bludge. She can hear the fat woman's breath straining in and out of her mountainous flesh. She tells her, 'The trouble with you coppers is you're so short on subtlety.' She turns on Wally's hot ring, which has escaped the devastation, and lays the crowbar across it. And when it's red hot, she rams it up Wally's arse. 'No less,' she tells Bludge, 'than the man deserves.' And Wally screams and screams. Bludge throws him away like a rag into the debris, the burning bar still dangling from his anus.

The girls walk out, Mary to collapse into a bed downstairs, and Bludge to leave the building — she wonders what to do with herself next. Slowly, Wally, juddering, moaning, pulls the bar out of his body; then, naked, white, bleeding all over, he rolls gradually up into the foetal position, save for the scarsprayed mess of his damaged leg. He thinks, perhaps, that the pain will fade; but it doesn't.

So he hauls himself inch by inch through the small hours over the smashed remains of his life spread out now all across the carpet, until he makes it to the base of a broken window. The rim of it along the floor still has bits of pane in it; fastidiously, he knocks these out with a buckled film can lying nearby, so as not to gouge himself more as he heaves his body at last over the edge and into space.

It is dawn. Washing down across him as he flies is more light, crisp, clear, clean, light blue light, more light than he's seen in years. His pain ebbs at the huge emptiness, the great open size of the world. Out from under the weight of the ocean, he floats down free towards the uprushing pavement.

Grief and Suzie are high as a snowy peak. The sun comes up across a gleaming sea, and they smile at each other with relief and excitement, watching the waves go crashing by.

When Mary wakes, she finds that Grief has left her, in her jacket pocket, a note giving the combination to his safe. Unlocking it, she finds that it contains enough cash to last her a month, at least. She heads off down the road in search of a dealer, not bothering to look at Wally's body. But later, the old woman who lives in the garbage examines it in detail. She peers at the stained arse and thighs, and all the blood; and then, chuckling, she comments, 'Too many of them cheap curries, my son.' She scurries on, pausing only to take a couple more of those nice new cheap tablets that make all her aches go away.

Above her as she goes, the humble television set burbles away, poking out from where it's hidden beneath the remnants of Wally's more sophisticated equipment. The sun climbs up between the tall empty buildings, and looks down at his crumpled body, alerting the flies with the steady glare of its heat. The voice of the TV drifts away into the golden emptiness of the sky. 'A deranged policewoman who made an attempt on our leader's life during last night's abortive terrorist fiasco has this morning been apprehended in the City of London. She is now in custody, awaiting trial. The attempt was, of course, unsuccessful. Our leader. . . .'

Cue film of Nanny reviewing the troops.

The Last Election was a walkover.

June '84 — January '85 RABAT/LIMA/LA PAZ

V I N T A G E
CONTEMPORARIES

"Today's novels for the readers of today."

— VANITY FAIR

"Real literature—originals and important reprints—in attractive, inexpensive paperbacks."

— THE LOS ANGELES TIMES

"Prestigious."

— THE CHICAGO TRIBUNE

"A very fine collection."
— THE CHRISTIAN SCIENCE MONITOR

"Adventurous and worthy."

— SATURDAY REVIEW

"If you want to know what's on the cutting edge of American fiction, then these are the books you should be reading."
— UNITED PRESS INTERNATIONAL

On sale at bookstores everywhere, but if otherwise unavailable, may be ordered from us. You can use this coupon, or phone (800) 638-6460.

Please send me the Vintage Contemporaries books I have checked on the reverse. I am enclosing $ _____ (add $1.00 per copy to cover postage and handling). Send check or money order—no cash or COD please. Prices are subject to change without notice.

NAME _____

ADDRESS _____

CITY _____ STATE _____ ZIP _____

Send coupons to:
RANDOM HOUSE, INC., 400 Hahn Road, Westminster, MD 21157
ATTN: ORDER ENTRY DEPARTMENT
Allow at least 4 weeks for delivery.

VINTAGE
CONTEMPORARIES

___ LOVE ALWAYS by Ann Beattie $5.95   74418-7

___ FIRST LOVE AND OTHER SORROWS
by Harold Brodkey $5.95   72970-6

___ THE DEBUT by Anita Brookner $5.95   72856-4

___ CATHEDRAL by Raymond Carver $4.95   71281-1

___ DANCING BEAR by James Crumley $5.95   72576-X

___ THE WRONG CASE by James Crumley $5.95   73558-7

___ THE LAST ELECTION by Pete Davies $6.95   74702-X

___ DAYS BETWEEN STATIONS by Steve Erickson $6.95   74685-6

___ A FAN'S NOTES by Frederick Exley $5.95   72915-3

___ A PIECE OF MY HEART by Richard Ford $5.95   72914-5

___ THE SPORTSWRITER by Richard Ford $6.95   74325-3

___ FAT CITY by Leonard Gardner $5.95   74316-4

___ AIRSHIPS by Barry Hannah $5.95   72913-7

___ DANCING IN THE DARK by Janet Hobhouse $5.95   72588-3

___ NOVEMBER by Janet Hobhouse $6.95   74665-1

___ FISKADORO by Denis Johnson $5.95   74367-9

___ A HANDBOOK FOR VISITORS FROM OUTER SPACE
by Kathryn Kramer $5.95   72989-7

___ THE CHOSEN PLACE, THE TIMELESS PEOPLE
by Paule Marshall $6.95   72633-2

___ FAR TORTUGA by Peter Matthiessen $6.95   72478-X

___ SUTTREE by Cormac McCarthy $6.95   74145-5

___ THE BUSHWHACKED PIANO by Thomas McGuane $5.95   72642-1

___ SOMETHING TO BE DESIRED by Thomas McGuane $4.95   73156-5

___ BRIGHT LIGHTS, BIG CITY by Jay McInerney $5.95   72641-3

___ RANSOM by Jay McInerney $5.95   74118-8

___ NORWOOD by Charles Portis $5.95   72931-5

___ MOHAWK by Richard Russo $6.95   74409-8

___ CARNIVAL FOR THE GODS by Gladys Swan $6.95   74330-X

___ TAKING CARE by Joy Williams $5.95   72912-9